SAVING MISS PRATT

Book 4 of The Hope Clinic

TRISHA MESSMER

DEDICATION

To writers block, you horrible, horrible thing. You kept me from finishing this book for far, far too long. But I beat you! And damn it if it didn't turn out pretty damn well. So take that and go sit in a corner.

ACKNOWLEDGMENTS

To the usual suspects—err people. First and foremost my wonderful family who supports me even if most of them don't have a clue what their mother does all day. Well, my daughter does, but the boys would really rather not know.

To my fantastic critique partners. I've developed such a wonderful friendship with these folks, I can't brag about them enough. They've continually pushed me to polish this story until it shines. Here's to all of you, and in alphabetical order: Brad, Clarissa, Dot, Ellie, Izzy, Jessica, Lisa, Michelle, Stacey. You are all the best! Love you guys so much.

To my wonderful cover artist, Johana Duran, who never fails to amaze me how she creates such beautiful backgrounds for my covers and really captures the tone of the story.

And to you, dear reader. I wouldn't be here without you. Thank you for allowing me to do the thing I love. Here's to many more happily ever after endings for us all.

CHAPTER 1—WHEN YOU HAVE LITTLE CHOICE

Priscilla fought a yawn, discreetly pressing her nails into the palm of her left hand. Mr. Netherborne expected a reply to his last question, no doubt. She struggled to remember what he'd just said. She opted for the safest answer.

"I completely agree." She pasted on a smile to accompany her answer and focused on his thick head of neatly combed blond hair.

Mr. Netherborne, on the other hand, furrowed his brows, the corners of them meeting in a pronounced V over his pale blue eyes. "Pardon, Miss Pratt? I asked if you would be willing to participate in distributing food baskets to the poor."

Oh that. "Forgive me, Mr. Netherborne. What I meant to say is I completely agree that the poor are in need of our charity." *What?* She cringed at the stupidity of the statement. Contrary to what many believed, Priscilla was *not* stupid.

Oh, she was many other things.

Foolish.

Over eager.

Too easily persuaded.

Or she had been.

Her willing participation in the forced compromise of the Duke of Ashton three years prior gave testament to that. Now she paid the price.

Dearly.

Oh, how she missed the city. When the *ton* discovered her part in her mother's nefarious plot to trap the duke into marriage, she'd been shunned—practically run out of London.

She longed for the busy Season with balls at Almack's—she'd never be allowed entrance there again—soirées, garden parties, nights at the opera, Vauxhall Gardens, Gunter's Tea Shop.

She had loved it all, but the mere thought of returning and facing the *ton* generated a sick sinking in her stomach. The glares, pointed fingers, and whispers behind fluttering fans would be the constant reminder of her disgrace. A brazen letter carved into her forehead would be no more condemning. There would be no welcome back with forgiving, open arms.

Instead, she and her mother were exiled to the family's estate in Lincolnshire, her only dancing partners the veritable Mr. Netherborne, the parish curate, and—well—sheep.

Lots of sheep.

Not that sheep could dance. They were frightfully stupid creatures.

And to make matters worse—if that were even possible—winter approached. The sky had grown gray and foreboding, the smell of snow heavy in the air.

Mr. Netherborne studied her. "Yes. Well, that is . . . yes, of course." He coughed, the sound forced.

Her mother eyed her from across the room, her head tilting toward the teapot lying on the table between Priscilla and Mr. Netherborne.

"More tea, sir?" Priscilla asked, her mother nodding her approval.

"Thank you, Miss Pratt." He held out his cup, still three-fourths full.

She added a tiny amount, not spilling a drop. She excelled at pouring, as she did with embroidery, and making small talk.

Except when it came to Mr. Netherborne, then her skills at conversation seemed to fly out the window, seeking the same escape she, herself, yearned for.

There wasn't anything *wrong* with Mr. Netherborne. Young, by his account, a mere eight-and-twenty, with even features on a moderately attractive face. He had all his hair and teeth—thank goodness. Not exceptionally tall, but taller than she was—which admittedly wasn't a difficult feat, as she stood barely over five-feet. He acquired his lanky build by spending hours upon hours studying scripture and visiting parishioners.

She'd managed to catch a glimpse of his forearms once during the autumn when he'd rolled up his shirtsleeves to help the tenants with harvest. She took heart that there had been a modicum of muscles visible. Perhaps other, more concealed, areas of his body would be similarly well-formed.

No. There wasn't anything *wrong* with him. But there wasn't anything especially *right* with him either. Aside from when he preached against moral turpitude, his face remained passive at all times, never exhibiting emotion, whether it be embarrassment, joy, or even anger. Mr. Netherborne was—in a word—unflappable.

The fiery passion he exhibited denouncing sin never found its way to other encounters. Try as she might, Priscilla never witnessed such heated fervor from Mr. Netherborne directed toward her.

More than anything, Priscilla longed to know she set a man's heart ablaze and to see the spark from that fire in his eyes. She'd seen it before, but not in relation to herself.

She vividly recalled it when Harrison Radcliffe, the Duke of Ashton, spoke of his—now—wife, Margaret.

The duke had that fire for Margaret, and Priscilla hoped one day to experience it for herself.

Priscilla's heart longed for passion, the soul-deep connection, as much as her body required air to breathe.

She met Mr. Netherborne's gaze and found . . . nothing.

"Mrs. Wilson's baby is expected in a month, is it not, Mr. Netherborne?" Priscilla's mother asked, obviously sensing the lull in conversation.

Priscilla expected a sound tongue lashing when Mr. Netherborne departed.

"It is indeed, Lady Cartwright. Perhaps our dear Miss Pratt might assist with the other children when the midwife is called?" He turned his gaze on Priscilla, his face passive and unemotional.

"I would be honored," she lied. She didn't dislike children, but being in the same house with a woman giving birth terrified her.

The briefest of smiles curled Mr. Netherborne's lips, then vanished as if a gentle breeze had blown it away.

An ominous shiver raced up Priscilla's spine when he turned and addressed her mother. "Lady Cartwright, might I impose upon you to give Miss Pratt and me a moment alone? If you deem it necessary, leave the door ajar for propriety."

Priscilla's mother practically bolted from the chair as if she'd suddenly found herself sitting on a bed of nettles. "Of course, sir. And I have the utmost confidence in your comportment."

As she passed Priscilla, her mother side-eyed her as if to say, "You know what to do."

Rather than leave the door ajar as Mr. Netherborne had suggested, her mother closed it with a firm *clack*.

So, this was it? She'd been expecting it for weeks. More like dreading it. Because once he asked, she'd have to answer. And as much as she didn't want to lose the only suitor she'd had in the three years since her disgrace, a tiny part of her still hoped that Mr. Netherborne would magically transform into an ardent and passionate lover.

He cleared his throat, as if deducing she'd not fully given her attention.

He was not wrong.

"Miss Pratt. Surely it hasn't escaped your notice during my frequent calls that I enjoy your company."

Really? What had she missed? Perhaps her mind had wandered or she'd blinked one too many times.

"As a member of the clergy, it is vital for me to lead an upright and moral life. One that is beyond reproach. To that end, the vicar has encouraged me to secure a wife to dissuade any of the young ladies of the parish from improper thoughts about me."

What? Did *anyone* have *improper* thoughts about Mr. Netherborne? She reminded herself he wasn't unattractive. Perhaps the other unmarried young ladies of the parish—all three of them under the age of fifty and over the age of thirteen—hadn't had the *pleasure* of becoming better acquainted with him as she had.

That indeed was possible. She remembered their first meeting when he moved to the small village outside of Grantham after completing his studies. Her heart had skipped a little at the first sight of him, then settled into a steady, unexciting *thump-thump* when he'd opened his mouth to speak. Thinking of him at night did wonders when she wanted to fall asleep.

She gave the expected answer. "The vicar is a wise man."

His smile made a quick in-and-out appearance, and he nodded. "He is, indeed." He cleared his throat again, the sound—irritating.

She wished to grab him by the coat lapels and shake him, shouting, "*Spit it out!*"

Instead, she smiled placidly, restraining her hands by clasping them on her lap.

"I've decided, given time, you would make a respectable wife, fitting for my aspirations as vicar when Mr. Evans departs this life to meet our maker."

He's decided? Given time? She stared at him, at a loss for words. It wasn't actually a proposal requiring a yes. Was it?

It appeared he did indeed expect an answer.

"I'm flattered you should think so, Mr. Netherborne," she said through clenched teeth.

He obviously didn't notice. "We could be married in spring after Easter. A longer engagement would seem prudent, allowing time to prove yourself."

Blink. Blink. "Prove myself?"

She would have appreciated it if he had displayed the least bit of embarrassment. But he did not. "Yes. To prove you've repented from your former life."

Ah, there, the lightest tinge of pink at the tips of his ears. Thank goodness. Perhaps he was human after all. "You must know that the . . . events three years prior while you were in London are common knowledge among the parishioners. However, I'm confident that in due time you will demonstrate you've renounced the hedonistic lifestyle many in London's society pursue. Dedication to serving the poor, tending the sick and suffering of our parish will prove to those around us your devotion to a simpler country life."

She supposed it was fortunate *one* of them was confident in the matter. She, however, was not.

"Shall I speak with your mother? It would be better to speak with your father, but I will write to him forthwith for his permission and blessing."

All the air in the room stilled, as if each particle hung on her answer. Should she accept and resign herself to a dull life as a country curate's wife? Or should she refuse, effectively losing what could be her only possible chance at marriage? At three-and-twenty, she edged closer and closer to being on the shelf.

She weighed her options carefully, neither palatable, but one decidedly more agreeable than the other. The one thing she swore she would never be was a spinster.

"That would be lovely, Mr. Netherborne."

Edinburgh, Scotland, December 14th, 1826

Timothy Marbry finished packing his valise, anxious to return home for Christmastide. He'd sent trunks with the bulk of his belongings ahead of him. It had been several months since he'd seen his family. He'd posted his letters—one to his parents and another to his sister Bea and her husband Laurence—a week prior, notifying them of his expected arrival. The families had decided to celebrate the holiday in London, no doubt to fuss over Bea's first child who had been born that spring.

His studies to finish his medical training had progressed nicely, and he passed all his exams. Perhaps the family would have a double celebration.

Unlike most people who loved Christmas, Timothy dreaded the holiday. Oh, he'd loved it in his youth: the festive decorations of holly and ivy around the estate, the family gatherings, the wassailing.

Now it dredged up memories of pain and loss along with the oppressive guilt.

Still, he would put on a cheerful face for his family—his mother mainly—grit his teeth, and suffer through as any good soldier was commanded to do.

A heaviness settled on him like a great weight pressing upon his chest as he lifted the valise, tying it to the saddle, and mounted the horse. He'd have eight days to prepare himself, practicing his polite smile and devising pranks to play on his sister—nothing too startling. Perhaps a toad disguised as a gift.

Scratch that. Bea would most likely declare it a perfect gift and devise some form of experimentation to perform on the poor creature.

A smile tugged at his lips at the thought of Beatrix. Who would have predicted that his bluestocking sister and his best friend would have made the perfect couple? He'd expected Bea to remain single all her days, and he'd been more than willing to have her join his household when his father died and left him the title.

Timothy took care of his own.

And he loved Bea.

Contrary to the belief that his sister's ability to make a love match would encourage hope for his own, Timothy had no such

7

ideation. He'd witnessed too much in his one-and-thirty years to believe in fairy tales.

Convinced that couples like his sister and Laurence deluded themselves, believing physical attraction equated a deep, undying love, Timothy took a much more practical approach.

When it came time for him to marry, he would choose a wife using reason rather than emotion. He didn't require much, but as the future Viscount Saxton, he would insist she be respectable and held in society's high esteem.

Of course, physical attraction of some degree was important. He would be expected to produce an heir after all, and being attracted to one's wife would further that goal. But he hoped to find a level-headed woman with whom he shared the same values and opinions.

But of all the criteria he demanded in a wife, passionate love was not among them. The passion of love—if the emotion existed at all—created turmoil, and Timothy wanted none of it. In his experience, passion only led to rash decisions, heartache, and guilt borne from deadly consequences. Not only was passion not required, it was to be avoided at all costs.

After an uneventful five days into his journey, he stopped for the night in Newark-On-Trent at a posting inn. Weary to the bone, he'd failed to heed the innkeeper's comments about the weather.

"Must be a bad storm coming. My rheumatism has been bothering me all day," the man said.

Timothy pulled out a packet of willow bark from his bag. "Steep two spoonfuls of this in some boiling water for a tea. Add honey to sweeten if you like, as it can be bitter. It should ease your discomfort."

The man thanked him, albeit glancing suspiciously at the package of bark.

When Timothy awoke the next morning, the man's prediction had come true. Fat, wet snowflakes drifted past the window. He'd have to hurry if he were to make it to the next posting inn by nightfall. He could hear Bea scolding him for his decision to travel on horseback rather than by coach, but he was in no mood for sharing his journey with strangers.

As his horse plodded along at an even pace, the snow changed from fat flakes to stinging ice.

Brittle as a heart betrayed by passion, the sleety mix crunched against the horse's hooves. Pellets bit into Timothy's cheeks, and he wrapped his scarf around his face, covering his mouth. His fingers began to numb beneath his calf-leather gloves, and he flexed them to drive more blood to his extremities.

Before long, the snow whipped fast and furious, coming at him in a blinding sideways slash.

Unsure how far he'd already traveled, he began searching for shelter, or at least a home where he could obtain information about the nearest inn. A pristine blanket of white covered the road, and he reined in the horse. He pulled out his pocket watch and gazed up at the sky to gauge his direction by the sun.

But all he saw was a white sheet of haze.

He urged his horse forward, hoping he remained on the road and would soon find shelter.

CHAPTER 2—WHEN DESTINIES COLLIDE

The sun had only begun peeking over the horizon when word arrived that Mrs. Wilson's time to deliver had come. Priscilla dragged herself from her warm bed and washed her face while her lady's maid, Lucinda, selected her gown.

"Not that one, Lucinda," she said, pointing at the cream-colored muslin Lucinda held up for inspection. "The skirt has an unsightly stain." She should have little concern about what the Wilson children thought of her gown, but even exiled to the country, Priscilla still prided herself on her appearance. Certain standards must be maintained.

Oh, it was vain, she admitted, but at least if she dressed the part, she could pretend she was amid London society. Why, once, she addressed a particularly stately ram as "my lord."

Instead, Lucinda selected a lovely pale blue gown trimmed in delicate lace at the bodice and edges of the sleeves, and Priscilla nodded her approval. Once dressed, she preened before the mirror.

She executed a deep curtsy. "The waltz, my lord? How scandalous! But of course, I must accept."

Lucinda snorted a laugh behind her. "Planning on giving the Wilson tykes a dancing lesson, miss?"

Priscilla shot her a quelling glance. Nancy, her abigail in London, would never have spoken so disrespectfully. Unfortunately, Nancy had refused to move to the country, preferring the city as much as Priscilla, and had sought employment in another household.

Although competent, Lucinda prided herself in her country roots, never failing to voice her opinion about London's high society. Priscilla suspected her mother assigned Lucinda to her as further punishment for failing to secure a titled husband.

The woman followed Priscilla down the stairs, on her heels like a loyal bloodhound. However, Lucinda's loyalty did not lie with Priscilla, but rather her mother. Priscilla couldn't eat an additional biscuit without it being reported to her mother. Thank goodness Lucinda wasn't accompanying her to the Wilsons'. A devilish idea rose in her mind. Perhaps, simply to spite Lucinda, Priscilla *would* give the Wilson children dancing lessons. At least her partner would be human.

"Don't wake mother. Tell her I'll have Mr. Wilson bring me home when they no longer have need of me."

After boarding her family's carriage, she settled against the squabs and dreamed of traveling to an elegant ball rather than playing nursemaid to three country bumpkin children.

❦

PRISCILLA GAZED OUT THE WINDOW OF MRS. WILSON'S COTTAGE. "Where is the midwife?" she muttered, more to herself than anyone. Mr. Wilson had left over an hour ago to fetch her.

Someone pulled at her skirt. Three pairs of blue eyes peered up at her, widening at the subsequent scream coming from the direction of their mother's bedroom.

"Shush, children. Your mama will be fine." Who was she trying to convince—the Wilson children or herself?

Two-year-old Molly stuck her thumb in her mouth and whimpered.

Priscilla knew she should comfort the child, but who would comfort *her*? Why had she agreed to this nightmare?

The snow that had started soon after she'd arrived at the Wilsons' continued to fall, increasing with intensity. She turned back to the window, hope rising in her chest. A lone rider approached, his head huddled down to shield himself from the frigid wind, white flakes covering the brim of his hat.

A gust of wind shot through the cottage as Mr. Wilson entered, shaking snow from his coat and hat.

"Mr. Wilson, where is the midwife?" Priscilla asked, her voice rising in pitch.

He moved to the hearth, holding his hands out to the radiating heat. "Can't come."

The tempo of Priscilla's heart increased. "But the baby—it's coming."

He turned, his nose and cheeks red, his eyes pleading. "You'll have to help her."

"I . . . I . . . I don't know how."

"It's a natural process. Have you never seen a calf or lamb birthed, girl?"

A calf or a lamb was hardly a human baby, but she answered his question. "No."

He huffed, and she cringed at his glare. "All you need to do is help it out and tie the cord. Lettie will do the rest."

"If it's so easy, why don't you do it? I'm here to mind the children."

He bellowed a laugh. Hardly fitting, in Priscilla's estimation, given the circumstances.

"Better I show you than tell you." He moved toward the door of the bedroom, knocking twice before entering.

Moments later, Mrs. Wilson shouted, "Out! Out! You did this to me! Don't come near me, you brute!" Something slammed against the door or perhaps the wall of the room—the sound of shattering glass followed.

Mr. Wilson exited, wiping his brow. "Be careful going in. She threw a pitcher at my head." He strolled to the kitchen, returning with a broom and a replacement pitcher full of water. He held them out to her. "I'll mind the little ones. I can't do no work in this blizzard anyway."

A collective cheer rose from his children. Priscilla wasn't certain how to take that.

She girded herself as she moved on leaden limbs toward the bedroom door where the screaming Mrs. Wilson waited. After pulling in a deep breath, she opened the door and entered.

ॐ

THREE HOURS LATER, PRISCILLA FINISHED CHANGING THE BED linens and Mrs. Wilson's night rail. Every muscle in her body stung from exhaustion as she placed the newborn baby boy into Mrs. Wilson's arms.

She gazed in amazement at the woman who cradled her baby and placed soft kisses on his fuzzy head. The beatific expression on the woman's face was even more astounding, considering what she'd just gone through. Why would anyone wish to go through such torture multiple times?

Priscilla's gaze drifted toward the tiny bundle. The creature reminded her of a wrinkled pug, only redder. Its loud wail pierced the room, and she jumped. Fear trickled up her spine, and she darted a glance toward Mrs. Wilson.

"A healthy cry is the best music to a mother's ears," Mrs. Wilson said, reassuring her.

Priscilla had serious doubts about that statement.

"You can let him in now," Mrs. Wilson said, placing the baby to her breast.

"Are you certain?" Priscilla wished to avoid any more hurled pitchers.

"Yes, love. I expect he's wearing out the floorboards. Best let him in to see his new son."

Priscilla had barely opened the door and four bodies practically poured into the room, the two-year-old tumbling to the floor at Priscilla's feet. They all raced over to greet the new member of the family, forgetting about Priscilla entirely.

"Mr. Wilson, I suppose I should leave now," Priscilla said to the excited crowd.

Too busy cooing over the newborn, the family ignored her. Even in the desolate country, she was superfluous, cast aside without a second thought once her usefulness ended. She stepped quietly from the room, feeling very much like an intruder and wishing to remove herself as quickly as possible.

With Grantham closer than home, she decided to walk to town. Once there, she would hire someone to take her home by carriage. She slipped her heavy woolen cloak around her shoulders and stuffed her hands into her kid-leather gloves, then opened the door and stepped outside.

Wind whipped against her, buffeting her body as she trudged through the snow toward town. Snowflakes, which had trailed lazily down from the sky earlier in the day, flew at her from angry angles, stinging her face. She tugged her hood up, pulling it closer around her face.

As she trudged through the snow, muscles in her body she didn't realize existed ached with each torturous step. Her mood grew as tumultuous as the storm around her. Why had she ever agreed to minding the Wilson children? What else could go wrong in this terrible, horrible, very bad day?

Too late, she realized the foolishness of even pondering the question.

When the storm eased, changing from slashing fury to soft, slow flakes, she gazed about. She should have arrived in town. How had she been turned around? The usual markers she used to gauge her location and distance disappeared under the blanket of snow. As she turned in a circle, trying to spot the telltale signs of chimney smoke, the only thing before her lay a field of white.

Panic seized her, and she turned to head back toward the Wilsons' cottage, retracing her footsteps. But after a while, even those disappeared. She forced down the urge to weep. It would serve no purpose and only leave her with frozen tears to further chill her already cold face.

She did the only thing she could think of, which admittedly she didn't do nearly often enough.

She prayed.

Would God abandon her, the future wife of a curate, to succumb to the weather? Or was there a higher purpose in store for her?

"Please let someone find me," she whispered.

Silence answered. Even the creatures of the woods apparently had found a much warmer place to wait out the storm.

She pressed forward, deciding to seek closer shelter rather than try to find her way back to the Wilsons'. She continued searching for familiar markers. There! Ahead stood the gnarled tree she'd passed on her way. She remembered a tiny home nearby recently left vacant when the tenant died.

There would be no signs of welcoming smoke to guide her, but she recalled the general direction of the building. She braced herself and trudged toward what she hoped would be her salvation.

TIMOTHY PULLED THE SCARF CLOSER AROUND HIS FACE, breathing through the soft wool. The lull in the storm provided a respite against the stinging ice and wind.

He flexed his hands, alternating from one to the other, his fingers so numb he couldn't feel the leather of the reins. He'd learned to suffer through severe winter conditions as a soldier. But he continued to search for shelter as his best chance for survival.

As the sheet of white stretched before him, he suddenly felt uncomfortably warm despite the frigid temperature. Dizziness threatened to unsettle him from the saddle, and his right ear ached like the devil. Something was amiss, and his mind scrambled to diagnose himself. He repositioned his scarf and scanned the area frantically for shelter.

In the distance, a ramshackle cottage rested on the crest of a nearby hill. No smoke rose from its dilapidated chimney, but the promise of shelter from the wind and the ability to find enough dry wood to light a fire in the hearth lifted his spirits.

He urged his mount forward, the poor beast as frozen as he was. "Maybe there's a stable or barn, old boy. Hang on."

The terrain dipped and rose in little waves, and the horse's feet slipped on the icy ground as he descended a steep slope to the flat plain of land lying before the elevated cottage. "Almost there," he muttered, his teeth chattering even as his head throbbed with heat.

Without warning, a woman appeared before him, stumbling out from a copse of trees. As he pulled back on the reins, the horse sidestepped, losing its footing and tumbling them both to the icy ground.

Trapped beneath the weight of the horse, he tugged at his leg to free it, then breathed a sigh of relief when the horse righted himself and rose.

His gaze darted toward the woman who stood stock still. "Grab the reins! Don't let him run off."

She bolted into action, thankfully restraining the horse, yet she took several steps back, staring at him with wide eyes.

Her cloak was caked with snow, flakes of it crusting the small bit of hair that peeked out from her hood, so coated with white he couldn't tell its true color. But her eyes were as blue as the summer skies on a cloudless day.

From the cut of her cloak and quality of her kid-leather gloves, she certainly wasn't a tenant. What the devil was she doing out in the storm? Perhaps he was closer to a home of a wealthy landowner than he'd first thought.

"Is your home nearby?" he asked.

She blinked and took another step back, taking the horse with her.

Damnation!

"I won't hurt you. We both are in need of shelter. I was headed to yonder cottage. Do you live there?" he asked, the question ludicrous given her attire and the lack of evident life within the small structure.

"No. I became lost in the storm on my way to Grantham." She pointed toward the cottage. "I was headed there as well."

His right leg pained him like the devil. He held out his hand. "Will you help me up?"

She hesitated a moment, then took a tentative step forward, grasping his hand with hers. Thankfully, she'd brought the horse closer, and he used the leverage not only from her hand, but by grabbing the strap of the saddle to pull himself upright.

With the cottage still some distance away, it would be ungentlemanly to ride while she walked. But when he put weight on his leg, the pain radiated up his calf. He assessed her approximate weight.

Groaning, he slipped his left foot into the stirrup and mounted the horse.

She narrowed her eyes and in a tone most indignant, she said, "You're leaving me?"

"No." He held out his hand. "Use my boot as a step. I'll lift you up."

Those blue eyes widened. "You want me to ride on your lap?"

He laughed at her outrage. "Or behind me. Who is going to see us in this snowstorm? If you'd prefer to walk and freeze, that's your choice." He waited a beat, watching her face as she agonized over her decision. "Well?"

She huffed, her eyes narrowing, and he pictured a cornered hellcat. He'd have to watch for her claws, grateful he had extensive knowledge about angry cats thanks to Bea's pet, Catpurrnicus.

When she slipped her gloved hand in his, her fingers felt stiff.

"Front or behind?" He stifled the chuckle at his improper innuendo. His weakened state played havoc with his manners. Luckily, the miss before him was too innocent and naïve to comprehend the implication.

"Behind."

"Very well. When I pull, swing your right leg up behind me. You'll have to lift your skirts."

Red colored her cheeks, but she did as he instructed, and he lifted her onto the horse.

"Hold on."

Her arms loosely slipped around his waist, but when he gave a nudge to the horse with the heels of his boots and the beast jerked forward, she tightened her grip.

It felt . . . good.

SURELY THE ICE CRUSTED UPON HER CHEEKS MELTED AT THE HEAT rushing to her face. What would her mother say if she witnessed Priscilla riding astride a horse—behind a stranger, no less?

On second thought, her mother would most likely ask if said stranger was a titled gentleman, and if so, to have more than a few witnesses document their embarrassing arrangement.

Thank goodness, as the handsome stranger said, no one would see them. Her mother's machinations were the reason Priscilla was isolated in the country and in this predicament to begin with.

As she clutched his waist, she contemplated the odd sensations flowing through her. Framed by thick auburn lashes, his moss-green eyes had studied her in an unnerving manner as he lay trapped beneath his horse.

When he'd risen, his right leg gave way slightly as he steadied himself with the saddle straps. The weight of the horse must have injured him, and her heart lurched with compassion. Guilt swarmed in her stomach that she might have played a role in his fall by startling his horse.

The lure of the cottage beckoned as they drew closer. Even through the frigid air around them, heat emanated from him where her arms wrapped around his body. She scooted a little closer, pressing her face against his back. Closing her eyes, she relished in the delicious warmth. A soft moan of pleasure escaped her lips.

When a rumble of laughter vibrated against her cheek, she jerked back, grateful he couldn't witness her—most likely—pinkened cheeks. The nerve he had to laugh at her! The man was probably a rake of the worst kind. She must be on her guard.

Somehow, the thought excited more than frightened her.

As he reined the horse to a halt before the cottage, he held out his hand again. "Grab hold and slide off."

Once they'd both dismounted, he limped toward the cottage door, knocking soundly.

"It's empty," she said. "Mr. Thatcher passed away two weeks ago."

One auburn eyebrow lifted as he turned toward her, but he remained silent. After tethering the horse, he tried the doorknob, but finding it locked, he pivoted toward her again. "You're certain no one lives here?"

She nodded, her whole body shivering with cold and missing the heat of him as she'd pressed against his body.

When he stepped back, her heart sank to her toes. Was he giving up? Ready to leave? Then, with a swift kick from his left boot, the door flew open, and he stumbled and fell to the ground, clutching his injured right leg. "Damnation!"

"Sir, your language!"

He shot her an angry look and muttered something under his breath.

Not bothering to assist him, she raced inside and out of the hostile elements.

Groans sounded behind her, resulting in a brief twisting sensation in her chest. Before she could return and help him up, he grasped the door frame, pulling himself upright, then hobbled inside.

With each press of his right foot to the floorboards, he winced and muttered a curse.

"Is it . . . is it broken?" Her whispered question breached the eerie stillness of the abandoned cottage.

He shook his head. "I don't think so. A twisted ankle more like it." He glared at her. "If you would be *so kind* to assist me to a chair and help me with my boot, I will assess the injury."

Was it a trick? He certainly appeared to be in pain. She took several tentative steps toward him.

A lopsided smile crossed his lips. "You need not worry. I'm in no condition for ravishing today."

The gall of the man!

She squared her shoulders and strode forward, this time with more assurance. In front of him, she glowered. "I'm not afraid of you."

"Ha! You have a strange way of showing your courage."

That decided it. She did *not* like this man. Nevertheless, he had been injured. Not to mention he brought her more quickly to Mr. Thatcher's cottage than she would have arrived on her own.

He lifted his arm, motioning toward her shoulders. "With your *permission*," he said, the last word uttered like a profanity.

She shifted her weight under his arm, finding it easier when she wrapped her arm around his waist, then assisted him to a wingback in the front parlor.

Muscles in his jaw tensed, each step a strange arrhythmic motion like a clumsy dance. *Ta-dum. Ta-dum. Ta-dum.*

He plopped in the chair, sending a tiny dust cloud into the cold air. "My boot." He held out his foot.

Did the man always speak so rudely? "I am *not* a valet, nor a maid, sir. Take off your own damn boot." *Oh, dear. If Mama had heard that!*

She braced herself for his censure, and, for a moment, his brows drew down, drawing her attention to his incredible eyes. Were they the color of moss or more like the dark leaves of an oak in summer? She couldn't decide.

The debate ended when he gave a hearty laugh, and she wondered if he'd been possessed by an entirely different person.

After watching him struggle dramatically with his boot for more than she deemed necessary, she acquiesced. "Very well. Since you seem incapable of managing without assistance."

"My feet are wet. I think they're frozen inside," he said, and to her ears, he sounded—sincere.

Her first attempt to remove the offending boot proved unsuccessful, her own wet gloves making it difficult to grasp the leather. So she stripped off the gloves, the action itself taking great effort.

His eyes trained on her as she pulled each finger free. Something hot burned in those green depths, and a shiver—not generated from the chilly air—raced up her spine.

Grasping the heel and rise of the boot with her bare hands, she tugged again, falling on her bottom—without the boot.

His lips quirked upward in one corner.

She scowled at him. "Stop laughing."

He drew a hand over his face as if to erase the smile. "Perhaps if you approach it from a different angle?" He demonstrated with a circular motion of his finger. "My valet usually straddles my leg, his back facing me."

So, he does have a valet? Although she should have guessed from the quality of his greatcoat and fine woolen scarf.

The prospect of having her rear end facing him did not appeal, yet she had seen the suggested action performed on her father.

"Very well." She huffed, pulling herself from the floor. "But this is most improper."

After lifting her skirts enough to step across his extended limb, she tugged at the boot again. It didn't budge. Something pressed against her bottom, and she froze.

"What is *that?*" she asked, the horror in her voice clear to her own ears.

"My other foot. Leverage."

The man was insufferable. She tugged again, the boot against her bottom pushing then propelling her forward, this time with the offending piece of footwear grasped firmly in her hands.

"Ah ha!" She held the blasted boot up in the air like a flag of victory.

He merely grinned, and she wanted to wipe that smug look off his face.

She crossed her arms over her chest. "I suppose you want the other removed as well?"

"If you would be so kind." He held his booted foot out, that lopsided smile playing across his face.

She threw the boot at his head.

CHAPTER 3—CONFINED IN A COTTAGE

Timothy ducked the flying piece of footwear.

The hellion! She completely shattered his first impression of a spoiled society miss—and nearly his skull in the process. The boot hit the floorboard behind him with a resounding *thud*.

"Good thing your aim is terrible," he grumbled, then tugged at his other boot. At least his left foot remained unswollen, allowing the leather to slip more easily from his leg. He tossed it behind him to join its brother.

The hellion continued to glare at him. He supposed he would have to ask her name. Referring to her as *hellion* to her face wasn't likely to win him any favors, and he needed her to tend to the horse and fetch his bag.

"I suppose I should introduce myself since I've placed my foot so intimately upon your person."

Red blossomed on her cheeks, the effect most attractive.

He pushed that from his mind. Being attracted to the wildcat was the last thing he needed. Regardless of their circumstances, he would remain a gentleman. Which speaking of, introductions were in order.

"I'm Timothy Marbry."

He waited for her to respond in kind, but she did not. Instead, something flashed across her face. Fear? Nervousness?

"I do apologize for the . . . familiarity, but as you can clearly see, my ankle is quite swollen."

Her eyes darted to his right foot which, freed from the constraints of the leather, had ballooned up.

"I need to wrap it and keep it elevated. If you would be so kind to fetch my bag from my horse, I have some bandages inside. And if there's a sheltered area around, perhaps settle my horse in and find him some hay."

She perched her fists on her hips. "Do it yourself. I'm not your servant."

Perhaps flattery would work. He needed her defenses down. "Of course you're not. It's clear you're a gently bred lady, and this is an untenable situation. I assure you, if I could do it myself, like any honorable gentleman, I would."

She huffed, sending him a dubious look.

"Do you question my ability to go outside and hobble around in my stockinged feet?"

"No. I question that you're a gentleman."

He drew a hand down his face. So much for flattery. "Would you like me to build a fire in the hearth, Miss . . .?"

"Since you provided your Christian name, you may call me . . . Emma."

Excellent. They were getting somewhere. "Please, Emma? If you fetch my bag so I may wrap my foot and ankle, I'll find some suitable dry wood here and start a fire. And please don't transfer your anger at me to my poor horse. After all, he did carry you here. Wouldn't finding him shelter and a bit of hay be the least you could do to repay the poor beast?"

She demonstrated a perfect eye roll, tugged her gloves on, pulled her cloak more firmly around her, then traipsed out, slamming the door behind her.

God help the man who winds up with that termagant.

As he waited, he gazed around, grateful to find a few pieces of firewood by the hearth, along with a flint and several tapers. Two candles sat within iron stands atop the mantle. They'd at least have heat and light.

Perhaps once she'd warmed herself, she'd be more amenable to searching the kitchen for some food, if any remained. His stomach growled at the mere idea. He hadn't eaten since morning, and the dim orange glow of sunset glinted through the windows. Nightfall arrived early this time of year. There would be no more traveling today.

Would someone be looking for Emma? A husband? Parents?

And what would they say if they discovered him alone with her?

THE NERVE OF THAT MAN! PRISCILLA STOMPED FROM THE COTTAGE, wishing the ground beneath her were his head.

What a day! Forced to deliver a baby. Lost in a snowstorm. How foolish to think her day could get no worse. And yet, here she was, stranded in a cottage with Mr. Timothy Marbry.

A moment of panic had seized her at the mention of his surname. Although she had never met him, she remembered Lord Saxton had a son named Timothy. Concerned he had heard of her blackened reputation, she struggled for a name to provide him which would allow her to maintain her anonymity. It would not do at all to have him racing from her presence for fear of compromise when he realized her true identity. Or worse, send her out into the cold on her own.

Which, at the moment, she in fact was.

Instead, she fabricated a name from a novel she recently read by Miss Jane Austen. Emma was such a lovely name, unlike Priscilla.

She hated her name.

Since it was highly unlikely she would ever cross paths with Mr. Timothy Marbry again once he went on his way, she seized the opportunity and created a whole new persona.

In fact, it might be most enjoyable to pretend to be someone else. It could become a cherished memory she would recall while sentenced to a secluded life in the country as Mrs. Abner Netherborne.

She exhaled a sigh, her breath forming puffs of white clouds, and strode toward the horse.

The animal neighed and shifted sideways as she approached.

She didn't really like horses. Truth be told, she'd never given them much thought. They pulled carriages and men liked to ride them. God knew why. She untied the bag from the saddle straps, and with two hands, flung it against the cottage door.

"I hope all your clothes fall out, you big oaf!"

"I heard that." His voice traveled through the walls. It seemed she wasn't the only one yelling.

Steam came from the horse's nostrils as it gave a sound snort, then tossed its head.

"Very well, you." She took a cautious step toward the beast, then untied it from the tethering post. "Let's find you somewhere warm."

As if answering her, the horse nodded its head. Perhaps they weren't so dumb after all.

She'd only been at Mr. Thatcher's twice, the last time distributing food baskets shortly before he'd passed, and she didn't remember if he had a stable or barn. With a quick scan around the back of the house, she noticed an outbuilding sitting a respectable distance away.

The snow covered her ankles, and in drifts reached her shins. Each step required more effort. After trudging through and barely clearing the shadow of the house cast from the setting sun, she gave in and lifted her cloak and skirts enough to place her foot in the stirrup.

Once she was seated in the saddle, her feet no longer reached the stirrups, which had been adjusted for Timothy's long legs. *Timothy*. Such a nice name for such a despicable man!

With her feet dangling, she nudged the horse forward with the heels of her half-boots. She barely had to guide him with the reins, as he seemed to sense their destination.

Although not warm, the stable was shelter, and she found some hay left in a storage area by the stall. Hands on her hips, she studied the horse, never having had to tend to one herself. With more than a little difficulty, she removed the tack, hoping that Timothy—*ugh* —would recover enough to brush the poor creature down later.

By the time she returned to the cottage, every muscle in her body, especially her legs, screamed. Without the aid of the horse, trudging back had been torturous, and she practically whooped for joy when she reached the front door.

Luckily for him, Timothy's—*ugh*—bag no longer sat by the open doorway. If it had, she would have tossed it at his head as she had his boot. The scent of woodsmoke greeted her as she stepped inside. The delicious warmth of being in the shelter of the cottage would alone have been enough—almost, but fledgling flames blazed with light and nipped at the logs in the hearth, the comforting crackling music to her ears. Candles burned atop corner tables, adding additional light to the growing dimness of the room.

Timothy—*ugh*—had wrapped his foot and ankle with a cloth, and half hopped, half hobbled from the hearth back to the chair from where he'd so unceremoniously placed his foot against her person.

Without removing her cloak, she took his place in front of the hearth, and after removing her gloves, held her hands before the fire. "Ah." She flexed her fingers, grateful they still moved. Once feeling came back into her fingertips, she removed her cloak, her back still toward him.

When she turned, his eyes widened, and he rose from the chair, apparently completely forgetting his injured ankle. "Good God, what happened to you?"

What?

"You're covered in blood. Are you injured?" He took a halting, uneven step toward her, muttering a curse as he placed weight on his injured foot.

27

Her gaze drifted down toward her gown. She'd completely forgotten how assisting Mrs. Wilson's birth had left her in such an unkempt state. Birthing children was a messy business. One she hoped to avoid for as long as possible.

"I'm a physician. I can assist."

"No. No. Other than half freezing, I'm fine. This isn't my blood."

If possible, his eyes widened further. "Did you kill someone?" From his serious tone, he obviously believed it was possible.

"No." She squinted at him. "But I'd like to." As she glared at him with all the malice she could muster, she took a seat across from him, not offering any explanation. A smile tugged at her lips, and she wondered what images his mind might be conjuring. She hoped it would be enough for him to keep his distance for fear of his life.

Silence passed between them, but she had perfected the waiting game.

Minutes later, he conceded. "Well, are you going to tell me why you're covered in blood?"

In her sauciest voice, she tilted her head and said, "I don't know. Why don't you guess?"

"If not murder, severe injury of some poor unsuspecting man who tried his best to be of service?"

She studied her nails. "Hmm, that does sound lovely. But, no."

He rolled his eyes and shook his head, his frustration most satisfying.

"I will give you a hint. You said you were a physician. Had your *services* been available earlier in the day, the blood would have been on you instead of ruining my gown."

"You operated on someone?" She found the rising pitch of his voice and the incredulous tone even more satisfying than his frustration.

"Not exactly an operation, but you're getting closer."

His brow furrowed, little lines forming between his eyes, making him look a bit like a beagle puppy she had as a child.

He snapped his fingers. "You delivered a baby." As soon as the words fell from his lips, he frowned again. "*You* delivered a baby? *You?*"

Before that morning, she would have doubted it as well. Still, she mustered her most indignant tone. "Why do you find that so hard to believe?"

"So, it's true?"

She straightened her shoulders. He didn't have to know how terrified she'd been during the ordeal, nor how she wished never to repeat it. "Yes. A fine, healthy little boy."

"Well, I'll be . . ." He frowned again. "So, my next question is, why? I mean no offense, but you appear rather young to be a midwife. And your cloak and gown are of fine quality, not to mention inappropriate for assisting with a birth."

Truth be told, having one of her favorite gowns ruined annoyed her. However, when she'd set out for the Wilsons' that morning, she had expected to be minding children, not delivering one. Part of her wished he would wrap his arms around her and tell her how brave she'd been, to console her for the loss of such a fine garment.

But she merely waved her hand in the air. "One does what one must. My original task was to care for the other children when Mrs. Wilson's pains grew worse. But when Mr. Wilson returned without the midwife, I had no other choice."

Not quite true. Had she followed her initial instinct, she would have run as far and fast from the Wilsons' home as her feet would have taken her. But she wouldn't give Timothy—*ugh*—the satisfaction of hearing her admit that.

"So, why were you out in this weather?" He sounded . . . *concerned*.

"Once the baby arrived and all was well, they had no need for me. I had no idea the snow would start coming so hard and fast. I became disoriented and lost my way."

He rose from his chair and stirred the fire. The flames jumped to life, sending delicious heat throughout the room.

"The winds from the North Sea are chilling the air at a furious pace. I expect things will ease by morning. Until then, I fear we're both stuck here for the night."

She would rather deliver another baby than be trapped in a cottage with *Timothy*. The reality of her horrendous day crashed in around her.

What on earth was she to do?

❧

IT WOULD BE AN UNDERSTATEMENT TO SAY THE BEAUTY BEFORE him surprised him. Astounded would have been more like it. He would never have expected such strength and determination from a gently bred young woman.

Except for Bea—but his sister had been the exception to practically every young woman he'd ever met.

But Emma was a puzzle. He tried to reconcile the juxtaposition of a woman who'd taken offense at helping him with his boot with a woman who would willingly deliver a baby.

And at the moment, she stared at him as if he'd suddenly grown horns from his head. Her perfect pink bow of lips had formed an erotic little *O* to match her widened blue eyes, her already fair complexion paling further.

"I . . . I . . . I cannot stay here overnight with *you*."

He pointed to the darkening windows. "If you got lost during the day, I'd highly advise against traversing this storm in the dark of night. You'll be much safer—and warmer—here. There might be wild animals."

She crossed her arms under her bosom, drawing his eyes to the perky flesh peeping up from her bodice.

"I think I would rather take my chances with the animals than with you." She frosted him with a glare.

He shrugged. "Suit yourself. But I rather thought we could scour the kitchen for something edible. I haven't eaten since this morning other than some hardtack left over from my military days."

She straightened, her arms dropping back to her sides.

Ah, there. That caught her attention.

"I thought you said you were a physician?"

"I am. But I was also in the military. The two aren't mutually exclusive." He grinned at her. "Much like being a prickly termagant and delivering a baby."

"I am *not* a termagant!"

Oh, but she was making this much too easy. "So, you do admit to being prickly, then?" He prepared himself to dodge another flying object.

She dropped onto the sofa like a recalcitrant child. "One thing you definitely are *not* is a gentleman."

"Do you prefer to continue arguing over what we are or are not, or would you rather see if there's anything here we can eat?"

"I did see some carrots, and apples in the stable."

He almost jumped from his seat before he remembered his sprained ankle. "Did you bring them back?" As if to mock him, his stomach growled.

"Well . . . no. I didn't think . . ."

"Of course you didn't," he muttered. The woman had no sense in her pretty head. He worried about the child she helped deliver. "Go back and get them."

"I am not some underling you can order about, sir. I've done your bidding with your bag and your horse, not to mention your boot. If you want to eat, go fetch them yourself."

His patience worn as thin as a whore's nightgown, he clenched his teeth. "I *would* if I could get my boot back on. But as you can surely see, my ankle is much too swollen."

"Pity." She studied the nails on her delicate hands. "Perhaps you shouldn't have removed it in the first place. Using my . . . person as leverage, I might add."

"I shall pray for your husband, as he surely has need of it."

"I'm not married . . . yet. But my future husband has no need for your prayers. He's a curate, soon to be a vicar."

Timothy couldn't imagine a man of God leg-shackled to this

harpy. The man truly must be a saint. He braced himself and rose, hopping toward the kitchen as best he could to avoid putting weight on his injured ankle.

"Oh, for goodness' sake. Must you be so dramatic?" Her words came out in a huff.

When he turned to face her, his ankle gave way, and he tumbled to the floor in a heap. Gritting his teeth, he cursed under his breath. He wouldn't want to offend her *delicate* sensibilities.

In his sweetest voice, he appealed to whatever shriveled heart still beat in her chest. "If you could find something I could use as a crutch, I would be most grateful. Something long enough to fit under my arm would be best."

She stomped off, expressing clearly how his request inconvenienced her, slamming and rattling every movable object in her wake.

While she searched, he crawled over to a table, and grasping it for support, pulled himself back to a standing position, carefully balancing himself on his good foot.

He breathed a grateful sigh when she returned, carrying an actual—albeit crudely made—crutch in her delicate hands.

"I remembered Mr. Thatcher saying he'd fallen once and needed to use this." She held the piece of wood before him with thumb and forefinger, as if the wood itself might attack her.

He snatched it and placed it underneath his armpit. Rather short, it would be difficult, but for the moment, it was like a shower of blessings.

"Thank you," he said, mustering as much sincerity as he could. "Shall we explore the kitchen together?"

She rolled her big blue eyes and pursed her mouth.

When he found himself wondering how those rosebud lips would taste, he shook himself back to reality. Sequestered in a cottage during a snowstorm with a single woman courted enough trouble. He didn't need to add the lure of seduction into the mix.

But oh, those lips . . .

CHAPTER 4—WRANGLING A CHICKEN

Priscilla refused to admit that her own stomach growled. Timothy's—*ugh*—had done a sufficient job on its own. She cursed herself for being so foolish as to leave the few carrots and apples in the stable with the horse.

But perhaps they would discover something edible left in the kitchen. Mr. Thatcher had only been dead for two weeks. Surely something remained they could eat. Regardless of what they might find in the kitchen, once feeling had returned to her extremities, she resigned herself to donning her cloak and heading back out to the stable to fetch what she had left behind.

She followed Timothy into the kitchen, watching him hobble on the crutch—gracefully, she reluctantly acknowledged. Her gaze dropped to his backside when the crutch snagged against his coat, drawing the side of it up high enough to expose his well-formed posterior.

"Do you know how to set a trap?"

She froze mid-step. *What?* Was he implying she was trying to trap him into a compromising situation? "Beg pardon?"

"For game. Rabbits, for example. If we could catch one, we could at least have some meat. And if you would be so kind to fetch the carrots and apples you discovered, we could make a nice rabbit stew."

She heaved a sigh of relief. "No, but if you explained it, perhaps I could try." The least she could do was attempt to be useful. The gnawing at her stomach grew uncomfortable.

His moss-green eyes narrowed as he stared at her. "You sound almost . . . willing."

She hated losing, but at the moment, her empty stomach demanded she give in. "I am. The sooner we can eat and restore our strength, the sooner we can leave this wretched place."

He nodded and finished hobbling into the kitchen. As he searched the cupboards and sideboard, she followed suit.

"What are we looking for?" she asked, hoping she didn't sound as stupid as her question seemed.

"Flour, salt, any spices or seasoning, though I doubt this time of year there's anything fresh. Perhaps before the man died, he dried some herbs. Also, search for any cooking items, pots, pans, spoons, that type of thing—huzzah!"

Startled by his sudden exclamation, she dropped the pot she'd discovered. It landed with a loud *clang* on the floor.

"What is it?" she asked, drawing closer to where he stood.

He held some feathery green leaves in his hands. "Herbs." He brought the shriveled leaves to his nose. "Fennel leaves. We're in luck. Even if we can't snare some meat, at least the carrots will have some flavoring."

Whatever those leaves were, they didn't look appetizing to her. She returned to searching where she had retrieved the pot and discovered more cookware.

"Flour and salt," he said from behind her, his voice full of excitement.

Truth be told, the mention of the food items had visions of steaming stew floating in her mind, and her stomach rumbled in anticipation.

He chuckled, the sound unnervingly pleasant. "I quite understand."

She peeked over her shoulder, expecting him to be mocking her, but he continued to hop around on his crutch, examining every nook and cranny in the kitchen.

"Since I'm much warmer now, I'll go back outside to the stable."

He nodded, but didn't face her, probably hoping to find a fully cooked meal somewhere inside the cupboards.

Twilight painted the snow in shades of bluish gray, and after donning her cloak and gloves, she hurried back to the stable. Noises from woodland creatures—the hoot of an owl, chattering of squirrels—encouraged her to make haste and not tarry.

The horse gave a snort of welcome as she entered the stable, and after giving him one of the precious apples, she tucked the rest of the items into a sack she found hanging from a hook on the stable wall.

Eager to return to the warmth of the cottage, she stiffened when a strange scratching caught her attention. Quickly scanning the area for something she could use as a weapon, she grabbed hold of a filthy shovel, most likely used for mucking out the single stall.

The scratching continued from outside the building. She tiptoed to the entrance and peered around the corner. A shadow grew larger as it crept around the corner. Shovel lifted like a cricket bat, she waited, ready to demobilize any assailant.

MORE THAN PLEASED WITH THE BOUNTY HE'D UNCOVERED IN THE deserted cottage's kitchen, Timothy stood back, assessing the various items. He opened the cottage door and scooped several pots of snow. Thank goodness the snow was wet, which would yield more water when melted. Although they wouldn't eat until later that evening, they would at least have something to fill their bellies.

If Emma ever returned with the carrots and apples. *Where in the devil is she?* Concern twisted his gut that she may have taken the horse and left. He not only worried that she might have abandoned him, injured as he was, but also that she was outside in the night defenseless.

Although he'd teased her about the animals lurking about in the night, his fears were not unfounded. However, the type of animal most threatening to her would be the two-legged kind.

He turned from the table, now displaying his treasure trove of ingredients and implements, and hitched the crutch under his arm, ready to go back to the parlor and attempt to pull on his boot so he could search for her. Before he made it out of the small kitchen, the front door burst open, and a gust of cold air blew through the home's small interior.

Unable to speak, his mouth opened and closed several times as he stared at Emma, clutching a brown sack to her chest. Scratches marred her fair complexion, and . . . feathers? . . . littered her hair.

His gaze darted again to the brown sack . . . which *moved,* then back to lock with hers. "What's in there?" he asked, his whispered tone conveying his amazement.

In answer to his question, the thing in the sack squawked in protest.

"I caught a chicken!" The grin beamed on her face as if she'd captured Napoleon himself. "It wasn't easy, mind you. I never realized they could jump. When I tried to pick it up, it leapt at me, nearly scratching my eyes out. But I smacked it with a shovel and stuck it in my sack. Apparently, I only incapacitated it."

She held up the sack like a pirate's booty.

"I could kiss you."

Her face reddened at his blurted words, and he wished he could take them back.

He rushed to put her at ease. "Forgive me. In my excitement at our prospective meal, I became overwhelmed."

Her cheeks still pink, she lowered her eyes. "I brought some potatoes I found and the carrots and apples as well. I gave one apple to your horse. It would be unfair not to share with him."

Had some magical transformation taken place during her trip

outside? Was this even the same termagant who'd argued with him before?

He rather missed her. But he liked this softer version as well. "That was most considerate of you. Now, would you like the honors?"

She tilted her head, her blond brows drawing in a delightful furrow. "For what?"

"To kill it."

Those blue eyes popped wide. "Do we have to?"

He bit back the laugh at her innocent expression. "Why else would you have risked your very life but to bring it back so we can cook it?"

She pursed her lips. "I suppose we can't wait for it to depart naturally. Although it appeared rather scrawny." She pushed the sack forward. "I think you should have the honors."

Not fooled by her reluctance to commit chicken murder, he took the sack as if it were his most prized possession—which, to be honest, at the moment, it truly was. "As you wish."

"How will you . . ." She waved her hand in his direction. "You know."

"Wring its neck. I'll be quick, I promise. The chicken will be making the greatest sacrifice for king and country."

"I doubt the chicken will see it that way."

At that, he did laugh. And it felt wonderful. "On that much, we agree."

⚘

PRISCILLA REMAINED IN THE SMALL PARLOR WHEN TIMOTHY—NO longer *ugh*—returned to the kitchen. She had no desire to witness the demise of the poor chicken, even though she eagerly anticipated devouring it later.

After some squawking and a few shouted curses from Timothy, silence followed, and Priscilla said a small prayer for the chicken's soul. Did they have souls?

She'd never given much thought to where the food placed before her at each meal had actually come from. Of course, she knew the lamb, beef, and—yes—chickens had been living creatures at one time, but until that moment, she'd never associated the two. She worried the chicken's pathetic appeal for mercy as Timothy wrung the life from the poor creature might forever taint her appetite.

Her stomach twisted and rumbled, reminding her it was a matter of survival. Hadn't the chicken committed the same act upon unsuspecting worms—or whatever chickens ate? Her knowledge of such matters was decidedly limited.

Might that change once she married Abner Netherborne? Would her life with a lowly curate entail tending chickens and geese, digging in the dirt of a garden to produce enough vegetables for their table? There would be no balls and fancy gowns, for certain. Her future appeared bleak and dull, nothing as exciting as being trapped during a snowstorm with a handsome doctor.

Handsome?

Well, in fairness, he was most attractive. Especially when his green eyes flashed with fire. She'd never so much as witnessed a hint of a spark in Abner Netherborne's eyes when he gazed at her.

She spread her cloak before the blazing fire and held out her hands to warm them. Sounds of chopping from the kitchen kept her rooted in place in the parlor. She had no desire to observe the dismemberment and vivisection of her impending meal.

Darkness poured from the windows. Since Timothy had moved the candles into the kitchen while he worked, the fire in the hearth provided the only light. Rather than an eerie atmosphere, she found the effect rather romantic.

As if reading her mind, Timothy emerged carrying some type of iron stand. "Because of the scarcity of firewood, I thought it best not to use what precious little we have to set a fire in the oven. We can cook here at the hearth. I'll need your assistance to assemble it."

With his instruction, she helped put together the stand while

Timothy returned to the kitchen to retrieve a round pot, which he hung from the stand over the open flame.

"Now," he said, "while our supper cooks, allow me to treat your scratches. I should have done so immediately, but my empty stomach seemed to cloud my judgment. I apologize for my selfishness."

After fetching his bag, he wet a cloth with a liquid from a flask. Next, he took a seat on the small sofa and patted the cushion next to him. "If you would."

Was it actually possible she'd forgotten about the injuries the chicken had inflicted? She yearned for a mirror to assess the damage.

She raised her hand to her face. "How bad are they?"

He hesitated a moment, and her chest constricted. Yes, she would seek out a mirror to see for herself.

"They appear superficial. I'm sure they'll heal with time and not leave any scars."

"Scars!" Panic slid up her spine, and her limbs became as numb and cold as they'd been after trudging in the snow.

"To prevent such an occurrence, it would be best if you allow me to tend them." He patted the cushion again.

She supposed she had little choice. And he said he was a doctor. She strode to the sofa, taking a seat next to him. "So, Dr. Marbry, how long have you been a physician? Did you serve as one in the military?" Not that she doubted his veracity, but why would the son of a viscount choose to become a physician?

She recalled reading something in the scandal sheets about his father's debt and the fiasco with his sister Beatrix, Lord Middlebury, and Lord Montgomery. Still, she had no desire to reveal her identity, so she played the innocent.

He dabbed at her face with the cloth. It stung at first, and he *shushed* her, his tone and his touch both surprisingly gentle. "Only as an assistant to the regimental doctor. I sold my commission approximately two years ago to pursue medicine. I've recently passed my exams. So, you're my first official patient."

She jerked back. "Do you even know what you're doing?" She gazed into his annoyingly beautiful eyes, reminding herself she was, but for all intents and purposes, an engaged woman.

"I think I can manage a few minor scratches."

"Minor? I recall you mentioned scars earlier."

"And if you *also* recall, I said I was confident your wounds would heal and not leave any scars." He grasped her chin with his hand. "Now. Hold still."

Regardless of the chill still permeating the room, heat flooded her face.

A ghost of a smile crossed his lips, but he remained silent and continued to cleanse the scratched area and even plucked a few feathers from her hair. Once he completed his task by applying a thin layer of salve, he gave a quick nod of satisfaction. "All finished. That wasn't so bad, now, was it?"

When she reached up to touch the tender skin, he grasped her hand, sending gooseflesh prickling her arms.

Yet she was anything but cold.

"Don't touch your face. Allow the salve to work." His eyes locked with hers, something flickering in their green depths, then darted to her lips.

Thickness clogged her throat, and she forced it down.

Even without trying, she'd landed in a world of trouble.

Timothy forced himself to focus on something other than Emma's blue eyes and rosy lips. Lord, help him make it through the upcoming night alone with her. He reminded himself she'd mentioned a fiancé. A clergyman, no less. "Since we're no longer at each other's throats, tell me a little about yourself," he said, hoping to put her at ease.

She stiffened before him.

What had he said? It seemed a simple, polite question. He tried another tactic. "You mentioned assisting a birth. I presume you live nearby? What is your father's occupation?"

If anything, she grew more agitated, her lips clamped as if they'd been sutured shut.

"I only thought we should get to know each other. Perhaps I'll start. My family owns an estate in Wiltshire. My father's a viscount. I have one sister, Beatrix, who recently married Viscount Montgomery, my close friend. They had a baby girl earlier this year, Elizabeth, although they call her Lizzie."

If any of his information surprised her, it didn't show on her face.

She smoothed the skirt of her blood-stained gown. "Am I to presume you're the spare, and hence your service in the military and occupation of physician?"

A reasonable assumption, he admitted, albeit false. "No. I'm in line to inherit. However, I much prefer to be productive. I've never cared much for idleness."

"Mr. Netherborne says idleness is the devil's workshop."

"I think he may have nicked that saying from someone else. Is Mr. Netherborne your intended?"

"He is."

Timothy studied her. No sign of affection crossed her face at the mention of her betrothed. "And have you been betrothed long?"

"A month. Mr. Netherborne believes in a long engagement. To prove myself." She blanched as if she hadn't meant for her last words to slip out.

Not wishing to embarrass her further, he kept silent, but the statement intrigued him to no end. What in the world did she have to prove?

CHAPTER 5—BEING NEEDED

Priscilla waited for Timothy to ask why she would have to prove herself. Yet he remained silent. The words had slipped out. What was it about Timothy that made her feel like she could speak her mind?

Not at all like Abner Netherborne, where she weighed each word carefully before allowing it to leave her lips. Simply being in the man's presence exhausted her. But being with Timothy was effortless.

She would say comfortable had it not been for the powerful pull of attraction when she brushed his hand or he examined her with those intriguing green eyes.

Of course, she had already known he was the heir, but his honesty impressed her. He could have easily lied.

As she had been doing.

It had been impetuous for her to claim to be someone she was not, then careless to give her fiancé's correct name. Timothy could easily make inquiries to determine her true identity.

But would he? It would serve neither of them well to make it known the snowstorm had stranded them together overnight with no appropriate chaperone. As a gentleman's son, he would be honor bound to marry her—precisely something her mother would encourage, especially given past events. And Timothy Marbry was exceedingly more preferable than a stodgy clergyman.

But did Timothy deserve to be trapped into a marriage he didn't want?

She rather thought not. She hated to admit it, but she had grown to like him—at least a little.

Especially when he studied her with those entrancing green eyes as he did in that moment. "I believe it's your turn to share about your family. Do you have siblings?"

"I have an older brother," she said, deciding to share what she could honestly. Victor had been abroad for the past five years studying painting with a master in Italy, but she withheld that bit of information. In order to pose as a merchant's daughter, having a well-traveled brother would raise suspicion.

When Timothy sent her a rakish smile, her heart did a little jig in her chest.

"Did he play pranks on you when you were children?"

She laughed remembering the affectionate teasing they shared. "He did. Sometimes the most awful things. Once he put a dead spider in my bed when I was sleeping. I screamed for hours."

Timothy laughed, a bright crack of sound that seemed to lighten the darkness of the room. "I did that once myself. Unfortunately, my sister was thrilled and set the creature aside to examine at a later time."

Minutes passed quickly as they settled into an easy conversation.

Unlike her time spent with Mr. Netherborne, Priscilla found herself enthralled as Timothy spoke with conviction and pride about his studies and his plans to work in the Hope Clinic under the tutelage of the unconventional Duke of Ashton.

"He has the most brilliant ideas, Emma." Timothy's chest puffed out with pride. "I impressed him when I discovered an effective treatment for my brother-in-law's allergic reaction to my sister's cat."

Priscilla smiled but remained silent. She was all too familiar with the duke's endeavor to provide medical care for the poor. Even under different circumstances, Timothy's association with the duke was yet another reason Priscilla could never seek an attachment with the increasingly attractive Dr. Marbry.

Delicious aromas of herbs and vegetables simmering in the pot by the hearth teased her nostrils, and her stomach voiced its desire to be filled. Heat crept up her neck, warming her cheeks, and she lowered her gaze to her hands.

He chuckled, the sound as pleasant as the scents of their soon-to-be supper. "No need to be embarrassed. My own stomach agrees with yours." He rose from the settee and hobbled to the hearth, using the crutch. He'd brought a ladle with him from the kitchen and stirred the mixture, then lifted the spoon to his lips, taking a cautious sip.

"Almost done," he said with a satisfied nod. "And none too soon. I'm feeling weak from hunger."

Indeed, even with the crutch, he stumbled back to his seat. His face appeared flushed, but it may have been due to standing over the open fire. Once seated, he sighed, and his eyelids drooped, giving him a sleepy look she found most alluring.

"My head is spinning like the devil. Talk to me, Emma. Keep me awake."

She searched for a safe topic, one that would flow from her with ease yet not reveal too much. She settled on telling him about Abner Netherborne's latest sermon.

"Mr. Netherborne is adamant about honesty. He said liars are an abomination to the Lord, and their tongues will burn like flames in the fires of hell." Her own tongue tingled in accusation. Why had she chosen that particular sermon?

Timothy's lips curved up. "Honesty is important, but have you ever told a lie because to speak the truth would inflict harm on someone?"

"Well. Once, I told a gentleman he was an excellent dancer even

44

though he trod on my slipper. My foot throbbed the remainder of the evening."

He chuckled again, the sound not nearly as hearty as it had been. "And do you believe that's something that will lead to your eternal damnation?"

"I certainly hope not." She'd told more than one such untruth during her Seasons in London, not to mention more than a few to Mr. Netherborne himself. "But I suspect Mr. Netherborne will demand complete truthfulness from me when we marry." The idea itself depressed her.

"And if he asks if you love him, what will you answer?"

"I . . . I . . . don't know. Perhaps I'll grow to love him."

"Perhaps. If you believe in love."

"Don't you?"

He delivered his response without hesitation. "No."

Why did her stomach drop to her toes at his answer? And why did she even care what he thought?

WHAT HAD POSSESSED HIM TO BRING UP THE SUBJECT OF LOVE? Timothy tried to focus as the room spun before him. The vertigo intensified as he had stirred the chicken stew. Something was definitely wrong.

Surely it wasn't the mention of love, but the mere thought of it constricted his chest. Love was for fools and dreamers, and believing in it only ended in disappointment and pain.

He'd been the recipient of that hard lesson from the beautiful, but betraying, Merilee. He vowed never to lower his guard again, instead shielding his heart by avoiding any romantic entanglements.

Yet he hadn't expected the jolt of energy shooting through him when he touched Emma. Her eyes had been wide and trusting as he'd cleaned her scratched face and hands, and his gaze had drifted unbidden to her lips more than once.

The ringing in his head muddled his thoughts, but he ordered himself to fortify his defenses lest he be subjected to a sneak attack. He brushed it off as simply physical attraction and shifted away from her, putting more space between them. His reaction would be the same with any beautiful woman. Would it not?

"Don't you intend to marry?" she asked, drawing his attention back to her.

"Of course. Someday."

"And don't you wish to love your wife?"

"Love isn't a requirement for marriage. Mutual respect and an understanding of what's expected is sufficient. Many people have less."

Her blue eyes narrowed. "That's not what I asked you."

Damnation! "No. I don't wish to love my wife. As I said, I don't believe love exists. Oh, there is attraction, and I hope to have enough to produce children. But love? I have no desire for such a weakness. People who believe in love have their hearts crushed when they discover that their idealized view of the other person is false."

His buzzing head now pounded, and he rose again, more to end Emma's interrogation than to check the stew. He only managed two steps when he stumbled and the overpowering vertigo sent him crashing to the floor.

So hot. Had the fire escaped the hearth?

"Timothy, Timothy. Wake up." Emma patted his cheeks. Her face spun before him.

Wake up? What is she on about? He blinked, trying to clear his blurry vision.

"Thank goodness. You were lying there so still for several minutes. I thought you died."

He braced himself on his elbows and tried to rise, but the vertigo returned. "Dizzy," he croaked.

Emma slipped her arm around his waist, and pulled him to his feet, returning him to the settee. She placed a cool hand to his forehead. "You're burning up with fever." Her touch was soft and gentle as a kiss.

Kiss. His fevered mind focused on the thought, and his eyes drifted to her lips.

"Here, lie down." She lifted his feet, attempting to stretch him out on the short settee, but his legs protruded over the arm. As uncomfortable as the position was, at that moment, he didn't care. He would curl up in a bog as long as he didn't have to move.

"Tell me what to do," she said. Genuine concern covered her face, her blue eyes expressive with worry.

"In my bag, there are several small pouches of medicine. Find the one that says willow bark." His words sounded muffled as if spoken from a distance. He watched her through half-open lids, scrambling to find his bag and digging through it.

"Aha!" She held up the pouch. "Now what?"

"Find a pot to boil water, then make a tea from it. Two spoonfuls of the bark per cup of hot water."

Sounds of Emma rattling around in the kitchen drifted in, the clanging of pots and pans like a hammer to his head.

Most definitely, something was wrong. Sharp pain pulsed in his ear accompanied by the infernal ringing. He struggled to self-diagnose, remembering the theorem presented in medical school about particles called animalcules that could be transmitted via the soil or even the air. Although he personally discounted the touted miasma theory, perhaps a tiny particle had blown into his ear from the punishing wind of the storm.

Then he waited for Emma to return, hoping the tea would at least reduce his fever and pain.

PRISCILLA FOUGHT THE PANIC SEIZING HER CHEST, CONSTRICTING it as if her stays had been too tight. Her hands shook as she rummaged through the assortment of pots and pans left in Mr. Thatcher's kitchen.

Water? Where would she get water? She spun in a circle, for

once in her life wishing she'd not been reared as an aristocrat's daughter.

Maybe he simply fainted from hunger. Once he'd eaten some of the stew, surely he would regain his strength. But it didn't explain the heat emanating from him. Her own hands were still cool to the touch, not yet absorbing the heat from the fire.

Quickly throwing her cloak on, she went outside to the pump by the well, praying it had not frozen over. She grasped the arm of the pump and bore down with all her might, barely budging it.

"Gah!" She banged the pot against the metal pump. "Come on, you!" She tried again, and with a squeak, the arm gave way. She threw her weight into it. Three solid pumps later, water trickled from the spout, and she held the pot underneath to collect the precious liquid.

Finished, she raced back inside the cottage and into the room where Timothy waited. Water sloshed in the pot as she skidded to a stop. His eyes were closed, and he lay so still she wondered if he had died.

Dear Lord, don't let him be dead! What would she do? She couldn't leave him there to rot, but how would she explain how she'd known he was there? Even worse than being discovered with a man in a compromising position was being discovered with one who was dead and couldn't marry her.

"Timothy," she whispered.

No answer.

Focusing on his chest, she watched for the telltale signs of rise and fall.

Why did he have to be wearing so many clothes?

Heat rose to her cheeks at the thought. Thank goodness he couldn't see her.

There. Not at his chest, but gentle movement near his abdomen reassured her that he still lived. She approached with cautious steps. "Timothy," she called again, a little louder.

His long auburn eyelashes fluttered against his cheeks. Could a man be beautiful? She rather thought in Timothy's case he could.

"Timothy!"

He startled, jerking awake, his eyes wide and searching. "What?" He tried to rise but fell back against the settee. "Good God, my head."

"I have the water."

He nodded. "Remove the pot with the stew. It should be done, then replace it with the pot of water. Use something to shield your hands so you don't burn yourself." His voice sounded gruff and raw, not the smooth baritone she'd heard before.

She nodded, even though his eyes had once again fallen shut and couldn't see her. She grabbed several cloths from the kitchen and did as he instructed. "Perhaps once you've eaten, you'll feel better."

He moaned. Was that a yes or a no?

After placing the pot of stew in the kitchen and spooning out two healthy servings, she returned to the parlor and set the bowls on a table near the settee.

She jostled his shoulder, fear taking root in her chest. "Timothy."

He opened a bleary eye and groaned.

"Can you sit up? Try to eat something."

He moved slowly, grasping the back of the settee and pulling himself upright.

She held out the bowl of stew.

From the way his hands shook as he reached for it, there would be more stew in his lap than in his stomach.

"Never mind." She gathered the thick mixture on the spoon, then lifted it to his mouth. "Open."

The aroma of the chicken and vegetables teased her nostrils, and she wanted nothing more than to shovel the stew into her own mouth. But Timothy needed her.

What a day it had been. No one had ever *needed* her before. Yet twice in one day—even as ill-equipped as she'd been for both situations—she'd been truly needed.

Timothy's eyes closed as he sucked the stew from the spoon,

and his lips tipped up ever so slightly. "Good," he said. He pushed her hand holding the spoon toward her. "Now you. Eat."

Her stomach growled again—as if she needed to be reminded of its emptiness. Instead of retrieving her own bowl, she dipped her spoon into Timothy's bowl and filled it with the savory stew. Lord, it smelled good.

As the herbs, chicken, and vegetables hit her tongue, she, too, closed her eyes, appreciating Timothy's reaction. It *was* good. Not only good—delicious.

"Good?" he asked, sounding more than a bit cocky.

She fought the smile. "It will do."

He snorted a laugh, then grabbed at his ear, uttering a curse.

She waited until he settled himself, then fed him another spoonful. They alternated until the spoon scraped against the sides of the bowl. She reached for hers, still full on the table.

He shook his head. "No more for me."

She shrugged and finished every morsel in the second bowl. Mr. Netherborne would accuse her of gluttony, but she didn't care.

After setting aside the empty bowl, she rose and checked the pot of water. "It's boiling."

"Two spoons of the willow bark. Let it steep for a few minutes."

She prepared the tea. Holding the cup to his lips, she placed her hand on his back, steadying him as he drank. If possible, he seemed even hotter than he had before they'd eaten.

"It would help if I could fully lie down. Surely there's a bed somewhere?"

"Upstairs, I believe. There is a stairway tucked behind the kitchen. Can you make it with your crutch?"

"I'll try." He rose and hobbled toward the kitchen.

Candle in hand, Priscilla remained one step behind, ready to catch him should he lose his balance. His arm holding the crutch shook, and perspiration dotted his forehead. He made it up two stairs, then sagged against the wall of the stairway.

"I'm afraid I will require your help again. I apologize."

The narrow passageway of the staircase barely allowed one

body, much less two. Pressed tight to his side, she wrapped her free arm around his waist and he draped his over her shoulders until they painstakingly made it up the flight of stairs and to the bedroom.

He landed on the bed in dramatic fashion, his feet still dangling off the side.

She fluffed the pillows under his head and lifted his stockinged feet onto the bed, then covered him with several blankets. As she pressed her hand against his forehead to test his temperature, he grasped her wrist.

"Emma, my angel."

CHAPTER 6—
MIS"CONCEPTIONS"

Everything about the situation was wrong, yet surprisingly right. Timothy strained to focus on Emma's face. Lord, she was beautiful, and when she leaned over him, placing her delicate hand upon his forehead, her touch was like heaven, cool and soothing.

How had he thought her a termagant?

"Emma, my angel." He closed his eyes, his body fluctuating between burning and freezing. At the moment, heat radiated from him, cooking him from the inside out. He yanked at his cravat to pull it off, but his fingers fumbled at the knot he had painstakingly tied that morning.

"Allow me," Emma said.

His hand dropped to his side, too weak to argue with her. It was improper for an unmarried woman to undress a man, yet he mumbled a weak, "Thank you."

Light flickered from the single candle Emma had carried upstairs, casting deepening shadows on the walls. With food in his stomach and the softness of the bed beneath him, Hypnos sang a seductive song, luring him closer to what he required—restful slumber.

"It's cold in here," she said, darting a glance toward the empty hearth.

Not to him, it wasn't. He struggled to rise from the bed. "I should start a fire." No sooner than he placed his feet on the floorboards, vertigo overcame him again, and he fell back onto the bed.

"Rest," she said. "I'll try. Can you tell me how?" The bossy, indignant tone with which she had addressed him earlier had vanished, replaced now with sincerity and perhaps a little humility.

He lifted his head from the bed, taking inventory of the wood left next to the fireplace.

"Take the kindling—the small pieces of wood. Set them under the grate. Put two logs on the grate at an angle to start. Then light the kindling with a taper. It should be dry enough to catch."

As she worked, he guided her with the only thing he could offer—his words of encouragement. Every few moments, she would glance over her shoulder to gauge his reaction, and he nodded his approval.

Soon the comforting smell of woodsmoke and crackle of flames licking the wood filled the room.

With her task complete, she collapsed into the single chair in the room. Her eyelids drooped, and her head bobbed against her chest. She had to be exhausted as well.

When they'd climbed the stairs, he noticed there was but one bedroom in the tiny cottage, and he was currently occupying the only bed.

"Emma," he called, knowing full well what he was about to propose would be considered indecent. Yet he couldn't allow her to sleep in a chair.

"Come join me."

PRISCILLA'S EYES SHOT OPEN AS IF SOMEONE SLAPPED HER ACROSS the face. Surely she had misheard him. He would not suggest something so improper. "I beg your pardon?"

When he patted the side of the bed next to him, her heart lurched, pounding so hard against her rib cage she thought it might burst from her chest.

"You can't be comfortable in that chair. Share the bed with me."

"But . . . But . . ." The idea terrified her, and although they were the only people present, she lowered her voice to whisper the scandalous words. "What if I get with child?"

What began as a laugh turned into a fit of coughing, and he wiped at his eyes. "We're both still clothed. I promise nothing will happen. I'm too ill to even consider it."

She rose from the chair and inched closer to the bed. "Are you certain I won't get with child? Mama said if I lie with a man, I would get with child." Her mother had explained little before Priscilla's nightmarish failed wedding to the duke, simply saying it would be necessary for Priscilla to lie with him. Her cheeks burned at the thought.

"Simply lying next to a man won't get you pregnant. It takes a bit more than that."

"Oh." Perhaps that's what her mother meant when she said the duke would explain things. She chewed her lip, debating if she should proceed—both with additional questions and her approach toward the bed.

Could she? Perhaps the precise question was—should she? Obviously, she *could*. The bed appeared considerably more comfortable than the lumpy chair upon which she had sat. Her neck had already begun to cramp. And he *was* ill. Certainly he wouldn't attempt anything indecent in his condition?

Or it could be an elaborate ruse, specifically designed to lure her into the bed next to him so he could force himself upon her.

The lure of the soft mattress won the battle regarding the second question, and before she knew it, she stood, gazing down at the patchwork quilt spreading across the bed. At first, she only sat on the edge, testing the softness beneath her. Lovely. After removing her half-boots, she stretched out flat on top of the counterpane, lying straight as a pin. Her arms remained glued to her sides for fear she might accidentally brush his body in case touching while lying next to a man would be the determining factor.

She cast a quick glance at him.

Although his eyes remained closed, his lips quirked at one corner. "Relax, Emma."

She jumped, the suddenness of his words having the opposite effect than their intention. "How can I relax when you're grinning like that?"

"I'm not grinning." His smile widened.

"You are. Do you find this funny?"

"Immensely."

"Oh, you!" She huffed, crossing her arms over her chest.

Men.

As she lay atop the brightly colored counterpane, she wished she could bury herself beneath its warmth. The fire had barely begun to burn, and the room was still unbearably chilly. Heat emanated from Timothy's body, and she scooted a tiny bit closer.

She worked her bottom lip again, pondering. "What does it take?"

"Hmm?" He practically groaned his mumbled response.

"You said it takes a bit more than lying next to a man. I should like to know what it takes, so I'm on guard lest you try it."

At that, his eyes shot open. "Obviously, your mother has not prepared you for your upcoming marriage. However, speaking about such things while we are both lying in bed together would not be conducive to preserving your innocence. I suggest you drop the subject and try to get some sleep. You have my word as a gentleman that I won't do anything to compromise you."

Did he not realize that merely being alone with him had compromised her beyond repair?

And yet, she still wondered what that *anything* would be.

EMMA'S QUESTIONS HAD DONE NOTHING TO AID IN TIMOTHY'S attempt to sleep. In fact, once she'd brought it up, even in his weakened state, all he could think about was making love to her. He turned on his side away from her in case she glanced down and noticed the rise of the counterpane beneath his stomach.

Damnation!

How could he become excited when he felt like bloody hell? Every muscle ached, and yet he still yearned to hold her in his arms and kiss her senseless, then bury himself deep within her. He struggled to push the thoughts from his fevered mind.

Was she really so innocent as to believe she could become pregnant by simply lying next to a man? Mothers did their daughters a disservice by not explaining things. Or perhaps that was their intent—filling girls' minds with such nonsense to keep them from placing themselves in what could be precarious situations. He stole a peek over his shoulder at Emma.

She had moved from her previously straight position to being curled in a tight ball, her slim body trembling. Why hadn't she crawled beneath the covers?

He rose, relieved when the vertigo remained at bay, then hobbled to the fire to stir it to life.

She'd done an adequate job for someone who had never started a fire. Everything about her puzzled him. She was obviously a woman of gentle breeding, used to having servants tend to basic needs such as preparing food and fires, and yet she'd delivered a baby. Nothing made sense to him.

His military training kicked in. Cautious to take anything at face value or trust in anyone's word, he wondered how much she had told him was truthful. And why did she only provide her Christian name?

When he tried to rouse her and encourage her to get beneath the covers, she merely moaned and rolled over. But it was enough for him to scoot the counterpane from beneath her and replace it on top. She sighed with pleasure, which did nothing for the desire he continued to tamp down.

After climbing back into bed next to her, he pulled the counterpane over himself. Emma snuggled up next to him, pressing her body to his.

God help him. It would be one of the longest nights of his life. But the softness of her next to him was a torture he both cursed and welcomed. He stared at the flickering light on the ceiling until the candle sputtered out and his eyelids grew heavy.

Dull throbbing of his ankle roused him from his slumber. A rooster crowed, probably mourning the loss of the hen they'd consumed in the stew the evening before. He cautiously cracked one eye open. Orange light of dawn filtered into the small room from the slit in the window curtains.

Mercifully, the pain in his ear subsided. His head no longer pounded, and the inferno blazing inside his body from the prior evening had died out, leaving him feeling comfortably cool except for the heat generated from the body next to him.

Emma's arm draped casually across his chest. She had snuggled next to him with her head against his shoulder, the gentle rhythmic rise and fall of her abdomen indicative of someone in deep slumber.

With a finger, he stroked her cheek, barely brushing the delicate skin. Her long eyelashes fluttered, and her lips twitched upward. His only thought—Mr. Netherborne was a lucky man. He pushed that aside, reminding himself he had given up on the notion of love and romance.

She wasn't his to lie next to, hold in his arms, or kiss her delectable lips. Yet here he was, doing all but the last. He should remove himself from the temptation all together. Yet, what would be the harm in remaining a few more moments while she slept?

Moments turned to minutes and before he knew it, the sun had fully risen and shone brightly, reflecting off the snow-covered ground outside and illuminating the small room. Emma's breathing changed from slow and even to quick and shallow, and her eyes moved beneath her lids.

She stretched against him, the sensation of her body so close to his doing nothing to assist in his resolve to be a gentleman.

With thumb and index finger, he carefully lifted a stray, blond lock of hair from her cheek and tucked it behind her ear. "Good morning."

❦

PRISCILLA HAD BEEN HAVING THE MOST PLEASANT OF DREAMS. Timothy held her in his arms and was preparing to kiss her.

His voice, no longer hoarse and raspy, whispered in her ear, "Good morning."

"Hmm," she moaned. She pressed against him. Still lost in her dream, her mind had not quite processed his words. What was he waiting for? She wanted that kiss. "Kiss me."

Lips brushed against hers, at first with the lightest of touches, then becoming more insistent. Something rigid pressed against her stomach. Was there something between them? Her mind clawed its way to consciousness while her body fought to remain in the lovely, dreamlike state, reluctant to forgo the euphoric sensation enveloping her.

She opened her eyes. Timothy's face pressed against hers in a deep, sensual kiss. This particular dream was unnervingly real.

A rooster crowed, and sunlight filtered through the curtains. In one horrific moment of clarity, she realized she was no longer dreaming.

With a sound shove, she pushed Timothy away and bolted upright. "What are you doing!?"

The devilish expression on his face appeared not at all contrite. "Kissing you."

For his honest answer, he received a blistering slap. "You promised!"

He sat up and rubbed his cheek. "Ow, that stings. What precisely did I promise?"

"To be a gentleman."

"You asked me to kiss you. As a gentleman, I simply obeyed your command."

She scrambled from the bed, pulling the counterpane with her and clutching it to her breast. "And how did I get under the covers?"

She paced in a circle around the room, muttering more to herself than to him. "Oh, no. No, no, no." She glanced over and pointed at the strange bulge rising from his breeches. "And *what* is *that?*"

He gazed down. "I can't help what my body does. It's morning, and you were especially enticing."

Her throat tightened as the magnitude of the situation slammed into her. What if his condition was the *anything*? "Am I . . . will I . . .?"

His brow furrowed. "What?"

She crept a few steps closer and lowered her voice to a whisper, lest even the dust motes overhear the frightening news. "Am I with child?"

Timothy threw himself back onto the bed and ran a hand across his face. "God save me from uneducated women."

CHAPTER 7—THE TANGLED WEB WE WEAVE

Timothy peeked through the gap in his fingers, worried Emma would throw a heavy object at his head. Although the boot she'd thrown at him the night before had missed him, it had been close, and the heel could have done serious damage had it struck him.

Emma glared down at him. "Well, am I?"

"No. Stop worrying. But please have your mother explain things to you in a little more detail before you marry your Mr. Netherborne. You'll be doing yourself—and Mr. Netherborne—a favor."

He swung his legs over the side of the bed and, placing a minimum amount of weight on his injured ankle, stood. Thankfully, the swelling and pain had subsided.

Gingerly he made his way to the window and threw back the curtains. Bright sunlight flooded the room. "It appears the storm had ended. I need to check on the horse."

Her eyes widened. "Will you . . . return?"

"Of course. I can take you home or wherever you wish."

Color drained from her face. "To preserve our reputations, perhaps it would be best that you not take me all the way. If we go toward town, we could stop outside, and I could travel the rest of the way on foot."

"Very well." He tucked the crutch under his arm, hobbled from the room, and closed the door behind him.

After sliding his boots on, thankfully without too much trouble, he donned his coat, scarf, and hat. Snow had piled outside, and he braced his shoulder against the wooden door, giving a sound shove. Wind had blown drifts against the house, but there was less accumulation farther out. Light from the clear blue sky reflected off the white blanket before him, half blinding him. He raised his hand to shield his eyes. Thank goodness clouds no longer threatened to add to the remnants of the snowstorm.

He inched his way to the ramshackle stables where his horse had, hopefully, survived the night. A soft whinny greeted him as he approached, and he breathed a sigh of relief. Grateful the dull ache in his ankle had subsided to a mere twinge, he placed the crutch aside and tended to the horse, forking up a bit of hay left in the corner.

"There's a good man," Timothy said, brushing the horse's brown coat. "We'll be back on our way in no time. There will be a fine reward of oats and maybe an apple for you when we reach the nearest inn."

With the horse contentedly munching on the hay, Timothy set about hoping to find eggs from any chickens that had escaped Emma's clutches. He laughed to himself, remembering the sight of her and her grin of victory as she held the chicken aloft in triumph.

Voices drifted across the white expanse from what, presumably, was the snow-covered road. As quickly as he could move on his injured foot, he hurried around the stable, hoping to catch their attention, yet stopping short when he heard one man call out.

"Miss Pratt!"

Was that Emma's last name? Timothy didn't recall her mentioning it, but it sounded vaguely familiar. Had he heard it from her or from someone else? He prepared to step forward and opened his mouth to call back, but the clarity of the situation halted him. It would ruin her if they discovered she had spent the night alone with him in the cottage, regardless of the fact nothing untoward had happened.

Except for that kiss.

As tempting and exciting as it had been, one kiss wasn't enough to give up his freedom as a bachelor. Not to mention what Emma wanted. Her request to leave her outside of town clearly indicated she desired their predicament remain a secret. Although she admitted she didn't harbor a tendre for her Mr. Netherborne, it would be unfair of Timothy to presume she wished out of the betrothal.

Instead, he remained hidden—and silent, but ready to spring into action should she need him.

The other man, who appeared older, pointed to the cottage. Wisps of smoke from the dying embers of the fire rose from the chimney. The men moved their horses toward the cottage, and the younger man called out once more. "Miss Pratt! Are you inside?"

Emma stepped outside, her cloak wrapped around her shoulders. She glanced around, her movements frantic and jerky, and although Timothy couldn't see her well, he imagined her panic, thinking they'd discovered her in a compromising situation.

The younger man dismounted and approached.

Strange, he didn't run toward her, gathering her in his arms in relief as Timothy expected, but instead, motioned about with his arm, speaking to her in words Timothy couldn't hear.

Emma shook her head, and once the other man dismounted, they joined her and entered the cottage.

ICY CHILLS HAVING NOTHING TO DO WITH THE WEATHER SNAKED up Priscilla's spine as she faced Mr. Netherborne and Mr. Wilson. Hearing someone call her by her last name—which she had purposely kept from Timothy, had set her on the verge of panic.

She pulled her cloak tighter around her shoulders as Mr. Netherborne approached.

"Thank the heavens, Miss Pratt. We've been looking for you for hours." Mr. Netherborne pointed a finger toward her face. "You're injured."

Memories of Timothy's gentle touch as he tended to her scratches flooded her mind. "No, I'm fine. Cold and hungry, but unharmed."

Mr. Wilson sent her a sheepish and apologetic glance. "I hadn't even realized you left until late last night. When I arrived at your home this morning to ensure you had returned safely, your poor mother panicked and insisted I enlist Mr. Netherborne in a search."

Mr. Netherborne nodded. "Praise God Mr. Wilson noticed the smoke from Mr. Thatcher's cottage. Perhaps we should step inside and warm ourselves a mite before returning you safely home?"

Priscilla nodded and led them inside. She quickly scanned the room, grateful that Timothy's boots, coat, scarf, and hat weren't lying about. What was keeping him? She cast a quick glance around again, worried he would appear any second and cause her ruination.

A small part of her almost hoped for it. Timothy Marbry seemed a much more amiable and exciting prospect for a husband than Abner Netherborne. But she had serious doubts he would offer to marry her. Especially when he discovered her true identity.

The fire in the living room hearth had long since died. The smoke Mr. Netherborne had mentioned must have come from the upstairs fireplace. "I'm afraid it's not very warm in here. I started a fire upstairs in the bedroom." At least that part was true.

Mr. Netherborne gazed around the room, his expression calm, his demeanor unflappable. "What happened, Miss Pratt?" Even his voice seemed serene, as if he had little concern for her welfare.

Rather than answer Mr. Netherborne directly, she turned toward Mr. Wilson, who seemed more concerned than her fiancé. "I'm sorry to have worried you. It appeared you no longer had need of me, and I didn't want to intrude further. I thought I could make it home by myself, but I became disoriented from the snow and wandered off the road."

"It's a blessing you remembered Mr. Thatcher's place here," Mr. Wilson said. "You could have frozen to death."

Mr. Netherborne grew pensive, his eyes focused on something behind her. "You started the fire yourself?" he asked, turning his attention back to her.

Did she note a touch of suspicion in his tone?

She squared her shoulders. "I did. I'm not completely useless."

"Forgive me. I didn't mean to imply . . ."

Priscilla grew tired of the interrogation. But more importantly, she needed to remove herself before Timothy reappeared.

Where the devil is he?

"If you don't mind, I'd like to go home now."

The men nodded. Mr. Netherborne had the decency to assist her onto his horse, choosing instead to walk and lead the animal back to Priscilla's home.

He remained silent throughout the short trip, but Mr. Wilson blathered on about the new babe, telling Priscilla what a fine job she had done delivering him.

Priscilla tried ignoring him, annoyed at listening to what a cute button nose the baby had and how he cooed upon seeing his father's face. She remembered the child as a red-faced, squalling bundle, looking strikingly like a monkey she'd seen in a drawing. How people viewed the creatures as adorable was beyond her understanding.

She breathed a sigh of relief upon seeing her home rising before her on the road.

If only she hadn't stumbled upon Timothy, she would have been home, safe and warm in her own bed, her stomach full from a delicious meal their cook had prepared. Instead, she'd wrangled a chicken, started a fire, and snuggled next to a handsome man to steal a bit of his warmth.

A tiny voice inside her head prodded her. *Perhaps becoming lost was a blessing.*

True, any regret she may have harbored had more to do with not having met Timothy under more acceptable circumstances. And even if she had, she would never have been able to be herself. Not when he most likely would give her the cut direct upon learning her true identity. No doubt he'd heard all about the debacle with the Duke of Ashton—perhaps even from the duke himself.

Yes, she admitted, it was better this way. Better to have one sweet memory of a kiss than to see loathing and rejection in his eyes. She'd cherish and relive that moment in the years ahead— years most likely trapped in a loveless and passionless marriage to Mr. Netherborne.

As Mr. Netherborne assisted her from the horse, her mother appeared at the doorway, a handkerchief clutched to her bosom.

"Where have you been!"

It seemed being welcomed home with open arms and smothered with kisses and hugs was not to be. No word of thankfulness fell from her mother's lips for Priscilla's safety at being found.

At the scowl on her mother's face, Priscilla steeled herself.

"You will be the death of me."

"I'm sorry, Mama. The snow blinded me, and I lost my way."

Her mother's eyes widened. "What's on your face?"

"Minor scratches, Mother." Priscilla wanted to add that she'd been assured they would heal and not leave scars, but she held her tongue. It would not do to have her mother question how Priscilla had received that particular information.

Mr. Wilson tipped his hat. "As you'll not be needing me further, I'll be on my way. Glad you're home safe, Miss Pratt. Do call to say hello to the fine little fellow you helped deliver. My wife wishes to thank you again."

"Thank you, Mr. Wilson. I shall." Mrs. Wilson might prove the perfect source of information regarding how those fine little fellows come to be. An explanation seemed the least the woman could do to repay Priscilla for her services.

"Well, come inside." Her mother motioned Priscilla and Mr. Netherborne in.

Priscilla could envision the flames shooting from her mother's eyes—flames that would have come in handy in lighting the fire the night before.

Her mother's tone softened, becoming sugary as she turned toward Mr. Netherborne. "Thank you, sir, for finding my wayward daughter. I pray she's learned a valuable lesson, which will benefit your marriage."

Mr. Netherborne shifted, his eyes darting to the floor. Not embarrassment—something darker—more foreboding, shadowed his face. "With your consent, may I have a word with Miss Pratt alone?"

"Of course. Of course. Please use the drawing room. Keep the door ajar a bit, if you would. For propriety, you understand."

Mr. Netherborne nodded, but again, the strange look in his eyes unsettled Priscilla.

Alone in the drawing room, Mr. Netherborne stood before her, not quite meeting her gaze directly, his hands clasped behind his back.

Awkward moments passed. She opened her mouth to enquire why he wished to speak with her, but clamped it shut when he raised his hand to silence her.

"Miss Pratt," he finally said. "Were you alone all night in Mr. Thatcher's cottage?"

A lump formed in her throat, and she tried to force it down along with the lie. "Yes. Of course."

His eyes narrowed, and his lips pressed together so tightly they almost disappeared. "Think carefully, Miss Pratt, and revise your answer if you must."

Although empty, her stomach roiled. "What are you saying, Mr. Netherborne?"

"There were two bowls on the table in the cottage." As if he needed emphasis, he held up two fingers. "Two."

In a perfect imitation of the man before her, she kept her face passive. "I had a second helping."

A condemning eyebrow quirked. "And you used a fresh bowl? What did you eat?"

Ah, this she could answer truthfully. "I captured one of Mr. Thatcher's remaining chickens for a stew."

"And you prepared this stew?"

She squared her shoulders. How dare he doubt her! "As I said in the cottage, I'm not completely helpless. One can do many things when one is forced to survive."

"I see. And did you don a man's boots to venture out into the snow, perhaps to retrieve firewood?"

Oh, dear.

Heat flooded her cheeks. "What are you implying, sir?"

"There were a man's boot tracks in the snow coming from the cottage. Fresh tracks. How do you explain that?"

"Perhaps a passerby such as yourself."

Mr. Netherborne, who had always been so reserved, so passionless, glared at her, red streaking up his neck to his ears and face. "Miss Pratt. Do you expect me to believe that? The direction of the footprints came from *inside* the cottage. I would advise you to think before answering my next question. Keep in mind, I can forgive many things, but dishonesty is not one of them."

Priscilla's heart pounded from his accusatory glare.

"I will ask you one more time. Was anyone else with you in the cottage?"

Finally swallowing that pesky lump, she straightened, facing her fate head on. "Yes. But nothing happened. A man fell from his horse and injured himself. The snow prevented us both from proceeding, so I assisted him to the cottage where we could warm ourselves. But I promise, nothing happened."

"And where is this man now?"

"I don't know," she answered truthfully. "Perhaps tending to his horse in Mr. Thatcher's stable."

His hands still clasped behind his back, Mr. Netherborne began pacing the room, muttering something unintelligible. When he stopped and faced her, his demeanor shifted.

"Thank you for being honest, Miss Pratt. Although I would have hoped you had been more forthright at the beginning. I must pray about this. Such deceit does not bode well for our marriage. And although I understand your reluctance to tell me, it gives me cause to doubt your honesty that nothing in fact happened between you and this mysterious man. As such, consider our betrothal suspended. I shall leave you now to go in search of this man and obtain his side of the story, if possible. I bid you good day."

Without allowing her a word of reply, he turned and marched from the room.

When the door opened, her mother practically fell inside, her eyes wide and mouth matching. "Priscilla, what in God's name have you done?!"

CHAPTER 8—BEING PRODUCTIVE

After tidying up and checking the cottage for anything he might have left inside, Timothy saddled and mounted his horse. Unease niggled at him as he recalled the scene that had played out before him with Emma and the two men.

She'd obviously known them. But something about the younger man didn't add up in Timothy's mind. Had he been her fiancé? Her brother perhaps? Yet the man's detached demeanor upon discovering her safe and unharmed seemed too dispassionate for someone betrothed or related.

If Bea had been missing during a blizzard, Timothy knew he would have been frantic with worry. And Laurence, Bea's husband, had ridden miles in a horrible lightning storm just to apologize to her.

No, something was definitely odd about the man's behavior. Nevertheless, it wasn't Timothy's concern, and he pushed Emma and her alluring blue eyes from his mind, nudging his horse forward.

More than likely, the remnants of his feverish state still muddied his mind, and he had misinterpreted the reunion. Emma wasn't his, and sharing one kiss—even an especially arousing one—did not give him any claim to her.

Surely his weakened condition had left him vulnerable to feelings of attraction he'd tamped down five years ago. He huddled into his coat and gritted his teeth against the chilly wind as his horse plodded forward—toward home and away from Emma.

He made it to Stilton by nightfall, with another full day's journey ahead before he reached London. Grateful to find an inn with an available room, he settled into the comfortable but small bed, his stomach full from a hearty meal and his muscles tired from the long ride.

Yet the fine meal of roast lamb and potatoes paled in comparison to the chicken stew he'd shared with Emma the night before. And although a fire roared in the hearth, heating the room to perfection, the lack of Emma lying beside him left him cold. He tossed and turned, pulling the counterpane over his head, trying to forget the image of her holding the chicken out like a trophy—her face scratched and feathers strewn in her hair.

He laughed out loud at the memory, then cursed himself for being a dolt.

How could being with a woman for one short day and night affect him so greatly?

Memories and emotions he'd believed long buried stirred to life when he'd held her in his arms, and he cursed himself for allowing them to be resurrected. He'd been much better off without feelings of romance and passion clouding his judgment.

He'd been a fool once.

Never again.

Hours later, he drifted off. But even in sleep, she haunted him.

Upon arising the next morning, he vowed again to put her from his mind. His ankle had improved greatly, and no sign of fever remained, suppressing reminders of his time with the hellion who had scratched her way under his skin.

Puddles of melted snow created patches of mud as Timothy's horse wove its way back to London. Throughout the journey, his mind kept returning to Emma and her clear blue eyes and sweet rosy lips. Hope boosted his spirits that being productive at the clinic would further eradicate any remnants of the fiery blonde.

Riding through the East End, he slowed his mount, his spirits plunging as men, women, and children in ragged clothes struggled to get warm as they huddled around fires burning in large containers. He tossed a few penny coins to a boy who reminded him of Manny, the Duke of Ashton's adopted son. The boy caught them with wide-eyed wonder, then raced off as though afraid someone would demand he give the small amount back.

Timothy's heart tumbled to his boots at the need and want surrounding him during a season that celebrated joy and abundance. Spurred by his maudlin thoughts, he took a detour to Hope Clinic, eager to begin making a difference. Dusk settled over the city, and for a moment, he wondered if his plan was folly. Perhaps Harry and Oliver had long since closed the doors for the day.

But a light shimmered from the window of the clinic. As he pulled his horse to a halt, a woman exited, leading a small girl by the hand.

Timothy dismounted and tethered his horse, tipping his hat to the woman. "Is the clinic still open?"

She paused, giving him the once-over. "It is, but if you're wantin' treatment, you'll 'ave a wait."

He thanked her, then removed his valise and entered, the little bell's tinkle announcing his arrival. The woman hadn't been exaggerating. People lined the small waiting area, occupying every seat. Some sat on the floor or leaned against the walls.

"Hello?" he called out.

"You'll 'ave to wait your turn like the rest of us," one man grumbled. "The doctors is busy."

Obviously.

"I'm also a physician. I've come to help."

The subdued moans mixed with conversation grew louder as the group clamored for his assistance.

He'd never been so grateful to have completed his studies and passed his exams. A sense of purpose filled him, and he shrugged off his coat and got to work. Curious eyes peered up at him. Was there any type of order or prioritizing of treatment? He hardly knew where to begin, so he started at the end of the long row of waiting patients.

A deep masculine voice rose behind him. "Mr. Marbry?"

Timothy straightened from where he'd been bent over an older woman's lacerated hand and turned, finding the Duke of Ashton staring at him with a bemused expression.

"It's Dr. Marbry, now." Timothy grinned, overjoyed to make his announcement.

Harry Radcliffe grasped his hand and slapped him good-naturedly on the back. Harry kept a low profile at the clinic, preferring to be called Dr. Radcliffe and reserving his title and status as duke for the *ton*. "And not a moment too soon. I see you've made yourself useful."

Timothy motioned to the elderly woman. "Mrs. Brown has a nasty cut, but I don't have supplies to clean the wound."

"Let's get you both into a treatment room."

After following Harry into one of the rooms, Timothy got back to work. The line of patients seemed never-ending. During Timothy's examination of a young boy, Dr. Oliver Somersby poked his head in.

"Harry told me you were here. Welcome, and may I say I'm certainly glad to see you. You couldn't have come at a better time."

Before Timothy could answer, Oliver disappeared to retrieve another patient from the waiting area.

Hours later, the dull roar of muted conversation from waiting patients diminished, and soon quiet settled over the clinic. Once he finished treating an older gentleman, Timothy escorted him out to find the waiting area empty save for Harry and Oliver, slumped in two of the chairs.

When the patient exited, Oliver rose and turned the sign in the window, announcing the clinic was officially closed for the day.

Timothy allowed his body to sink into a chair next to Harry. "Is it always like this?"

Harry shook his head. "No, but the bad weather always seems to take a toll on the less fortunate."

Oliver returned to his seat. "So, tell me. Have we scared you off yet?"

"Hell, no." Timothy grimaced at his slip of cursing in front of the duke.

Harry laughed and patted him on the back. "Good."

"To be honest," Timothy said, "it feels damn good to be productive." His mind drifted unbidden back to Emma, his first official patient, and the scratches on her face from the angry chicken.

"We can promise you that," Oliver said. "But if you both don't mind, I'll be off. I promised Camilla I'd be home for supper—for once." He rose and pulled on his greatcoat and hat. "And trust me, I don't want to disappoint Camilla. There would be no end to my penance."

Harry tipped his head back, his eyelids falling shut. For a moment, Timothy thought he'd actually fallen asleep. "How long have you been back in London?"

"I only just arrived. I'd planned to head to my family's townhouse, but riding through here and seeing the faces of the poor, I felt compelled to stop and see if the clinic was still open for the day."

Harry's eyes popped wide open. "You haven't even been home?"

Timothy shook his head.

"Good God, man. Go home."

When Timothy rose and strode over to retrieve his coat, his ankle gave way, and he stumbled.

Harry shot from his chair. "What is it? You're limping."

"My ankle. I took a tumble from my horse two days ago and twisted it. To be honest, I hadn't even noticed the ache while I was treating the patients. But now . . ."

"Is your horse outside?"

Timothy looked out the window, cursing his naiveté. "Um. It appears it's missing."

Drawing a hand down his face, Harry sighed. "I can't say it surprises me. Come. I'll take you home in my carriage. And tomorrow I'll arrange for another horse to be sent to your home. If I had known, I would have advised you where to stable your mount."

Settling against the plush squabs of the ducal carriage, Timothy exhaled a contented sigh.

Harry's eyes crinkled at the corner as he gave a soft chuckle. "Exhausted?"

"Completely. But it's a good exhaustion." His stomach growled, the sound filling the compartment of the carriage.

"And hungry. If I didn't know you would be eager to see your family, I'd invite you to join Maggie and me for dinner."

"Perhaps another time, Your Grace?"

Harry smiled and swatted Timothy on the leg with his hat. "None of that Your Grace business. Call me Harry, both inside and outside of the clinic. I've finally strong-armed your sister into it. Of course, Laurence helped persuade her."

"I can't wait to see the baby. I'm sure she's grown considerably."

"And thriving. I'm honored that both Beatrix and Laurence have requested me personally to see to little Lizzie's health."

"They want the best for their children." The idea of his sister as a parent still surprised him, but from her letters, it had become clear that Bea was a devoted and excellent mother.

The carriage jerked to a halt. Timothy gave his thanks, bidding Harry goodbye, and strode up to the steps of his parents' townhouse. He'd given up his own rented apartments when he'd returned to Edinburgh to finish his studies. First on his list of things to do now that he was back home would be finding a new residence.

Preston, his parents' butler, opened the door at the first knock. His dour expression hadn't changed a bit. He took Timothy's hat and coat and said in his typically droll voice, "Your mother and father are in the upstairs parlor. Your mother has expressed her concern regarding your late arrival."

Translation: I am in for a severe tongue lashing.

Timothy ran a hand through his unruly hair. Then, tugging briefly on the edges of his coat to straighten it, he took a deep breath and climbed the stairs to face the dragon.

Boughs of greenery and holly decorated the hall and wound through the spindles of the staircase, the festive mood not matching his own. Servants bustled around him, each giving him a quick but courteous nod and "Welcome home, Master Timothy."

Excited chatter drifted down the staircase as he ascended one torturous step at a time, his ankle still throbbing mercilessly. A baby's mournful wail alerted him that Bea and Laurence had joined them, and he breathed easier that there would be some friendlier faces to greet him.

His parents had been none too happy about his decision to pursue medicine, especially his mother. And though his father didn't oppose his choice outright, he remained silent when Timothy would rather have had his support.

At least, other than little Lizzie's cry, everyone sounded in festive spirits.

When Timothy entered the parlor, Laurence peered up from where he cradled little Lizzie in his arms. Her chubby hands wrapped around his cravat, attempting to either untie the neckcloth or choke her father with it. Laurence nudged Bea, and her eyes flew wide, the smile on her face as blinding as the snow outside the abandoned cottage.

Damnation! He must stop thinking about Emma!

"Timothy!" Bea bounded from her seat and raced toward him, pulling him into her arms. With ease, he picked her up and swung her around in a circle, much as he had when they were children.

She appeared well, and marriage had obviously agreed with her. Of course, much of that had to do with the fact she'd married the man she'd loved for eight years. Why she'd never confided in him—

her own brother—about her feelings for his best friend had baffled him to that very day.

His parents followed suit, each coming to embrace him and welcome him home.

"Where have you been?" his mother scolded. "We've been worried sick. We expected you days ago."

"Now, Matilda. He's here now. That's all that matters."

Timothy gaped at his father and blinked. Was the man actually standing up to his wife for once?

"Welcome home, son." His father clasped Timothy's hand, giving it a firm shake. "Ignore your mother," he whispered, and Timothy had an unsettling feeling perhaps he'd slipped into the home of some other Timothy.

His father patted him on the back and addressed his mother. "He appears no worse for wear. No need to question him about his whereabouts."

Timothy darted a glance toward his mother, whose lips had pressed into a tight line. He turned a questioning look toward Bea.

"Much has changed, Timothy," she whispered in his ear. "We'll speak privately later."

"Come and sit by your mother." His mother returned to the settee and patted a cushion next to her. "Let me look at you."

With the first two steps, his limp announced all was not as well as his parents believed.

His mother's hand shot to her chest. "Oh, dear. You're injured."

"A minor sprain. I had a bit of a tumble from my horse. Snow had fallen heavily in Lincolnshire, and the beast lost his footing, trapping me under him. I had to seek shelter and wait out the storm before continuing onward."

He recounted the details of his time at the cottage, sans one important element. With no mention of Emma in his story, his tale suffered from her exclusion.

"Why in the world didn't you obtain passage on a coach?" Laurence asked, jostling eight-month-old Lizzie in the air, which resulted in a fit of giggles from the imp of a child.

"To be honest, I thought I would travel faster by horse. I didn't expect the blizzard."

"Oh, you poor dear," his mother cooed as he settled next to her. "Quick, Beatrix, fetch a stool for your brother to prop his injured foot."

Bea did as instructed, but not without giving him a solid eye roll as she positioned the stool under his booted foot. Perhaps things hadn't changed as much as he first suspected.

⚜

WITH BLEARY EYES, PRISCILLA STARED OUT THE WINDOW AT THE snow-covered ground. Everything appeared bleak and barren and, although others found joy in the blanket of white, it only reminded her of her life.

Dull. With nothing of interest to catch the eye and spark the imagination.

After the severe dressing down she'd received from her mother, she'd cried herself to sleep. At least she'd resisted the pressure to name Timothy as the man with whom she'd spent the day and night alone in Mr. Thatcher's cottage.

The glorious day and night.

She stroked the window's lace curtain, running the material through her thumb and forefinger. Something about the texture reminded her of the kiss she'd shared with Timothy. How could something be both soft and rough at the same time?

She had little faith that Mr. Netherborne would forgive her transgression, but in truth, the fact she had most likely lost yet another chance at marriage didn't upset her as it might have. Oh, she still wished to be married, but life as Mrs. Netherborne had become even less appealing after spending time with Timothy. Never had she experienced that spark of excitement when in Mr. Netherborne's presence. And the fire sizzling in Timothy's eyes never once flickered in Mr. Netherborne's.

Out of desperation, she'd risen early the next morning and

wrote to her father, who remained in London, living separately from her mother. Although she didn't expect to be welcomed back into London society, she much preferred to spend the remainder of what would be her life as a spinster in the bustle of the city.

And away from sheep.

She'd confessed everything to him. Well, all except Timothy's name. No good would come of that. Even living in the same city, she would remain on the fringes and out of Timothy's circle. However, a small part of her wondered what would happen should they chance upon each other.

Of course, all depended on her father's answer. She had tried living with her father after her initial disgrace, but the wagging tongues of the *ton* had been more than her young heart could bear. She had been desperate to get away.

She'd grown up a bit in the last three years, and it wasn't as if she was going to regain her voucher to Almack's or be admitted to homes of the more elite. But while strolling through the park on her father's arm, she would square her shoulders and hold her head high when passing the gossip mongers.

If he allowed her to come home.

For two days, her mother refused to speak with Priscilla directly, instead mumbling to herself what a disappointment her daughter had been—again. Within Priscilla's earshot, of course.

Priscilla wished there were a way to fly her letter to her father, that she might receive his response with greater rapidity.

Fortunately, her mother did not prohibit her from visiting the Wilsons and their new babe. Mrs. Wilson had been most gracious with Priscilla's thinly veiled questions about marital intimacy. And although not precisely detailed, Mrs. Wilson's accounting eased Priscilla's mind that nothing she and Timothy shared would result in a child.

Four days after her return, on Christmas Day, her mother tapped on her door. "Priscilla. Mr. Netherborne is here to see you."

She smoothed her skirts and patted her hair. The least she could do was look presentable when he broke off their engagement. As she entered the small parlor, she found him with his hands clasped behind his back, facing the window away from her.

"Mr. Netherborne." Relief eased the tension in her neck. Her voice sounded strong and not filled with desperation.

He turned, his expression unreadable, his demeanor unflappable. In short, as he always appeared. "Miss Pratt."

She moved toward a chair and motioned for him to take a seat.

He declined. "I will not stay long." He paced before her.

Not a good sign.

Eyes downcast, he pursed his lips before speaking. "I spent the past few days in prayerful consideration."

Clenching her fists, she tamped down an urge to grab his lapels and give him a firm shake to get on with it. However, one did not interrupt Mr. Netherborne when he prepared to make a pronouncement.

"I have decided to give you another chance."

She blinked, unsure she'd heard him correctly. "Pardon?"

"It would be most uncharitable of me to not give my future wife the benefit of the doubt."

She should be happy.

Relieved.

Yet, as she gazed at her future husband, she was anything but.

"There is one condition," he added.

A chill trickled down her spine.

"Which is?"

"I demand to know the name of the man. Surely you at least obtained his name? I searched around the cottage when I left, but found no trace of him, although it was clear a rider had left the stable and traveled south."

"And why do you wish to know his name? What good can come from such knowledge?"

"I wish to question him. To determine what type of man he is and if he is . . . honorable."

Priscilla sensed a trap. Would Abner Netherborne, a man of God, purposely mislead her in order to reveal Timothy's identity?

Something was afoot. She straightened before him, determined to protect Timothy at all costs. "You say you wish to be charitable. To give me the benefit of the doubt. And yet, you demand—your words—information which I do not have."

"I suggest you think about this, Miss Pratt." He paced again, his austere expression chilling the air around them. "I understand you have requested to return to London to see your father."

"How did you . . .?"

"Your mother intercepted your letter."

Anger boiled within her, and she opened her mouth.

He held up a hand to silence her. "Rest assured. You shall have your wish. Your mother has suggested that time in the busy city will help you rethink your priorities and come to realize your place is here . . . with me. I agree. It's my belief once you return to that devil's pit, you will see the error of your ways. I shall give you six months, at which time I shall come to London personally for your answer."

With that, he nodded and strode from the room.

She wanted to shout at him she didn't need his bloody six months, and he could take it and shove it up his . . .

But all she could think about was—she was going back to London!

CHAPTER 9—MARRIAGE CONVERSATIONS

Timothy bounced baby Lizzy on his knee as the family gathered to celebrate Christmas. "Mother says she looks exactly like you did as an infant, Bea." Indeed, the child had a shock of red hair and green eyes like her mother.

"Oh, but she is like her father through and through," his sister answered, glancing up from her book. "If we deviate from her schedule by mere seconds, she howls for hours. You can set a clock to her cries when she wants to eat. Exactly like Laurence. In fact . . ."

Laurence strode into the room, stopping beside his wife and kissing her on the cheek. "Did I hear my name?"

Timothy exchanged a smile with Bea. "Bea was saying what a delightful child Lizzie is and how she takes after you."

One of Laurence's eyebrows quirked. "Why do I have the feeling there is an insult buried in that statement?"

Bea covered her mouth to stifle a laugh. However, Timothy hid nothing from his best friend and guffawed. "Because you know I cannot ignore any opportunity to get in a sound dig."

Laurence lifted his daughter from Timothy's grasp. "That's true.

Insult *me* all you like. Lizzie, however, is perfect." He jostled the child gently. "Aren't you my sweetling?"

As if to contradict her father, Lizzie wailed.

Bea set down her book and stood, retrieving her daughter. "As I was about to say, it's her feeding time."

Laurence's gaze remained on Bea as she exited the room with their daughter.

"Tell me." Timothy said. "What is it that makes a man so besotted? I should like to avoid it at all costs."

Laurence turned toward him, his eyebrows tugged down in confusion. "Beg pardon?"

"My point, exactly. Has marriage caused your renowned mind to rot? You watch my sister like a forlorn puppy."

Laurence sent him a sheepish glance. "I suppose I do. But that's what love does to a man—at least this man."

"As I said, I shall avoid it then." Timothy rose and poured them both a brandy. "I have no desire to mope about after a woman."

Laurence accepted the drink and tipped his glass toward Timothy. "You just haven't met the right one."

Unbidden, a vision of Emma popped into Timothy's mind. He pushed it aside. "There is no *right one*. Other than my sister, they're all a pack of schemers, waiting to trap a man into marriage before he realizes it's too late to run. No thank you." He swallowed his brandy in one gulp, the burn trickling down his throat and settling in his chest.

About to take a drink, Laurence lowered the glass from his lips. "What has happened to you? I don't remember you being this jaded about marriage."

The haunting memory loomed, and Timothy glared at his friend. "I've grown up."

"As have we all," Laurence continued apparently oblivious to Timothy's warning. "I realize we haven't spoken much about women since you've returned home from the military, but I seem to remember you writing about someone named—"

"Stop!" Timothy slammed his empty glass so forcefully against the table the crystal decanter rang in response. "I don't wish to speak of her. Ever."

Laurence remained unfazed. "Very well. But should you wish to talk about it in the future, you'll receive no judgment from me. You're not the only one to pursue the wrong woman."

Timothy knew he should drop the subject, yet he couldn't help but ask. "What's it like?"

"What's what like?"

Timothy couldn't resist rolling his eyes. "Good God, your mind really has rotted. What we've been talking about. Being in love. Being loved in return."

"Ah. Now that I can answer in one word. Bliss. It's as if everything in your world fits together, jagged edges, misshapen pieces and all. It doesn't matter if things aren't perfect because you're so damn happy you don't care."

Laurence's eyes glazed over for a moment, and Timothy had the urge to take his pulse to see if he'd had a stroke. "It's an overall feeling of goodwill toward everyone. Much like the atmosphere of Christmastide year-round. And for those you care about who remain unattached? Well. Your greatest wish is for them to experience the same joy."

Timothy shifted uncomfortably at Laurence's pointed stare. "Am I to presume this means you intend to take on the role of matchmaking mama? Because if so, I might remind you I have one of those who can rival the best."

Laurence rose and slapped Timothy on the back before proceeding to pour them both another drink. "No. Have no fear. I won't push any debutantes into your path. You need to find the right woman yourself."

When Laurence handed him the brandy, Timothy sipped it.

What if he'd already found the right woman but she belonged to someone else?

SIX DAYS AFTER PRISCILLA HAD WRITTEN TO HER FATHER, HE arrived personally to fetch her, promptly giving her mother a severe tongue lashing.

"How could you even think to send our daughter out unchaperoned?" he bellowed at her mother.

There was little love lost between her parents, especially after the fiasco that had brought about Priscilla's disgrace.

For once, her mother remained speechless, twisting a lace handkerchief in her hands.

He narrowed his eyes, his own hands clenched into fists. "Or was this another attempt to snare a man into the parson's trap? I would have thought you'd learned your lesson, woman."

Priscilla almost felt sorry for her mother as tears shimmered in her eyes.

"You have judged me harshly," she answered, finally finding her voice. "Priscilla has an offer from Mr. Netherborne. Or at least she did."

"Which your total inability to function as a mother has now placed in jeopardy, I understand."

"It was Mr. Netherborne himself who suggested she assist with Mrs. Wilson's children when it came time for her to deliver. I merely acted to please Priscilla's future husband."

Her father gave a loud harrumph in answer, then instructed a servant to pack Priscilla's belongings so they could leave at once.

It would be a lie to say she was sorry to leave Belton, but the expression on her mother's face tugged at Priscilla's heart. The woman wasn't perfect, but she was Priscilla's mother nonetheless.

Once inside the carriage and heading back to London, Priscilla stared across the compartment at her father's unreadable face and gave a heavy sigh. "Won't you ever forgive Mama?"

"Some things can be forgiven but not forgotten, child. Your mother has made her own bed. I was a fool for allowing you to leave London to live with her."

His expression softened, and a wan smile crossed his lips. "Tell me the truth. Do you wish to marry this Mr. Netherborne?"

Timothy's visage coalesced in her mind. Would the man never leave her in peace? "Not particularly. But I do wish to marry, and he has been my only prospect. Now, I suppose I shall be a spinster." She blinked back the tears welling in her eyes. "But if I am to be a spinster, I should much rather be one in London than in the country."

"You're hardly ancient, my girl. People's memories grow cloudy with time." He grew pensive, staring out the window at the passing countryside. "Eligible gentlemen are more abundant in London. I shall increase your dowry. A number of men, titled or not, are in need of an infusion of funds that an agreeable match would remedy."

Something about the prospect of becoming nothing more than a walking purse rankled Priscilla. "So, he would be marrying my dowry to fill his coffers?"

Her father turned his gaze back toward her. "People have made matches for less. You could have your pick, the ultimate choice to accept would be completely up to you. Of course, other options exist. Lord Middlebury is still looking for a wife."

He waited, as if gauging her response.

Horror must have shown on her face, for he broke out in a grin. "Relax, Cilla. If you ever accepted a man like Middlebury, I would disown you. I'll admit that dangling the incentive of a large dowry in front of a man's nose isn't the most palatable idea, but why don't we try?"

"Very well."

"Perhaps I'll host a small soirée to test the waters. A bit of a welcome home party for you. Let's see how the *ton* responds to your return and go from there, shall we?"

A party did sound lovely. "Would there be dancing? Oh, how I miss dancing."

"Of course. Now, if you don't mind, I'm going to rest. The journey has tired me."

At that, he closed his eyes and rested his head against the back squabs of the carriage.

But Priscilla couldn't sleep. Her mind raced with images of new gowns, lavish table settings overflowing with rich food, beautiful music, and—most of all—dancing in the arms of handsome gentlemen.

Foremost among them—Timothy Marbry.

⚜

Timothy trudged up the steps of his parents' townhouse, exhausted from another day at Hope Clinic. Word had spread about the new young doctor assisting Doctors Radcliffe and Somersby, and Timothy had quickly developed a list of regular patients. Many of them giggling young women.

Both Harry and Oliver exchanged knowing glances and strongly suggested that Timothy might wish to consider finding a wife with alacrity.

It was the one thing his fellow doctors had suggested that he adamantly refused to consider.

Preston took his hat as he lumbered into the foyer of the house. "Your father wishes to speak with you in his study, sir."

"Can't it wait?" Timothy's only wish was for a hot meal and a glass of whisky to numb his already overworked brain.

"I'm afraid not, sir. Lord Saxton specifically requested to speak with you immediately upon your arrival home."

Timothy nodded and made his way to his father's study. After knocking softly, he entered without waiting for a response.

His father lifted his gaze from the journal before him. "Ah, son. Perfect timing. Take a seat."

Hours spent at the clinic during the past week had made examining his father's features an automatic response. No sign of illness was evident, although a trace of concern furrowed his father's brow. "What is it? Preston said it was urgent."

His father harrumphed and settled against the high-backed chair at his desk. "Preston exaggerates everything. I swear the man

86

thrives on drama. But I'm glad you're here. I wished to speak with you regarding the finances of the estate."

Timothy's gut clenched. Had his father been gambling again? He'd hoped the man had learned his lesson after the previous year's fiasco. "Are you ill, or is there another . . . problem?"

His father lifted a hand. "No, no. I know what you're thinking. But I'm not getting any younger. Now that you're home, it's time you grow accustomed to running things once I die."

"Can't it wait? I've been rather busy at the clinic."

"About that."

"If you're going to join Mother and start in about how it's unseemly for a viscount to have an occupation—"

"Calm yourself. I wasn't going to lecture you. Quite the opposite. I think it's an excellent idea. Of course, I would prefer you performed your duties for those more able to pay commensurate to your skills. But I admire your desire to assist the poor. Your sister would have my head if I weren't supportive."

His father pinned him with serious eyes. "Having a source of income not dependent on the estate will be advantageous when you inherit. If I can't convince your mother to stop her infuriating habit of buying every bonnet she comes across, I'm not sure if there will be much coin to leave you."

"Is it truly that bad?"

"Although Montgomery saved my sorry hide from disgrace and penury with his fool-hardy wager, I'm not out of the woods. My steward has reported numerous necessary repairs, and the crop harvests didn't meet expectations."

He ran a hand down his face, and at that moment, he aged before Timothy's eyes. "Running an estate requires more than simple reliance on a trusted advisor. It requires personal involvement. With an outside occupation, you will need additional assistance. My man is training his son to succeed him. But if you truly mean to devote your time to the clinic, you will want to find a secondary steward, one skilled in managing the books. That requires funds to pay them, more than your salary at the clinic provides."

"So, either way, I'll need money."

"Yes. An infusion of funds to shore up things."

The air in the room stilled. Timothy swore he could see dust motes floating in slow motion before him. A dark foreboding pressed in on him, making it difficult to breathe.

"There is one way." Solemness filled his father's eyes, an apology waiting to be delivered.

Timothy swallowed down the lump forming in his throat.

"If you marry a woman with a healthy dowry . . ."

Timothy shot from his chair. "Dear God, Father. Have you not learned anything from Bea's predicament?" Although, in fairness, his sister's situation had turned out to be beneficial for all parties. But he would never forget the pain in his sister's eyes when she believed she would have to marry Lord Middlebury.

Yet if it hadn't been for Bea's untenable situation, she would never have concocted the scheme that ultimately led to her compromise and subsequent marriage to Laurence—who loved her to distraction.

His father slammed a hand down on his desk. "For your information, I've learned everything from that. Ever since the day you and your brother-in-law humiliated me at White's, I've not sat down at a gaming table. I've apologized to Bea profusely." He took a breath, his voice softening. "I'm not insisting you marry a wealthy woman. I'm giving you an option. A way to care for the estate and pursue your ambition."

Pain shot through Timothy's jaw as he ground his teeth. "And do you have a woman in mind, or am I at least free to do my own choosing of whom to be leg-shackled to for the remainder of my days?"

"The Marquess of Stratford has been eager to find a husband for his daughter, Lady Honoria, ever since the scandal with that commoner. He wants a titled husband for her."

Nausea roiled in Timothy's stomach at how aristocratic men so easily bartered or sold their own daughters for coin or prestige.

"Pay her a call. See if you two get along."

"And the marquess would settle for a lowly viscount as a son-in-law?"

"He'd be thrilled. He's mentioned you to me specifically. I believe his words were, 'Dashing and young. Perfect for my girl.'"

Timothy harrumphed. Lady Honoria was pleasant enough. Attractive—enough to manage his marital duties. Quiet and reserved, she'd definitely be a biddable wife. She sounded positively, absolutely—wrong.

"I'll give it some thought," he answered, not sure why he agreed to even that much.

As he rose to take his leave, the image of Emma flooded his mind, and his mood darkened further.

The next day, during an unexpected lull in the deluge of patients, Timothy approached Harry in an empty examination room.

"Your Gr—Harry?"

Harry lifted his head from where he'd been filling a jar with willow bark and greeted Timothy with a smile. "Everything all right?"

"I wish to speak with you about a private matter." Normally, Timothy would discuss his predicament with Laurence, but his friend and sister had returned to their home in Dorset after the holidays to spend some time with Laurence's family before the new Season began.

Harry's blond eyebrows rose. "Oh? Let me close the door." After securing the door, Harry turned, his face solemn. "Now, what is it? You're not ill, are you? Your ankle paining you again?"

"No. No. I'm fine. My ankle is completely healed. It's regarding . . . a woman."

A smile ghosted Harry's lips so briefly, Timothy wondered if he'd imagined it. "You've been back in London for what—a week—and already have woman troubles?"

"Not troubles precisely. I need your advice."

"Very well. But I warn you, I gave Oliver advice several years ago, and now he's happily married. Although admittedly he trod an extremely crooked path to get there."

Bea had recounted how Oliver had withheld his parentage from Camilla, nearly costing their relationship and even his life. Timothy had only recently returned from the military after the uprising at the Romani camp where Oliver had nearly been hanged. The mere thought had Timothy running a finger around his cravat to loosen it.

"I fear there is no such happy ending for me. I'm sure you're aware of my father's financial difficulties that led to the fiasco with my sister."

Harry nodded. "Although, thankfully, that turned out well for her. I have much admiration for your sister."

"Yes. Well, my father has confided things still look rather bleak for the viscountcy. My position here affords additional income, but it doesn't appear to be enough to sustain the estate's coffers."

Harry shifted. "I wish I could pay you more, but things are stretched thin as they are. Perhaps another ball to raise—"

"No. I don't mean to imply I'm requesting an increase. I've only begun my duties here. You've already been more than generous."

He stared at a shelf over Harry's head holding supplies, thinking how many more they could purchase with the salary Harry paid him. "Father has suggested I make a match with a woman with a large dowry."

"I see," Harry said. "And how do you feel about that?"

"I'm not sure. It's not like I expected to marry for love. No offense, Your Grace, but I believe you, my sister, and Dr. Somersby are exceptions. I really don't believe in love, especially within the aristocracy."

Expecting Harry to become enraged or insulted, Timothy braced himself for the duke's censure.

As he often did, Harry surprised him. "I can understand that. When I was in America, I held the hope of making a love match.

At least there, I wasn't burdened by title-seeking mamas or debutantes. When I returned here to England, that hope was crushed. Even more so when I fell in love with Margaret. It truly seemed hopeless for us. But we persevered, risking all to be together."

Harry ran a hand across the back of his neck. "In truth, we still do. But we're not talking about me. Does your father have anyone in mind?"

"Yes. That's what I wanted to speak to you about. What do you know of Lady Honoria Bell?"

"The Marquess of Stratford's daughter? Not much. I remember calling on her as a courtesy to her father when I was seeking a bride. She's young, she'd just had her come-out that Season. Pretty in a quiet, understated way. Other than that, I can't tell you much."

Timothy nodded, the information not providing him much to assist in his decision.

"You would be more than likely guaranteed to have red-headed children."

"Are you talking pangenesis?"

"Of a sort. I've been keeping a journal with some observations regarding inherited traits and tendencies, hoping it might explain certain illnesses."

"From what I've heard about Lady Honoria, she's mild-mannered."

Harry nodded. "She seemed deathly afraid of me, as if she would incinerate if I touched her. Of course, some of that might have been my brother's reputation preceding me. Even Margaret took time to adjust to me."

"Could she carry on a decent conversation? What are her interests? Do you think she would be supportive of my work here at the clinic?"

"That I couldn't tell you. I called on so many women it became a blur. And truthfully, the only person who occupied my thoughts was Margaret. There are only two women, other than Maggie, who stand out in my memory during that time—your sister and one woman I refuse to think about."

Timothy's mind jolted at the mention of his sister in such a context. "Bea stood out?"

Harry nodded again. "Because of her bluntness and honesty. She told me she had no desire to marry me. Even then, I suspected her heart belonged to another. She proved a very handy—and willing—partner when I was avoiding the matchmaking mamas. However, I regret I gave your own mother false hope."

"And the other woman?"

"As I mentioned, I'd prefer not to speak of her. It was a most unpleasant situation."

Timothy presumed it was regarding the scandal Bea had written to him about. "Of course. Forgive me."

Harry waved a hand, dismissing it. "It sounds as if you're seriously considering a match with Lady Honoria. I would suggest you call upon her and discover the answer to your questions yourself. Perhaps a match between you has merit. Stranger things have happened than a marriage of convenience evolving into a love match."

Knowing the duke had a point, Timothy nodded. But he harbored no hope of such an evolution.

CHAPTER 10—INVITATIONS AND ATTACHMENTS

"A ny invitations?" Priscilla asked, nibbling at a slice of buttered toast. The hope she harbored each morning fluttered in her chest. Although not nearly as dull as Lincolnshire, she'd been practically a recluse since she'd returned to London over a month ago. She yearned to go somewhere—see anything other than the townhouse walls.

Destined to be an utter failure, the soirée her father had planned did not bode well for her overall return to London society. Most of the *ton* chose not to respond at all, but the majority who did, sent their regrets. The sole acceptance came from Lord Middlebury.

Calling it a *Welcome Home* party had been the death knell, but Priscilla bit back the criticism of her father's decision. It appeared society's memory hadn't grown as cloudy as he'd believed. Mercifully, her father sent Lord Middlebury a note informing him the party had been cancelled due to unforeseen circumstances, sparing her the torture of spending the entire evening with the odious man.

Her father's gaze lifted from the correspondence on the silver salver, his brow furrowed—whether from concern or concentration, Priscilla couldn't tell. He refused to use the spectacles his physician had recommended.

Hope fizzled out like a dying ember when he shook his head. "Only business correspondence and a letter from your mother." He held the parchment aloft, annoyance simmering in his eyes.

"Is she well?" Priscilla thought it best to keep the topic of her mother on a general basis.

"Um," he muttered. Not exactly an answer, but the bob of his head indicated the affirmative. "Mr. Netherborne has asked about you, it seems."

And here she hoped to have a pleasant day. "Is his holiness going to forgive me?"

Amusement shone in her father's eyes, and his lips twitched. "Now, Priscilla, is that any way to speak about your intended?"

"He's not my intended any longer. Not unless he gets off his high and mighty morals and forgives me for something I didn't even do." She took a less dainty bite of toast and chewed a bit more viciously, masticating it to mush.

Her father ignored her. "Your mother says he's enquired if you've given any thought to your actions and plan to come home before the six months are up."

She squared her shoulders. "I *am* home."

"Very well, then. We shall say 'goodbye' to Mr. Netherborne." He rose and tossed the letter into the blazing fire.

"And good riddance," she mumbled.

Piece by piece, the pile of correspondence dwindled before her, and she rose, prepared to return to her room—once again disappointed.

"Aha!"

Her father's words stopped her mid-stride. The tone in his voice alone caused her breath to hitch. "What is it?"

"The Duke of Ashton is hosting another masquerade ball in a

month to raise funds for his clinic. It would appear it's become an annual event."

The giddy excitement she'd experienced a moment before deflated. *The Duke of Ashton?* Of course, she couldn't go. "Oh." Even to her own ears, the dejection in her voice was evident. "Will you go?"

Her father met her gaze, and her heart melted at the love she witnessed in their depths. "*We* shall go. Together. It's a masquerade, after all. The invitation requests a response with the number of guests planning to attend. I shall respond with two."

She raced over, threw her arms around her father's neck, and placed a kiss on his cheek. "And may I have a new gown?"

He patted her arm. "I think I can arrange that."

Literally dancing from the room, she twirled a bit as she exited —which she thought was fitting.

She was going to a ball!

🪷

AIR IN THE ROOM GREW UNCOMFORTABLY WARM. TIMOTHY resisted the urge to tug at the cravat currently strangling him. Perhaps if he moved farther away from the roaring fire in the hearth? A buzzing like an annoying insect reached his ears, and he jerked his head toward the sound.

"More tea, Dr. Marbry?" Lady Honoria Bell motioned toward the tea service on the table before her.

He stared down into his still half-filled cup. Or was it half-empty? "No, thank you," he answered. What he wanted—needed— was a good stiff glass of Scottish whisky, preferably some that Laurence's cousin had sent to him for Christmas.

It had been delicious.

"How do you find the weather, Dr. Marbry?"

Did the woman need to say his name each time she addressed him?

"Cold," he answered truthfully.

95

Poor Lady Honoria looked as uncomfortable as he felt. Surely there must be something they had in common. He cleared his throat. "I understand you paint." Not that he painted. He left that up to his brother-in-law, the supplier of fine whisky Timothy sorely needed at the moment.

"I do, although my attempts are feeble compared to most."

Self-deprecating as well as quiet. No over-exaggerated talents for her. He rather liked her honesty. "I'm sure you are being too harsh on yourself. I should very much like to see your attempts and judge for myself."

Not really. So much for honesty.

Her cheeks flushed, and—at that moment—she appeared quite lovely.

"My daughter is quite accomplished on the pianoforte, sir," her mother, who accompanied them as chaperone, piped up from where she sat in the corner.

"Might you favor me with a song?" He sent her his best smile, but it felt more like a grimace.

Lord, he wished he were at the clinic lancing a boil.

Her cheeks flushed again, wiping the thought of a festering boil from his mind.

"I'm nowhere near as accomplished as your sister, Dr. Marbry. Lady Montgomery is extraordinary. I had the privilege of hearing her play at a musicale during my first Season."

Apparently, Lady Honoria had difficulty with compliments. This courting business was more difficult than he remembered.

Still, she rose and moved toward the instrument, settling herself on the bench.

Throughout her rendition of Mozart's "Rondo Alla Turca," he smiled and leaned forward, feigning interest. She played well, her fingers never missing a note, but something was lacking. He struggled to place it.

Passion.

It was as if she were only going through the motions. There was no life exuded in the tones ringing from the instrument.

Yet he applauded enthusiastically when she finished.

He was, after all, a gentleman.

And he was courting Lady Honoria Bell.

Why did he feel so hollow inside? As if a surgeon had slit him open and scooped out all of his organs and intestines.

As Lady Honoria retook her seat and smoothed her skirts, no spark of excitement rose in him.

One thing was certain. Marriage to Honoria Bell would not risk his heart.

And that was fine with him.

❦

"YOUR SMILE IS BLINDING ME, MISS." NANCY, PRISCILLA'S MAID, shaped the last strand of blond hair in the intricate coiffure she'd created. Priscilla's father had gone above and beyond to woo Nancy back into his employ.

Priscilla rose and assessed her image in the cheval mirror. Tiny seed pearls wove throughout her hair's intricate design—the effect most attractive. "You've outdone yourself, Nancy." She ran her hands down the pale blue satin of her gown, bouncing on her toes in excitement. Delicate Venetian lace edged the scandalously low neckline and puff sleeves. She slipped on the long white gloves, relishing in the silk's feel against her skin.

"You'll be the most sought-after lady there, miss."

She lifted the edge of her gown, revealing a dainty foot under the hem. "I do hope my slippers hold up. I plan to dance all night. No man will be too disagreeable." She met Nancy's dubious gaze. "They will all be wearing masks. I won't have to look at their faces. I only want to dance!"

Nancy chuckled and, nodding, left Priscilla alone.

Priscilla twirled around her room, her arms spread wide. It had been ages since she danced and, oh, how she'd missed it. She had little care with whom she partnered. Although she hoped at least one would be young, dashing, and perhaps a tiny bit flirtatious.

97

Would he suggest they slip away to a secluded spot?

Would he attempt to steal a kiss?

Sensations like tiny birds fluttered in her stomach, and her heart beat furiously.

Would she let him?

Oh, to have one magical night where no one judged or shunned her. She closed her eyes, picturing it before her.

A soft knock broke the spell.

Her father poked his head around the door. "Are you ready, my dear?"

She nodded, too excited to speak. Her father looked quite handsome in his formal attire. He'd commissioned a new waistcoat in a subtle shade of green.

Priscilla's thoughts drifted to Timothy and his moss-green eyes.

Nervous energy pulsated through her during the brief carriage ride to the Duke and Duchess's stately home on Grosvenor Square. Unconsciously, her feet tapped a happy rhythm against the carriage floor, practicing the movements of several dances.

"Anxious?"

"Hmm?" She peered up from the clasped hands in her lap.

Crinkles formed at the corners of her father's eyes. "From the movement of your feet, I half expect them to carry you from the carriage immediately when the door opens—perhaps without even trying. They seem to have a mind of their own."

"Oh." Heat rose up her neck to her cheeks. "I suppose I am a bit eager."

When they slowed to a stop, she peered out the window. A line of coaches, not unlike their own, queued in front of the grand home. Worry seeped in, replacing her excited anticipation. "Do you think anyone will recognize me?"

"You've grown up, my dear. Not only your physical appearance, although I'll admit, as your father, I'll be watching the young—and old—men carefully around you. But you've matured as well." He chuckled. "Although your exuberant feet belie the girl within.

Besides"—he tied the black demi-mask to his head—"we have these. Now don yours before we arrive."

After tying and adjusting the white mask dotted with sapphire-like stones along the edges to her face, she took a deep breath before exiting the carriage.

Remnants of the hopeful debutante she'd been surfaced, and she said a silent prayer that perhaps, tonight, she would find her one true love.

※

Timothy sipped a glass of ratafia, scrunching his nose at the overly sweet drink. "Lord, how can people drink this abomination?"

Laurence chuckled beside him. "I hear there is some brandy in a side parlor that is excellent. Shall we seek it out?" Although they were both masked, Timothy had hounded his friend for a description of his mask prior to the evening. He counted on Laurence to save him from the empty-headed chits sure to make him wish to run screaming from the ballroom.

"Even brandy seems too weak to calm my nerves. I wish we had some of your cousin's whisky."

Laurence turned toward him, his amiable smile disappearing. "What's wrong? I don't remember you being uncomfortable at one of these. That was usually left up to me."

"Ah, but now you have Bea to rescue you from boredom. So someone must take up the mantle."

Laurence scanned the crowd. "How are things progressing with Lady Honoria? Is she planning on attending this evening?"

Timothy nodded. "It's the one thing she actually talked about the other day. I swear it seems like she's afraid to speak her mind about anything. It's most frustrating."

Laurence chuffed. "You're just used to Bea. Most ladies hold their opinions to themselves around an eligible gentleman. Miranda informed me it's how they trap you before you realize what they're really like."

Timothy snorted a laugh. "Our sisters are a pair, are they not? If only all women could be like them."

"Hmm." Laurence nodded. "Speaking of . . ." Laurence straightened to attention.

Timothy followed his gaze.

Ah, there. Across the room, Bea had finished dancing with a tall, blond gentleman Timothy suspected was the duke. No matter what he did, Harry seemed to stand out in a crowd. Of course, it could also be that he was one of the first to seek Bea out for a dance.

"Go on, then," Timothy said. "Abandon your poor old friend in order to dance with your wife."

Laurence didn't answer, but made a straight path toward the spitfire redhead Timothy claimed as the best sibling.

Left alone, Timothy felt exposed, as if all feminine eyes were upon him. As if each woman took it as a personal challenge to make sure a man didn't have a moment's peace.

"A lord and a lady," the footman announced—the standard introduction at one of the Duke of Ashton's masquerades. Titled or not, the footman announced everyone in the same manner, with no names ever mentioned.

Timothy darted a glance toward the entrance, ready to dismiss yet another pair of society nobs. The glass of ratafia hovered halfway to his lips as the air in the room seemed to press in around him. Everything moved in slow motion as the woman entered the ballroom.

He pressed a hand to his chest, checking to ensure his heart still beat.

Breathe, man.

Something about her seemed so familiar—and so alluring. The way she moved with such grace, her blond hair fashioned softly, the swell of her bosom as it peeked boldly from her gown—all tickled his mind, taunting him as if he should *know* her.

Pulled like the gravitational force Bea had waxed poetic about, he drifted unbidden across the room toward her. The man with her —who knows if he was actually a lord—appeared some years her senior, providing Timothy the courage to presume she remained unattached.

The pale blue satin of her gown draped elegantly over her form, the color complementing her coloring to perfection. The lower waistline, keeping with the latest fashion, accentuated her tiny waist.

He imagined placing his hands around her, wondering if he could make his fingers meet. Tiny pearls decorated her hair, and he wished to pull them, one by one, from her tresses.

He pushed aside the guilt poking at his brain, telling him he should seek Lady Honoria. With his quickened pace, his weakened ankle gave way, and he stumbled, albeit briefly, as he approached the mysterious woman.

Her head turned his way, and she gave him a bright smile, which immediately vanished the moment his steps faltered.

Buffoon! Had his clumsiness ruined his chances of requesting a dance?

The man with her smiled in greeting, and Timothy dipped in a bow.

"May I have the pleasure of the next set, my lady?" He turned toward the man. "With your permission, of course."

The man smiled warmly, supporting Timothy's suspicions he was the father rather than an aged husband or suitor. "You have it, sir, but it will be up to my daughter if she agrees."

Color rose to her cheeks, barely visible underneath her white demi-mask, and she squeaked out her answer, "Yes."

He held out a hand to escort her to the dance floor, and as she slipped her gloved fingers into his, a familiar energy shot through him, once again nudging his brain, demanding recognition.

Masquerade balls had always been a double-edged sword. Anonymity proved useful when faced with a partner with whom you no longer desired any further acquaintance, but a detriment when meeting someone with whom you made a strong connection.

Again, he reminded himself, although they were not officially engaged, he had an understanding with Lady Honoria, and the wicked thought of enjoying a night of pleasure before settling into dull married life both tempted and shamed him.

A simple country dance was hardly a reason to feel guilty. It wasn't as if he planned anything scandalous with his blond dance partner.

Yet.

CHAPTER 11—THE PRICE OF EAVESDROPPING

Priscilla's heart skipped a beat as the handsome man approached her. She practically vibrated from the thrill of being back among society and at an elegant ball. She'd barely walked into the ballroom and had already gained the attention of a dance partner.

As the man grew closer, his gaze never left hers. But when he had stumbled, then limped the rest of the way, her blood chilled slightly.

Red hair.

Handsome.

Young.

Limping.

Gracious. Could it be Timothy?

Here? At her first foray back into society?

It was both wondrous and frightening at the same time.

When they came together during the steps of the dance, she leaned closer, keeping her voice low. "Are you injured, my lord?"

"Pardon?"

"You appear to be limping."

"A minor injury to my ankle. Nothing to worry about."

She shifted her gaze sideways, trying to catch his expression. Did he recognize her voice?

Ninnyhammer. Of course he doesn't remember you.

"Are you quite certain you're able to dance, my lord?"

At that, he faced her, his moss-green eyes locked onto hers, his lips curling into a smile. "Are you suggesting I'm unfit?"

Movement of the other dancers prevented her from stopping mid-step lest she break the form of the line—although the urge to run and hide became almost unbearable. "Well . . . no . . . I didn't mean to imply." Since she didn't trip over her own feet, her tongue more than compensated. Tiny hairs prickled the back of her neck.

"And I'm not a lord. So you can drop the pretense."

His words faltered a bit after the word *lord,* as if he wanted to add something but thought better of it. The bite to his words sent a warning to Priscilla.

Was he angry? Priscilla scrambled to redeem herself and salvage the situation. "Yet, tonight are we not all considered lords and ladies per the duke's requirement? We would be ungrateful guests if we were to disobey his instructions."

Slipping his hand in hers as they executed the steps of the dance, he leaned in, whispering, "I merely suggest that if you're seeking to form an attachment with a titled gentleman, not all here are of the peerage."

Rancor narrowed her eyes. His words cut like a blade across her tattered reputation. Would she never escape the ignominy of her past? "I'm here to dance and enjoy myself. Not seek a husband. And I resent your implication, sir. I would remind you it was you who approached me."

All doubt fled from her mind. This had to be Timothy. No other man could raise her ire so quickly and yet send shivers of attraction throughout her body.

Chagrin painted his face—what she could see of it under his blue demi-mask. "I beg your pardon. You are correct. That was quite rude. Perhaps we might start over?"

She jerked her chin at him. "That depends. Do you plan to

continue such boorish behavior, or will you act like a gentleman—lord or not?"

"I accept your chastisement and promise to be on my best behavior."

"Very well, then." She kept her tone cool—reserved, but inside heat pooled in her belly as she remembered the repartee they'd shared in the cottage. Not to mention the warmth of the bed they'd shared. Her face burned with the memory.

"You're flushed," he said, the concern in his voice touching and reminding her of the softer side of Timothy Marbry.

"It is a bit warm in here."

He scanned the room as if searching for something, his gaze landing on the double doors leading to a balcony outside of the ballroom. "It's too cold to go outside. Perhaps a less crowded room?"

Less pleasant memories flooded Priscilla's mind. The compromise with the duke and the scandal that followed. Her knees grew weak from the memory. "Oh, no. I couldn't. It wouldn't be proper."

His demeanor shifted, and he appeared almost deferential. "My apologies. I didn't mean to imply I expected you to join me somewhere private. Your virtue is safe with me."

The words, so similar to the ones he'd spoken at Mr. Thatcher's cottage, did little to put her at ease. Truth be told, it was not his intentions that concerned her, but her own desire to run her fingers through his hair and feel his arms around her.

He gently grasped her elbow. "I shall escort you back to your father. Would you like a glass of ratafia? Or I could see if there is any lemonade, if that is to your liking."

"Lemonade would be lovely," she croaked the words, her throat thick with emotion more than parched from dryness.

After depositing her back at her father's side, he strode toward the refreshment table.

"Is something wrong?" her father asked. "You seem upset. Should I have a word with that young man?"

"No!" She blurted the answer much too rapidly, and her father lifted a brow. She took a deep breath and composed herself. "Everything is fine. I became a bit overheated on the dance floor. He's going to fetch me something to drink."

Even though the mask hid his face, she imagined the dubious look that her father was no doubt sending. "I should have arranged for a chaperone to accompany us."

Lovingly, she patted his arm. "You are a fine chaperone. However, I know you, and if there's been word of gentlemen withdrawing to the card room, I would be perfectly safe without you. I promise not to do anything that would cause you embarrassment."

Placing his hand on top of hers, he squeezed. "I have no doubt, my dear. It's clear you've paid the price of your mother's machinations long enough."

Priscilla's attention traveled to the refreshment table where her dance partner waited in line. "Father, any idea who the young man is?"

"Hmm? The one who danced with you?" His gaze followed hers, settling on the man she presumed to be Timothy. "Red hair. Could be one of the Weatherbys." He returned his attention to her. "Why? Are you certain nothing untoward happened between the two of you?"

"On the dance floor? Really, Father."

"It would surprise you how many assignations people have made between the moves of a country dance."

His statement did, in fact, surprise her. There was so much she didn't know about her father. She considered interrogating him later, but for the moment, her only concern was the man approaching with a glass of lemonade in his hand.

PEOPLE PAUSED IN CONVERSATION AS TIMOTHY THREADED HIS way through the crowd to return to the alluring blonde with sparkling blue eyes. He'd noticed them as soon as he'd asked her to dance.

Clear as a sunny day in June, they'd studied him with an intensity that sent his blood surging. The nagging sense of familiarity took further root in his mind. Yet he couldn't place her.

After mustering out of the military, he'd spent less than a year back in London before going to Edinburgh and less than three months since he'd returned. Since then, he'd spent the majority of time at the clinic and the remainder paying calls on Lady Honoria Bell.

No matter how he searched his memory, he couldn't recall meeting anyone in London fitting his dance partner's description.

She graced him with a smile as he handed her the tart drink. "Thank you." She sipped daintily, barely touching the liquid to her lips.

His eyes instinctively dipped to her mouth. When her tongue darted out and licked the drops of moisture away, he felt the urgent need to adjust his trousers.

"If you will both excuse me, I think I'll adjourn to the card room."

Timothy's head jerked up at the man's words. He'd completely forgotten her father had been standing right next to her. His brain fumbled for a respectable response, but before he could form one, the man turned and left them alone.

"He's left you unchaperoned?" Timothy couldn't believe his luck.

"I would hardly call being in the room with at least a hundred people unchaperoned, sir. And I might remind you I've already rejected your suggestion to go to a more private room."

"Ah, but I didn't say 'private.' I said, 'less crowded.' For example, we could take a turn in the hallway. Somewhere quieter, with more room to breathe."

Before his lovely dance partner could answer, a petite redhead, who was most definitely not his sister and too bold to be Lady Honoria, touched his arm. "I believe this is our set, sir."

Drat. He'd almost forgotten the woman who accosted him the moment he'd entered the ballroom. "Ah, so it is." He turned an apologetic smile toward his former partner and bowed, holding her gaze. "If you would excuse me."

"But of course."

As the redhead led him to the dance floor, he craned his head back toward the blonde. Masculine satisfaction swelled in his chest at the disappointment etching her face.

THE EARLIER EXCITEMENT THAT HAD BUBBLED UP WITHIN HER settled to a low thrum. Sorry to have lost Timothy's company when his new dance partner pulled him away, Priscilla hoped for a distraction from her preoccupied mind. Scanning the room, she noticed a group of women huddled together at the refreshment table.

Perhaps another glass of lemonade would serve as an excuse to work her way into the enclave of women and gather a bit of gossip. With care to appear as if she was not eavesdropping—which in fact she truly was—she sipped the glass of lemonade and perked up her ears.

Among the group were two older women. Their graying hair and large bosoms draped in strands of pearls gave testament to both their age and station. One of them nodded vigorously, apparently agreeing with what someone else had said.

"It's true,' the woman said. "I heard it from my lady's maid, who heard it from Lord Cartwright's footman."

Priscilla straightened at the mention of her father.

"Although I don't always trust a servant's word, I'm concerned my maid is becoming a little too familiar with Cartwright's man. I may have to put my foot down and insist she no longer keep company with him. I would hate to lose an excellent servant simply because a footman seduced her away from me."

Priscilla wanted to stamp her foot and tell the old biddy to get back to what she had heard. Who cared about the servants' love lives? Well, she supposed the servants did, but that was neither here nor there. Thank heaven one of the other women brought the gossiping woman back to the matter at hand.

"Such news is disconcerting. We should warn our sons to be most cautious should they see her. Such a disgrace to the *ton*. Why, she's nothing but a scheming doxy."

Who?

"She should have stayed in the country with her mother and away from polite society. What she put our dear duke through is unforgivable."

Oh!

With blinding clarity, Priscilla needed no further explanation of whom they spoke. The lemonade, although sweetened with the finest sugar, soured in her stomach and threatened to make another appearance.

All eyes in the group turned to her as she gave a tiny, choked gurgle. The old gossip reached out, placing a hand on Priscilla's arm. "My dear, are you quite all right?"

Unable to force the words, Priscilla simply nodded. Tears welled in her eyes, her chest constricting with each nasty word bouncing around in her head.

Doxy.

Disgrace.

Warn our sons.

Her head spun, and she found it hard to breathe. She choked out a strangled cry.

A younger, dark-haired woman, who had been standing nearby but not part of the group, reached out. "Are you certain you're not ill, my dear? I could fetch Ha—the duke."

"No." She shook her head frantically, realizing the woman was the duchess herself. Who else would refer to him as Harry in front of a group of gossiping busybodies?

She pushed past the group and fought her way through the crowds, desperate to find the exit and a quiet room where she could safely fall apart. Heads turned as she bumped into unsuspecting guests, but she didn't bother to stop and apologize. Why should she when they all hated her so much already?

On shaky limbs, she stumbled out into the hallway and searched for an empty room. Light spilled from a room to her left, and she raced toward it. When she placed her hand on the half-open doorway, widening the entry, a gasp sounded from within.

Quickly backing out, she muttered an apology and turned back into the hallway. At the end of the long passage, a door stood open, the room cast in shadows from a single lit candle. She hurried inside, not bothering to shut the door, hoping the darkness would be sufficient protection from any possible intruders.

Her hands trembled as she undid the ties holding the beautiful mask in place. Wetness pooled on both her cheeks and the inside of the mask. She wiped at her tear-stained skin, the action useless— each swipe immediately followed by a guttural sob and fresh tears.

Why did she ever think she could re-enter London society? Had she really believed that a few short years would erase her shame? It would appear that the ugly blot on her reputation was as difficult to remove as ink spilled on a white gown.

And although she was loathe to admit it, her heart sank knowing perhaps Mr. Netherborne, the countryside, and sheep were her only future.

CHAPTER 12—UNMASKED

Timothy finished his dance set with the woman he suspected was Andrew Weatherby's sister, Anne. Not only had she asked him point-blank if he was unmarried, but she also touched him repeatedly on the arm, running her hand up and down as if she were brushing a well-groomed dog.

He liked Andrew, but Timothy wondered if he should have a talk with the man about keeping a tighter rein on his sister. Luckily, Anne, if that's who his partner had been, made quick work of finding another dance partner as soon as Timothy had mentioned that, although not betrothed, he had formed an attachment with someone.

At least courting Lady Honoria had some perks. Although, he'd yet to see her, or at least he hadn't recognized her if he had—that thought more than a tad disconcerting. Shouldn't a man recognize the woman he planned to marry, even if she wore a mask?

For the moment, the need for a bit of peace took priority, and he threaded his way out of the ballroom in search of a bit of respite in a vacant parlor. Passing one room, which he discovered someone already occupied, his eyes trained on a darkened room at the far end of the long hallway.

Ah, solitude! With quickened steps, he approached, but before he could enter, the sound of someone weeping drifted out from the room's shadowed depths. He paused, his fingertips skimming the door frame. Should he enquire if the person within needed assistance, or should he leave them to their sorrow in silence?

The physician in him won out. He'd heard rumors of women being accosted in secluded rooms. Had they not been best friends, Timothy would have beaten Laurence to a pulp when he'd been found with Bea in a state of undress.

Keeping his voice low so as not to frighten the woman any further, he announced himself. "Pardon me. Are you in need of help?"

She turned, her face barely illuminated in the soft light of the single candle, but from her gown, he recognized the woman who had captured his attention when she first arrived. Emboldened, he stepped farther into the room, only to realize she no longer wore her mask.

He had witnessed many shocking things in his military career, but little prepared him for seeing the face of Emma before him.

Here.

In London.

At the Duke of Ashton's masquerade ball.

As if in slow motion, her gaze rose, locking with his.

His heart stuttered as he stared into those startling blue eyes.

"Emma?" He choked out her name. Was she a figment of his imagination? Had he projected his longing onto another woman's face? If he blinked, would he find his vision cleared only to find another, less alluring blonde?

"What are you doing here?" He choked out the words, both elated and perplexed when the vision before him didn't shift into something more easily explained.

"Marbry? Is all well?" the masculine voice called from behind him.

Timothy turned to find Laurence, whose gaze slid toward

Emma, then immediately returned to Timothy. "I saw you exit the room as if it were on fire."

"I sought some solitude, but I heard sounds of weeping." He faced Emma again. "Emma, what's wrong?"

"Emma?" The surprised tone in Laurence's voice had Timothy pivoting again. Lord, he was like a child's top. "This is Miss Priscilla Pratt. Why did you call her Emma?"

Priscilla Pratt? Why did that name sound so familiar? And why did she look just like his Emma?

His Emma? *Good grief, man, get hold of yourself.*

He failed miserably. "What the devil is going on here?" He veritably shouted the words as he yanked off his mask. The need to confront her—literally face-to-face—overruled the pretext of the masquerade's anonymity.

Emma—err—Miss Pratt stumbled against a nearby settee. "I can explain, Dr. Marbry."

Heedless of the impropriety of the situation, he strode forward, grasping her upper arm with a punishing grip. "Damn right, you will explain," he replied, lowering his voice to a more subdued level.

Laurence was on his heels. "Careful, man. Regardless of her reputation, there is no cause to mistreat her."

"Mind your own business." Timothy snarled the command, then pointed a finger at Emma—err—Miss Pratt. "She lied to me! I demand to know why."

"You can't interrogate her without another woman present. It simply isn't done."

Laurence and his infernal rules!

"It's fine, sir," she said, her voice soft with resignation. "My reputation is already in tatters. What does it matter if the gossips receive more fodder?"

Laurence's usually easy-going manner turned lethal. "Allow me to fetch my wife. I'm more concerned about *his* reputation and the consequences of being alone with *you*."

The blow found a direct hit. Even in the dim light, Timothy could tell that Emma—err—Miss Pratt's face blanched.

Timothy needed to diffuse the volatile situation, although his own blood was boiling. "Don't bother Bea. I can take care of myself. If Emma, I mean Miss Pratt, wanted to trap me, she would have had ample opportunity already."

Laurence's mouth formed a taut line below his demi-mask, but he nodded and left them alone in the room.

The air crackled between them. Or was that the fire in the hearth? He glanced over toward the fireplace, finding the blaze he expected within a mere sputter.

Definitely the air between them.

"That was Lord Montgomery?" she asked, as if she were casually enquiring about the weather.

"Don't change the subject. Explain yourself." His head pounded. He could almost feel the blood shooting through his veins to find a home inside his skull.

"Should we sit?" she asked. Gone was the hellion he'd spent the night with in Lincolnshire. In her place, a frightened, timid woman quaked before him. She rubbed at the red oval marks marring the delicate white skin of her arm.

Evidence from his own hand. Guilt soured his stomach. "Please." He pointed to the settee and took a seat on a comfortable wingback opposite.

Color returned to her face, but she twisted the fabric of her gown in tightly coiled fists.

"I'm waiting." He veritably barked the words.

Fire returned to her eyes. Ah, there was the woman he remembered. "If you would be patient, sir. I'm trying to determine where to begin."

Unable to resist the eye roll, he said, "At the beginning."

Her eyes narrowed. "Very well. I was born." A slight smirk played at her lips, and he had the urge to throttle her.

Or perhaps kiss her.

Irritation at his own reaction fueled his anger. "You know very well what I meant. Stop stalling. Why did you lie to me about your identity?"

Heavy silence stretched between them, yet he waited, crossing his arms over his chest for emphasis.

Emotions flickered across her face, changing so rapidly he wondered what exactly was going on in that mind of hers.

At last, she spoke. "At first, I only wished to be judged by my own merit rather than my tattered reputation. I recognized your name and knew if I revealed my true identity, you would treat me poorly."

He harrumphed. "Throwing a boot at my head was supposed to paint you in a favorable light?"

"And *you* know very well what I meant. I wished to avoid having you make a snap judgment against me."

"So you judged me instead?" He wanted the words to have a bite, but he failed, cringing internally at the injured tone in his voice.

Her expression softened, and she cast her gaze to her hands clutching her gown. She released the fabric, smoothing it, then folded her hands neatly onto her lap. "I did. I apologize."

The moment of contrition was short-lived, though, and she lifted her eyes to meet his directly. "But can you blame me for wanting to be known for something other than a conniving shrew who's willing to trap a man into marriage?"

Disjointed pieces slid together. When he'd asked Bea about the woman Harry refused to speak of, his sister had told him of the compromise orchestrated by one Miss Priscilla Pratt. And wasn't Pratt the name the men used when discovering her at the snowbound cottage?

He brought the matter back to the present. "You said at first."

She sighed. "When it became clear we were to be confined in the cottage together, I wished to alleviate any concern you might have regarding your duty toward me. If you would but think on the matter, you might understand why. I had no intention of trapping you, yet would you not have immediately arrived at that conclusion had you known I was the infamous Priscilla Pratt? Wasn't Lord Montgomery's protest proof of that?"

She had a point. She could have informed her rescuers of his presence and accused him of compromising her. Even his statement to Laurence admitted as much. Given the knowledge that even then she knew his name, the fact that no one sought him out, especially her father, gave testament to her silence.

"I suppose you had no wish to jeopardize your betrothal to Mr. Netheregions."

Her lips quirked upward. "Netherborne. Unfortunately, he is aware that I was not alone in Mr. Thatcher's cottage."

A chill raced up Timothy's spine, even though the room was unbearably warm. "Oh? And why has no one confronted me?"

It was her turn to give an eye roll. "Because I refused to name you, sir. I am no longer the girl who wishes to marry a man who doesn't want me."

The tightness banding his chest lessened, and he found he could breathe more easily. Yet an inexplicable sadness remained. "Your betrothed knows you spent the night with another man? Has he broken the engagement?"

"Suspended it, if there is such a thing. He is giving me time to repent and prove myself." With the final two words, her chin lifted as if mimicking the man's words.

"In London?" Incredulity rang in his voice.

⚜

THE ASTONISHED LOOK ON TIMOTHY'S FACE WAS LAUGHABLE. Priscilla bit back the urge to react, reminding herself of the seriousness of the matter. "Mr. Netherborne is unfamiliar with London society."

He lifted an eyebrow, giving him a rather rakish appearance. "Clearly."

Must he be so deliciously handsome?

"How am I to explain myself if you continue with your rude interruptions?"

His mouth opened, drawing her gaze, but apparently reconsidering, he closed it and motioned with his hand for her to continue.

"As I was saying." She squared her shoulders with what, she hoped, was a dramatic flair. "Mr. Netherborne believes I shall find London society brash and superficial, sending me running back to find refuge in the country with him and . . . sheep."

Oh, how he wanted to respond. She could see it on his face. Yet he kept silent, with only his lips quirking in a delightful little smile.

She waited long enough to have the desired effect. "Have you nothing to say about that?"

"I thought I was to keep silent?"

"It's clear you wish to reply. I give you my permission."

"Just who is interrogating whom? Don't turn this around to have the upper hand."

Oh, how she adored him.

Wait. What?

Her cheeks heated, and she ducked her head lest he see her embarrassment.

"And have you?" he asked, interrupting and unsettling her thoughts. "Found London society unpleasant? Do you wish to return to the country and Mr. Netherborne?"

There was a tinge of something in his question she couldn't quite place. Worry? Surely not?

"Categorically no. My return to London was more of an escape from the country."

A muscle in his jaw pulsed, and his posture straightened, leaning toward her. "Escape? Were you in danger?"

"If there is danger in being bored to death. I detest the country. I've missed the activity of the city, the parties, the teas—the balls. Granted, this is the first I've attended, but merely being in the thick of things has invigorated me. If I hadn't been able to return, I seriously considered running away."

He quirked a brow.

"When Mr. Netherborne confronted me, it forced my hand, and I wrote to my father. All things considered, it worked out for the best. If I had run away, I'm ill-equipped to fend for myself."

He grinned, the sight perfectly adorable. "Except for catching chickens. You seem very adept at that."

She waggled a finger at him. "Ah, but I was completely ignorant as to how to prepare the poor thing."

"And your plans for repentance?"

"Contrary to belief, I have already repented. Not a day passes where I do not regret my actions against the duke. However, convincing others of my contrition and repairing my reputation is another matter and a much more arduous task."

He said nothing, but tilted his head in question. Had he already forgotten the state in which he had found her?

"Upon discovering me here, and before learning my true identity, you asked about my well-being. Although surprised, you at least seemed concerned."

His gaze slid away, pink rising to the tips of his ears. "I did, and I apologize for my abrupt change. What caused your unhappiness?"

"It would appear no one expected me to be so bold as to attend a ball given by the man I so grievously wronged. I overheard a conversation regarding my past sins, which remain not only unforgotten but unforgiven."

She took a deep breath, tears welling again in her eyes at the mere memory of the unkind words. "Already I have suffered the scrutiny of self-serving dowagers and their perfect progeny. It seems mothers are being told to warn their sons about the scheming *doxy* who has returned to London intent on trapping them into marriage."

Compassion shone in his eyes, as if he wished to apologize for those who had harmed her. "Surely they didn't use that term in reference to you?"

"I'm afraid they did."

"And do you still intend to move forward with your plan to redeem yourself?"

The deflating defeat that had crushed her upon entering the room transformed into determination, and she met his gaze with renewed purpose. If she could face Timothy, she could face them all. "What better place to prove myself than where I fell into ignominy?"

That eyebrow quirked again. "That's . . . wise. And brave."

His praise shouldn't have affected her as much as it did. But the fluttering sensation in her stomach gave testament to how much his good opinion mattered. No one had *ever* called her either wise or brave. But coming from Timothy Marbry made the words even sweeter.

"And besides redemption, do you hope to accomplish anything else here in London?"

"As I am determined not to return to Belton and marry Mr. Netherborne, I hope to find a suitable husband here."

He shifted in his seat, and she could envision the cogs turning in his brain.

"Have you not heard a word I've said? You may rest easy, sir. I have no plans to cry compromise to secure a husband—even one as *desirable* as you." She poured every bit of sarcasm into the last as she could muster.

Red blotches formed on his cheeks. So the man had a conscience, after all.

"I had no idea I would see you again." Never mind that she'd thought about it and even hoped on a daily basis. "I'm as surprised to find you here as you are to find me."

"I doubt that—considering I thought you a merchant's daughter."

She laughed. "I should be insulted, but I'm not. It would appear my ruse worked as planned."

She considered him for a moment, wondering if possibly their meeting could be more fortuitous than expected. "I would like to be completely honest with you."

He frowned. "Have you not been?"

"Well, yes. But stumbling into you has given me a brilliant idea."

"Which is?"

"I want you to help me."

"How?"

"I would like you to help me find a husband."

CHAPTER 13—THE REQUEST

An overwhelming urge to clean out his ears overcame Timothy. Surely he'd heard incorrectly.

"Wha . . . What?" He sputtered the question. "How in the devil can I help you find a husband?"

A chill skittered up his spine, and he rose from the chair in one fluid motion. "Now see here. I thought you said you had no intention of compromising me into a marriage."

She waved him off as if he'd said the most ridiculous thing in the world. However, it certainly didn't seem ridiculous to him.

"Heavens, no. But as you can clearly see, it has become a challenge for me to find my way back into society. I thought with your influence, you could recommend me to some eligible gentlemen of your acquaintance."

"Wouldn't a woman better serve in that capacity?"

"Do you really think many women would be willing to help me after I staged a compromise with the beloved Duke of Ashton?"

She had an excellent point.

"Besides, I've heard you've taken a position at the duke's clinic. If you appear to have accepted me, given your close relationship with Ashton, perhaps others would be more willing to forgive and forget."

Another well-reasoned argument. And yet . . .

"I still don't understand what I can do to help. Do you expect me to go around mentioning you as a prospective bride to every unattached man I know?"

She exhaled an audible sigh, her body closing in on itself. "No. I suppose not. It *would* appear rather suspicious."

"Quite."

Her face brightened. "But perhaps if you made it known that my father has increased my dowry?"

His thoughts turned to Lady Honoria, and the interminable afternoons spent between them with nothing of interest to share. Such a difference from his time with Emma—err—Miss Pratt.

A rather unsettling idea flitted through his mind. "What if I enlisted Lady Honoria's help as well?"

"Lady Honoria?" Confusion followed by a flicker of—was that regret?—passed over her face. "Is there an understanding between the two of you?"

"Not exactly an understanding yet. However, I have been calling on her regularly." Why did those words stick in his throat?

She winced. Or did the flickering candle in the dim room play tricks on his eyes? "I see. Then forgive me for putting you in such an awkward position. Forget all about my request."

She rose, smoothed her skirts, and turned to leave.

"No, wait!" he called, tempted to reach out and grasp her hand. "Allow me to speak with Lady Honoria. Perhaps being seen in both her and my company will assuage some of the wagging tongues and start smoothing the path to your acceptance back into society."

"If you insist. However, I doubt Lady Honoria would be pleased to assist the likes of me—especially if it involves her own suitor. I wish you joy, Mr. Marbry." Her voice shook as if flustered.

"Dr. Marbry, Miss Pratt." He delivered the reminder gently, not wishing to cause her more discomfort.

Her gaze lifted to his. "Of course. Now, if you'll excuse me, I shall return and leave you to it." She secured her mask back in place, hiding her face.

With a whisk of lemon verbena trailing in her wake, she quit the room, her head held high and shoulders squared as if she were heading back into the fray of battle.

Timothy thought it most fitting.

After waiting several minutes for Miss Pratt to return to the ballroom, Timothy donned his mask and peeked around the corner to ensure no one lurked to witness his own departure. His mind reeled from Miss Pratt's—damned if he could only stop thinking of her as Emma—unusual request.

Absurd?

No doubt.

Was he considering it?

Oddly, yes.

The idea of having Em—err—Miss Pratt included in his time with Lady Honoria strangely appealed to him. However, the greatest hurdle would be Lady Honoria herself.

He called on his military training to develop a strategy for his attack—err—proposition. One thing he had learned about the proper daughter of the Marquess of Stratford—she had a compassionate heart. Often during their strolls in Hyde Park, she would question him about the patients at the clinic, asking if there was anything she could do to help.

"Keep them in your prayers, my lady," he had said.

"Oh, but Dr. Marbry, I wish to do something more actionable than pray." She had darted a quick apologetic look his way, color draining slightly from her rosy cheeks. "Not that I believe prayer ineffective. But I would like to do something more . . . personal."

"Perhaps assist Her Grace in raising funds for the clinic? Also, the poor have need of work. If you know of any position with which they could be employed . . ."

"I shall do so forthwith," she answered.

Yes. Lady Honoria had a good heart. Of that, he was certain. But would she help a woman who could be considered her rival?

Wait? What? Where had that thought come from? Miss Priscilla Pratt would not be a suitable bride.

Would she?

No! If her reputation alone didn't disqualify her, his tumultuous feelings toward her certainly did.

He shook his head to clear the unsavory notion. He needed to maintain his focus on Lady Honoria. Yet, would he be sabotaging himself with such an outrageous request? Would Lady Honoria respond by telling him to go to the devil?

And if she did, why didn't the prospect bother him?

Now that he knew the lady in the blue gown was Emma—err—Miss Pratt, he found his attention continually diverted, scanning the room for her. The evening had taken a strange turn.

Someone tapped his arm. "You appear to be off in a distant land," the familiar voice said.

He turned toward his sister, Bea. "Hmm?"

"Is all well? Laurence told me about your encounter with Miss Pratt."

"Of course he did." He ground out the words, reminding himself to have a *talk* with his friend later about minding his own business.

"Really, Timothy. You must be on guard."

"Not you, too? Is she sentenced to carry one mistake to her grave?"

Bea's eyes blinked behind her mask. "I hadn't realized you were her defender. What have I missed? Laurence said you called her Emma."

"And as I told your husband, he needs to mind his own business."

She reeled back from the sharpness of his tone.

Regret pinged in his chest. "I'm sorry, Bea. I didn't mean to snap. All I ask is to give her a chance. She desperately wants to redeem herself. You, of all people, should understand what it's like to be the butt of gossip."

And yet again, he offended his sister, but although he knew his words stung her, she remained stalwart. "Your sword has become more pointed as of late. I shall remember to be on guard." She turned, searching the room, her gaze stopping in the direction where Miss Pratt stood speaking with a gentleman.

⚜

AFTER LEAVING THE SMALL PARLOR, PRISCILLA HAD WANDERED the hallways of the duke's home in need of air. That which remained in the small parlor had been sucked out with Timothy's words about Lady Honoria Bell.

Did she expect him to remain unattached and waiting for her—considering he didn't even know who she truly was?

But now he did, and he didn't seem to hate her. In fact, his offer to assist, albeit with Lady Honoria's help, indicated he'd forgiven her deceit.

Still, pain knifed through her chest at the thought of Timothy in Lady Honoria's arms—forever.

Gah!

Finally gathering courage, she re-entered the ballroom and inserted herself into a small cluster of people, hoping to find distraction from her maudlin thoughts within the idle conversation. Yet, try as she might, she couldn't focus on whatever the devil the man next to her was saying. Something about purchasing a new horse at Tattersall's.

"Beg pardon? A horse?" Priscilla squinted to determine the color of his eyes behind his blue mask. Dull, lifeless brown. The color of dirt.

"Yes. I can't decide on the chestnut or the gray. Although I suppose I should go with the chestnut in case I wish to have a spare for the matched set I use for my curricle."

Lord, could he be more boring? "That sounds wise." She smiled prettily, hoping her words sounded sincere. Her mother always advised her a smile would come across in her voice. As lackluster as he was, she didn't want him to leave her alone. He'd been one of the few gentlemen who had bothered to speak with her during the evening.

Once again, her attention turned to Timothy who spoke with a petite redhead across the room. Was that his sister? He did say he was courting Lady Honoria, and she had red hair. Pain twisted in her chest. A brunette joined them, and when Timothy led her to the dance floor, the pain eased—somewhat.

"I do love to dance," she said, hoping the imbecile next to her would catch her meaning. If she could get closer and hear whatever conversation Timothy shared with his partner, she might be able to determine her identity.

"Can't abide it myself," the man answered. "What's the point of moving about aimlessly? I prefer things with purpose and direction."

Of course he did. Like buying horses.

"But if you would like to . . ." His tone practically begged her to say no.

She wasn't that unselfish. "Oh, yes. I'd love to."

His mouth drooped a little as he held out his hand. "Very well."

Not caring her partner was unenthusiastic, she slid her hand into his and followed him to the dance floor. She would have enough enthusiasm for both of them.

As the set began, they took their place in line with the other dancers, positioning themselves next to Timothy and his partner. Although they exchanged no words Priscilla could hear, upon closer inspection, she was convinced Timothy partnered with Lady Miranda, Lord Montgomery's sister.

Tingles of energy shot through her each time she touched Timothy's hand during the steps of the country dance. At one point, she could have sworn he gave it a little squeeze, and her gaze shot to his, finding a tiny smile ghosting his lips.

Such a tease!

On the other hand, her own partner's dislike for the pastime was evident with each fumbling pass and stilted bow. More than once, he even trod upon her foot. When she yelped aloud, she swore Timothy chuckled.

It would have been more advisable to not have forced the matter and allowed her partner to wander off to find another victim . . . lady with whom he could converse about horses.

All the excitement she'd felt at the beginning of the evening shriveled to nothingness. For the first time in her life, she no longer wished to dance. She wilted with relief when the set ended and her partner wandered off to bore someone else about horses. Her only thought—to return to the safety and seclusion of her room.

Once she located her father in the card room, she implored him to send for their carriage. "Please take me home, Papa. I've had enough festivities for the evening."

Concern shone in his eyes, and she loved him for it. He didn't question, merely instructed a footman to have his carriage brought around.

During the ride home, she remained silent, Timothy's handsome face dancing in her mind. Then, without warning, Lady Honoria would intrude, laughing gaily as Timothy complimented her beauty and gracefully maneuvered her around the dance floor.

Ugh!

Had she gone too far asking for his help? What did she hope to accomplish? Did she expect him to fall on his knees before her, begging her to consider him as a suitor?

He had no desire to marry her. Lady Honoria, well, that was another matter. One that Priscilla was loathe to contemplate.

As she expected, she doused her pillow with tears that night, sobbing herself to sleep. Was she doomed to a lonely, unexciting life in the country with the likes of Mr. Netherborne?

Spinsterhood almost seemed preferable.

Almost.

Timothy gave a nervous tug to his cravat as he waited in the drawing room for Lady Honoria's arrival. The precise purpose of his call was to enlist her aid in assisting Miss Pratt and developing a stratagem. A sour taste filled his mouth at the negative connotation of the word, but in order to convince a well-heeled gentleman to consider Miss Pratt as a desirable marriage prospect, the use of devious methods might be necessary.

Certainly nothing as straightforward as being seen about town with her would be sufficient. He didn't delude himself that he held that much sway with the *ton*, and Lady Honoria had suffered her own troubles with the gossips, a fact he refused to use to secure her assistance.

When Lady Honoria entered, her lady's maid in tow, he rose and bowed in greeting.

"Did you attend the Duke of Ashton's masquerade last evening?" she asked.

Timothy expected to hear censure in her tone, but found it absent. "I did. Did you?" Guilt swirled in his gut that, by all rights, if she had attended, he should have recognized her. "I'd hope to request a dance. But alas, I'm horrible telling people apart when disguised."

Not entirely a falsity, and he prayed she would excuse him if he'd slighted her in any manner.

"No. Unfortunately, Papa developed a terrible cough, and I insisted on staying to care for him. The duke and duchess are such gracious hosts. I've thoroughly enjoyed myself when attending in the past."

"Has your father's physician attended to him? If not, I could examine him."

"Yes. Dr. Mason came by last evening."

Dr. Mason. Concern rose in Timothy's mind. Harry had dismissed Mason from the clinic, and Timothy had taken his place. "A second opinion is often recommended. If your father would permit, I could examine him." He left it at that, hoping Lord

Stratford would agree, and more so that Mason had not done further harm.

"He's resting at the moment, but I will ask him before you leave."

Timothy nodded, accepting it was the best he could hope for at the moment. As for the other matter and his principal reason for his call, he hoped for a more definitive and positive result.

"Tell me about the ball," she said, providing him the perfect segue into the topic he planned to discuss.

"I had a most unusual encounter. With Miss Priscilla Pratt."

She blinked twice. "Oh? How is it you recognized her at a masquerade? You mentioned you have difficulty identifying people when they're disguised."

Although no tone of accusation tinged Honoria's words, Timothy cringed internally how his own words had tripped him. Obviously, she'd paid more attention to their conversations than he did. He studied her face, finding no anger, only eyes wide with curiosity.

"I stepped out of the ballroom to get some air and heard weeping coming from a small parlor. Miss Pratt had removed her mask. She asked for my assistance."

Honoria's head tilted, and try as he might to find the curve of her neck alluring and seductive, he could not. It was but a neck, and he studied it with dispassionate medical interest. He had no desire to dip his head and kiss the delicate skin as he had with Emma—err —Miss Pratt. Damnation if he needed to not only stop thinking of her as Emma, but stop thinking of her altogether.

"Assistance with what, pray tell? Was she harmed? Injured?" Honoria asked, drawing his attention back to the present. Genuine concern shone on her face.

"Not harmed physically. Apparently, she overhead rather unkind words about her. She requested my assistance to redeem herself with society."

It bode well that Honoria didn't scoff or scrunch her face up in disgust. Perhaps she would be amenable to the idea.

He pressed forward. "She's quite remorseful over what happened with the Duke of Ashton. However, society has not been forgiving. She suggested being seen in our company might smooth the way for her to be accepted once again and help her secure a favorable marriage."

"But why you? Do you have a former acquaintance with Miss Pratt?"

He listened for the telltale sign of jealousy in her tone or demeanor, but found none. Lady Honoria remained a perfect example of aristocratic decorum. This would be much harder to explain. But if he proceeded with his plans to make Lady Honoria his wife, honesty seemed the best path, even if he couched the truth in a fog of vagueness. "Our paths crossed on my way back to London from Edinburgh."

"I see." Sharp intelligence shone in Honoria's eyes, and Timothy had to respect her for not asking the question she no doubt pondered.

Yet he sought to ease her mind. "There is nothing between us, my lady, if that is your concern." How was it that the lie tripped so easily off his tongue? For there was indeed something between himself and Miss Pratt, albeit innocent enough.

Honoria's green eyes narrowed the tiniest amount. "And it is *your* wish to assist her in this quest? There is no coercion on her part?"

"None whatsoever. She's thrown herself at my mercy." Drat his poor choice of words.

"I still fail to see why she's singled you out from others who might prove helpful."

He took a deep breath. It would seem his intended was harder to convince than he'd thought. "When we met outside of Grantham, she gave me the name Emma because she feared if I knew her true identity, I would judge her harshly. I only discovered it at the ball last evening. Of course, her deception outraged me, so I demanded an explanation. She is most contrite and confided in me she is doing her utmost to escape an unwanted marriage proposal. She feels she has no one to turn to here in London, and because we had a . . . friendly exchange when she presented herself as Emma, she implored me to come to her aid."

He studied her face, gradually softening as she heard Miss Pratt's tale. He waited but a heartbeat longer. "You and I spoke recently of your desire to assist those in need." He lifted his hand when she opened her mouth, no doubt to protest she'd meant the poor. "Is Miss Pratt any less deserving of compassion and aid simply because she is not destitute?"

For a moment, she wrestled with his challenge, but he could tell the instant she conceded. "I suppose not."

"And of course, it wouldn't do for me, as a gentleman, to be her sole champion. Especially given our understanding."

Her gaze shot to his. "*Do* we have an understanding, Dr. Marbry?"

With forced sincerity, he answered, "I fervently hope so, Lady Honoria."

She gave a firm nod. "Then we shall endeavor to assist Miss Pratt by all means necessary."

He wanted to thank her, but the words stuck in his throat.

This was a terrible idea indeed.

CHAPTER 14—THE LIST

How is your father this morning?" Timothy asked Lady Honoria when she greeted him the next morning. He'd been unable to examine the man prior to leaving the day before, but had prescribed a poultice for congestion and willow bark tea with a generous amount of lemon for his fever and sore throat.

"Improved, thank goodness. He has requested that you consult, if you would be so kind."

"It would be my honor." Relief eased Timothy's nerves. Not only that Lord Stratford had indeed improved, but that he agreed to a second opinion. Perhaps it was a good omen of things to come.

Honoria seemed particularly animated, giving him a generous smile before seating herself. "Father was most impressed you are concerned for his health. He has a very good opinion of you, Dr. Marbry."

"You seem in good spirits, my lady," he offered, returning her smile and resuming his seat.

"I must admit that our task has invigorated me." She held a slip of paper in her hands. "I've made a list of prospective suitors for Miss Pratt."

He leaned forward, eager to hear her findings.

"With the Duke of Burwood's recent passing, his heir is a distant relative and has been away from London for some time. I understand he's still young and unmarried."

"A duke. It would definitely please Miss Pratt's mother, Lady Cartwright. But as a duke, he would most likely wish to avoid any whiff of scandal."

She pursed her lips, frowning at her list. "Oh, I suppose you're correct. However, it may depend on if he's been privy to the scandal sheets. I understand he's been called home from India. Far enough away to be shielded from the gossips."

She consulted her list. "Lord Felix Davies, the second son of Viscount Scarborough, recently arrived from the continent after his grand tour. He will be popular among the unmarried ladies, but nevertheless I've added him. His eldest brother is already married with a son, so it's unlikely Lord Felix will inherit, but his family is held in high regard. Like Burwood's heir, we have a chance he won't have heard about Miss Pratt's . . . incident."

Timothy nodded. "Who else?"

"Well, he's not titled, but Mr. Francis Ugbrooke is landed gentry, with a good living and an estate in Somerset. His wife died in childbirth several years ago, and I understand he's in dire need of a mother for the children."

Somehow, Timothy didn't imagine marriage to Mr. Ugbrooke and rearing his children would appeal to Priscilla. He motioned for Lady Honoria to continue.

"He's a bit long in the tooth, but Viscount Highbottom is still unmarried."

And not likely to satisfy Priscilla in the bedroom.

She'd probably be happier with Netherborne in the country. Timothy kept his knowledge to himself. Besides, it was best not to think about Priscilla in conjunction with a bedroom. "Anyone else?"

Honoria stared at her list and chewed her lip, the action failing to generate the same reaction in Timothy as when Priscilla had performed it.

Drat if his mind didn't return to her at every turn.

Well—he reminded himself—they *were* discussing finding a suitor for Miss Pratt. It was natural his mind drifted to her.

Wasn't it?

"Well, there is another gentleman, though he's not on my list," Honoria said, shifting in her seat and looking rather uncomfortable. "But he is unattached and still in his prime."

Ignoring the latter portion of her statement, Timothy's mind latched onto the first. "Why isn't he on your list?"

"He has a rather unsavory reputation, I'm afraid. In addition, I'm uncertain he would be amenable to the idea of marriage."

She couldn't be suggesting *him*? Surely not. "Are you going to tell me?" Timothy held his breath.

"Lord Nash. I considered him, but discarded the notion almost immediately."

It was enough that Nash had meddled in Bea's affairs. Although, truth be told, it had worked out rather nicely for his sister and Laurence. Even Laurence admitted he had thanked Nash for his hand in things.

But Nash and Priscilla? An unsettling panic crept up his spine.

One thing was certain—unlike Highbottom, by all accounts, Priscilla would have no complaints in the bedroom from Nash. The image of them together had Timothy ready to pound something.

"Perhaps I discarded the idea too hastily," Honoria said. "Given his own reputation, he may be more amenable to securing an attachment with a lady in similar circumstances."

"No," Timothy uttered the single word with express finality.

Lady Honoria blinked. Once. Twice. Three times in rapid succession. "Is there a reason you seem so adamantly opposed to Lord Nash? Other than his reputation? I heard Edgerton has been eager to see his brother married, no doubt hoping to quell some of the wagging tongues."

For the life of him, Timothy could think of no rational reason. In fact, Nash might be the only viable prospect, whether he be on Honoria's list or not.

"No. I concede to your logic. I only hoped there would be a more respectable and desirable choice."

Honoria studied him, her lips pressed in a tight line. "We shall not give up, Dr. Marbry. But as I can attest, the choice of truly desirable, eligible men has become quite limited. You are the one rare exception, and I am fortunate you have sought an attachment with me."

Although the gratitude she expressed with her words was no doubt flattering, her belief in them did not quite reach her eyes. Sadness lingered there as if she, like himself, had resigned herself to a life of mediocrity rather than the exceptional. The realization took him aback. She heralded him as a considerable catch, but in her eyes, he was but a mere consolation prize.

They were both settling, and he found it most unnerving.

Priscilla nearly spilled her tea when Digby, her father's butler, appeared by her side, holding the silver salver with an invitation addressed to her. As if she had found a prize of great value, she lifted it with care from the tray, running her fingers over the quality parchment.

"What is it?" her father asked. He'd been mercifully silent not only on their ride home from the Duke of Ashton's masquerade ball, but also in the days following. He'd simply asked if he had enjoyed the ball and upon her curt answer of "I suppose" had left the matter at that.

Her eyes widened at the design pressed into the red wax sealing the letter. *The Marquess of Stratford's crest?* After opening the missive, she scanned the contents, not sure if they were even more surprising than the identity of the sender. "It's an invitation from Lady Honoria Bell to a card party." The parchment dropped to her lap, her hands too shaky to retain their grasp.

"I hadn't realized you and Lady Honoria were on friendly terms."

Her father's statement, although not spoken harshly, still took her aback.

"We're not. Other than a few social gatherings prior to my . . . stay in Lincolnshire, we had little contact with each other." Her mind drifted to Timothy and her plea for help. As promised, he must have appealed to Lady Honoria. However, it would not serve to share that bit of news with her father.

He lifted his cup of tea and, after taking a sip, peered at her over the rim. "She had to deal with her own bit of opprobrium several years ago, so perhaps she sees you as a kindred spirit."

Priscilla hadn't considered that. Perhaps she and Honoria had more in common than their mutual attraction to one red-headed and very attractive doctor. "It's a week from Tuesday. Will you accompany me, Papa?"

His eyes crinkled as he peered over the rim of his cup. "I would be delighted. A rousing game of whist sounds marvelous."

Renewed hope and excitement bubbled within her, and she excused herself to go through her gowns in preparation for the upcoming event.

When the day of the card party arrived, the sky threatened to mar the occasion with rain. Ominous clouds hovered overhead, some forming the shapes of warriors upon horses, ready to attack.

She sighed, allowing the curtain she had pulled aside to fall back into position at the window. Nothing like storms and dreary weather to dampen both her gown and her spirits.

However, the point was, she reminded herself, that she had actually been invited to a social event, no matter what the weather.

Thunder mixed with the clatter of the carriage wheels and clopping of the horses' hooves as they journeyed toward the Marquess of Stratford's elegant home. A fat drop of rain plopped against the carriage window, followed by another and another.

Priscilla's delicate pink parasol, edged with white ruffles, had been more designed for appearance rather than practicality. Her father patted the sturdy black umbrella, leaning against the seat. "I've come prepared."

When they arrived, the footman held an umbrella over them as they exited the carriage, and her father, as any gentleman would, used his own to shelter her more than himself. She'd made it inside the entry with only slightly dampened skirts.

The butler greeted and directed them to a large parlor where they waited for their hostess. "Some guests have already arrived. Lady Honoria should join you shortly."

Priscilla shot her father a wary look. *Who had Lady Honoria invited?* What if some of the women who had shared such disparaging comments at the duke's ball were in attendance? Would they give her the cut direct?

Her father gave her arm, threaded through his, a comforting pat. "I shall not leave your side, my dear."

She took a deep breath, held her head high, and entered the room. Men and women in approximately equal numbers were chatting amiably but stopped short.

Every head turned in her direction and stared. It appeared Honoria had not informed her other guests that she'd invited society's foremost pariah. Priscilla's lips quivered as she forced a smile, and her father tightened his hold on her arm.

If anyone had dropped the proverbial pin, she would not only have heard it drop, but every speck of dust, had there been any, would make a swooshing sound as it floated in the air from where it had been discharged.

The Duchess of Ashton's gaze locked on Priscilla's. "Miss Pratt, how lovely to see you. Won't you take a seat by me?" She motioned toward the empty chair. Gasps echoed from several other women, drawing a quelling, but not unkind, look from the duchess.

Priscilla nodded and walked on shaky limbs toward the group. "Thank you, Your Grace." Once seated—her father remaining steadfastly by her side and taking the seat next to her—she focused on her hands, folded neatly on her lap.

"Have you found London much changed since your return?" the duchess asked.

Was the question designed to trap her? She jerked her attention to the duchess, finding no ill intent on her face. "No, madam. It appears much as I'd left it."

Her Grace leaned in closer. "Pay them no heed. You are Lady Honoria's guest as much as any other. Now, chin up and smile."

Unlike the forced expression of happiness Priscilla had presented when she'd first entered, a genuine expression of contentment not only spread across her face, but warmed her heart. The duchess was the one woman in the room who had every right to hate her, spurn her—and yet she did not.

"You are too kind, Your Grace."

Before the duchess could say another word, Lady Honoria entered. "My apologies for my tardiness, everyone. I was overseeing the arrangement of card tables in the solar for our games. If we have the appropriate number, we shall pair up in sets of four." Honoria quietly counted off the attendees, pointing a discreet finger as she calculated the total.

"Oh, dear, we seem to be one short. But Dr. Marbry has yet to arrive."

Priscilla's heart lurched.

❦

Timothy arrived late to Lady Honoria's card party, having requested time off from his duties at the clinic. Harry questioned him, and upon giving his permission, informed Timothy that he hoped it didn't become a habit. With Harry's duties in Lords, leaving the clinic only with Dr. Somersby to tend to patients was a burden.

Although Lady Honoria had claimed Timothy's presence wasn't necessary, he insisted, finding it difficult to remain uninvolved regarding Priscilla's search for a suitable husband. Indeed, Timothy felt as if he needed to oversee each and every encounter.

Why, he couldn't say.

Or perhaps *wouldn't* was the more likely word.

The thought of Priscilla in the arms of another man put him in the foulest of moods. In fairness, he had no right to such thoughts and emotions, and it certainly wasn't fair to Honoria, who, without so many words, waited patiently for him to speak with her father and ask for her hand.

Each time he convinced himself it was the proper day and hour, an emergency at the clinic, or a call at Bea and Laurence's to bounce little Lizzie on his knee seemed to crop up.

Once Priscilla had chosen someone—Timothy told himself—he would proceed with his proposal, and he and Honoria would be married.

Neither thought brought him joy.

Rain splattered against his hat as he descended from his carriage at the marquess's home. Although he'd been there numerous times when calling upon Honoria, the expansive, ostentatious home never failed to make him feel insignificant.

Would he become used to its impressiveness once he and Honoria were married? Would he take for granted all the things money could buy and forget what it was like to struggle to put bread on the table as his patients at the clinic did? He certainly hoped not. Yet, he'd seen the kind of complacency that allowed many in the *ton* to disregard the needs of the less fortunate. What were Priscilla's thoughts about the poor? Would she support his work at the clinic?

He bounded up the stairs and gave a firm knock against the door, reminding himself that it was Honoria he should think about rather than Priscilla.

Higgins, the marquess's butler, led him to the parlor where everyone waited.

Honoria welcomed him. "Perfect timing, Dr. Marbry. We were about to adjourn to the solar, and we were one short for a full set of four at the six tables."

He darted a glance around the room, catching Priscilla studying him. He hoped she would be seated at a table on the far side of the room from him. Otherwise, how could he ever concentrate on his cards?

Everyone followed Honoria to the solar, where she began dividing up the teams and tables. "In the spirit of fairness, we shall switch groupings after we've played two hands."

As the number of guests whittled down, Timothy grew more anxious. For the most part, married women and gentlemen were assigned tables together, but not with their spouses, which Timothy admitted was an excellent tactic. Much to Timothy's relief, Honoria assigned Lord Nash to a table with Lady Miranda, Lord Middlebury, and Lady Charlotte.

Once five tables had been filled, only Priscilla, Lord Felix, Honoria, and he remained.

"Partner with me, Marbry," Lord Felix said, "I like to win."

Honoria saved Timothy from being rude. "Now, sir, it's my party, and to be fair, I suggest we partner a gentleman with a lady."

"Are you implying that partnering two men gives them the advantage?" Priscilla asked.

Timothy admired the hint of confrontation in her voice. He'd missed her fire.

"Not at all, Miss Pratt. In fact, quite the opposite. I believe pairing two ladies would place the gentlemen at a distinct disadvantage. Don't you agree?"

The loveliest of smiles broke across Priscilla's face, and suddenly the dreary day seemed brighter. "I do, Lady Honoria. I most certainly do."

Honoria tapped a finger to her chin. "Hmm. I think I shall pair you with Lord Felix, and Dr. Marbry will partner with me."

Honoria handed Timothy the deck of cards. "Would you be so kind as to deal, Dr. Marbry?"

He shuffled and dealt the cards, his eyes constantly following Priscilla's graceful fingers, so long and supple, as she retrieved each card and placed it in position. Oh, what she could do with those fingers.

Finishing the deal, he turned up a five of spades for the trump suit.

Desperately, he tried to concentrate on the cards and the plays, yet found himself constantly sneaking glimpses of Priscilla.

In contrast, the concentration on her face during each play was intense as she considered the cards before her and in her hand.

Timothy had won the last trick, so he selected a ten of hearts and placed it in the middle of the table. Priscilla's rosebud lips curved upward, and she placed a queen of hearts atop his card. Honoria gave a frustrated little huff and played a nine of hearts, which made Priscilla's beam of happiness even greater. She and Lord Felix had already won the majority of tricks so far.

Then Lord Felix played a three of spades, trumping everyone.

"Why in the world would you do that?" The tone of Priscilla's voice practically called Felix an idiot, which, in Timothy's estimation, he was. "We had already won the trick. We're supposed to be a team."

Felix scooped up the cards. "We still won the trick." He turned toward Timothy. "Women. Am I right?"

"No, sir, you are not right. Miss Pratt has a valid point. Why waste a trump card on a trick your team has already won?"

Lord Felix waved him off, casting a disdainful expression toward Timothy.

Honoria stared, appearing quite flabbergasted. At least they could cross one pairing off their list of prospective suitors.

A fact that Timothy found most comforting.

CHAPTER 15—WHIST WHISPERS

Nodcock," Priscilla muttered under her breath. The fool Lord Felix had more interest in capturing the trick himself than playing as a team. She wanted to kick him under the table, good and hard right in his skinny shins.

Next to her, Timothy chuckled. The sound, so low and sensual, made her skin pebble in direct contradiction to the heat rushing up her neck to her face. As Timothy dealt the next hand, his fingers brushed against hers, fanning the flame burning within her even more. She had a sudden need for either some cool air or a refreshing drink.

Settling on the next best thing, she retrieved the fan lying in her lap, snapped it open and began waving it in front of her face.

An angry roar soared from another table, drawing everyone's attention to where Nash was scooping up the trick from the middle of his table. Lord Middlebury—his face blotched with red—shouted his accusation. "You cheated! I demand to see that you have no diamonds in your hand, sir!"

Nash settled back in his chair but refused to show his cards. "I'm afraid the stickpin in my cravat holds the only diamond on my person, sir."

Lady Miranda attempted to diffuse the situation. "From my tally, that gives us five points, Lord Nash. Perhaps show him your cards, so we may be done with this unpleasantness."

Nash shrugged and laid his cards out for all to see. True to his word, the only remaining cards in his hand were spades and hearts.

"I don't believe it. Check his coat sleeves," Middlebury blustered.

Nash responded with a laugh. "You give me more credit than I'm due. Now stop being a poor loser and apologize for insulting me with your accusations."

Middlebury rose, his chair scraping across the stone floor of the solar with a painful screech, sending a shiver up Priscilla's arms and spine. He bowed to Lady Charlotte, then stomped from the room.

"Oh, dear." Honoria rose from her seat. "I apologize for Lord Middlebury's hasty departure. Since that leaves us with uneven pairs, as the hostess, I will sit out. But we will still be short two players."

"Perhaps a footman could take Lord Middlebury's place?" Priscilla suggested.

Lord Felix glared down his long nose at Priscilla, his eyebrows arching. "A footman? You can't be serious? I refuse to play at a table with a servant!"

Regret surged through Priscilla, and she wished she could retract her words. It was one thing to have a footman or her lady's maid sit in for a round of cards while she was in the country with so few visitors, and quite another when in the height of London's society.

"I think that is an excellent idea," Lady Honoria said, although her tremulous voice hinted she wasn't entirely convinced of her statement.

"Hear, hear," Timothy said.

Tears pricked the corners of Priscilla's eyes that she had made such kind friends in Lady Honoria and Timothy Marbry. She even felt contrition for lobbing a boot at Timothy's head. Catching Honoria's eye, she whispered, "Thank you."

During her childhood, Priscilla had few friends, even those of the feminine variety. And when she'd grown older, her mother had even discouraged her from associating with too many other young ladies. "They are your competition, my dear. If you are to develop a relationship, let your goal be to learn their weaknesses rather than support their strengths."

She'd doubted the wisdom of her mother's words then, but as a dutiful daughter, she'd followed them. Now, sadness seeped through her soul at the happiness she'd missed by not having a female confidant, one to share her joys and troubles. At that very moment, she vowed to do everything in her power to befriend Lady Honoria, even if it meant enduring the pain of seeing her new friend form an attachment with the one man who made Priscilla's heart skip a beat.

TIMOTHY DEVELOPED A NEW RESPECT FOR PRISCILLA. HE WOULD never have imagined the hellion who complained so vehemently about assisting him with his boot would suggest a servant take the place of an aristocrat in a game of cards. Perhaps catching chickens and tending to an ill stranger had given her a new perspective as well.

With a willing footman taking Lord Middlebury's spot, Honoria assigned the new partners and tables. She paired Timothy with Lady Miranda at a table with Priscilla's father, Lord Cartwright, and the duchess. Miranda proved a worthy teammate, as Timothy knew she would. With Laurence as her brother, she would have learned the art of strategy with cards at an early age. She appeared especially adept at taking a trick when least expected.

"Did Montgomery teach you that move?" Timothy asked when she trumped with a three of spades, taking the final trick.

A tiny smirk crossed her lips. "Not that one."

"Maybe Middlebury should have kept his eye on you instead of Nash," Timothy said.

Lord Cartwright chuckled, shuffling the deck. He dealt the next hand, turning up a three of hearts for the trump suit. "It's a good thing White's doesn't allow women."

When Miranda raised her brows, he said, "A compliment, my dear. You would fleece us all."

Timothy led the first trick with an eight of clubs.

Her Grace frowned at her cards. "How are you enjoying your position at the clinic?" She laid down a ten of clubs.

Timothy glanced up at Miranda, who gave him an infinitesimal smile, then laid down the jack of clubs.

"I'm finding it most rewarding. The patients appreciate everything we do for them. It's exhausting but exhilarating at the same time, if that makes any sense."

The duchess's laugh, like bells, chimed next to him. "That's what Harry says. Although he always seems to have enough energy to bounce little Edmund on his knee when he returns home at the end of the day."

It was something to be admired for certain. He hoped he would be as successful at juggling all his duties when the time came for him to start his own family.

Lord Cartwright played a queen of clubs, taking the trick. "I saved us, Your Grace."

"Blast!" Miranda said.

Lord Cartwright glanced at Timothy and tilted his head to the table where Honoria sat. "I understand you've been keeping company with Lady Honoria."

Discomfort itched at his neck. "Yes. Well . . . umm."

"Don't misunderstand," Cartwright said. "I like her. You could do a lot worse." Then he muttered something which sounded like, "Trust me."

Truer words, but Timothy still found his eyes seeking Priscilla where she sat paired with Mr. Ugbrooke. The man looked as though he'd been drinking castor oil, his face pinched and dour. Priscilla turned slightly, catching Timothy staring at her, then laughed perhaps a little too loudly at something Mr. Ugbrooke had said.

Lord Cartwright's voice pulled him back to the matter at hand. "Your play, Marbry."

The two hands progressed in much the same manner, and when they switched tables, Timothy found himself once more in a group which included Priscilla. Honoria insisted Priscilla pair with Lord Highbottom, leaving Timothy to pair with Lady Charlotte.

Lord Highbottom made a disappointed face. As Timothy had suspected, arranging an attachment between Priscilla and Highbottom had a colossal chance of failure.

When they took their seats, Timothy had to admit, he also had a modicum of disappointment at the pairing, but seated with Priscilla on his left eased it considerably.

On the right, Highbottom kept nudging Timothy's knee under the table. Surreptitiously, he scooted his chair to the left, only to have his long legs bump into Priscilla's instead.

"I beg your pardon," he whispered.

A blush blossomed across her cheeks, but she kept her gaze down and her lids shuttered. Her long eyelashes brushing against her fair skin only drew his attention more.

"Lord Highbottom," Lady Charlotte said, placing a card on the table. "I understand you purchased a new curricle."

Highbottom's gaze shot to Timothy. "I did, my lady. It's most grand. Fast, too." He winked in Timothy's direction.

Red flashed in Timothy's vision at the lovely smile Priscilla sent to Highbottom. "I would so enjoy a ride through Hyde Park in such a vehicle. Were a gentleman to ask me, of course."

"Hmm," Highbottom muttered, not bothering to acknowledge her thinly veiled hint for an invitation.

Timothy mentally crossed off another suitor from Honoria's list, leaving Mr. Ugbrooke and, God help him, Lord Nash.

Time passed in a blur, and the party disbanded around three. Timothy gladly returned to the comfort of his home, where he didn't have to worry about unmarried women and finding them husbands.

Slouched against the sofa in his bachelor townhouse, he pulled at his neckcloth. There had been times during the card party when he'd have rather been dressing a gaping wound than sitting so close to Miss Pratt and not be able to touch her as he wished.

Why couldn't he feel such attraction to Lady Honoria? She impressed him, for certain. Her delicacy at handling the situation when Priscilla had suggested a footman join them at the card tables was admirable, to say the least.

When the guests had dispersed and left for their homes, he'd lingered, thanking Honoria for her kindness. However, they both agreed that they could safely remove both Lord Felix and Lord Highbottom from the list of prospective suitors.

It should have been a relief, but the later pairing of Priscilla and Lord Nash had caused Timothy great distress. Although seated at a different table than Timothy, the constant giggles from Priscilla and the low seductive chuckles coming from Nash had Timothy's blood boiling.

Timothy ripped the cravat from his neck, grasping the ends of the white cloth between his hands, and imagined wrapping it around Nash's throat.

Maybe he needed to move forward with his plans to propose to Honoria. He hadn't even attempted to kiss her. If they were engaged, wouldn't she expect such familiarity?

In truth, he hadn't missed sharing such gestures of affection. A sad statement for one who hoped to seek a contract of marriage. He needed to get his mind off Priscilla and on to something else, something that made him feel productive.

He slipped the cravat back around his neck and tied it, not bothering to create the elaborate folds his valet, Rivers, had managed earlier that day. No one would care at the clinic.

Work would divert his traitorous thoughts.

Arriving at the clinic provided the diversion and much more. People spilled from the waiting area out the front door. He hurried to the examination rooms, searching for Harry or Oliver regarding the enormous influx of people.

"Thank God you're here," Oliver said, as he finished bandaging a patient's hand. What appeared to be soot blackened the man's face.

"What happened?"

"An accident on the docks. We need every pair of hands. The other medical facilities are overflowing, and all physicians have been asked to help."

"I'll get to work." Thank goodness Oliver didn't chastise him for taking the day off to go to a card party. Perhaps that would come later from either him or Harry. But of course, emergencies were emergencies because one didn't schedule them.

By the time the last patient left, every muscle in his body ached with exhaustion.

Harry stumbled into the waiting area, locked the door, turned the sign to "closed," then slumped in the nearest chair. "Reminiscent of your first day working here, true, Marbry?"

Timothy found the strength to nod his head, but barely. "There must be a way to help more people. Is there nothing we can do to entice another physician to join us?"

Harry drew a hand down his face. "Unless someone will work for free, I'm afraid not. Although another pair of hands would be a godsend."

Unease soured Timothy's stomach that Harry had been most generous with his salary. The need to improve his financial situation pressed in on Timothy, reminding him that Honoria's dowry would solve many problems—not only those of the Saxton estate, but his ability to donate his time to the less fortunate.

He became resolute to do what he must. "I may be able to help with that shortly."

"DID YOU ENJOY THE CARD PARTY, MY DEAR?" PRISCILLA'S FATHER asked on their journey home.

Sighing, she settled against the soft squabs. "Yes. I did. I understand only Lord Nash surpassed you in taking the largest number of tricks."

He grinned at her. "I do love a good game of whist. Both Nash and I had the good fortune of being paired with competent players. Although I would never say this to her face, Her Grace didn't seem to have her mind on the game."

"Do you think she resented me being there? She was exceedingly kind to me when we arrived, but I don't know . . ."

"Rest easy, girl. She spoke to me briefly before she left and apologized for her lack of attention to the game. Although she didn't confess the reason, she did state she'd been feeling inordinately tired lately."

"Oh, I hope she's not ill. But surely the duke would know, wouldn't he?"

Her father gave her an enigmatic little smile. "I think she will be just fine. And as far as I could tell, she's completely forgiven you for what happened." He turned toward the carriage window, muttering, "If only others were as generous."

Indeed.

During the session when she paired with Mr. Ugbrooke, with the way he had stared at her, she expected him to pull out his lorgnette for a closer examination. Perhaps he would even open her mouth to inspect her teeth. She shuddered at the thought.

However, he did suggest he might call on her in the coming days, which was more than she could say for any other eligible man at the party.

She was unsure how she felt about that prospect. He wasn't hideous. Certainly nothing like Lord Middlebury, who had come perilously close to pinching her bottom when they first dispersed to join their respective tables. Quick sidestepping on her part allowed her escape.

Not precisely objectionable, Mr. Ugbrooke came nowhere near

Timothy in attractiveness. And unlike Timothy's exotic scent of sandalwood, Mr. Ugbrooke reeked of garlic.

Oh, Timothy. She exhaled another sigh at her dilemma. Before her disgrace, she would have loathed Lady Honoria, perhaps even done something underhanded to sabotage her attachment to Timothy. However, as much as she secretly wished either of them would break off their association, she admitted a strange kinship to the quiet woman.

And who could blame Timothy for seeking her affections? She was pretty, wealthy, and as far as Priscilla knew, well respected by those in the peerage. Yet what did her father say?

"Papa, you said something about Lady Honoria having some difficulty with society. I don't recall what happened."

He turned from the window, meeting her gaze directly. "I thought you'd learned your lesson about gossiping?"

Although no harsh accusation tainted his voice, his judgment sliced through her. "I only hoped to understand. She was very kind to me today. Even defended me against Lord Felix's disparaging comments."

Her father snorted. "He's a fine one to talk." He grew serious, his eyebrows drawing together. "What did he say? Should I have words with him?"

"No. No. Dr. Marbry and Lady Honoria defended me. It was a silly disagreement. But I should like to become friends with Lady Honoria, if she will permit, and I thought it might help to know a bit more about her."

Closing his eyes, he seemed to mull it over. "Very well. Six years ago, the year before your come-out, she developed a tendre for a young man who did not meet with her father's approval."

"That seems hardly enough to cause gossip."

He nodded. "As you're aware, it doesn't take much for the *ton's* tongues to wag. To hear your mother tell it, there was a degree of impropriety between them, and Stratford ran the young man out of London under threat of bringing legal charges."

Priscilla's eyes grew wide. "Could he do that?"

"Practically anything's possible if you have the power Stratford does. As I understand it, the young man had no title or money, and Stratford accused him of being a fortune hunter." He paused as if gauging her reaction. "However, I would take anything your mother says with more than a pinch of salt."

Years ago, such information about a rival would have been like finding gold. But at that moment, it caused her pain for her new friend. No wonder Honoria was still unmarried, and perhaps Timothy was her last chance for a titled husband.

Torn between her first female friend and the man who held her affection, she decided to make her best attempt to find a husband who wasn't an attractive red-headed doctor.

CHAPTER 16—ENCOUNTER AT THE BOOKSELLER'S

Signs of spring began making welcomed appearances. Snowdrops popped up from wet patches of earth. Birds fluttered about, gathering bits of twigs and string to build nests to lay their eggs. Buds on trees unfurled into tender leaves. The temperature rose enough to forgo wearing a heavy greatcoat. Worst of all, couples strolled along in the park, some even arm in arm.

It was enough to make a man curse.

Not that Timothy didn't enjoy spring. He did—especially the warmer weather. It was the infernal mating call all around him that put him in a foul mood. Each happy couple he passed, each chirp of a baby bird, each new litter of kittens mewing under a secluded stairway reminded him he needed to stop beating around the bush and offer for Lady Honoria.

Granted, the lady herself hadn't pressed the matter. She seemed content to spend time with him without any promises being made, which was curious. Her father, on the other hand, was not as patient. When Timothy arrived one morning to escort Lady Honoria to the booksellers, the butler directed him to Lord Stratford's study rather than the parlor where he usually waited.

Giving one solid knock to the open door, Timothy waited at the entrance.

Stratford did not rise from behind his desk, but instead nodded and motioned Timothy to enter. "Dr. Marbry." The man's intense blue eyes studied Timothy as if he were a specimen under a microscope.

Timothy swallowed the rather large lump that had found a home in his throat, unsure what, if anything, he should say. He forced the most polite and logical thing he could think of at the moment. "Sir." He nodded. "How are you feeling? Recovered fully from your malady of a few weeks ago?"

Stratford waved him off. "Yes. Yes. Although I will admit, the poultice and tea you provided did more for me than those damnable leeches my personal physician insists upon using."

Pride swelled in Timothy's chest. At least he'd done something right in the marquess's eyes. He waited, anticipating the direction of the conversation, but not wishing to presume lest he be completely off the mark.

A man used to controlling the situation, the marquess continued to eye Timothy, his fingers drumming a steady rhythm against the fine-grained wood of his desk. "How familiar are you with Honoria's past?"

Confusion shifted the course of Timothy's thoughts. What was Stratford fishing for? "I'm not sure of your meaning, sir."

"It's simple enough. Are you aware of her past?"

"If you're asking if I've heard gossip, to be honest, yes. However, I'm not one to believe such hearsay."

"Hmm." He stopped his infernal drumming and thumbed some papers. "If what you heard is that she was involved with a man beneath her, your sources are correct."

Timothy resisted the urge to squirm under the man's direct gaze, but heat inched up his neck.

"To a point," the marquess continued. "There was an unsavory part that circulated about Honoria's . . . virtue. I hope you don't give credence to such lies."

"No, sir. Of course not."

The tension that Timothy had initially attributed to the man's formidable reputation eased. Perhaps the marquess was more concerned about what Timothy thought than first expected.

"Lady Honoria has conducted herself with grace and dignity, sir. You need not worry about her behavior with me."

Of course, much of that had to do with Timothy's own lack of physical desire for his future intended. Had it been Lord Cartwright interrogating him about Priscilla, would he have been able to say the same?

He brushed it aside, reminding himself, yet again, he was *not* courting Priscilla.

"Is that all?" Timothy began to rise, hoping he would be dismissed.

Stratford held out his hand, urging him back to his seat. "Not quite. I'm wondering why my daughter hasn't brought you up to scratch. What exactly are your intentions regarding her, if I may ask?"

Although phrased politely, there was no question that he demanded an answer. Timothy scrambled for the precise words that would appease the man before him, yet buy him a little more time before placing himself in the parson's trap.

"My intentions are honorable, sir. Rest assured of that much. With my duties at the clinic, I fear I cannot spend as much time courting Lady Honoria as I would like, and I wish for us to become better acquainted before I make an offer."

The man's auburn eyebrow quirked. "So you *do* intend to offer for her?"

That lump rose, lodging itself firmly in the middle of Timothy's throat. "Yes, sir. When the time is right, and if you approve."

Stratford nodded. "Very well. That will be all."

And with that, Timothy was summarily dismissed, making his way to the parlor and Lady Honoria.

More spirited than usual, Honoria greeted him warmly and

motioned for him to take a seat. She poured and handed him a cup of tea. "It would appear the card party was a mixed success."

He took a quick sip before answering. "How do you mean?"

"Well, as we agreed, I've crossed Lord Highbottom and Lord Felix off my list. But perhaps we should reconsider Lord Nash."

He practically choked on his tea. "Pardon?"

"As a suitor for Miss Pratt. They appear to get along well. He seemed most attentive when they partnered together."

"He did, did he?" Timothy bit down so hard, he swore he cracked a tooth. He'd spent several days blotting out the image of Priscilla's flirtatious laughter at everything the scoundrel Nash had said.

Apparently, Honoria found his words amusing, for her laugh rang through the red haze clouding his vision.

"Dr. Marbry. From your reaction, one would think you're jealous." Her expression was all innocence, completely free from accusation.

"I'm merely concerned for her safety, and she is trying to rebuild her reputation. Keeping company with Nash is hardly the best approach to accomplishing an already difficult task."

She grew pensive, her brows drawing down over her green eyes. "I think there is much more to Lord Nash than meets the eye— that there is good in him he keeps hidden."

Timothy gave a boisterous laugh at her naivety but stopped short. From the serious look on her face, she truly believed it. "You are too good, Lady Honoria, especially for blackguards in the world like Lord Nash."

"Cressida Cox, who is a friend of Camilla Somersby, said that Lord Nash was instrumental in saving Dr. Somersby's life during the uprising at the gypsy encampment. I ask you, Dr. Marbry, would he do that if there wasn't good in him?"

Timothy had heard the same rumor and was tempted to ask Oliver himself. "People have motivations for seemingly selfless acts that aren't entirely selfless."

The lines between her eyes deepened. "I . . . that is a most perplexing statement."

"What I mean is, he must have had some ulterior motive, something that worked to his advantage."

"Yet, because of him, a man lives who could have died."

He couldn't argue with her there. In fact, it seemed futile and ill advised to argue with her at all. Arguing wasn't the best approach to wooing a woman.

"I concede to your wisdom, my lady. Please consider me thoroughly enlightened. Now, shall we cease speaking of Miss Pratt and Lord Nash and move to more pleasant topics?"

As she chatted amiably about Lord knows what, his mind drifted to a certain blonde with clear blue eyes.

"Dr. Marbry. Is everything all right?" Lady Honoria's soft voice jolted him and reminded him of his priorities.

A sickening feeling swept over him at the concern on her face, and he swallowed hard. Although compassion shone in her eyes, there was no trace of desire, and any affection he found therein seemed more of a filial nature.

Could he continue to pursue her, knowing they might never have the type of connection that Bea and Laurence had found?

He reminded himself he no longer believed in love, and that a marriage based on mutual respect was good enough for most of the *ton* and better than many experienced.

There had been a time when he'd wanted more, believed in more. Young and foolish, full of dreams and hopes, he'd trusted and believed, which had made him vulnerable to a scheming, deceitful woman.

He'd grown up since then. He wasn't that innocent, trusting lad any longer.

Honoria would be the perfect wife.

Respectable.

Compassionate.

Safe.

It should have brought him joy to know he had the approval of her father, but instead, he felt a tightening around his neck, choking the freedom right out of him.

NOTHING ABOUT THE SITUATION WAS PLEASANT. FOUR-YEAR-OLD Mary cried and pulled at Priscilla's skirts. Six-year-old Vincent had a runny nose and wiped it on his own sleeve. Mr. Ugbrooke watched Priscilla's every move, as if she were taking some sort of examination.

"Children need a firm hand, Miss Pratt." Mr. Ugbrooke sniffed. "Spare the rod and spoil the child."

If she had a rod, she wouldn't spare it on Mr. Ugbrooke. That was a certainty. If he was such a proponent of discipline, why didn't he do it? Priscilla decided she really had no use for the miniature creatures. She thought back to the red, wrinkly babe Mrs. Wilson had delivered and shuddered.

Still, Mr. Ugbrooke had made it clear he seriously considered her as a wife, so she stiffened her back, put on her most authoritative expression, and did her best to mimic the voice her mother used. "Mary, there is no need to cry over every little thing, especially simply because Vincent looked at you."

The girl wailed even louder, and Priscilla sent a pleading look toward Mr. Ugbrooke.

Priscilla pitied Nancy, her abigail, who stood to the side and grimaced, holding her hands over her ears. No doubt, the woman would pray that Priscilla made a match quickly so she could be relieved of her onerous duties as chaperone and focus only on those of lady's maid.

Vincent stuck his tongue out at his sister, causing her to howl again.

Priscilla's head felt like it would explode if the horrible caterwauling didn't cease soon. She practically jumped a foot in the air when Mr. Ugbrooke slapped his large hands together.

"Children. You will cease this instant!"

The crying stopped. Thank goodness.

How did he do that? Hadn't she exhibited the same amount of firmness and vigor in her demand?

A remnant of a quiet sob left Mary's lips, but she peered up at her father and nodded.

Inspiration took hold. As a child, she'd always been on her best behavior with the promise of an outing. Surely things hadn't changed that much in twenty-some-odd years? "Mr. Ugbrooke. If the children promise to be on their best behavior, why don't we take them to the park?"

Victorious joy filled her when the children's eyes lit with excitement at the prospect. "Please, Papa," little Vincent said, tugging on his father's coat sleeve with a snotty hand.

Mr. Ugbrooke brushed the child's hand away, then pulled out his handkerchief to wipe away the remaining residue. "Too much idleness at the park. But you may have an idea, Miss Pratt. Something educational, perhaps, to build their minds as well as their bodies. We shall take them to the booksellers."

All the joy on Vincent's face vanished the instant his father mentioned books. Mary didn't seem to care one way or the other. She probably only wished to take leave of the house long enough to breathe something fresher than the stale air circulating throughout the dank home. Priscilla decided if she were to marry Mr. Ugbrooke, serious redecorating would be in order.

"An excellent idea, Mr. Ugbrooke," she lied. Truth be told, she didn't *hate* books, but she loved the park more. *Ah ha!* "And perhaps on our return, we could detour through the park?"

Vincent perked right back up.

Mr. Ugbrooke pursed his lips, his face scrunched up as if the idea caused him pain. "We shall see. *If* the children can behave at the booksellers—and only *if*."

Vincent jumped up and down. "We will, Papa. We will."

With the matter settled, they made their way to the bookseller's, Mr. Ugbrooke discussing a volume of political essays and *Coelebs in*

Search of a Wife he'd been hoping to read. Priscilla thought they sounded frightfully dull and hoped to find the latest romantic novel. Of course, reading such books only depressed her spirits further. There would be no Mr. Darcy, Colonel Brandon, or Captain Wentworth for her. At this point, she'd even take a Willoughby or a Wickham.

She glanced at Mr. Ugbrooke. Nothing scandalous at all about him. But Timothy, on the other hand . . .

Good Lord, would she ever stop thinking about the man she couldn't have? She was pathetic.

⚜

TINKLE. THE BELL CHIMED AS TIMOTHY, HONORIA, AND HER lady's maid entered the bookseller's shop. The earthy scent of books prickled Timothy's nose, and he fought the sneeze.

Honoria chattered excitedly about a book she hoped to find as they waited for the bookseller to assist them. "It sounds so thrilling. A murder, an interrupted wedding, secrets, and a *ghost.*" She veritably whispered the last part. "I hope it lives up to Miss Radcliffe's *The Mysteries of Udolpho.* I did so love that one."

Timothy couldn't help but smile at her enthusiasm. He patted her hand wrapped around his forearm. "Then I hope they have it. I shall purchase it for you." It was an extravagance, to be certain. Timothy found his purse decreasing each month, what with contributing to help with his father's expenses in addition to his own. All the more reason to move along with his proposal and marriage to Honoria, who promised a substantial dowry.

After the bookseller greeted them and assured them he had a copy of *Gaston de Blondeville*, he raced off to retrieve a copy. As they waited, Timothy and Honoria passed the time browsing the shelves, each wandering in a different direction.

Without warning, a shriek pierced the quiet of the shop. Timothy slipped the book he was perusing back onto the shelf and hurried in the direction of the alarming cry. Rounding the corner of one of the stacks, he skidded to a halt when he came face to face—or should he say—chest to bosom with Miss Pratt.

She stumbled back, tottering precariously for a moment, and out of reflex, he wrapped an arm around her waist to steady her. Their eyes locked, the moment stretching between them, the silence of unspoken words deafening.

Scents of Priscilla's lemon verbena replaced the mustier smell of the books, and he drew in a deep breath.

The scent and softness of her pressed against the hard planes of his chest made him dizzy. Heat from her fingers, grasping his arms, seared him through the fabric of his coat.

Unbidden, his gaze dipped to her mouth. When the pink tip of her tongue poked out, licking her lips, he groaned. Rustling noises broke the silence and brought him to his senses. He quickly dropped his arms and stepped away from his temptation.

"I heard someone in distress," he said, the words sounding ridiculous even to his own ears.

"One of the children poked me in my . . ." She blushed and pointed to her derrière—as if he needed direction or incentive to look.

But one word stopped him cold. *Children?*

Heedless of the confusion that must have shown on his face, she continued. "Please don't say anything. If they don't behave, we won't be able to go to the park. And I did so wish to go."

He shook his head as if that might clear the wool filling it. "I beg your pardon? Who are *we?*"

"Mr. Ugbrooke and his children, Vincent and Mary. I have no idea who poked me, but I suspect it was Mary. I scolded her earlier. Although it could have as easily been Vincent."

As if summoned by the ghost from Honoria's book, two tow-headed children raced around the corner, slamming directly into Priscilla and propelling her once again into Timothy's arms.

If only he could keep her there.

Giggles eddied up around him, the small child placing a hand over her mouth as if to hold them in. "Who is *he*, Miss Pratt?"

Timothy extracted himself once again and gazed down at the girl. "Dr. Marbry. And you, I presume, are Mary Ugbrooke."

She giggled again. "Why were you holding Miss Pratt like that?"

Priscilla salvaged the delicate situation. "Because you knocked me into him." She sent the girl a censorious look, one his own mother would have been proud of. "I suggest you don't mention it. If your father knows you've been running in the store, he will prohibit our walk in the park."

Heavy footsteps approached, and Timothy took several more steps back, further distancing himself mere moments before the gaunt Mr. Ugbrooke made an appearance.

He stopped short, his gaze jerking between Priscilla and Timothy. "Marbry." He nodded the greeting.

Priscilla flashed him a smile that didn't reach her eyes. "I was just telling Dr. Marbry about our planned excursion to the park."

Timothy stifled a chuckle at how the children snapped to attention, the speed at which would have made his old commanding officer proud.

Ugbrooke's eyebrow quirked. "*If* they behave."

"We've been oh so good, Papa. Truly," Vincent lied, his eyes darting toward Priscilla in conspiratorial pleading.

Priscilla's blue eyes pinned Timothy, matching the same beseeching quality of the child's. "Perhaps you would care to join us, Dr. Marbry?"

"Dr. Marbry?" Honoria's voice called out.

Timothy turned toward Honoria's call, but not before he caught the withering look on Priscilla's face. "Over here."

Honoria's face brightened upon finding him with Priscilla and the Ugbrooke family. "Miss Pratt. How lovely to see you! And you Mr. Ugbrooke. Are these your children?"

Ugbrooke had the decency to bow. "They are, my lady. May I introduce Vincent and Mary?"

"Miss Pratt extended a kind invitation to join them in a stroll through the park," Timothy said, barely taking a breath before continuing. "But I was about to inform them we must respectfully decline. I've completely forgotten I'm expected at the clinic this afternoon to relieve Dr. Somersby." It was a lie. Harry had given him the day off. However, spending more time with Priscilla was decidedly not a good idea. He needed distance from her and her tempting lips.

If Honoria was disappointed, she hid it well. "Perhaps another time then." She turned toward Timothy, holding up a book. "Success! While you toil away at the clinic, I shall pass the time with my nose in my new book."

What a biddable wife she would make. So accommodating. So undemanding. So . . . unexciting. He didn't blame Honoria. She was a fine woman, kind, honest, generous. But she wasn't . . . *No!* He wouldn't allow his mind to finish that sentence.

"Did you find anything of interest?" Honoria asked.

Timothy forced himself not to look at Priscilla. "Yes, I think I did. I'll grab it on the way out. Allow me." He removed the book from Honoria's hands. "My treat."

With a curt nod of his head, he bid Priscilla, Ugbrooke, and the two rambunctious children goodbye, then grabbing the book he'd been considering when so pleasantly interrupted, he guided Honoria to the counter to pay.

The sooner he removed himself from Priscilla's presence, the better.

CHAPTER 17—THE PURLOINED RETICULE

Priscilla blinked, her mind whirling at the speed with which Timothy hurried away. One would think either she, Mr. Ugbrooke, or the children had some horrible contagious disease. She gazed down at Vincent, wiping his snotty nose on his sleeve.

Then again . . .

"Have you selected anything of interest, Miss Pratt?" Mr. Ugbrooke asked.

Oh, indeed. Unfortunately, it was something she could not purchase. "I've sent the shopkeeper on a quest for a new romantic novel."

Mr. Ugbrooke snorted in disapproval. "I suggest you ask what Lady Honoria acquired. As a lady of quality, I'm sure her taste is impeccable."

His dig hit its mark with resounding precision, but Priscilla feigned ignorance and forced another smile. "An excellent idea, Mr. Ugbrooke." God help her if this was any indication of life with Mr. Ugbrooke. Constantly looking down his nose at her, criticizing every choice she made, and holding her up to standards she would never meet did not bode well for wedded bliss.

He held several primers in his hands. "I've found these for the children. Lessons on moral development."

Even though she suspected Vincent didn't fully understand the words, the boy groaned.

Silently, she commiserated.

After enquiring with the bookseller, they discovered Honoria had purchased the last copy of *Gaston de Blondeville*.

"I shouldn't comment," the shopkeeper said. "But I found it dreadfully boring. I fear the good lady might wish to return it. If she does, I could notify you."

Priscilla stifled a laugh. "That's quite all right, sir. And knowing Lady Honoria as I do, even if she doesn't enjoy it, I doubt she would return it." Curiosity spurred her. "What of Dr. Marbry? Is the book he purchased available?"

The man's eyes lit up. "Indeed. I have one more copy of it." He motioned for her to follow, then stopped at a stack a short distance away. He scrunched up his nose. "It's by an American author, James Fenimore Cooper, but it has become very popular. It seems there is an interest in the wilds and natives of America."

He placed the book in her hands. *The Last of the Mohicans*. It didn't sound very exciting. Why would she want to read about the *last* of anything? But reading the same thing as Timothy held a certain appeal. "I'll take it." She avoided Mr. Ugbrooke's response, not wishing to witness if he disapproved nor caring if he did.

Purchases in hand, they exited the shop, the children and Priscilla waiting for Mr. Ugbrooke's verdict regarding their behavior. The children were blessedly silent, exchanging glances with each other and with her, but avoiding their father's scowl. Their restraint made her believe all was not lost regarding the park.

Impatience won out, and Priscilla breached the interminable quiet. She threaded her hand through Mr. Ugbrooke's arm, giving it the lightest of squeezes. "I would so love a stroll in the park. It would be a shame to waste the sunshine by sitting indoors."

He turned his steely gray eyes toward her and gave a sharp nod. "Very well."

Thank the stars!

"But the moment you misbehave, we leave."

Priscilla wasn't entirely sure if Mr. Ugbrooke had directed the warning toward the children or her, but she resolved to be on her most agreeable behavior, and the children nodded their little blond heads.

All appeared to be going well until they approached the Serpentine. Vincent tugged at her hand in an effort to hurry their pace. "I want to go swimming!" In his exuberance, he pulled so hard her reticule slipped from her wrist and fell to the ground when he released her hand. Before she could stoop to retrieve it, someone shot past, scooping it up and dashing off.

"Stop!" she yelled at the figure of a child, moving so fast he was almost a blur.

Ignoring her, the child continued along his escape route. The children, no doubt thinking it a merry game, gave chase. The thief looked over his shoulder to gauge the distance of his pursuers at the same moment he approached a large oak.

Luck was on her side when the boy tripped and fell at the foot of the tree. He attempted to rise, but wobbled on his feet and, howling in pain, tumbled back to the ground just as the Ugbrooke children arrived, followed closely by Mr. Ugbrooke, Priscilla, and Nancy.

Pain seared Priscilla's side from running with too tight stays, and she fought to pull air into her deprived lungs.

Vincent reached for the reticule, still clutched in the thief's hands, resulting in a tug-of-war.

"Give it back!" Vincent bellowed, sounding very much like his father.

Mr. Ugbrooke raised his walking stick as if to use it as a weapon on the child. Before he could swing, Priscilla stepped in front of the injured thief, blocking the attack.

"Step aside, Miss Pratt."

"I forbid you to strike this child. Can't you see he's injured and unable to run away?"

The little thief released the reticule to Vincent's grubby, snotty hands, who waved it in the air in victory. "I've got it! I've got it!" He jumped up and down as if his feet had springs.

"Thank you, Vincent."

"I'm going to locate a constable," Mr. Ugbrooke said.

The thieving boy's eyes widened, and his chin trembled.

It was true, Priscilla had no great love for children, at least not like most women. But something about the child before her dredged up a memory that caused shame to slither in her stomach.

She took in the child's appearance. His breeches, much too short for his growing body, were torn and frayed. Mud and bits of grass matted the cap covering his overly long hair. Blue eyes shimmering brightly stared at her and contrasted sharply with the mask of dirt on his face. She recalled another excursion in the park where the duke had attended to Manny, who had become his ward.

She'd been disgusted at Manny's appearance. Encouraged by her mother, she had tried to turn the situation to her advantage—and failed miserably. Shame burned her cheeks, remembering her selfishness when a child was in need. No doubt the duke and duchess had reacted to Priscilla's manipulations with the same disgust she now felt for Mr. Ugbrooke's threats.

"There is no need for that, sir. My reticule has been safely returned. No harm done, except to the child himself."

Mr. Ugbrooke turned an unsettling shade of red. "No harm? You cannot allow a thief to go free. He must be punished."

The boy groaned, and he wiped his nose, muffling the sound of a sniffle, clearly doing his best to mask an onslaught of tears.

Priscilla cast a quick glance at the boy. She was not one to wager, but she would put up the eight shillings in her reticule to bet the child had once belonged to the same gang as Manny and the child with the strange name the Somersbys were rearing.

Could she really allow Mr. Ugbrooke to ask the constable to throw the child into gaol? She shuddered at what would await him there.

"He's injured," she insisted, the pitch of her voice raising as it was wont to do when she became frustrated. "He needs medical attention."

"You"—Mr. Ugbrooke pointed a finger at her—"are too soft. It's precisely such a lack of moral fiber that has led this child astray. He needs a firm hand and punishment for his crimes."

Priscilla scrambled for a solution—one that wouldn't involve the incarceration of a child. "Very well, then. Go fetch a constable, but take the children with you. My abigail and I shall stay with the boy."

He huffed off, his children twisting their necks to stare back as they followed behind him.

"You ain't really goin' to turn me in, are you?" The boy sniffled again.

She stooped toward him. "Of course not. I only wished to remove Mr. Ugbrooke from the vicinity until I could decide what to do."

"'E's a right mean bloke."

She couldn't argue with that. "He has strict beliefs in morality. I don't think he understands that there are often extenuating circumstances for one's behavior."

"Huh?" The boy stared at her, the creases in his brow accentuating the dirt on his face.

"Never mind. What's your name?"

He sniffled again. "They call me Fingers."

She smiled in spite of herself. He definitely must be a remnant of the dispersed gang. Was Manny the only one with an actual name? "Now, where are you injured?"

"My ankle. It's twisted right good, it is. Tripped on that damn root."

Her mind drifted back to Timothy and his tumble from his horse. "You need a physician."

If possible, the child's face paled under the layers of caked dirt. "I ain't gettin' poked and prodded by no fancy doctor. I ain't got no money." He slid a sorrowful glance toward Priscilla's reticule. "At least not anymore. Besides, them fancy doctors gots leeches." The child shuddered. She couldn't blame him.

"What about the clinic? Will you allow me to take you there? I know one of the doctors, and he's very kind. He knows all about twisted ankles."

"It ain't no trick? You ain't goin' take me to the constable?"

She rose and put her hands on her hips and shook her head. "If I were going to do that, I would simply wait for Mr. Ugbrooke to return with one. Perhaps the pain has clouded your thinking. I would imagine it takes a modicum of intelligence to live off thieving."

The boy grinned at her, apparently pleased with the compliment.

"Now," she said, "Can you stand a little? Nancy and I will assist you, and we'll hire a hackney to take us to the clinic."

She motioned for Nancy to stand on the other side of the child, and together, they lifted him to his feet, supporting him under the arms as he hopped on one foot.

Priscilla gazed around. "We must hurry before Mr. Ugbrooke returns." They moved in the opposite direction from where Mr. Ugbrooke had gone, finally making it to Knightsbridge. Luckily, a hackney waited for a paying customer.

Priscilla flagged it down, and as they climbed in, she said, "The Hope Clinic. And do hurry."

❧

AFTER ESCORTING HONORIA HOME, TIMOTHY TOOK A HACKNEY to the East End. Since he'd fabricated the need to be at the clinic in order to put some distance between himself and Priscilla, he decided to make the best of it. It wouldn't do to admit to Honoria the real reasons for his excuse. Thank goodness she appeared content to have the afternoon alone with her book.

The tinkle of the bell on the clinic door announced his

entrance. Harry glanced up from where he was calling the next patient, and his brow puckered. "Didn't you request the day off?"

Timothy nodded. "Change of plans." He gazed around the waiting area. "Who's next?"

Harry shook his head and left to tend to his next patient, leaving Timothy alone to do the same. On the way to the examination rooms, he passed Oliver in the hallway.

Oliver raised a dark eyebrow. "What are you doing here?"

"Glad to see I've been missed," Timothy muttered under his breath.

"What's that?" The grin on Oliver's face indicated his hearing functioned perfectly well. "I thought you were going to call on your intended. Trouble in paradise?"

"Not at all. We simply called our outing short. Lady Honoria purchased a book she wished to read."

Oliver's gaze dipped to the book Timothy held, his grin widening enough to display the dimple in his cheek. "Planning on doing a bit of reading yourself between patients?"

Drat. He should have stopped at home to deposit his book. "Didn't want to waste time stopping at home. Thought I might be needed here."

Oliver patted him on the back. "Always. Now get to work."

Thank goodness the interrogation from his fellow physicians ceased, and he could distract himself with work. All was working well. He filled his time lancing a boil, dressing a laceration, and providing a poultice for a nasty cough. Why he hardly thought of Priscilla at all in the last—he peeked at his pocket watch—hour.

Except when he treated Mrs. Owens' laceration, and he remembered Priscilla's scratched face from the chicken when they were at the cottage. Oh, and when he lanced six-year-old Gordon's boil, and the lad stared up at him with those big blue eyes. And of course there was the poultice for Mrs.—

"Help! We need help!" a woman's voice called out from the waiting area—a very familiar woman's voice.

He'd just finished washing his hands in the chlorinated lime, his shirt sleeves rolled to his elbows, so he shook his wet hands off and rushed to the front of the clinic.

The frantic calls apparently captured Harry and Oliver's attention as well, for they also filed out of the adjacent examination rooms to investigate the commotion.

Timothy skidded to a stop as suddenly as if he'd come face to face with a brick wall. All heads had turned in one direction—toward Priscilla Pratt, who stood in the middle of the waiting area, supporting a rather grubby looking child. The boy—at least he thought it was a boy—balanced on one foot, his filthy hands holding on to Priscilla for dear life.

At that moment, he would have wagered nothing could have surprised him more. "Pri—Miss Pratt," he choked out the words. "What has happened?"

"The child needs attention. He's injured."

Harry appeared to be as dumbfounded as Timothy felt. He gaped at Priscilla, and Timothy wasn't certain if his expression was one of surprise or suspicion.

Oliver seemed to be the only one unaffected by the sight and was the first to jump into action, stooping before the child. "What hurts?"

Interestingly, the child looked at Priscilla. "Is 'e your friend? The kind one?"

Priscilla momentarily pinned Timothy with her gaze, then addressed the child. "No. This is Dr. Somersby. He's not my friend, but he's very kind and is an excellent physician."

Warmth spread through Timothy's chest at the implication of both the child's and Priscilla's words. She described him as a friend and kind.

"I want your friend. The one who don't use leeches."

Oliver chuckled and looked over his shoulder. "Dr. Marbry? Would you like to take this case?" He turned his attention back to the boy. "And we only use leeches on boys who don't behave during examination."

The child clung more tightly to Priscilla. Surely her gown would be covered with dirt from the encounter.

"He's bamming you," Timothy said, scooping the child in his arms and carrying him to an examination room.

Priscilla was on his heels.

"Perhaps you should wait outside," Timothy called over his shoulder.

The child's eyes widened. "No. She stays."

Timothy shook his head. It seemed no matter what he tried, he could not escape Miss Priscilla Pratt.

⚜

PRISCILLA DID HER BEST TO AVOID THE DUKE'S STARE. YET HIS icy glare made her awash in the stench of shame.

Or perhaps that was a product of the child's unwashed body. Nevertheless, she skirted past him to follow Timothy into the examination room with the child.

"What's your name?" Timothy asked, placing the child on the examination table. The sole on one of the child's shoes flapped like a lazy tongue as his feet dangled over the edge.

"He said he doesn't have a real one," Priscilla volunteered.

"I ain't mute." The child sent her a glare that could rival the one she'd received from the duke, then returned his attention to Timothy. "You can call me Fingers."

The name elicited a laugh from Timothy, the sound sending the sensation of fluttering wings in her stomach. "Well, Fingers, what hurts?"

"My ankle. Twisted it somefin' fierce."

Priscilla watched as Timothy gently pressed on the child's ankle. "Ow!"

"It's already swelling." Timothy removed the child's worn shoe, revealing a dirty stockingless foot.

Priscilla's eyes were riveted on Timothy's forearms, exposed from his shirtsleeves rolled to his elbows. Fine auburn hair dusted them, muscle cording when he squeezed the cloth he'd dipped in a strange smelling liquid and began washing the boy's foot. The room swayed as if she'd imbibed too much sherry.

"I must ask, Miss Pratt, should you be wandering the East End? Is that how you came upon Master Fingers?"

She shook herself from the wave of dizziness. "We were in the park as planned for our stroll. The boy, umm . . ." She caught the child's wide-eyed look of terror, no doubt preparing to be carted off by the constable. "He retrieved my reticule when I dropped it."

Timothy began binding the injured ankle. Although he didn't remove his gaze from his task, a smile ghosted his lips.

"As for my abigail, she is outside. She declined to enter."

"She would be safer inside than out, I'm afraid. Perhaps you should fetch her."

Priscilla nodded and quickly made her way back to the front of the clinic. Worry clamped against her chest that Timothy might dig the truth from the boy before she returned. She had no wish to send the child to gaol. He'd probably snatched her reticule hoping to find a few coins to purchase a bit of much-needed food.

When Priscilla exited the examination room, Nancy had already sought safety within the walls of the clinic. The woman was pacing the floor of the waiting area, wringing her hands, her eyes as big as saucers. "Oh, there you are, miss." Her gaze jerked around to the few remaining patients. Lifting a handkerchief to her mouth, in sotto voce, she said, "Who knows what manner of illness these people have."

Priscilla wanted to roll her eyes. One advantage to being married would be ridding herself of the nuisance of a chaperone. "For heaven's sake, Nancy. It's no worse than being in a crowded room at Almack's."

"Hear, hear," a portly man said, lifting an imaginary glass of something—most likely ale or whisky, judging from his red nose—in toast.

"If it makes you more comfortable, return with me to the examination room."

"Is there . . . blood?"

Priscilla succumbed to the eye roll. "Of course not. The child twisted an ankle. He didn't cut off an arm."

The portly toaster guffawed, then belched. Yes, definitely a connoisseur of alcohol.

Priscilla quickened her pace as Timothy's stern words drifted into the hallway. "Tell me the truth, boy. Did you abscond with Miss Pratt's reticule?"

She stepped into the room, drawing upon her courage. "Dr. Marbry, may I have a word outside?"

Timothy spun on his heel to face her, then, after giving the boy a reprimanding look, nodded.

"I see you've located your abigail," he said, jerking his chin toward Nancy.

Priscilla waved it off. Her chaperone was the least of her concerns. "I forbid you to interrogate that child."

Timothy's green eyes sparkled, his lips tipping up at the corners. "You forbid me, do you? Have you joined the ranks of His Grace and the Somersbys and decided to adopt street rats?"

"No . . . I mean . . . yes, I forbid you, but no, I am not adopting the boy. But look at him, Dr. Marbry. He's probably hungry and only wanted to buy something to eat. Besides, my reticule has been returned, and no harm has been done . . . except to him. Please don't call the constable. I've already had to sneak away from Mr. Ugbrooke, who demanded it."

Footsteps sounded behind them, and she turned to once again find the duke watching them intently. "If you're planning on calling the constable, I'm afraid you're too late. The lad just hobbled off behind you while you two were in your heated discussion."

With a jerk, Timothy swiveled around and peered into the examination room. "Blast. He's gone."

"Oh, dear. I wanted to give him some money before he left."

The duke's eyebrows rose as he continued to stare at her as if she had two heads.

Timothy explained, "Miss Pratt thinks he's hungry, and that's why he tried to nick her reticule."

"Indeed? And since when have you been concerned with those less fortunate, Miss Pratt?" Surprise tinged the duke's accusation.

She squared her shoulders and met his gaze. "A person can change, Your Grace."

The question remaining was, had she changed enough?

◈

WITH THE CHILD GONE, PRISCILLA AND HER MAID LEFT THE clinic, leaving Timothy with much to think about. As he washed his hands in the chlorinated lime again, he sensed eyes on him, and he peered over his shoulder.

Harry stood in the doorway, looking very serious. "A word, Marbry?"

"Of course," Timothy shook the water from his hands and rolled down his shirt sleeves. "Something wrong, Your Grace?"

Harry waved the title aside. "None of that here, remember? I would like to speak to you as a friend, if I may." He motioned to the chair, indicating Timothy should make himself comfortable.

Unease built in Timothy's chest when Harry failed to proceed, but out of respect, he waited.

Harry's serious gaze pinned Timothy to his seat. "About Miss Pratt."

Timothy swallowed the lump lodged in his throat.

"I hadn't realized you were *friends*."

Timothy scrambled for an explanation that wouldn't betray his feelings but would appease Harry. "We're acquaintances. She's enlisted my help in repairing her reputation and securing a suitable husband."

The duke's blond eyebrows raised, nearly touching his scalp, and his body stiffened as if called to attention. "Enlisted the help of an *unmarried* man to seek a husband? Are you certain that's wise?"

"I should have clarified. Lady Honoria and I are assisting her."

"Nevertheless," Harry continued, "I would caution you when dealing with Miss Pratt. She cannot be trusted. No doubt you've

174

heard the gossip surrounding my own dealings with her. She nearly cost me the woman I love, Marbry. Take care she doesn't do the same to you and Lady Honoria."

There would be little chance of that since he didn't love Honoria. "I understand your concern, Your . . . Harry. But she truly is sorry for the trouble she caused and wishes to rejoin polite society and make a favorable match."

Harry ran a hand across the back of his neck, shifting awkwardly on his feet. "I must admit, she was the last person I expected to bring in a street urchin for treatment."

And as much as Timothy hated to admit it, so did he.

One thing was certain. Priscilla would never fail to surprise him.

CHAPTER 18—RESCUE ON ROTTEN ROW

O n Sunday, after Timothy attended church services with his family—where he came perilously close to nodding off from boredom during the sermon—he ordered his horse saddled and rode to the Marquess of Stratford's to collect Lady Honoria.

She'd sent him a missive the day before, suggesting, if the weather permitted, they might enjoy an invigorating ride along Rotten Row.

When Timothy arrived, Higgins the butler gave him a note along with a disapproving glare.

What in the world had he done now?

> *Dr. Marbry,*
>   *Deciding to take full advantage of the day, my maid and I have gone ahead. We will wait for you at the entrance near Hyde Park Corner.*
>   *Lady Honoria*

He pulled out his pocket watch and, with a quick glance, realized he was forty minutes late. Had he truly procrastinated so long speaking with Bea and Laurence after the church service? And what did that say about his eagerness to see Lady Honoria?

Not wishing to make matters worse, he urged his horse onward at a quick gait, vowing he would apologize for his tardiness.

When he approached the park, throngs of eager riders gathered at the entrance, and he would be hard pressed to find Honoria. It would have been an ideal time to have the same sense of awareness he seemed to experience whenever Miss Pratt was in proximity.

He scanned the crowds and—speaking of—there, off to the right, Priscilla sat regally on a dappled gray mount as if posing for a portrait. A jaunty little bonnet in a fashionable blue velvet perched on her blond curls, a few of which trailed temptingly down her neck. Her matching blue riding habit draped her body, accenting every curve to perfection. She had a magnificent seat.

Unfortunately for Timothy, his mind drifted to another time wherein Priscilla rode on horseback, astride on his mount and holding on to his waist as they made their way through the snow to the cottage. Which led to more memories he'd been trying to scrub from his mind. Specifically, sharing a bed and lying next to her.

Kissing her.

Blast.

"Dr. Marbry," a feminine voice called, jolting him from his unwelcome thoughts.

Lady Honoria approached on a gentle chestnut mare, her maid following several strides back.

He tried to view her in the same manner as he'd viewed Priscilla, taking in the fine cut of her emerald-green riding habit and bonnet with the feather bobbing in rhythm as her horse trotted toward him.

But he could not. No desire stirred. No warmth spread within his chest.

He pasted on a smile and tipped his hat. "Lady Honoria. I apologize for my tardiness. You look remarkably lovely this fine afternoon." The least he could do was pay the lady a compliment. And she *did* look lovely. Just not as lovely as . . .

He forced that thought from his mind.

"Wonderful," Honoria said, her attention drawn to where his had been moments ago. "I see Miss Pratt has arrived."

At that, Timothy's head jerked between Priscilla and Honoria. "You knew she would be here?" He winced at his accusatory tone, yet Honoria seemed unfazed.

"I hoped. I extended the invitation to Lord Nash and suggested he invite Miss Pratt."

Nash?

Timothy bit back the unkind words bouncing on his tongue and itching to take flight. He held his gloved hand over his mouth and gave a cleansing cough. "Nash? Why?"

For a fleeting moment, something flashed across Honoria's face that said *Are you daft?* But she quickly schooled her features and smiled prettily. "That should be obvious, should it not? From our encounter with her last week at the bookseller, she doesn't seem very taken with Mr. Ugbrooke, so I thought perhaps a completely different sort of man might appeal to her. I know you don't believe she and Lord Nash might suit, but"—she turned toward Priscilla and tilted her head the way women do when they're thinking—"I believe you might be mistaken." She returned her gaze to Timothy. "Why don't we find out?"

Hope flew in on feathered wings that perhaps Nash might not show, then promptly exited as Nash, tall in the saddle, edged his mount toward Priscilla.

Tension snaked in Timothy's chest when Nash tipped his hat toward Priscilla. *The cad.*

"Shall we join them?" Honoria waved a hand toward the *happy* couple.

After giving Honoria a curt nod, his jaw clenching so tight he feared he might crack a tooth, Timothy nudged his mount forward to join their riding companions.

"Good afternoon, Lady Honoria." Nash touched the brim of his hat again, his smile faltering and turning glacial when he addressed Timothy. "Marbry."

"Nash." Timothy ground out the man's name.

Priscilla darted a glance at Timothy, her eyes wide in surprise. Clearly, the arrangement had blindsided her as well.

Nash made a show of gazing about, his head tilting up to the sky. "A fine day for a ride, wouldn't you say?"

Timothy grunted a response he hoped would be interpreted as a yes and motioned for everyone to proceed.

Nash simply smirked and focused his attention on Priscilla, taking the lead with her riding by his side. "You look especially lovely today, Miss Pratt. Your riding habit brings out the depth of blue in your striking eyes." He glanced over his shoulder as if gauging Timothy's reaction.

Timothy's fingers twitched, imagining them tightening around Nash's neck.

۞

WHEN THE EXPECTED HEAT DIDN'T FLOOD HER FACE, PRISCILLA provided the polite response to Nash's compliment. "Thank you, sir." Why didn't Nash's words evoke the same reactions she knew they would have if Timothy had spoken them?

It was a conundrum. Nash was handsome, in a dangerous sort of way, and he had been nothing but polite and attentive to her in all of their encounters, not at all living up to his rakish reputation.

"I must say, my lord," she reciprocated. "You sit your mount most excellently."

A grunt of—was it disapproval?—drifted from behind her.

"That is most kind, Miss Pratt. I've always been a fairly gifted horseman, but recently I've taken some instruction from Dr. Somersby. Are you familiar with the gentleman?"

"I've met him. Although I can't say I know him well. How is it you came to take riding instruction from him? I would think a doctor's skills would be in, well, doctoring."

Nash laughed, the sound deep and genuine. "A logical conclusion, and a correct one, I would presume, although I've yet to need his medical services. Let us say his heritage is one in which he's become most adept at riding. He taught me a few tricks. Would you like to see?"

Priscilla nodded, wondering what he might do.

"Oh, please show us, Lord Nash," Honoria chimed in.

"Yes. Do show us." Timothy's encouragement reeked with sarcasm, and Priscilla couldn't resist sneaking a peek over her shoulder to see if his expression matched.

It was foul indeed.

The cut didn't appear to faze Nash in the least. He continued to smile charmingly. "Very well. Would it offend you if I removed my coat? For ease of movement, you understand."

At that, Priscilla's cheeks *did* warm. "Of course not."

He removed his coat and his hat, and handed them to her, then studied the path before them. For what, she didn't know. Riders approached from the opposite direction and passed, leaving the stretch before them relatively clear.

"I'll start with something easy." With a nudge of his boots, the horse took off in a trot. He slipped his boots from the stirrups, pointing his toes down, released the reins, and held his arms out to the side.

She clapped her hands in delight. "Marvelous!"

"Show off," Timothy muttered behind her. "It's something any cavalry man worth his salt can do."

"Are you able to do that, Dr. Marbry?" Honoria asked.

"If I wanted to show off, certainly. However, some of us have more restraint."

Nash reined in the horse and trotted back to them.

"Child's play," Timothy said.

Nash chuckled. "Is that a challenge?"

Timothy jerked his chin. "I don't stoop to such foolishness."

Priscilla darted a glance toward Honoria, whose lips tipped up in a show of camaraderie. What was it about men?

Nash snorted a laugh, then directed his attention back to Priscilla. "Would you like to see something else? Something more daring, perhaps?"

Excitement tripped up her spine. "Is it dangerous?" Her words came out in a combination of a gasp and a whisper.

Nash gave a careless shrug. "Depends on whom you ask. However, I promise you, I will be perfectly safe."

"Then, yes, please."

Checking again, presumably to make sure the path remained clear, Nash dismounted. With one hand grabbing on to the horse's withers and the other the mane, he urged his horse into a quick trot as he ran along beside. He bounced three times, then vaulted up into the saddle in one fluid motion.

Priscilla's hand rose unbidden to her throat. "Oh, my goodness!" She cast a surreptitious glance back at Timothy, who simply continued to glare.

Reseated on his mount, Nash trotted back. After he retrieved and donned his coat and hat, he grinned at Priscilla. "I'd wager not many of your suitors can perform that trick, my lady."

"Didn't you learn anything about wagering, Nash? You didn't fare so well from that last one with my brother-in-law." That retort came from Timothy.

Nash waved a dismissive hand. "A figure of speech, dear fellow."

When Timothy appeared as if he were ready to take offense, Priscilla intervened. "I, for one, am duly impressed, my lord. Wouldn't it be marvelous if women could ride astride and perform such daring acrobatics, Lady Honoria?"

"You're a braver soul than I, Miss Pratt."

Priscilla admired Honoria's self-deprecating statement. "Not at all. I have enough difficulty remaining seated riding sidesaddle." She had grown to like the quiet redhead.

Even if Honoria had secured the attention of one annoyingly handsome Dr. Timothy Marbry.

TIMOTHY HAD ABOUT ENOUGH OF NASH. HE EDGED HIS HORSE forward, hoping to take the lead so he wouldn't have to watch him flirting with Priscilla. "If we've finished with the tomfoolery, I suggest we get on with our ride."

"My, my," Nash whispered, barely loud enough for Timothy to hear as he moved parallel to Nash's mount. "One would think you're jealous, Marbry. You seem inordinately fascinated with Miss Pratt. Yet, aren't you supposed to be courting Lady Honoria?"

Biting back the comment, partly because there was truth in Nash's accusation, and partly because he didn't want to exacerbate his already sour mood by getting into an argument, Timothy ignored the jab.

Although, he found the idea of planting Nash a facer most appealing.

Nash raised his voice for his next taunt. "And they call *me* a cad."

The anger bubbling just beneath the surface burst forth, and Timothy jerked on the reins of his mount, pulling the horse around with such force, the horse bucked, then stumbled into Priscilla's mount.

Frightened, the poor beast took off like a shot, becoming nothing more than a gray blur and taking Priscilla with it. Heads from everyone around turned at the scream she emitted. Horses and riders scattered to the side, giving her a wide berth.

Fear lanced through him, not unlike the time he came face-to-face with an enemy's bayonet. Priscilla must have relaxed her hold on the reins, for they'd slipped from her fingers. She leaned precariously forward in the saddle, trying to gain purchase and recapture them.

The jaunty blue bonnet flew off her head, sending her blond curls flying unrestrained.

Before Timothy had the perspicacity to react quickly, Nash kicked his mount into action, riding furiously to catch up. But Timothy was not to be outdone by Nash's show of bravado.

Heels of his boots jabbed mercilessly into his horse's sides and he followed suit. Nash may have had the ability to perform audacious stunts to impress the ladies, but Timothy had the faster horse. Of that, he was certain.

Plus, Timothy was leaner than Nash, who outweighed him by about a stone.

Pushing his horse to the limit, he soon found himself neck and neck with Nash as if they were racing for a prize. Timothy supposed they were—the award being gratitude for rescuing Miss Pratt.

They split apart, riding on opposite sides alongside Priscilla's gray. Unfortunately for Timothy, the dangling reins seemed to wave toward Nash's black gelding on the left.

But rather than reach for them, with one hand holding the reins of his own mount, Nash reached out to Priscilla with his free hand. "Miss Pratt. Lean toward me."

She hesitated a moment, and she turned toward Timothy. Terror widened her blue eyes.

Arrogance filled Timothy that she would seek him for her salvation rather than Nash, who had the advantage. And to prove the saying true, pride went before Timothy's fall.

Nash called out to her again. Once he regained her attention, he wrapped the reins around his wrist and, using both hands, plucked her from her saddle, settling her on his lap.

With Priscilla safe, Nash slowed his horse, but Priscilla's riderless mount continued on. Rather than admit he'd been completely ineffectual, Timothy maneuvered around to the other side of the gray and grabbed hold of the dangling reins, finally pulling the horse to a halt.

As he turned both animals around, the sight of Priscilla's arms around Nash's neck drove home the one cruel fact to Timothy.

Jealousy bloomed in his chest.

CHAPTER 19—THE GARDEN PARTY

“How are things progressing, Miss Pratt?” Honoria's lips curved in a shy smile over her glass of lemonade.

Unlike so many others who could have asked the same question, Honoria appeared completely without guile. Her efforts to assist Priscilla in finding a suitable husband had been tireless.

“Nothing new to report, I’m afraid,” Priscilla answered truthfully, and honestly, the lack of progress was a relief.

“Lord Nash’s gallantry was most admirable. Has he not called further?”

Priscilla shook her head. No loss there, either. Even Nash—who was decidedly preferable to Mr. Ugbrooke—held little appeal for her, if nothing more than the simple fact he was not Timothy.

Honoria’s smile faded. “Well, it was only a few days ago. Perhaps he’ll be in attendance today.”

“I fear not. If I remember correctly, there was no love lost between Lord Nash and Lord Montgomery.” Interestingly, both men had also played a part in the forced compromise Priscilla and her mother had orchestrated with the duke, something that might tie them together. However, Lord Montgomery’s involvement had been involuntary, a matter of omission rather than commission.

"Did I hear my husband's name mentioned?"

Priscilla turned to find Beatrix Townsend, Lady Montgomery, approaching, her narrowed eyes pinning Priscilla.

In truth, Priscilla had been surprised, albeit pleasantly, Lady Montgomery had invited her to the garden party. As a staunch supporter of the duke's, Beatrix held little affection for Priscilla, and most likely only invited her on Timothy's behest.

Priscilla swallowed her fear and faced the fiery redhead. "Lady Honoria wondered if Lord Nash would be in attendance. I merely stated my doubts based on his relationship with your husband."

"Oh, that." Beatrix waved her hand as if she were swatting away a pesky fly. "That's all in the past. They will never be bosom friends, but they've come to a peaceable agreement to maintain a cordial relationship."

Well, that was a surprise. If Nash could mend broken fences, perhaps there was hope for her as well.

"How very magnanimous of Lord Montgomery," Priscilla said.

"My husband isn't perfect, but he is generous. Not to mention, he's made his own share of blunders." A faraway look flitted across Beatrix's face, her smile much like that of the enigmatic Mona Lisa. "Besides, both Laurence and I owe Lord Nash a debt of sorts."

Honoria brought the topic back to the matter at hand. "So, will he be in attendance today?"

"We have invited him, although he's yet to arrive. And speaking of tardiness, where is my wayward brother? I thought you would have him better in hand, Honoria."

Jealousy pinged in Priscilla's stomach when Honoria blushed.

Beatrix's gaze drifted to a place over Priscilla's shoulder. "Ah, there is the culprit now!"

Envy morphed into a thousand fluttering wings, and Priscilla turned, holding her breath in anticipation.

Timothy loomed in the open doorway of the terrace, his eyes scanning the crowd. When they locked on Priscilla's, the fluttering in her stomach increased, and her heart took flight.

She fought to contain her excited anticipation as he strode toward them, each step infused with purpose and determination.

He bowed, then took Lady Honoria's hand and kissed it.

Abruptly, the giddiness in her stomach turned into an eagle's death dive, sinking so fast she feared she might cast up her accounts on Timothy's boots.

After his greeting to Honoria, he placed a gentle kiss on his sister's cheek. "Bea. I apologize for my tardiness."

Finally, as if she were an afterthought, he turned toward Priscilla. "Miss Pratt." Cold. So cold, as if the sun, which was shining brightly in the sky on the late spring day, had been snuffed out with those two simple words.

She wanted to weep.

Her gaze still locked on Timothy, she sensed Beatrix's and Honoria's eyes on her. Could they tell? Did they know of her feelings for him?

Oh, God. The words both an internal cry and a prayer, she screwed up her courage. "Dr. Marbry." Although not encased in ice as his greeting had been, she deliberately forced all emotion from her own.

"It would seem all tardy parties are now present and accounted for," Honoria said, nodding toward the entrance from where Timothy had come. "Lord Nash has arrived."

Rather than peer in Nash's direction, Priscilla returned her attention to Timothy's face.

It gave her great satisfaction when he winced.

⁂

Bea grabbed Timothy by the elbow. "May I speak with you in private?"

As much as he hated leaving Priscilla to Nash's advances, he nodded and followed Bea inside to a quiet corner of the house.

"Please have the courtesy to explain yourself, dear brother." Bea's glare was positively frigid.

"I offered to spend a few hours at the clinic prior to coming here. Surely you don't object to my tending to the poor, *dear sister*."

Bea rolled her eyes. Lord, but she executed it to perfection. At least she had learned something at their mother's knee. "I'm not talking about the fact you were late to my party. I'm talking about your romantic entanglements."

"Entanglements, plural? I have no idea what you might be implying."

"Really, Timothy. You've been courting Lady Honoria for five months, but the way you looked at Miss Pratt mere moments ago . . ."

He opened his mouth to object, and Bea held out a silencing hand.

"Don't deny it. Years spent as a wallflower have honed my observation skills quite well, thank you very much. Besides, I know you better than most people know themselves. There is something between you and Miss Pratt, and I, for one, wish to know what it is."

He narrowed his eyes, hoping to imitate their mother's look of disapproval. "I don't owe you anything. I might remind you I'm a grown man and capable of managing my own love life."

She met him stare for stare. "Are you? Truly?"

"Motherhood has softened your brain. You're imagining things."

"And you are evading the question. So apparently my brain has not become as *soft* as you think. Are you about to break Lady Honoria's heart for the likes of Miss Priscilla Pratt?"

Fury boiled inside his chest, his voice escalating in volume. "What on earth do you have against Miss Pratt?"

Andrew Weatherby—who had been passing—stopped, blinked twice, sent a concerned look toward Bea, then hurried away when she shook her head.

Timothy lowered his voice. "What has Miss Pratt done to deserve such vitriol from you, of all people?"

"Do you really have to ask me that? What she did to Ashton is unforgivable."

"She's trying to make amends. Haven't you ever made mistakes you regretted, Bea? Might I remind you that you yourself staged a compromise? With none other than Lord Nash Talbot?" He wanted to spit the man's name out to rid his mouth of the foul taste.

"That was entirely different." She at least had the decency to blush.

"Oh, so the fact you were attempting to extricate yourself from an engagement rather than enter one excuses you? Deceit is deceit, Bea."

Bea recoiled as if he'd actually struck her. Guilt swirled in his gut. The fact that he himself experienced the effects of such deceit only made his accusation more egregious.

Reaching out, he took her hand, but she slipped from his grasp as if his touch burned her skin. "Bea," he said, his voice softening with regret. "I'm asking you to give Miss Pratt a chance. She's a friend, nothing more." The lie pricked his conscience.

"Friend?" Bea's chin dipped and her lips pressed together in a straight line as if she wished to say more but exhibited an uncharacteristic bit of restraint.

"Lady Honoria and I are helping her rebuild her reputation. She's truly sorry for what happened and only wishes to make amends so she may secure a good marriage within society. Can you blame her for that?"

"No. I suppose not. But I would be remiss in my duties as your sister were I not to caution you about her. Promise me you will be on your guard."

"I promise." In truth, an invincible fortress surrounded his heart, guarding it against any interloper.

"As for Lady Honoria, it would be best to make your intentions known as soon as possible. Propose and announce your engagement. That should protect you from any unwelcome advances from unscrupulous females."

Truth rested in Bea's words, and Timothy saw the wisdom in them. Yet, knowing what he should do and doing it were two different matters.

Masculine laughter drifted in from the terrace, reminding Timothy that Nash still lurked about, leaving Priscilla open to his advances.

"Now, we should get back. Your guests will be missing you."

Bea gave him one more eye roll for good measure, then threaded her arm through his and led him back outside.

NEVER IN HER LIFE HAD PRISCILLA ENJOYED A GARDEN PARTY less. Oh, it was a perfectly lovely party, to be certain. Fresh flowers scented the cool spring breeze. Liveried servants offered refreshment for every imaginable taste, artfully displayed on shining silver trays. Dulcet notes from a string quartet rose from the side of the terrace.

No, it wasn't the party. It was Priscilla's preoccupation with a particular male attendee. Try as she might to pay attention to Lord Nash as he relayed the details of her eventful ride on Rotten Row to Dr. Somersby, her attention kept drifting to the house where Timothy had gone with his sister.

Bands of worry tightened Priscilla's chest over what Lady Montgomery was saying to her brother at that very moment. She pushed the thought from her mind, reminding herself that not everything was about her.

"You're quite fortunate, Miss Pratt."

What?

Dr. Somersby watched her expectantly.

"I beg your pardon?"

Dr. Somersby's attention drifted to the entranceway where she had watched Timothy leave, then refocused back on her. The ghost of a dimple appeared on his cheek. "Your riding accident. It could have been much worse had Lord Nash not come to your rescue."

"Oh, yes. I'm most grateful. He stated he learned many of the riding techniques from you."

Dr. Somersby waved it off. "It was nothing, really. He's a quick study." His gaze shot to the entrance of the house once again. "What happened with the street urchin you brought into the clinic? Ashton said he escaped before Dr. Marbry finished treating him."

Nash raised a questioning eyebrow. "You're rescuing street rats?"

"I wouldn't call it a rescue precisely. We had an . . . encounter in Hyde Park."

The low chuckle emanating from Nash should have sent a shiver of pleasure up her spine. If the scandal sheets were to be believed—and she had come to doubt the dependability of such gossip—Nash's rakish reputation had sent many an innocent young lady into swoons. Yet she remained unaffected. Strange.

"I hope you counted your coins after the . . . encounter." Nash turned toward Dr. Somersby. "I thought that rag-tag bunch had been disbanded. Didn't you take one of them into your care?"

Dr. Somersby nodded. "Pockets. Although my wife deserves the credit for that. But the boy has become an integral part of our family." He paused briefly. "Miss Pratt, did the child give his name? If he's part of the same gang, perhaps Pockets knows him."

"Fingers," she answered. "Although even he admitted it wasn't his real name. There was something slightly *off* about him."

Dr. Somersby laughed, shaking his head. "When Eva was born, I teased Camilla that we should name her Waistcoat."

Nash burst out in laughter. "I can imagine how that went over."

"Not well, I assure you."

Light sparkled in Dr. Somersby's eyes when he spoke of his wife, and Priscilla's heart lurched. Oh, how she longed to see a man direct that type of passion toward her. Although Nash—contrary to the tongue-wagging of society—had treated her kindly and respectfully, no such fire shone in his eyes when he gazed at her. Not even when he rescued her during the riding incident.

Determination, concern, yes.

Passion, no.

And if she were completely honest, such lack of interest on Nash's part didn't disappoint her.

No, the only man who had remotely exhibited such fire was also the only man from whom she desired it.

Timothy Marbry.

Speak of the devil, he strode from the house on his sister's arm. Once again, his gaze locked with hers, but he jerked it away as if it pained him. As expected, Beatrix led him to a group where Lady Honoria now chatted with Lord and Lady Saxton.

As the men beside her chatted about horses, Priscilla studied the faces of Timothy's parents. They seemed especially enamored with Lady Honoria. And why shouldn't they? She was everything a man like Timothy Marbry would want in a wife. Wealthy, a well-bred daughter of an aristocrat, quiet, and unassuming.

Of those qualities, Priscilla only possessed two, and even the well-bred part had been under scrutiny thanks to her mother.

And although they'd both had the whiff of scandal dogging their heels, Lady Honoria had been the victim, not the perpetrator. People not only sympathized with victims, they typically forgave them.

Unlike herself.

Oh yes, everyone would cheer a union of Dr. Timothy Marbry and Lady Honoria Bell.

Everyone except Priscilla.

As if to prove a point, Camilla Somersby appeared at her husband's side. "Lord Nash. Miss Pratt." Her voice was chipped ice.

At least Priscilla wasn't the only one receiving the chilly reception.

"Oliver," his wife said, "Margaret and Harry have arrived." She nodded toward the entrance of the terrace.

Priscilla's stomach churned. She should have expected another encounter with the duke. It was common knowledge that he and Lord and Lady Montgomery were close friends. She took courage remembering the duchess's kindness at the card party and hoped she would have a softening effect on her husband's approbation.

She glanced toward Lord Nash. His mouth was pressed in a

firm, straight line, his jaw pulsing erratically. Once more, she found herself sharing a commonality with Lord Nash Talbot.

After the Somersbys excused themselves and made their way through the crowds toward the duke and duchess, Nash whispered low, "I hate to abandon you, but being seen in my presence by the duke and duchess will not advance the cause of repairing your reputation."

What a curious man. She peered into his dark eyes, hoping to see . . . something.

She found compassion.

Odd. But perhaps not.

And truth be told, he was more than likely right. An alliance between the two of them would only sully her reputation further.

How did he stand it?

Sending her a pained smile, he bowed and left her alone.

Again.

CHAPTER 20—CONFRONTING FEELINGS

If Timothy heard about the weather one more time, he would pull out his hair. Thank heaven Harry and Margaret had arrived. At least they would share some more meaningful conversation.

Timothy's mother executed a deep curtsy. "Your Graces. My daughter and her husband are honored by your presence."

Timothy pulled in his lips, stifling a laugh as he caught Harry's slight eye roll. Thank goodness his mother was too busy complimenting the duchess's gown to notice.

"You must give me the name of your modiste, Your Grace."

Timothy's father groaned. No doubt concerned over the cost of new gowns.

Unlike Harry, if Margaret found his mother's request obsequious, she gave no indication. "Madame Tredwell." A model of grace and decorum, Margaret was not only the ideal duchess but also the ideal partner for Harry. They complemented each other perfectly.

Timothy's gaze slipped to Honoria. She would certainly be the perfect viscountess. However, the question remained if she would complete his other half as well as Margaret did for Harry.

Unbidden, his fickle gaze sought Priscilla like a magnetized force, unable to resist no matter how hard he fought against the pull. The small group she'd been part of had dispersed. The Somersbys threaded through the crowd, advancing toward Timothy —or more likely Harry and Margaret. Even Nash—the cad—had abandoned her, and Timothy wasn't certain if he was relieved or saddened on her behalf.

Their eyes held, and his heart squeezed uncomfortably as a flush of what he supposed was embarrassment darkened Priscilla's cheeks. Abruptly, she broke eye contact with him and moved toward another cluster of attendees composed of Lady Miranda and Lord and Lady Easton.

Timothy's discomfort grew as Lady Easton turned toward Priscilla then, taking her husband's arm, walked away, giving Priscilla the cut direct.

After exchanging some words with Priscilla, Lady Miranda turned up her nose and left as well.

Someone squeezed his forearm, and he returned his attention to the small group before him.

Honoria nodded discreetly in Priscilla's direction, her concerned expression indicating she too witnessed the affront. "I should speak with her," she whispered.

Before either he or Honoria could make a move, Priscilla rushed through the crowd and darted inside the house.

Knowing well it was ill-advised, Timothy interjected, "No. Allow me." He patted Honoria's hand resting on his arm and made his excuses to the group.

Apparently, he and Honoria weren't the only ones to notice the slight. Oliver grasped Timothy's coat sleeve as he turned to leave. "Might I be of assistance? I know something of the repercussions of the *ton's* disapproval."

"Let me speak with her first. But thank you."

Oliver nodded and released his grip on Timothy's arm.

A flash of pink, the color of Priscilla's gown, rounded a corner as Timothy hurried inside his sister's home. He increased his speed, nearly knocking over a footman carrying a large tray of canapés. The man spun but kept the tray and its contents upright, clearly up to the task of his position.

After a quick apology, Timothy continued his pursuit. Resisting the urge to yell her name, he finally caught up with her and grabbed her elbow, stopping her. "Priscilla, wait."

She turned toward him, her face a mask of pain. Tears streaked her cheeks, still hot with the blush of shame, and she wiped them away. "This is impossible. I've been a fool to think things would change and I would be forgiven."

"That's not true," he said, knowing full well his words held little weight.

The look on her face told him she recognized the lie. "Even if it weren't"—she directed a glare his way—"which it is. My prospects have not improved. Mr. Ugbrooke sent his apologies that he would no longer be calling. He was my only hope here in London."

The unholy name forced its way to the tip of his tongue. "What about Nash? He seems to have become your champion." Lord, how the thought churned his stomach.

"Contrary to your belief, although he has been nothing but kind"—she held up her hand to silence his oncoming protest—"it's clear he has no genuine interest in me. I'm a fool, but I hoped for passion. To know the kind of love the duke and duchess have. There is no fire in Nash's heart for me, not like I see in . . ."

She jerked back, averting her eyes as if he would see the truth in them.

Was he that transparent? Were his efforts to tamp down the building—and unwanted—emotion an utter failure? He should have held his tongue, maintaining his innocence of her meaning.

Yet he could not. "See where? In whom?"

Her gaze swung back, her own eyes blazing with the passion of which she spoke. But unlike the passion of love, hers burned with anger. "You know very well in whom. Although you refuse to admit it."

"Out with it, Priscilla. Let's not play these games."

"You. Damn you. In your eyes."

⁂

HOW COULD HE BE SO NONPLUSSED? HIS MOSS-GREEN EYES stared blankly at her as if she'd spoken in a foreign tongue, his jaw hanging ajar.

She wanted to scream, but she kept her voice low lest they be overheard. "Don't deny it. At least have the decency to be honest with me, even if it comes to naught."

From the corner of her eye, a black cat lurked stealthily from the shadows, diverting her attention. She loved cats.

Timothy's gaze dropped to follow hers, his eyes widening even further in horror. "Hurry." He grabbed Priscilla's arm and veritably yanked her into an adjacent room, slamming the door behind them.

"What in the world? It was only a little cat."

"That was no cat. That was a demon. My sister's, to be precise, named Catpurrnicus. We're lucky to have escaped unscathed."

Surely he jested? "If this is your not-so-subtle attempt to get me alone, you only needed to ask. It's not like we haven't been unchaperoned before, if you recall."

Was he truly so quick to forget their time together in Mr. Thatcher's cottage?

"You're the one accusing me of having some feelings you seem to have conjured in your imagination."

Oh, she wanted to slap him. Stamp her foot on his. Throw a boot. How could he be so infuriating! "Do you deny it then? You hold no desire for me?"

He tore his gaze away. "Desire isn't love, Priscilla. You shouldn't confuse the two."

"I'm not. I know you don't love me," she bit the words out. Pain lanced through her with every syllable, and she choked back the tears clogging her throat. "But you do want me. Desire me. At least admit that much."

He paced before her, dragging a hand through his thick hair.

196

"What do you want from me?" The words were spoken so softly, she wasn't sure they were actually meant for her ears.

"The truth. Nothing more. Contrary to what the *ton* believes, I'm not some scheming termagant, only out to trap a husband into marriage by any means necessary."

Halting at her words, he pinned her with his stare, his eyebrows lifting in challenge.

She threw up her hands and flashed him a grim smile. "Oh, very well. I *am* a termagant, and I do wish to find a husband." She held up a finger. "But I do not wish to secure one by nefarious methods, which I've proven to you before."

Emotional fatigue overcame her, and her knees suddenly became weak and unable to support her slight frame. When she teetered unsteadily toward the settee, Timothy grasped her arm, but she jerked it away. She would not allow him to interpret her weakness as evidence of a plot to compromise him.

Once she had settled on the settee, she drew a deep breath, summoning the strength to continue with her confession.

Before she could proceed, Timothy sat beside her, taking her hand in his. "What can I do?" All the anger and accusation from his voice had melted away like snow flurries meeting the rising sun. Instinctively, she understood his question was not directed to her momentary bout of weakness but to the heart of their heated conversation.

"Admit that what you feel for me is more than that of a friend. I fully acknowledge I'm not the type of woman you wish to marry, the respectable wife you need by your side. And I know you don't love me. But I've seen it in your eyes, Timothy. You do want me. Just once before I resign myself to marry a man who holds no passion for me, I'd like to hear it from the lips of the man who does."

From his taut jaw and closed eyes, a war of indecision raged in Timothy's mind. Was it truly so difficult for him to admit he wanted her? Was she so tainted by scandal that a man would be ashamed of desiring her?

"Your answer will not leave this room, I promise. I will take it to my grave." Silently, she added *and cherish all my days.*

Yet, he failed to respond.

"Whether or not you admit it, you should know that ever since our kiss in Mr. Thatcher's cottage, all I can think about is you. I want you so much it hurts—here." She rubbed the place over her sternum.

"I don't love you." Although not spoken harshly, his words lashed against her already aching heart.

"I know. There is softness in Dr. Somersby's eyes when he gazes upon his wife. Such affection, respect . . . worship. There is none of that in yours."

"You don't understand," he said. And at that moment, he couldn't have been more right. What about his admission was there to understand other than his failure to love her?

"It's not simply that I don't. It's that I can't. I will never love anyone." He shook his head. "I love my family. I love my work. But romantic love. Never. I've sworn to never allow myself to be that vulnerable again. It causes nothing but anguish and grief."

She blinked, astounded by his confession. What in the world had happened to him? Speechless, she could only wait for him to continue, and she sent up a prayer of thanks when he did.

"But I will admit I want you. More than I've ever wanted any woman. That kiss we shared in the snowbound cottage affected me as well. I thought I'd never see you again. That you would be married to your Mr. Netherborne, and that would be that. Since finding you here in London, you've thrown my world into chaos."

He scrubbed a hand down his face. "Are you satisfied now? Happy that we've both admitted to feelings neither of us can pursue?"

No. She was not. The joy she anticipated upon hearing his words did not arrive. Instead, they left her confused and saddened.

When she didn't answer, he said, "I thought not. Why else do you think I've withheld these feelings from you? I don't wish to cause you pain, Priscilla. And yet I have."

The tears she'd been fighting to contain trickled down her cheeks. Unlike a lover, Timothy did nothing to soothe them away. He sat next to her unmoving, his hands clenched into fists on his lap.

"So you don't love Honoria?" The question seemed absurd, even though she was the one asking it.

"No. I like her. She will make an excellent wife. An excellent viscountess when the time comes. She's safe."

"Safe?" Both a question and an accusation, the word came out as a bark.

"I run no risk of falling in love with her." He dragged his hands through his hair again, leaving it adorably tousled. "You desire passion, and I avoid it at all costs. We are at a crossroads, Priscilla, and now we must go our different directions."

Anger lit up her chest like a blazing inferno. "At least one of us will get what we want, then. I hope you're happy in your loveless marriage. I know I will not be."

She stormed from the room. Upon opening the door, she found the black cat sitting patiently, its yellow eyes peering up at her. She leaned down and scratched it behind the ears. "Go get him."

⚜

BEFORE TIMOTHY COULD RISE FROM THE SETTEE AND GO AFTER her, Priscilla left in a swirl of pink. Lord, fire bolts had shot from her eyes, scorching him to his soul. He hung his head, cradling it in his hands.

"Damnation!"

Time stopped, and his skin iced over at the answering hiss. His head jerked up to find Catpurrnicus preparing to pounce. With one fluid and terrifying motion, the demon cat launched itself at Timothy. Stupidly, Timothy jerked back in defense, affording the monster more available landing space.

More frightening than when Timothy had stared down the blade of a sword during battle—which might have been an

199

exaggeration, but only barely—the cat perched on Timothy's thighs.

He held his breath and waited.

Catpurrnicus was anything but predictable. He'd been known to purr and cuddle like any ordinary domesticated house cat one moment, then viciously attack without provocation the next. To Timothy's knowledge, the only two people consistently graced with Catpurrnicus's lovable side were Bea and Laurence.

The black tail thumped on Timothy's knees. What had Bea said that movement meant? Timothy searched his brain and came up with nothing. Fear had a way of evacuating all rational thought from one's mind.

He did not need to wait long to find out. Claws dug into Timothy's breeches, most likely drawing blood. Then the cat lifted its lithe body and placed its paws on Timothy's face.

Dear God, the demon would scar him for life!

He swallowed his panic like a bitter potion, determined not to allow a small beastie to get the best of him. Yellow eyes met his green ones in a stare down while Timothy prayed those razor-sharp claws would remain retracted.

"That's a good fellow," he said, not entirely sure his voice conveyed the conviction he intended. The smile he forced to his face must have appeared as a body in rigor mortis, grim and horrible. Small pricking sensations poked at his right cheek, and without moving his head lest he spur the attack, he glanced down.

It appeared breaking eye contact proved to be the solution, as Catpurrnicus lowered his body and leapt down, landing soundlessly on the floor. As he strolled nonchalantly toward the door, most likely knowing full well he had been the victor in their battle of wills, he turned once, sending a message of warning Timothy fully comprehended.

Odd that a cat would make him reconsider his behavior to the one woman who stirred his blood. And yet that was precisely how Timothy interpreted the strange encounter with the black menace.

Pulling a handkerchief from his pocket, he dabbed at his

wounded face. Six tiny spots of red stained the cloth. At least his breeches were black and would conceal the claw marks on his thighs. But perhaps evidence of his encounter with Catpurrnicus would elicit some sympathy from Priscilla and make her more amenable to his apology.

Although he had yet to decide what exactly he would apologize for. He'd wounded her, no doubt. Her tears were testament to that as surely as the claw marks on his face. And although the evidence of her pain would not be visible to others, it ran much deeper than a few pricks from an unpredictable cat.

He'd spoken the truth. He wouldn't apologize for that. Honesty was of utmost importance. He didn't even anticipate speaking words of love to his future wife. But he would apologize for his insensitivity to her pain and for having wounded her thusly.

Once he'd straightened his hair and cravat, which had somehow become askew, he made his way out to the terrace with the direct intention of finding Priscilla, determined to take charge of the situation and have the last word.

They say men are fools.

CHAPTER 21—UNEXPECTED WORDS OF WISDOM

Priscilla stopped at a small mirror in the hallway to gauge her appearance. Red discolored the whites surrounding the blue of her eyes, and droplets of remaining tears still glistened on her lashes. With a hasty swipe, she brushed them away, wishing she'd thought to pack a handkerchief in her reticule.

Ninnyhammer!

What had she expected?

For Timothy to fall upon his knees and confess his undying love?

To proclaim he only courted Honoria to make Priscilla jealous?

To beg her to marry him?

Fury at her own foolish dreams only brought forth a swell of new tears. Oh, how she hated that she cried when angry.

No!

She would not succumb to such weakness, if for no other reason than to not afford the self-righteous *ton* more fodder for their wagging tongues. Her one hope to remain unnoticed hinged on what had, up to that moment, caused her such discomfort—the overall snub she'd received from many of the attendees, many of whom were a hair's breadth from giving her the cut direct. Of course, that didn't ensure they weren't paying attention, simply that they chose not to interact with her.

When she stepped out onto the terrace, a few heads turned, but just as quickly looked away. Invisibility had its advantages at times. However, she refused to be cast out from the party and instead sought out someone who might provide a bit of companionship and comfort. Her father appeared deep in conversation with Lord and Lady Easton. She had no desire to have him witness another snub if she joined them.

Her eyes latched onto Lord Nash, leaning casually against the terrace railing. Alone. Like her.

With her reputation already shredded and apparently beyond repair, she wove her way through the crowd. Knots of people parted accommodatingly as sure as if she had been Moses extending his staff across the Red Sea.

Wouldn't Mr. Netherborne be proud of her for such a biblical reference?

Upon her approach, Nash's lips tipped up into a welcoming smile, only to fall when she reached his side. "Miss Pratt. What has happened?"

"May we walk? Perhaps a turn in the garden?" Anything to get away from prying eyes and ears.

He lifted a dark eyebrow. "Are you certain that's wise? Speaking with me in the sight of others is one thing, but walking alone, unchaperoned . . ." He shook his head.

"What does it matter? They will never forgive me, even if King George himself were to bless me."

His chuckle didn't match the concern in his eyes. "Considering the number of scandals following him, it might be more of a possibility than you'd imagine. However, I commend you for keeping your sense of humor in all of this. Even so, I would caution you to give thought to what you ask."

"Must everyone assume they know my mind better than I do? Besides, you are the one person who can even possibly understand."

"Very well. But I must insist I don't offer my arm. For your protection, not mine."

Acutely aware of the eyes focused on her, eyes that had so intentionally refused to meet her gaze before, Priscilla proceeded down the steps of the terrace with Nash by her side.

"So, tell me. What has prompted this complete lack of concern for propriety? Have you abandoned your quest to find a husband here in London?"

Priscilla jerked in surprise toward Nash. "You knew about that?"

"Society may not often include me in their inner circles, but talk has made its way to me by other means. Besides, it is rather obvious. Lady Honoria's attempts at matchmaking are less than subtle." His chuckle reassured her he had not taken affront at such a forced pairing—at least where he was concerned.

She found herself smiling in return. "I suppose so."

He clasped his hands behind his back as he strode beside her, mindfully keeping his distance. "Have you then? Given up on finding a husband here, and does it have any connection to the redness of your eyes?"

She'd have never pegged him for a perceptive man, at least not based on his reputation. Perhaps that's what made a successful rake —understanding the workings of a woman's mind. "I fear it's more that London has abandoned me rather than the other way around. As for the redness of my eyes, that is because of an entirely different but not unconnected reason."

"Hmm." His gaze slid sideways, and something about his muttered response suggested he understood more than she imagined possible. His next words confirmed her suspicions. "Might that reason be a certain physician?"

Pain seared her heart anew from the mere thought of Timothy's harsh words. "It's of no consequence. There is no future for me here in London or with . . . him. He's made that perfectly clear."

Upon reaching the outer edge of the garden, Nash motioned with his hand, indicating they turn around to remain in view of those on the terrace. "And is that unobtainable future the only one able to secure your happiness?"

Her gaze locked with his dark eyes. No mockery shone within them. He'd simply asked a question, one perhaps more rhetorical than literal. Yet she answered, "I don't know."

"Taking the good doctor out of the equation, what exactly is required to make you happy?"

Hadn't she just had a similar conversation with Timothy? "I want passion. For a man to truly desire me, love me, accept me for who I am." She blushed admitting this to Nash, who could so easily use this to his advantage.

"There is no need to be embarrassed, Miss Pratt. What you've stated is a basic human need. I would wager—and as you know, I *am* a betting man—that if pressed, many if not all people would admit to wanting the same things. It's simply that most people settle for much, much less."

She nodded, the wisdom in his words sinking in and taking root. Isn't that what she had decided to do? Settle? "May I ask you a question?"

"Of course."

Heat scalded her cheeks, and she plucked up her courage to ask the one person who wouldn't judge her. "Is physical passion truly as wonderful as I've heard?"

Both eyebrows raised at her scandalous enquiry. "You've heard? I assumed gently bred young ladies were sheltered from such talk."

"People in the country aren't as guarded with their conversation as those in London, and I confess, I may have both eavesdropped and enquired directly."

His eyes crinkled at the corners, matching the smile on his lips. "Have you ever been kissed, Miss Pratt? And if so, was it pleasant?"

Unbidden, her gaze darted toward the terrace and landed squarely on Timothy, who was in animated conversation with his sister. Quickly, she turned back to Nash.

The gleam in his eye indicated he deduced where she had

directed her attention. "Ah. So that is a yes. Well, imagine the pleasure of that kiss magnified one thousand times."

"Truly?"

He nodded. "I would say that with the right person, the experience surpasses any other in physical pleasure."

Oh, my.

"By the right person, are you implying someone with experience, such as yourself?"

He emitted a short crack of laughter before turning to her, his expression serious. "Are you asking me to seduce you?"

"No . . . I . . . oh, dear." She had the sudden desire to curl up into the tiniest ball and hide from sight.

"Have no fear, Miss Pratt. Even if you were making such a request, I would respectfully decline. Contrary to belief—although I find you most attractive—I don't seduce innocent women. I merely meant you should share the experience with someone you truly care about, perhaps love. Especially for the first time."

He pinned her with his gaze, sharp with understanding.

Desperate to divert his attention, she said, "One personal question, if I may."

He quirked a dark eyebrow. "Considering you've practically bared your soul to me, it seems only fair that I reciprocate—although much depends on your question, and I reserve the right to not answer."

"How do you stand it? Staying in London, I mean. Where people are so judgmental and cruel to you. It seems to me your reputation is most undeserved."

Dark shadows passed across his face. "Don't delude yourself, Miss Pratt. I've done many things—despicable things—to deserve my reputation. But people are slow to forgive, and even slower to forget. As for how I stand it"—he shrugged—"I suppose it's easier for a man. Being the son, then brother of a marquess has its advantages. Should I decide to marry, the association with the title might be more than enough to aid my bride in *forgetting* my past indiscretions."

"Do you have any practical advice for me as a woman?"

A deep chuckle erupted. "Another area where my reputation far exceeds reality. Like all other men on the planet, I have yet to understand the mind of a woman. However, if I were to give advice to a man, I would tell him not to run from his problems, but rather pursue what he wants—within limits, of course. I would rather have tried and failed than be riddled with doubts and regrets over what might have been."

"Regardless, I know whatever I decide, I can't stay in London whether I marry someone else or not. To see him at parties and in the park with Lady Honoria on his arm, it would eat at me on the inside. Much better to be away entirely."

"Out of sight, out of mind, 'eh?"

"Does it work?"

He shrugged. "I wouldn't know. I've never been in love myself. Not to the extent that the object of your affection has consumed you so thoroughly it destroys you when that affection is not returned."

They strolled in silence while she pondered his advice. What she wanted was to experience the type of passion that could consume her—if only once before she sentenced herself to a loveless marriage in the country with Mr. Netherborne.

But did she have the courage necessary to take what she so desperately wanted?

STEPPING OUT ONTO THE TERRACE ONCE AGAIN, TIMOTHY scanned the crowd. No sign of Priscilla's pretty pink gown greeted him. Had she left? Surely she would have bid goodbye to her hosts before departing? He strolled over to his sister, formulating a way to ask without giving himself away.

Bea glanced over from where she'd been in conversation with her husband, her eyes widening. "Whatever ha—? Did Purrny do that?"

His sister was nothing if not quick to make correct deductions. "Who else? I swear, Bea, that cat is a menace."

Her eyes narrowed. "What did you do to provoke him?"

"*Me?* Nothing."

"Must have done something. Catpurrnicus is gentle as a lamb if he likes you and you treat him well," Laurence said—the traitor.

"Not you, too? Has my sister changed you so much that you would take her side over your best friend?"

Laurence simply shrugged. "When she's right, she's right."

Bea beamed and tugged affectionately on her husband's arm. "My husband is the most intelligent of men."

Lord, those two were enough to make Timothy cast up his accounts right there on the terrace. "Please tell me that this married bliss you two exhibit will be short-lived. I don't think I can stomach much more of it."

With a wave of her hand and a roll of her eyes, Bea said. "You'll change your tune someday. Mark my words."

"God forbid," he muttered.

Unfortunately, Bea had exceptional hearing. "Why in the world are you so opposed to love? Is that why you're dragging your feet with Honoria? Is it because you're afraid you'll fall in love with her?"

Not a chance. "Nonsense. The clinic keeps me busy. Which speaking of, I need to speak with Ashton." Timothy would thank him later for his timely rescue.

Unfortunately, the duke's furrowed brow created a wave of turmoil in Timothy's chest as he approached. Timothy prepared himself as Harry reached his side. "Is something wrong, Your Grace?"

"Do you recall our conversation the other day in the clinic regarding Miss Pratt?"

What? "Of course."

Harry pointed his chin toward the garden. "It would seem she's not as keen on repairing her reputation as you had believed. Walking unchaperoned with Nash Talbot will do little to aid in her efforts." Harry paused as if only then noticing. "And what happened to your face?"

Timothy brushed it aside. "Bea's cat." More pressing was Harry's first observation. Priscilla strolled in the garden by Nash's side, both apparently deep in conversation. As if sensing him watching, Priscilla lifted her gaze in his direction, then glanced away. Nash wasn't as discreet. He met him stare for stare, and as it had been with Catpurrnicus, Timothy was the first to back down.

Damnation! What was she thinking?

"Your Grace, forgive me for interrupting," a feminine voice broke Timothy's train of thought.

Honoria performed a perfect curtsy before the duke. How could Timothy have spent five months in her presence and still not recognize her voice without looking? Certain he could pick out Priscilla's laugh and speech from a large crowd, he cringed with shame.

Honoria deserved better than the likes of him.

Harry smiled warmly at Honoria, and Timothy couldn't help but notice the difference in reception she received compared to Harry's reaction when Priscilla arrived at the clinic. "Think nothing of it. I was just leaving to find my wife. Marbry, I urge you to think about what we've discussed."

He turned to walk away, calling over his shoulder, "And ask Beatrix if she has some chlorinated lime to wash that wound."

Before Honoria could ask the obvious, Timothy answered, "Bea's cat."

"Truly? I encountered the little sweetling in the hallway when I went inside to the lady's retiring room. What ever could have provoked it to inflict such damage?"

Was everyone on that demon cat's side? Irritation roiled, and without realizing, he lashed out. "What is so urgent you had to interrupt?" He wanted to reel the words back in before they found their mark, but it was too late.

Honoria blanched, her eyes blinking rapidly.

He was an arse. More than that, a horse's arse. No, an elephant.

"I apologize. That was uncalled for and most ungentlemanly. Everyone has been asking about my face, and that cat is not the sweet, cuddly creature everyone imagines."

"Does it hurt?" Clearly, she meant to ease his burden of guilt, but the tremor in her voice indicated the pain he'd inflicted had not dissipated.

"No. Truly." He softened his own tone. "Now, what did you wish to tell me?"

"Miss Pratt and Lord Nash. It seems our efforts may have been successful after all." She dipped her bonnet in the garden's direction, where Harry had already diverted his attention.

"Yes. I've seen. Ashton already pointed them out. Although he views the pairing differently than you do."

"Oh." Honoria's mouth dipped at the corners, and unlike when something had saddened Priscilla, Timothy had no urge to kiss and cheer her. "Well, I suppose with their history . . ."

"He questions her sincerity about repairing her reputation with society, especially—all things considered—with Lord Nash."

"I see his point. It was my concern when we began this endeavor. But if the ultimate purpose was to secure a husband, does it matter what society thinks?"

Now Timothy was the one nonplussed. Who was this woman before him? "I can't believe my ears. Do you really believe that?"

She lifted a shoulder. "I suppose not. But wouldn't it be wonderful if we didn't have to worry about pleasing everyone else rather than ourselves?"

"Indeed."

"Perhaps that's what Miss Pratt and Lord Nash have decided." She nodded back toward the garden, where the aforementioned scorners of society's rules ascended the steps back onto the terrace.

To Timothy's relief, Priscilla refrained from using Nash's arm for support, and they kept a respectable distance between them. However, they garnered enough disapproving stares to support his argument that society was still quick to judge and slow to forgive.

Nash caught Timothy staring, his dark eyes drilling into

Timothy's skull as if to extract the secrets held within regarding his feelings for Priscilla. The cad turned toward Priscilla, lifted her hand, and placed a chaste kiss upon her knuckles, having the gall to slide his gaze toward Timothy in the process. With that one fluid motion, an ugly churning in Timothy's stomach replaced his momentary relief.

Was Honoria's assessment correct? Was Nash truly pursuing Priscilla?

More importantly, why did that matter?

CHAPTER 22—LIES WE TELL OURSELVES

Unseen forces propelled Timothy forward toward Nash—the blackguard—and Priscilla. The audacity of the man to flaunt such familiarity in public. How dare he!

Aware that Honoria was on his heels, Timothy knew he should curb his reaction.

Yet he could not.

"Dr. Marbry, whatever is the matter?" The poor woman's words came out breathy.

Had his pace truly been so fast it made it difficult for her to keep up?

Volcanic fury built within him, the pressure reaching dangerous levels. "He kissed her hand." He ground out the words through clenched teeth.

"Why . . . yes. A good . . . sign, wouldn't you . . . say?"

Refusing to look at her, Timothy pressed forward. "I would not."

He skidded to a halt a few feet before the unlikely pair, sensing Honoria's hand on his forearm. He spun toward her.

Face flushed, she gawked at him, her eyes searching, probing. A quick shake of her head brought him to his senses.

Apparently, Honoria wasn't the only one present who was aghast at his indecorous display. Fans paused mid-flutter. Glasses of lemonade were poised inches from waiting lips. Music from the string quartet stopped mid-measure. His own mother held a canapé mere moments away from consumption.

If not for the chirp of a bird, who obviously hadn't received the message to cease its song, Timothy would have believed time had frozen before him.

He could have easily borne those things. But the smug look of satisfaction on Nash's face? Never!

The cad's gaze refocused on Priscilla. "Will you permit me to call upon you tomorrow, Miss Pratt?" The unctuous tone in his voice made Timothy's stomach churn anew.

A flicker of hope ignited when Priscilla appeared taken aback by Nash's request, then sputtered out with her answer. "I will look forward to it, my lord."

My lord, my foot. Well, in truth, Nash *was* a lord, but only through familial association.

Nash—the cad—executed a deep bow. "If you will excuse me while I bid goodbye to our hosts. I shall count the minutes until tomorrow." A smirk played across his lips as he passed Timothy, who half expected Nash to bump into him, adding insult to injury.

Instead, Nash nodded. "Lady Honoria. Marbry." Moments later, he stood before Bea and Laurence, then mercifully, he left.

So focused on the blackguard Nash, when Timothy turned around, Priscilla was gone. "Where did she go?"

"To join her father," Honoria said, nodding to a small cluster of attendees to their left. Concern shone in Honoria's green eyes. And although he expected a touch of condemnation, he saw none. Perhaps he had not betrayed his feelings as much as he feared. Either that, or she didn't care, which was both disconcerting and strangely comforting.

"It is what she requested of us, is it not?" she asked. "To aid in securing a husband."

"A *respectable* husband who would reestablish her place in society. I fail to see how a marriage to Nash Talbot would provide either."

"As I said before, perhaps she simply no longer cares."

"Hmm."

"And perhaps," she said, her voice becoming a bit more emphatic, "she is not the only one who needs to consider what is most important."

Honoria's enigmatic words bounced against his hardened heart and stubborn mind.

For the rest of the afternoon, he sulked like a schoolboy who'd lost at cricket and subsequently been ridiculed by his friends.

Even Laurence couldn't cajole him out of his foul mood. "What say we go to White's after this? Have a rousing game of cards? These parties are a drain on my nerves."

"Then why on earth did you have one?" Timothy veritably barked the words at his best friend.

Laurence, being the even-tempered, good-natured man he was, didn't bat an eye. "Because Bea wanted to. And if I've learned one thing about being married, it's to do what my wife wishes." He leaned in to whisper. "Often it's something of great enjoyment." He waggled his eyebrows. Waggled! Marriage had turned the man's typically sharp mind to mush.

"Eww. I did *not* need to have that image in my mind. She's my sister, man. Remember yourself!"

Laurence simply laughed and patted Timothy on the back. "White's. As soon as this is over." Then he wandered off, presumably to annoy someone else.

If it weren't for the infernal feline predator lying in wait, Timothy would have gone inside and located the fine Scottish whisky Laurence hoarded in his study. Strike that. Timothy had done that once only to discover in horror a scandalous portrait of his sister hanging on the wall. Never again. He'd die of thirst first.

He sipped his much too sweet lemonade and watched Priscilla chatting with Lady Charlotte. Was she cozying up to Nash's sister as well?

Damnation!

Unable to stand much more, he wound his way through the crowds and found his sister. "Bea, I'm leaving. I would thank you for inviting me, but considering that beast you call a pet attacked me, I'll withhold my gratitude."

"You should thank me regardless. I did this for you."

"Me? What the deuce are you talking about?"

"Shush. Mother's right there. She'll hear you cursing."

He brushed it aside. "She'll survive. Now, what's this about doing this for me?"

"Lady Honoria suggested it. She told me how you both are trying to help Miss Pratt find a husband. Although Lord knows why. Sometimes I think Lady Honoria is too good for this world. Certainly too good for my rapscallion of a brother." Her grin softened her words.

But there was truth in them. "She is too good for me. I don't deserve her."

"Then you best make haste before someone else steals her from under your nose. Besides, now that I'm married, Mother is eager for another wedding."

"What's that I hear about a wedding?" Their mother scurried over in a rustle of silks, lace, and overabundance of rosewater. "Has Lady Honoria finally brought you up to scratch? Goodness, I don't know what you're waiting for."

"That's what I said." Bea shot him a little smirk.

They were ganging up on him. "At that, I shall bid you both adieu. Bea, tell your annoyingly lovesick husband that I'll be at White's waiting for him." He kissed his mother on the cheek. "Goodbye, Mother. Don't send out the wedding invitations just yet."

He hurried away before anything else could go wrong, only to run into Priscilla again in the hallway.

Bees buzzed in his head, and he swayed unsteadily on his feet. "Nash? Really?"

Her icy glare chilled him to the bone. "What should it matter to you? At least with him, I might experience passion. Given freely and not withheld like a miser."

As she brushed past him, he reached for her arm. "Priscilla, wait."

"Unhand me." Cold and controlled, the passion of which she spoke—which she admitted she craved—was eerily absent from her words.

In a wave of lemon verbena, she was gone, leaving his world empty and bleached of color.

❦

WHAT LITTLE SPARK OF LIFE THE PARTY HELD LEFT WITH Timothy, and Priscilla found it growing ever more difficult to withstand the snubs from the remaining attendees. Even though she rarely indulged in strong spirits, as she sipped the lemonade, which admittedly was a perfect balance of tart and sweet, she wished it were something stronger. Anything to numb the sharp pain in her chest that knifed through her at Timothy's words.

If only she had taken the time to cultivate a close relationship with a woman her age, someone to confide in. She needed—wanted —a friend.

She turned at the delicate clearing of a throat to find Lady Honoria.

"Miss Pratt, may I have a word?"

If Priscilla could choose a friend, it would be Honoria. True, they had little in common, different in temperament as night to day. But Honoria had treated her kindly and had an unfailing ability to see the best in people, something Priscilla sorely lacked. Rather than solidify a friendship, the one thing they did have in common was precisely that which prevented Priscilla from confiding in her.

Dr. Timothy Marbry.

How could Priscilla unburden her heart to the very woman the man had been courting?

Earnest urgency shimmered in Honoria's eyes, and a prick of

anxiety trickled down the pathway of Priscilla's spine. "Of course." They moved to a quiet corner of the terrace unpopulated by others.

"I'm not sure how to approach this," Honoria said, her gaze fixed on the stone terrace beneath them.

"I'd rather have you say it to my face than behind my back where I might hear it from the wagging tongues or read it in a scandal sheet."

Again, Priscilla's words proved why the two would have a fraught friendship. Presuming Honoria had words of criticism, as Priscilla no doubt would have for one such as herself, she'd jumped to the worst conclusion.

Erroneously.

Honoria's fair skin paled. "Oh, no. You misunderstand. If anything, I admire how you've conducted yourself this afternoon. The courage you've shown is quite extraordinary."

Courage? Priscilla glanced at the lemonade, wondering if perhaps something stronger *had* been added which had undoubtedly altered Honoria's perception.

It rendered Priscilla practically speechless. Still, she choked out two words she truly meant. "I apologize."

"You have nothing to apologize for. It's no wonder you would think that, considering the treatment you've received." Honoria sent her a look that somehow conveyed sympathy without pity.

Doing her best to mimic the expression, she said, "Whatever you have to say, I'm listening."

"I wished to speak with you about Dr. Marbry."

Whump! An object the size of a boulder dropped in her stomach, heavy and foreboding. "What about him?" The words came out in a croak that would rival any bullfrog's nightly call.

"He's very kind and considerate. Attentive in all that matters. It's just that . . ." She shook her head, as if debating what to say next.

Priscilla held her breath. Had Honoria noticed the desperate look in Priscilla's eyes each time she gazed at Timothy? The longing, the desire? And worse, had she noticed that Timothy returned those looks with as much feeling?

In short, had they been found out? She waited for Honoria to continue, learning from her past mistakes.

Pain lanced her heart afresh that Honoria would suffer as well. "Just what, Honoria?" She knew she should address her properly as was befitting her station, but something inside told her that Honoria needed the friendship she herself sought.

"It's only that I'd hoped . . . foolishly, perhaps, that I might experience a love match."

Priscilla swallowed, forcing down the lump that had risen to her throat. "And Dr. Marbry hasn't met your expectations?"

Honoria's gaze shot to Priscilla's, and their eyes locked in sisterly camaraderie. "Oh, please don't blame Dr. Marbry, Miss Pratt."

"Priscilla, please."

Honoria gave her a wan smile. "Priscilla, yes. It's not his fault he doesn't hold such affection for me. As I said, he's kind and thoughtful. However, I must shoulder some of the responsibility. I fear my feelings for him are more like those for a brother." Pink flushed her cheeks. "And I hoped for more . . . ardent feelings."

Unsure how she should respond, Priscilla held her tongue and waited.

"Am I expecting too much? My father said Dr. Marbry has expressed his intention of offering for me, although he has yet to do so. I have a suspicion he might hold a tendre for someone else."

Ah, that Priscilla could address honestly. "I don't think you need to worry about Dr. Marbry loving another. If it is what you wish, I believe he would make you a faithful and loyal husband."

Honoria's lips curved into a tiny smile. "You make it sound more like I'm looking for a new English Spaniel puppy."

Priscilla's hand flew to her mouth, seconds too late to stifle the giggle. "I suppose I did. But I do understand what you're saying. I, too, hoped for the type of match others have found, one filled with passion. We have only to witness the affection of our hosts to see that it's possible."

Both women sighed as they turned their attention to Beatrix and Laurence. He had his arm wrapped around her waist, and her hand rested on his chest, her fingers stroking him affectionately.

"Lord Nash appears to have taken an interest," Honoria said, her attention returning to Priscilla. "Do you think something will come of it?"

"No. Not that I wish it would. However, he's been inordinately kind to me, and I will be forever grateful."

Honoria nodded. "As I am to Dr. Marbry. The question remains. Do we wait, or do we settle?"

That, indeed, was the question. "I can't answer for you. But I believe I have no choice but to settle."

❂

ENSCONCED IN A COMFORTABLE CHAIR IN THE READING ROOM AT White's, Timothy poured himself a well-deserved brandy while he waited for Laurence. The burn of the amber liquid did little to ease the taut frustration banding his chest.

The image of Nash kissing Priscilla's hand, the echo of his promise to call upon her on the morrow, pinged in his mind like a musket ball ricocheting against metal. Where in the devil was Laurence?

He took another healthy sip of the liquor, Honoria's strange words joining the ranks to torture him.

"Perhaps she is not the only one who needs to consider what is most important."

Surely she was not implying that he didn't know his own mind? He was well aware of his duty—of what mattered. He needed a wife —eventually. A respectable wife with a healthy purse.

More than his family coffers needed restoration, his father's notorious large gaming debt had also sullied the family's reputation. Not to mention the depths to which his father sank, arranging a marriage for Beatrix to Lord Middlebury to expunge the debt. If it hadn't been for Laurence, both Bea and their family's financial security would have been lambs to the slaughter. Their family's still-suffering reputation was another matter entirely.

And above all, Timothy needed a wife with whom he would not fall in love. Succumbing to love opened a man to the subsequent grief and guilt left in its wake. He vowed never to repeat the experience and to protect his heart at all costs. That, in his estimation, was truly what mattered most.

No, Honoria certainly could not have been speaking of him.

He downed the remainder of the brandy and set the glass aside as Laurence entered the room. "It's about time."

Laurence raised a brow. "Nothing prevented you from playing without me. There are a number of other people willing and able to take your blunt."

"This was your bloody idea."

"You've been in a foul mood since your run-in with Catpurrnicus. Surely a little cat isn't the sole cause of your foul humor."

"First of all, that *thing* is a demon in disguise. And no, I will admit he's not the only reason."

They strolled into the card room, and Laurence settled himself at a table with two empty seats. "A woman, then."

"It's always a woman," Lord Harcourt said, shuffling the cards.

"You don't even know what we were talking about," Timothy said, peeved that the man contributed to a conversation of which he was not a part.

Harcourt chuckled. "Don't have to. When a man has such a look of utter confusion on his face as you do, Marbry, the only logical reason is a woman."

Lord Trentwith, who occupied the other seat, chimed in, "I have to agree. Now, are you going to shuffle those cards all day, Harcourt, or are we going to play?"

Harcourt began dealing. "Don't mind Trentwith. He's anxious to take someone else's money. Middlebury just left in a huff, having lost twenty pounds, and Highbottom hightailed his way out after him."

"Bea was disappointed to receive your regrets to our party today, Trentwith, as she was yours, Harcourt."

"Sabina isn't comfortable around society, and I refuse to go anywhere socially without her." Trentwith winked. "Except here, of course, but since White's doesn't allow women, well . . ." He shrugged.

"I volunteered to look after the children for Camilla and Oliver," Harcourt said. "Victoria has proclaimed she's too old for a nanny."

Timothy glanced at his cards, excited to see several of the trump suit in his hand. "Then why are you here? Shouldn't you be with them?"

Harcourt laughed. "I quickly discovered that chasing after a healthy toddler at my age is more difficult than it appears. Eva is as rambunctious as her mother at that age. Trentwith and Sabina had come over to assist, and Sabina shooed us both off. What did she say, Trentwith?"

"Something derogatory about men." Oliver's father closed his eyes. "If I recall, her precise words were, 'Be gone. You both are more work than the children.'" He grinned. "I do love that woman."

What's most important.

Propriety dictated Timothy not press, but he couldn't resist asking. "Is it difficult? Foregoing societal events? How do you deal with the wagging tongues?"

Trentwith tapped the ashes off his cheroot into a crystal ashtray. "Not for me. I've attended enough balls and soirées to last a lifetime. We attend small dinner parties with close friends and family"—he nodded toward Harcourt—"but if Sabina wanted to attend a ball, I wouldn't hesitate for a moment. I would stand by her side proudly, and anyone who had something negative to say about it, well, let's say they would be putting themselves at risk for bodily injury."

"Hear, hear," Laurence added. "I'll ask Bea to plan an intimate gathering. Perhaps the duke and duchess, your son and daughter-in-law, Harcourt, the Weatherbys, and Marbry, of course. I should very much like to get to know your wife better, Trentwith."

"Just keep Catpurrnicus locked up," Timothy said, half-joking.

Harcourt led out a guffaw. "Is that what happened to your face? Since the conversation started with talk of a woman, I suspected . . ."

Everyone broke into gales of laughter, even Timothy, albeit perhaps not as heartily as the others. However, his amusement was cut short when Nash stalked into the card room.

The exuberance Timothy felt looking at his cards vanished, as if suddenly the trump suit had magically changed. "What's he doing here?"

All three pairs of masculine eyes turned toward him, the same shocked expression on their faces as if painted by an unimaginative artist.

"Surely you've not been away from London so long as to have forgotten White's is one of Nash's favorite haunts," Trentwith said.

Laurence stared at Timothy as if attempting to discern the workings of a complicated machine. Mercifully, he turned his attention back to the game, offering an eight of hearts as the first play.

Lulled into a sense that Laurence's attention had refocused on the game, Timothy breathed a sigh of relief when Nash settled at an adjacent table. Too soon it would appear.

Laurence tapped the cards against the table as he retrieved them, having won the trick. "Although I cannot blame you, it hasn't escaped my notice that your persistent foul mood today seems to increase whenever Nash is in proximity."

"Humph," Timothy grunted. "Lately, wherever I go, it seems he appears just to sour my mood. Like when you stroll in a garden and inadvertently tip over a rock to expose a hoard of wriggling insects beneath."

Harcourt bellowed a laugh, drawing the attention of said insect —err—person.

In a voice loud enough to reach Timothy's ears—without a doubt intentionally—Nash said, "Miss Pratt was a vision today at Montgomery's garden party. I don't think I've ever seen her quite so radiant."

Timothy bit back the words threatening to attack. Letting them loose would only give Laurence more ammunition.

"Careful, Marbry, that's a new deck."

Timothy followed Trentwith's gaze, embarrassed to find the cards he'd clutched so tightly now possessed markedly bent edges. He muttered a quick apology, his mind barely registering the numbering or suits they displayed.

"We'll play out this hand and then request a new deck," Harcourt offered.

Laurence simply returned to his previous scrutiny and uttered a condemning, "Ah."

Somehow Timothy knew his friend's judgmental declaration had nothing to do with the misshapen cards.

CHAPTER 23—DECISIONS MADE IN HASTE

"Are you all right, my dear?" Priscilla's father asked on their way home. "I am concerned about your reception at the Montgomerys' party." He studied her in the way, she supposed, most fathers did when worried about their daughter's state of mind.

She couldn't blame him.

Bitter resignation had permeated the compartment of the carriage from the moment she ascended and took her place across from the man who loved her unconditionally. With Timothy's declaration, she accepted she would never gain his heart—although she'd not held much hope in the first place.

Yet, like many women, she held on to her dreams and hopes with tenacious claws, digging in and refusing to release until they lay dead in her hands.

Her conversations with both Lord Nash and Lady Honoria had been illuminating, not only for her own decisions, but for insights into two of the people who had exhibited acceptance and kindness. She prayed that, unlike hers, the hopes and dreams in their fragile hearts still beat with vigor and would bring them happiness in their lives.

Her father waited patiently for her answer. She didn't want to lie to him, but she also wished to withhold the pain she knew he would undoubtedly shoulder if she spoke the bare truth. "It was enlightening."

"Although I'd hoped for a more respectable man as your husband, Lord Nash seems to have taken an interest."

Contrary to what many believed, Priscilla was not stupid. Nash's bold-faced attempts to make Timothy jealous were as clear to her as a priceless diamond, and as ineffectual as a sheep in Parliament. Oh, there was no doubt it aroused Timothy's displeasure, but Priscilla suspected Timothy's disapproval had more to do with Nash than her.

"As I've become better acquainted with him, I've discovered there are many layers to Lord Nash Talbot. However, what you witnessed was simply kindness on his part and an attempt to spur other gentlemen into action."

Hands resting on the top of his cane, her father leaned forward, his eyes widening with interest. "Which other gentlemen?"

Oh, dear. She hadn't meant that last part to slip out. "No one in particular." The lie scorched her tongue. She assuaged her guilt with the knowledge that nothing would come of Timothy's admitted desire for her, so it seemed a reasonable price to pay for keeping her father in the dark.

Priscilla wilted with relief when the carriage came to a rest in front of her father's townhouse. Strange how she'd never been one for solitude before her infamous fall from grace, but after the momentous events of the day, she yearned for time to reflect on her prospects—or lack thereof. She must decide her next step.

Once again, disappointment waited.

Before they'd even arrived at the entrance, Digby threw open the front door. From the panicked look in his eyes, something had rattled his usual unflappable demeanor. "Sir, Lady Cartwright has arrived. She's in the front parlor."

Mother?

Her father heaved a sigh, then turned toward her. "Did you know she was coming?"

Priscilla shook her head.

"She brought a gentleman with her, sir." Digby's eyes darted toward Priscilla. "A Mr. Netherborne. They said they're here for Miss Pratt."

To fend off her father's likely subsequent question, Priscilla shook her head again. "He did say something about coming here after he'd given me time to *think*. But I'd completely forgotten about him."

"Very well, Digby. I trust you've provided refreshments. Tell them Priscilla and I will be in shortly."

After Digby scurried off like a frightened mouse, her father pinned her with a serious gaze. "You think he's here to offer for you?"

"I suspect so. Surely he wouldn't travel all the way from Belton for any other reason."

"Let them stew a while longer. Personally, I need time to fortify myself with a snifter of brandy before facing your mother. Meet me at the top of the stairs in fifteen minutes. Use the time as you see fit, and then we shall face them together."

Oh, how she loved her father.

For fifteen minutes, she prayed and paced, then prayed and paced some more, asking, nay, begging God for guidance as she weighed each of her minimal options.

If she stayed in London, with some—oh, all right, a lot—of luck, she might convince Mr. Ugbrooke to reconsider. He could provide her the security of marriage and the ability to stay in London. The negatives, however, admittedly outweighed the positives. She had more pity than affection for the Ugbrooke children, and even less for Mr. Ugbrooke himself.

Her other option would be to remain in London with her father as a spinster. Although she adored her father, her status as a spinster would only add to her disgrace with the *ton*, and she would be forever branded as undesirable.

But the biggest draw of London also presented the biggest drawback. Any parties she would attend, as a wallflower or as Mrs.

Ugbrooke, she would no doubt encounter a certain handsome, red-headed doctor. Seeing Timothy with Lady Honoria, or whomever he married, would be too great of an obstacle. Even if she gave up on the idea of happiness, she at least hoped for contentment and peace, neither of which she would have if she remained in London with a constant reminder of what she had lost.

The resignation that had enveloped her on the carriage ride home settled deep in her soul, and she knew what she had to do. Glancing at the clock, she had precisely two minutes to meet her father and face her fate.

She squared her shoulders and exited her room, armed with her decision to accept Abner Netherborne and a life in the country with sheep—and more importantly—away from Dr. Timothy Marbry.

❦

TIMOTHY STEWED OVER THE EVENTS OF THE GARDEN PARTY FOR three weeks. Thank goodness his duties at the clinic had—for the most part—kept him busy and his mind occupied. He threw himself into his work, offering to arrive early to open and staying late to close, often leaving so late at night he would return home to fall into bed exhausted.

And those were his good days.

On less favorable days, Harry insisted he leave early, or worse, take a day off. "You'll be no use to anyone if you work yourself to the bone only to become ill yourself. I don't want to see your face here until tomorrow. Is that understood?"

On one such day, as he stared at the ceiling of his bedroom, Timothy realized that in his efforts to avoid thinking about Priscilla, he'd completely ignored Honoria. After dressing and forcing down a light breakfast, he mounted his horse and rode to the Marquess of Stratford's elegant home.

Once there, he paced the floor of the front parlor, wondering what he would even say to her.

"Dr. Marbry." Honoria greeted him as she whisked into the parlor amid the light scent of lavender. Her abigail, like an ever-present shadow, took a seat in the corner. "Please sit. I hope you were offered refreshment."

Was he? He'd been scrambling over what to say and quite forgotten if the butler had mentioned it. Having no intention of causing problems for the servants, he found the best solution was to err on the side of caution. "Of course." He smiled, hoping she wouldn't press him to indicate if he'd agreed or declined. The arrival, or lack thereof, of refreshments would be her answer.

Her green eyes narrowed, her lips pursing as she was wont to do when in thought. It pleased him that at least he'd noticed that much about her during their time together. "Forgive my boldness. Are you unwell?"

Ah, she'd most likely noticed the dark circles under his eyes. "Tired. Things have been busy at the clinic." At least they were for him. "Please forgive me for not calling upon you since the garden party."

Unlike many other women, who no doubt would be thoroughly put out from his lack of attentiveness, Honoria's eyes shone with warmth and understanding. "Think nothing of it. I admire your dedication to the poor, sir."

Everything about her indicated she would be a perfect wife, meeting all of his needs with kindness and acquiescence. There would be no temper tantrums if he came home late at night, no complaints for his inattentiveness at parties, no demands of his time at mundane social gatherings. She would most likely perform all her wifely duties with the same calm acceptance. Lord, she probably wouldn't even complain if he took a mistress.

And the thought chilled him to his marrow.

Was that really what he wanted? A marriage between relative strangers?

More importantly, was that what Honoria wanted? She certainly deserved better.

In answer to her previous question, the butler brought in a

silver tray holding the tea service and some finger sandwiches, placing them on the table before Honoria, bowing, then taking his leave.

She poured, glancing up in question, pink blossoming on her cheeks. "I'm sorry, I've forgotten how you take it?"

"Milk, no sugar."

She nodded, then prepared his tea.

He paid particular attention to how she prepared her own, admitting to himself his own ignorance in the matter. *Milk, two sugars.*

When he sipped the warm liquid, he searched his mind for a mutually enjoyable topic of conversation. He didn't even know much about her interests.

He recalled their trip to the booksellers—how long ago? "Did you enjoy your book?"

She tilted her head, her brows drawing down in question. It seemed to have slipped her mind as well. "Book? Oh, yes. The Anne Radcliffe novel." She sighed. "Not as enjoyable as her other one, I'm afraid. And yours? Although I expect you may not have had as much free time to read as I."

Although he'd wager she hadn't intended it, her comment still illustrated how much he had neglected her. "Most interesting. I've been meaning to ask Ashton about it, to compare his experiences. Although I understand he spent time in Boston, which is a bustling city rather than the rugged wilderness portrayed in the book."

"Perhaps you might loan it to me? Then I would be equipped to discuss it intelligently."

Her attempt to engage him, to connect on some deeper level, twisted the knife in his gut. Would he allow her to be solely responsible for any real interaction between them? Why couldn't he make a better effort?

"I would be happy to, although I fear there are some rather unpleasant details that might upset your feminine sensibilities."

She blinked. Once. Twice. Three times. A dark shadow passed over her face. "I'm not a delicate flower who needs to be shielded and sheltered from unpleasantness." She sipped her tea, perhaps attempting to compose herself. "Is that why you don't discuss your cases at the clinic? That you believe they would upset my *feminine sensibilities?*"

He stared at her, certain his mouth hung open and that he was the one to blink in surprise.

In an instant, she reined in the indignation painted on her features, the color on her cheeks morphing from rosy pink to stark white. "I beg your pardon." She cast her eyes down, seeking something within her teacup.

"Don't apologize. You were quite right. I presumed rather than asked. As for my cases at the clinic, I thought more not to bore you with the details of lancing boils and prescribing poultices for chest congestion. Besides, Ashton is adamant about preserving the privacy of our patients in the same manner he would in tending to those in society."

She nodded, but he feared the damage had been done.

He was an arse. Perhaps Honoria would provide more in their relationship than mindless obedience. The idea should have given him hope.

But it did not.

An uncomfortable silence settled around them, and he feared opening his mouth again lest his boot seek the opening. He resisted pulling out his pocket watch to see how much time had passed. His fingers tapped an uneven rhythm against his leg.

"Oh," Honoria said, jolting him out of his stupor. "Have you heard the news?"

He shook his head. Even if she imparted something he'd already known, at least it would break the interminable silence.

"Miss Pratt is engaged."

What the devil was in the tea? The room began to spin, Honoria's words hitting him like a punch to his stomach. "Wh— what?" he croaked, coughing and pointing to the tea as if to blame it, even though he hadn't even had a sip in the last few minutes.

"To a Mr. Netherborne. I believe they are keeping things rather quiet. Father heard it from Lord Cartwright at his club. I understand, he's a curate she met during her time in Lincolnshire."

"But she told me she didn't want to marry him."

"She did? I don't recall that conversation."

"It was . . ." He stopped himself. Was it when they'd spent time together in the cottage and she'd called herself Emma, or here in London? "I don't recall precisely when she said it, but I believe it's why she decided to seek a husband here." There. Not a lie.

"Perhaps being apart from him has made her reconsider."

He doubted it, especially if the man was still as judgmental as Priscilla had implied.

Honoria leaned forward, concern shining in her eyes. "Forgive me, but you look unwell."

"Perhaps I'm more exhausted than I imagined. If you will excuse me, I think I shall return home and rest." He rose and bowed, hoping he didn't appear too anxious.

"Of course," she said, rising to ring for a servant to escort him out.

Not willing to wait, he practically raced from the room.

He hated lying to Honoria, although he seemed to be doing it more often, but he had no intention of returning home and resting. Instead, he made his way to Lord Cartwright's townhouse to hear the news directly from Priscilla's own lips.

IN NO HURRY TO RETURN TO THE COUNTRY, PRISCILLA requested a London wedding, and Mr. Netherborne reluctantly agreed. Oh, he'd blustered and argued that they should marry in Lincolnshire where he served, but Priscilla's father insisted, and how could a lowly country curate refuse a viscount?

Despite Mr. Netherborne's protests over an elaborate wedding, Priscilla's mother flitted about like a nervous bird, making the arrangements. However, at Priscilla's insistence, her mother made one concession. Lord Cartwright procured a common license to eliminate the reading of the banns, and no other announcements were made. Priscilla had no wish to be the topic of society's scandal sheets again, and surely her less than prestigious match would set tongues wagging. She had no illusions of avoiding the gossips forever, but she hoped to be out of London by then.

Two times she prepared to be a bride, both times fraught with guilt. Shouldn't brides be joyous, anticipating a happy life with their new husband? Of course, it had been different with the duke than it was with Mr. Netherborne. She had done the duke a great disservice by trapping him, and her guilt at wounding him still ate at her to that day. But at least he had escaped and found happiness.

This time, she had trapped and doomed herself to a loveless marriage. She prayed she would find a way to grow in affection toward Abner, but the fanciful dreams of a young girl had vanished the moment he had placed a chaste kiss on her lips at their engagement.

The resulting comparison to the magnificent kiss she shared with Timothy was inevitable, and she found Mr. Netherborne's attempt sorely lacking.

It was like kissing a snake. Not that she had ever kissed a snake, but she did have a vivid imagination. Lips as dry as parchment barely brushed against hers, cold, perfunctory, and—passionless.

In the four days he remained in London after their engagement, he made no further attempt, presumably *saving* himself for the marriage. When he returned to Belton almost three weeks ago, she did not feel the loss.

She slumped against her chair and gazed out the window of her bedroom. Sun bounced against the pavement, casting short shadows from the people strolling leisurely along the streets of Mayfair. Why couldn't it be the typical London weather—gloomy and rainy? Something to match her mood.

A carriage pulled up in front of the house, and a gentleman descended, his form familiar. Priscilla's heart rose to her throat. When he craned his neck and caught her peering down at him, he gave a little wave. She shot from her seat as if propelled by a cannon.

"Victor!" she shouted as she raced down the stairs, caring little she would receive a severe dressing down for her unladylike behavior. "He's come! Victor's come home!"

She hadn't seen her brother in five years since he'd been touring the continent and taking painting instruction from a master in Italy. He must have received her letter announcing her upcoming nuptials. Tears of happiness slid down her cheeks that he'd come home.

He'd barely made it inside when she hurled herself at him, knocking his hat off in the process.

Digby muttered something about not needing to announce anyone as he picked up Victor's hat.

Her brother wrapped his arms around her and lifted her off the floor, swinging her in an arc.

She squealed like a schoolgirl until he set her back down.

"I see old Digby hasn't changed," he whispered in her ear. Then he grasped her arms, holding her from him in appraisal. "You, on the other hand. Well, is it possible you've grown even more beautiful? You were a mere child when I left."

He, too, had changed. A healthy golden tan had darkened his typically fair complexion, accentuating his blue eyes. The unexpected removal of his hat had left his unfashionably long hair disheveled, and a golden lock fell over his forehead.

"Mother will insist you get a haircut, but I love it." It curled over the tops of his ears and at the nape of his neck.

"So do the ladies." He wiggled his eyebrows.

She slapped his arm playfully. "You rake! As I recall, you've never had a problem attracting women."

He gazed around. "Speaking of Mother, I'm surprised she hasn't laid siege. Is she here?"

Priscilla shook her head. "She's at the modiste, and father is at his club." She threaded her arm through his and led him to the drawing room, grinning like a ninny. "I have you all to myself."

He became uncharacteristically somber. "Good. I wanted to talk to you."

Panic snaked up her spine. "Is something wrong? You're not ill, are you? You look wonderful—so tan."

"It's that unrelenting Italian sun. But no, it's not about me. I'm concerned about you. Your letter didn't contain the joyous anticipation of a bride I would have expected, and I left immediately upon receiving it. This isn't another of Mother's schemes?"

"No." How could she tell him she'd managed this particular mess herself?

"But you're not happy about it." It was not a question.

They settled on a sofa in the drawing room. "I've given up on happy."

A blond eyebrow raised. "Cilla. You have your whole life ahead of you. If you don't want to marry this man, then don't."

"It's not that simple. You've been gone these past five years. You don't understand how difficult it's been trying to reestablish myself in society. To be forgiven for what I'd done."

"That was mainly Mother."

She shook her head. "No. I can't allow her to take the blame any longer. The duke pleaded with me to release him. Pleaded, Victor. I knew it was wrong. I won't excuse myself any longer."

His blue eyes studied her. "You *have* grown up." Taking her hands in his, he said ever so gently, "But Cilla, you did release him. Father wrote and told me what happened both at the wedding and after. Perhaps the first step is to forgive yourself."

A tear escaped and trickled down her cheek onto her lips, the taste salty, and she brushed another away with the back of her hand. "It's not only that. I tried to find a husband here in London, but circumstances make it too painful to stay here. A quiet life in the country with Mr. Netherborne will be my penance."

She should have known better than to make even a vague reference of Timothy to her brother. He'd always had a sharp mind.

"What circumstances?" He bristled before her. "Has someone

taken advantage of you? Give me his name, and I shall have his head."

"No. Yes. No, not like you think. There is someone here, but he's not taken anything from me except my heart."

"Still. A man who would toy with a woman's affections so carelessly should be brought to task. Does Father know?"

Again, she shook her head, more vehemently this time. "And I don't want you to do anything either. He's been perfectly honest with me. He never made me any promises."

"Humph. And this Mr. Netherborne? Where is he? I should like to meet him to determine if he's good enough for my sister."

"He returned to his parish in Lincolnshire until the wedding."

"And he's not aware of your feelings for this other man?"

"Goodness, no. Promise me you won't say anything to anyone."

"Very well. Although I won't agree to like it." He patted her hands. "Now, what do you say we take advantage of this exceptionally beautiful day and go for a stroll in the park? My legs are cramped from my long journey and in need of exercise."

He winked, his face assuming the mischievous expression she had loved since they were children. "Besides, I'd rather delay my reunion with Mother as long as possible."

She laughed, the sound almost foreign to her ears. At least her upcoming nuptials had resulted in one bright spot of her life.

CHAPTER 24—THE LETTER

Timothy walked the short distance from the Marquess of Stratford's home to Lord Cartwright's, instructing the groom he would return for his mount. He needed the extra time it would take him on foot to prepare what he would say to Priscilla.

First and foremost, he would apologize as he'd intended immediately after their heated conversation at Bea's garden party. Those words had been corralled and trapped on his tongue at Nash's flagrant display of attention.

Initially, he'd decided if Priscilla's intention had been to flaunt a relationship with such a rake to wound him, he would not give her the satisfaction of knowing she succeeded. However, the news of her engagement gave rise to new questions and the second reason for his call.

Was this a further attempt to make him jealous?

To coerce him into a declaration he was unwilling to make?

Or had she truly resigned herself to give up on her dream of a love match filled with the passion she desired?

And why to Mr. Netherborne when she admitted to loathing life in the country?

Why now?

And what precisely did he hope to accomplish by seeing her?

Such questions did little to assist in the formation of an apology and only confused his already tortured mind more. Before he realized it, he had neared her father's townhouse. Several houses away, he paused to gather both his courage and a few words with which to begin.

Movement at the Cartwrights' front door caught his attention. Priscilla exited on the arm of a man—a young man, of perhaps Timothy's age.

Mr. Netherborne? Timothy tried in vain to recall what the man looked like when he'd seen him from a distance at the cottage.

But the man's appearance was not what caused jealousy to band Timothy's chest.

Oh, no. It was the look of pure adoration on Priscilla's face as she gazed up at the fellow.

The man leaned down and said something in Priscilla's ear, eliciting laughter that drifted on the breeze toward Timothy. With one arm linked in the man's, she used her free hand to touch his chest, the action intimate and familiar—and like a scalpel slicing Timothy's heart.

What had changed? Had Mr. Netherborne proven himself to be an ardent and passionate suitor?

The thought rankled.

Timothy ducked behind a waiting carriage and observed the couple as they crossed the street toward the park. Intrusion on their moment now out of the question, he waited until they disappeared among the crowd, then turned to retrieve his horse and head home.

His apology was no longer only obligatory but paramount. But he could not offer it in person. Feelings he refused to acknowledge would betray him if he were to gaze into her inordinately blue eyes —the risk too great, the price too dear. Instead, once he arrived home, he settled himself at his writing desk and retrieved foolscap, pen, and ink to write, perhaps, the most important letter of his life.

"REALLY, VICTOR! YOU MUST CURTAIL SUCH OUTLANDISH STORIES while in Mother's presence." Priscilla had blushed more than a few times at Victor's tales of exploits and romantic entanglements while studying art in Italy. His descriptions of the female models and aristocratic Italian women were enough to put curl in her hair.

He winked again, the devilish glint in his eye lighting up her world. "They're not outlandish if they're true."

"They most certainly are. And I have serious doubts you've not exaggerated."

He smoothed the front of his coat with his hand. "Can I help it if I'm irresistible?"

"Incorrigible is what you are. With a gargantuan opinion of yourself."

He threw his head back, hand pressed against his heart. "You wound me, sister."

The easy lightness of their conversation dissipated when they arrived back at their father's townhouse and Digby opened the door. "Your parents are in the drawing room. They're most eager to see you, sir."

Priscilla tried not to take the slight to heart. Victor had been away from home for five years and naturally her parents would focus their attention on him.

She turned to go upstairs. "I'll go to my room and give you some time with Mother and Father."

He grasped her arm. "Oh, no you don't. You're not leaving me alone with the tigress." Holding her hand, he pulled her with him into the arena.

In an instant, their mother sprang from her chair and enveloped Victor in her arms. Over her shoulder, he mouthed a silent *Help me!* to Priscilla, making her giggle. Their father waited patiently, finally having a chance to shake his son's hand and pat him on the back.

As expected, Priscilla was forgotten while her parents bombarded Victor with countless questions. Before long, their chatter became nothing more than the buzzing of insects as her mind drifted.

"Cilla?" Victor stared at her, his head tilted in question.

She blinked. "Beg pardon? What?"

He smiled, popping his deep dimples. "Everything all right? Mother asked if you would like to invite Lord and Lady Saxton to the wedding breakfast. She heard from Lady Saxton that you've become friendly with her son, Timothy Marbry."

Priscilla squirmed under Victor's astute gaze. She tried to deflect the conversation, sending an icy glare toward her mother. "You told Lady Saxton?! I thought we decided to keep the engagement and wedding quiet so as not to attract more gossip."

Her mother straightened her already stiff back. "Certainly you don't expect me to remain silent, especially with Mathilda going on and on about her new grandchild?"

"It's not a competition, Mother." Victor leveled that particular admonishment. "Besides, it's Priscilla's express wish to avoid attention. You don't see Father gadding about town announcing it from the rooftops."

A queasy feeling settled in Priscilla's stomach at the sheepish look on her father's face. "Well, to be honest . . ."

"Father, what did you do?" Priscilla veritably squeaked the words.

"I may have mentioned it to Stratford at White's. He said Lady Honoria had been asking about you."

"Is she also your friend?" Victor chimed in.

Why couldn't they have continued discussing Italy?

However, it provided a perfectly acceptable solution to Victor's previous enquiry. "Lady Honoria has been most kind, doing her utmost to help me salvage my reputation in society. And Dr. Marbry is courting her, so naturally I would have made his acquaintance."

There. She commended herself on her relatively quick thinking. Surely that would satisfy Victor's curiosity.

His narrowed eyes told her otherwise. "Hmm."

Victor most likely inherited his tenacity from their mother, for she reiterated the question Priscilla had, up to that point, avoided. "Well, do you wish to invite Lord and Lady Saxton and I suppose the Marquess of Stratford as well to the wedding breakfast?"

The last thing she wanted was to gaze upon Timothy Marbry's face while she sat next to her new husband. "I'd prefer not. We're not that close."

If only they were. She needed to remove herself from Victor's probing eyes. "If you would all excuse me. I would like to pen a letter to Mr. Netherborne." She sent—what she hoped was—a pointed glare toward Victor. "After all, he is my betrothed."

As she rose, Digby entered, carrying a silver salver. "A letter for Miss Priscilla. The person delivering it said it was urgent."

She plucked the missive from the tray and turned it over. The sealing wax bore no crest, and although the handwriting's bold, even strokes indicated a masculine hand, she did not recognize it.

"Who is it from?" her mother called. "A well-wisher?"

"That would hardly be urgent, Mother," Victor said.

Victor's words fell on deaf ears, the sound itself muted as Priscilla opened and glanced down at the signature. Her hand rose to her throat. "Please excuse me, I . . . I shall read this in private."

And without another word, she dashed off to the safety of her bedroom.

With shaking hands, Priscilla read the precious letter.

My dearest Miss Pratt,

It is my understanding felicitations are in order. I received word that you have renewed your betrothal to Mr. Netherborne.

Initially, upon hearing the news, I reflected upon our heated exchange at my sister's garden party a mere few weeks ago. Permit me to offer my apologies for my words that so grievously injured you, as I have no intention of ever causing you pain.

That being said, it was precisely your insistence on what you expressed as your utmost desire that made me ponder your reasons for reestablishing your attachment to your betrothed. Please forgive my boldness in my

assumptions, but I believed you held no great affection for your intended—
at least not to the degree you communicated to me during our conversation
as being paramount. For propriety's sake, I will refrain from naming it lest
eyes other than your own read this, but certainly you know of what I speak.

I will admit it perplexed me as to why you had agreed to a match that,
from my understanding, did not meet your ideal criterion. Therefore, I fully
intended to speak with you and urge you not to settle for something that
may not ensure your happiness.

Much to my surprise, when I witnessed you and your intended outside
of your home in Mayfair this very day, my presumptions appeared utterly
false. Unless you aspire to tread the floorboards of the theater, the genuine
affection with which you gazed upon his face could not have been
fabricated, nor could the returned esteem shining upon his.

Such revelation has only led to more questions on my part.

Was your confession to me false?

Had you overestimated your feelings for me? (I must admit, although I
have no right to feel thus, this possibility has wounded my male pride.)

Had you underestimated your affection for Mr. Netherborne?

What has changed in so short a time?

Is there more to this hasty change of heart than meets the eye?

Forgive me for my impertinent questions. I have no right to ask them.

My only concern is for your happiness. If you have found that which
you seek with Mr. Netherborne, I can do nothing but wish you joy.

However, rest assured that I will forever cherish fond memories of a
girl named Emma who hurled boots and captured chickens.

Ever your servant,

Timothy Marbry

Tears welled in her eyes. Her attempt to blink them back only
served to flick them from her lashes and land in splotches against
the parchment.

Three times she read the letter, trying desperately to discern
the additional meaning couched within his words. Every instinct in
her screamed that he cared. Perhaps more than he ever wished to
admit.

She concentrated on one particular paragraph. He'd seen her with Mr. Netherborne? That day? Gazing affectionately?

Impossible.

Victor! It had to be. There was no other explanation. If Timothy knew, would such knowledge change anything he'd said in his letter?

New possibilities whispered seductive promises in her mind.

A soft knock on her door disrupted her fanciful musings.

"Cilla? It's me."

The door cracked a few inches, and Victor poked his head around the corner. One look at her, and he threw the door wide, marched to her side, and settled on the bed next to her. Eyes darting to the letter in her hands, he reached out. "May I?"

She hesitated but a moment before placing the missive in his waiting grasp. "Swear to me you'll keep this secret."

Pinning her with his gaze, he gave a curt nod, clearly unhappy with her demand.

Breath trapped in her lungs as she watched his eyes skim over the contents of the letter.

He stopped several times to look up with unvoiced questions. Silence stretched between them like a taut bowstring ready to snap.

She braced herself for the eventual onslaught.

When he finally broke the silence, it was not with angry condemnation but hushed compassion. "Oh, Cilla." He gazed down at the letter again. "Timothy Marbry is the man of whom you spoke —the one who has stolen your heart."

"Yes."

"And this confession he speaks of? Was it your declaration of love?"

"Not precisely. I didn't tell him I loved him."

There was no need for him to voice his next question. His quirked brows were enough.

"I told him I wanted him."

Victor shot upright from his seat. "Dear God, tell me you did not say that?"

Squaring her shoulders, she met his glare. "I most certainly did, so much that it hurts. And I demanded he admit he wanted me too."

He paced before her. "Are you mad?"

"Perhaps. I told him I desire a marriage filled with passion." She pointed to the letter dangling from Victor's fingers. "That's what he refused to name. But he made it perfectly clear that although he desires me, he would not—could not—love me, nor anyone else for that matter."

"But you said he's courting Lady Honoria Bell. And who is this Emma woman? This man should be horsewhipped for toying with women's feelings so cavalierly."

"He is courting Honoria, in his own words, because she's safe. He would never risk his heart married to her."

Victor shook his head as if trying to clear it. "I can't believe you would have affection for such a man."

"You misjudge him, brother. He's kind and caring. Something has hurt him, I just know it. He admitted to protecting himself."

"And this Emma?"

"I am Emma."

At Victor's confused expression, Priscilla told him about the time in the cottage, Timothy's injury, the chicken, even the kiss.

"I never thought I'd see him again. I wanted someone to see me without the shadow of disgrace looming over me. To have someone like me for who I am."

Victor chuckled. "By throwing a boot at them?"

A sly smile tugged at her lips. "Well, perhaps not that."

"Well, that does sound like *you*. But a chicken? Truly?"

She nodded. "And it was delicious."

The fleeting amusement faded from Victor's face. "This was in winter?" His gaze dipped, then locked on her belly. "I should strangle him with my bare hands. Are you certain you only shared a kiss?"

"Yes." But it was a glorious kiss, one she had mentally reprised countless times since.

"I could confront him. As a gentleman, he would be honor bound to marry you. He could be yours, Cilla."

She shook her head. "I don't want him like that. If he can't give himself to me freely, I don't want him at all." She plucked the letter from Victor's grasp, once again gazing at the paragraph mentioning Mr. Netherborne. "But there's something here, something hidden within the words that gives me hope. Perhaps I'm a fool."

"I won't insult you with my response to that statement."

She pointed to the words in question. "He thinks I care for Mr. Netherborne, but what he witnessed was my affection for you. I must tell him the truth."

"Shall I accompany you?"

Oh, how could she ask and not raise suspicion? It was an impossible task. "Do you trust me?"

His lips parted, readying an answer, then he tilted his head, exhaling the unspoken word.

"I need to see him alone. Will you help me?

"I don't like this."

"No one has asked you to. But Victor, I need to do this. Then I will marry Mr. Netherborne and resign myself to a life in the country. No one shall be the wiser."

"When?"

If she was going to do this reckless thing, she would do it before her courage failed. "Tonight."

CHAPTER 25—THE PROPOSITION

Bands of light from the setting sun striped the floor in Timothy's small study, painting it in a soft glow. He rose and lit a few more candles, hoping to coax the upcoming night into hastening its arrival.

Not that it would matter. Sleep would most likely not come easily, if at all. He hadn't slept well for weeks, ever since Bea's garden party. The impetuous letter he'd sent to Priscilla did nothing to further his cause. Indeed, the moment he released it into the hands of the footman for delivery, a knot had formed in his stomach, refusing to ease.

He gripped the edge of the mantle over the unlit hearth, his knuckles whitening with coiled tension. Would the infernal day ever end?

After pushing himself from the abused mantle, he poured another glass of whisky and swirled the amber liquid around the crystal glass.

With one large gulp, he let the prescriptive liquid sear his throat and prayed it would dull the razor-sharp edge of his thoughts.

Instead of relief, painful memories elbowed their way to the forefront.

Merilee.

Like Priscilla, she, too, had said she desired him—loved him. And green boy that he was, he believed her, returning her *love* in full measure.

And it was all a lie.

Stationed outside of Antwerp and unable to return home for Christmastide, he planned to commemorate the holiday with another joyous occasion. Intoxicating anticipation bubbled in his veins when he'd gone to her apartments with every intention of asking her to be his wife.

Only to find her in the arms of a second lieutenant in his regiment—in flagrante delicto.

After pulling the offending officer from her bed, Timothy flung the man's clothing at him, and as his superior officer, ordered him to get dressed and meet him outside.

Merilee pleaded with him, begging him to forgive her. But he demanded satisfaction, not only for her honor, but for his own.

Seconds were hastily obtained from a group of soldiers in a nearby tavern. Although dueling was illegal in England, many in the military turned a blind eye when away from home, accepting it as part and parcel of a soldier's precarious life.

Pistols at ten paces. Timothy stood back-to-back with the second lieutenant, his blood bubbling for an entirely different reason. With each count, he gripped his pistol tighter, and any thought to fire at the ground vanished when he heard Merilee call the man's name, her voice in utter anguish.

He aimed low, but before the command was given, his opponent fired, disregarding the rules. Hastily, he pulled the trigger at the same moment a bullet slammed into his shoulder, propelling him back and his pistol upward.

Merilee's screams rent the air.

Gray encroached on Timothy's vision, and he stumbled, falling to the ground. He waited for Merilee to rush to his side, to speak words of contrition and love.

Such words did indeed pour from her lips, but not for Timothy.

She knelt beside the crumpled body of the second lieutenant, motionless on the ground, her body draped across his in a death shroud.

Soldiers in the regiment carried Timothy off to the physician. The second lieutenant was beyond assistance.

Burning pain seared Timothy's shoulder as the doctor probed inside. "I expected you to be assisting me in *removing* bullets, Marbry, not be on the receiving end."

Clink.

The bullet dropped into the metal bowl, and Timothy made a vow.

He would excise love and passion from his heart as surely as the surgeon removed the piece of metal from his shoulder.

Physician, heal thyself.

And so he had. For five years, he'd kept her from his thoughts. But the pill had been bitter. Of course, it helped when he'd found out Merilee had only pursued him for his title and money, with every intention of keeping her lover secreted away.

But then Priscilla had barged into his life.

He poured more whisky, desperately trying to erase the sight of her on the arm of Mr. Netherborne, her face shining with adoration.

Just like Merilee.

What a fool he'd been.

He jerked at the soft knock on the open door.

Rivers, his valet, stood at the opening. Financial matters being what they were, Timothy kept a small staff, a cook, a maid, one footman, and Rivers, who served as butler as well.

"Sir, you have a caller."

Timothy glanced at the clock on the mantle, shocked at how much time had passed, lost as he was in his maudlin thoughts. "At this hour?"

"She says it's urgent."

She? "Is it my sister?" Panic snaked up his spine that perhaps Lizzie had taken ill.

"No, sir." Rivers squirmed as if uncomfortable. "She said to tell you Emma wishes to speak with you."

Perhaps the liquor had dulled his senses more than he'd hoped. "Em—" *Oh!* "Send her in, Rivers."

Muted voices drifted in, and footsteps followed.

"Miss Emma, sir," Rivers announced.

Timothy scraped a hand through his hair, well aware of his disheveled appearance.

Priscilla, on the other hand, looked exquisite.

A royal blue cloak covered her from head to toe, and even in the shadowed light, the clear bright blue of her eyes put the rich color to shame. Blond curls, so soft his fingers itched to touch them, peeked out from the hood.

"Do you require anything else, sir? Would you like me to have the cook prepare some tea?"

Timothy wrenched his gaze from Priscilla to his valet. "No, thank you, Rivers. It's late. Don't disturb her. Miss *Emma* won't be staying long."

Priscilla cringed.

Good.

Despite his adamant assertions that he did not wish to cause her pain, Timothy had an unhealthy satisfaction of wounding her just a little.

Rivers nodded and made a hasty exit, leaving the door open.

The simple act sharpened Timothy's awareness, and he stared at Priscilla. "Where is your maid? Aren't you taking a terrible chance coming unchaperoned to see an unmarried man so close to your nuptials, *Emma?*" His words came out cold and unfeeling, even though they sliced through him.

Her pink tongue darted out and licked her rosebud lips.

He groaned inwardly as his groin tightened.

"I . . . I . . ."

"For God's sake, Priscilla, spit it out."

Fire blazed in her eyes. "You don't have to be so rude and blaspheme."

He rolled his eyes. Bea would be proud. He flashed Priscilla a grim smile. "Very well. To what do I owe the honor of your presence so late at night? Aren't you concerned about propriety?"

"I wanted to see you, speak with you alone."

He refrained from another eye roll. "Obviously."

"I received your letter."

No longer able to look at her and maintain control, he turned his back and reached for the whisky decanter. "Let me guess. You came here to rub it in my face personally. 'Ha ha, Timothy. Surprise! Everything was a ruse.' Giving me a false name should have been my first clue, *Emma*."

Fresh drink in his hand, he spun back around to face her. The glass nearly slipped from his fingers as his heart tumbled in his chest.

Suspicious brightness shimmered in her eyes, shaming him.

"No," she said, the word choked. "You had questions. I came to answer them."

He lifted the glass of whisky. "Go ahead. I'm listening."

"May I have one?" She pointed to the glass.

"Strong for a lady of delicate sensibilities, but I would be an ungracious host to refuse." He poured a finger of whisky into a crystal glass, then, on second thought, poured another finger's worth.

After handing her the drink, he tipped his forward, clinking the glass to hers. "To truth."

She stared into the amber liquid, swirling it gently, but didn't drink. "Truth. Yes. The man you saw me with was not Mr. Netherborne." She lifted her impossibly blue eyes to his. "He is my brother, Victor, recently arrived home from Italy. And yes, I love him dearly, so the affection you witnessed was truly genuine, as his is for me."

A strange mixture of shame and hope churned in his stomach. "But you *are* engaged to Mr. Netherborne?"

She nodded. "But to answer your questions, my feelings for him haven't changed. Nor have mine for you. If anything, I've underestimated them."

"Then why? Why agree to marry a man you don't love when, by your own admission, it is passion and love you seek most?"

Silent tears rolled down her cheeks, and the anguish in her eyes speared him square in his heart. "Because by *your own* admission, although you desire me, you cannot love me, and you seek a wife whom you neither love nor desire."

Her words propelled him back as sure as if she'd struck him. "I never said that."

"You did. You said you seek to marry Honoria because she is safe. How else am I supposed to interpret that?"

"That doesn't explain why you are choosing to marry a man you don't love. To relegate yourself to a life in the country—which, by your admission, you detest."

"It's preferable to a life here where I remain the object of scorn and derision. Sheep do not judge."

"So you're running away? I would have never pegged you as a coward."

"If gossips were the only thing to contend with, I might withstand it, but to remain here and see you across a ballroom, in the park, to long for you, knowing what I feel could never come to fruition, would be too much to bear." She shook her head, then took a large drink of the whisky.

Fitful coughing followed, and her eyes watered not from sadness but from the reaction to the strong spirits.

His physician's instincts kicked in, and he raced to her side and pulled the glass from her grip. "Trust me." Moving quickly, he unfastened and removed her cloak, not caring that it tumbled in a pile at her feet. With the cloak out of the way, he grasped her wrists, lifting her arms over her head. "Slow breaths."

They stood together, dangerously close, as he held her arms aloft. Her coughing eased, yet he didn't release his hold. The nearness of her heightened each of his senses. He heard her slow exhales as she caught her breath, saw the droplets of tears lingering on her lashes, smelled the faint remnants of liquor on her lips, and felt the heat from her body seeping into his own.

And every inch of him burned for her.

❦

ALTHOUGH HER COUGHING HAD SUBSIDED, PRISCILLA FOUND IT exceedingly difficult to breathe. He stood so close the fabric of his coat scraped against her breasts through the thin muslin of her gown.

He did not release her. "You were saying?"

What exactly had she been saying? Her mind blanked. The nearness of Timothy's lips to hers overshadowed everything else.

He'd kissed her before—as Emma. Perhaps . . .

"In your letter, you mentioned your memories of Emma. Would that we could return to that cottage and I could be her again. To have you kiss me once more."

The incredible moss-green of his eyes darkened, his lids lowering to half-mast, then dipped to her lips.

Her breath hitched as he closed the distance between them and pressed his mouth to hers, nipping gently at first, teasing, tasting, testing, then becoming more insistent.

With one large hand, he grasped both of her wrists, still holding her arms aloft, then snaked his other arm around her waist, pulling her tight against him.

She sighed, her lips parting with the exhalation, and Timothy's tongue swept inside, setting her afire.

More glorious than the first kiss, presumably because she was awake to appreciate it and participate fully, she prayed it would never end. If she could but stay like this with Timothy forever, her life would be complete.

And yet . . . she wanted more. Bits and pieces of Nash's words broke through her muddled mind. *Pleasure of a kiss magnified one thousand times. Surpassing any other. With someone you care about, perhaps love, especially the first time.*

She would marry Mr. Netherborne in five days. Did she want her first time to be with him, a man who elicited none of the effervescent excitement currently bubbling through her like champagne?

Unequivocally not.

Was it wrong?

Perhaps.

Probably.

Very well—yes.

However, she wasn't about to hone her moral conscience at such a moment, at least not concerning Mr. Netherborne and his strict standards for behavior. There would be plenty of time to do her penance in the countryside—years, in fact.

Honoria was another matter entirely. Priscilla had no wish to cause her injury.

Timothy pulled back, breaking the heavenly contact, and rested his forehead against hers.

She gathered her wits—what little remained after that mind-numbing kiss. "Have you proposed to Lady Honoria?"

His arm around her waist grew taut, and his fingers pressed against her back more firmly. "No."

Thank goodness.

"And your feelings for her haven't changed, grown deeper?"

He shook his head. "What concern of it is yours?"

"Your answer determines the course of my next action. Had you secured a betrothal to Honoria, or even admitted to a greater affection, I would have bid you goodnight and left."

Releasing her, he stepped away, putting respectable distance between them and taking all the glorious heat with him. "And since I haven't? What now, Priscilla?"

A warning sounded in her head. Upon arriving at Timothy's, her intention had been precisely as she'd stated—to answer his questions and correct his misunderstanding. To have a maid, or even Victor, with her would have kept her from speaking the truth fully and freely.

The kiss changed everything. She would spend the remainder of her life in regret if she did not make her request. He could very well say no and send her packing with a sound shove out the door. Nash's advice, albeit designed for a man, rang in her ears.

I would rather have tried and failed than be riddled with doubts and regrets over what might have been.

Fully aware that her request—her actions—might precipitate other regrets, she summoned what little courage she possessed and pressed forward. "I shall be out of your life within the week. You shall neither see me nor hear from me again. Might you grant me a parting favor?"

He said nothing—the silence hanging between them like an unwanted houseguest.

She licked her parched lips.

Timothy's gaze dipped to her mouth, and the black centers of his eyes grew, making the lovely rings of green almost nonexistent.

"The favor?" He croaked the words, his voice deep and raspy, the sort that scraped along the skin, sending gooseflesh on end.

Her heart pounded against her ribcage, silent and fierce. Words clustered together on her tongue like a herd of sheep, and the image of her future in the country urged her forward.

"One night of passion. With you."

⊛

BLINK. BLINK, BLINK, BLINK. TIMOTHY SHOOK HIS HEAD, TRYING to clear it. Surely he had misheard her. This from the woman who believed merely lying next to a man, fully clothed no less, would lead to pregnancy? "Have you run mad?"

He took a dangerous step forward. "Do you even know what you're asking?"

"I believe so, yes."

He laughed, the sound of it brittle to his own ears. "Go home, Priscilla. I have no desire to deflower you and then send you off to marry another man."

"You lie!"

The accusation punched the air from his lungs. "Not the best approach to seduce a man."

"Do you deny you desire me?"

He turned away. "We've had this conversation. Ad nauseam."

"I want to hear you say it. Do you deny it? Say yes, and I shall go. But do me the courtesy of speaking the truth."

He spun and pulled her into his arms, the passion which she sought raging dangerously close to erupting. "Yes, I desire you, though I wish it were not so. Giving in to these desires can only bring pain, Priscilla. To us both. Don't you see? I cannot offer you anything more than physical pleasure."

If he expected her to pull from his embrace and run away, he was sorely mistaken. She remained rooted before him, no trace of fear in her eyes.

Fool.

Although he wasn't certain if he should apply such an insult to her or himself.

"I have no misconceptions regarding your feelings or rather the lack thereof, sir. You've made it abundantly clear you do not— cannot love me. I accept that fully and without reservation. All I ask is that you leave me with one fond memory to live upon while I spend my days in the country, just as you have memories of a girl named Emma."

"And your knowledge of the act?" He had to know what she expected lest he go too far. Lord, was he truly considering her outlandish request? Had *he* run mad?

"More than it had been. I made . . . inquiries in the country before returning to London. Mrs. Wilson, the woman I assisted in childbirth, was more than helpful."

The flush of her cheeks, visible even in the low candlelight, indicated she spoke the truth.

Foolishly, he appealed to her reason. "You're not concerned your Mr. Netherborne will know?"

"I don't plan to tell him."

As if it were that simple. He almost barked a laugh at the serious expression on her face. Good God, must he spell it out? "I meant that you no longer would be untouched."

Her eyes widened. "He could tell that?"

"If he has experience, yes."

She pursed her lips as if deep in thought. "Would he, do you think? He's a curate after all."

The conversation had become ludicrous. How could he be discussing such matters with her as if they were negotiating the price of a gelding at Tattersall's? "He's a man, Priscilla. But I suppose in the throes of passion he might not notice." He *had* lost his mind.

She squared her shoulders and pinned him with those incredible blue eyes. "I'll take that chance."

He ran a hand down his face, the sigh escaping his lungs. "Go home, Priscilla."

"How can you be so selfish!"

He darted a glance down at the floor, expecting her to stamp her dainty foot. "I'm protecting you."

She glared at him. "Why? Because you care more than you will admit? What are you afraid of?"

Where all her pleading and rationalizations had failed, his resistance snapped with her accusation of cowardice.

Closing the distance between them in one long stride, he grasped her upper arms and lowered his mouth to hers in one searing kiss.

CHAPTER 26—THE SURRENDER

All rational thought left Priscilla when Timothy captured her mouth with his. Different from his other kisses, an urgency —a need—imbued the way he kissed her, as if his very soul was parched and her lips held the life-giving water he craved.

And here she'd thought the previous kisses were glorious.

Silly girl.

She grew faint, her knees weak and unable to support her. And contrary to the persona she'd presented in the past, she was not a woman prone to swoon.

The intensity of his grip relaxed on her arms, and he inched one hand up, trailing along her shoulder, her neck, and finally resting against her cheek. Her skin purred with pleasure from his touch.

His mouth left hers, and she immediately mourned the loss.

Soft puffs of his breath brushed against her ear as he whispered, "Do you wish to continue?"

Words failed her, and she could only nod.

"Come with me." Taking her hand, he led her from the room.

Was he escorting her to the door? "Where are we going?"

A lopsided grin spread across his face. "Somewhere more

comfortable. Surely you don't wish your first time to be on the desk of my study?"

"Oh." *Ninny*. Had the kiss jumbled her brain so thoroughly? A blush scalded her face. When Mrs. Wilson explained relations between a man and a woman, Priscilla never imagined the act could be performed anywhere other than a bed. But Timothy's comment opened new possibilities.

Of course, marriage to Mr. Netherborne would not likely afford any opportunity to explore those possibilities. He seemed exceptionally traditional.

Which was rather disappointing.

Forcing any thought of her dreary future with Mr. Netherborne from her mind, her gaze darted nervously about the hallway. "What of the servants? Will they see us?"

"You need not worry. I keep a small staff, and they know how to be discreet. Besides, at this hour, they're all abed."

Bed. Heat burned her face anew as she followed Timothy into a modest bedchamber.

Light from candles on the mantle and on a nightstand cast the room in a warm glow. A small fire in the hearth eased the chill of the late spring night, and a sizzling pop greeted her. Servants had pulled back the counterpane of the bed in preparation for Timothy's slumber.

With his hand resting upon the doorknob, he faced her. "Are you certain this is what you wish? Say the word, and I'll escort you safely home."

"No. I mean, yes, I want this—more than anything." The truth of the words vibrated in her chest.

"Very well." He closed the door with a click of finality.

For a moment, he merely stood before her. His gaze raked over her, igniting gooseflesh everywhere it touched, driving her mad.

"Are we simply to stand here, then? I was under the impression there was much more involved."

He laughed at that, the bright crack of sound generating the sensation of a thousand fluttering wings taking flight in her stomach. His laughter ceased, and his expression grew dark and seductive, creating an altogether different, but no less exciting, sensation. Warmth flooded low in her belly.

He strode forward, each leisurely step like a dangerous animal stalking its prey. "If the ultimate goal is to create a lasting memory, rushing seems contradictory, wouldn't you agree?"

Her gaze darted toward the bed. Was she really going to do this? When she turned back, Timothy stood before her, silent and waiting.

She swallowed her remaining doubts, which, much to her surprise, went down without a struggle. "What should I do?"

An auburn eyebrow quirked. "Do you wish to go? The door is unlocked."

"No." She croaked out the word, her throat becoming as dry as the desert. "I wish to . . . take part fully, but I don't know where to begin. Since this is to be our only time together, I wish to perform to satisfaction."

If she had learned nothing else at her mother's knee, it was to strive for perfection at all times. Besides, she hoped that the experience would be memorable for Timothy as well. She would derive a small—possibly unhealthy—satisfaction if she knew Timothy could not so easily forget their time together.

"Ah. Listen to your body, it will tell you what you need to know. Then simply do it, or tell me what you wish me to do."

"Kiss me again?"

He chuckled, the rich sound warming her like a cup of hot chocolate on a cold winter's night. "You don't sound certain. Is that a command or a question?"

"Kiss me—now."

Without hesitation, he obeyed, his mouth at first covering her own, then traveling along her jaw, tracing the shell of her ear with his tongue, then trailing down the column of her neck.

She shivered with anticipation as he neared the bodice of her gown.

"You didn't specify where to kiss you"—his teeth nipped at the edge of fabric above her breasts—"so I had better consider all possibilities."

Listen to your body. Well, she would if anything made sense in her chaotic brain. Yet, her fingers itched to test the silkiness of his hair, and she heeded their instruction, threading them through his thick auburn locks.

She held him in place for a few moments longer, debating her next request.

As he placed hot kisses on a sensitive spot of her throat, wicked images flooded her mind.

The room had suddenly grown uncomfortably warm, and she peeked over at the hearth, expecting to see the once meager flames transformed into a blazing inferno, but naught had changed.

She had on far too many items of clothing. As did he. She remembered the corded muscles of his forearms when she'd watched him at the clinic, and she yearned to see them again.

Filled with confidence, she made her next demand. "Take off your coat."

He peered up at her, his eyes mirroring her own wicked intentions.

With one hand, he unbuttoned the garment, his gaze never leaving hers, then shrugged out of it, allowing it to drop carelessly to the floor.

Although she found it quite enticing to watch him disrobe, she reminded herself she wanted to participate fully. After a moment's hesitation, she reached for his cravat. Her fingers worked the intricate knot, untying, unwrapping until it draped loosely over his shoulders and down his chest, leaving his shirt gaping seductively at the neck. "Your valet is quite talented."

"I'll send him your compliments." His lips quirked up at one corner.

She grasped each end of the neckcloth and pulled him toward her. "Kiss me again."

"My, you are bossy." And yet he complied forthwith, most satisfactorily so.

He kept his hands at his sides while he plundered her mouth with his tongue.

Knees going weak, she sagged against him, and he banded her with strong arms, keeping her upright. Heat from his touch seared her through the fabric of her gown. Notes of sandalwood and fresh pine made her dizzy with desire.

For long, luscious moments, she savored the kiss, meeting his tongue play for play.

Wanton. You are wanton, Priscilla Pratt.

She pushed aside the accusatory voice in her head and remembered her objective. Still trapped between their bodies, her hands released their grip on the neckcloth and fumbled with the buttons on his waistcoat.

Timothy's lips curved against hers, his body inching back to give her more room to work.

After slipping the garment off his shoulders, she broke the kiss. Although she missed the nearness—the heat—of him, she needed to see him more clearly for her next demand. "Off with your shirt! And be quick about it."

⚜

A LAUGH BUILT IN TIMOTHY'S CHEST AT THE FIERCE LOOK ON Priscilla's face as she gave her order, but he bit it back. And here he foolishly thought he was finished with barked commands when he sold his commission in the military.

He gave a quick salute and fought the smile tugging at his lips. "Yes, General!" He slid his braces off his shoulders, then pulled the shirt over his head, tossing it onto the floor by his coat.

Priscilla devoured him with her gaze, and as it inched up and down his body, he burned with desire everywhere it touched.

Clad only in his trousers—braces hanging loosely down the sides and back—stockings and boots, he felt exposed. But it was not for his lack of clothing.

Oh, no. Surely, if she lifted her gaze from his body and probed his eyes, she could see, sense that more than desire coursed through his veins.

When she stepped forward and placed one fingertip on his chest, he shivered, but not from the cold. Truth be told, she scorched his skin with her touch. Whisper soft, she trailed the finger along his pectoral muscles, stopping at the tiny pink peak of his nipple.

A groan, guttural and primitive, escaped his lips at the same time his groin tightened, his arousal straining against the fall of his trousers.

Her eyes snapped to his, her mouth forming an erotic little *O*. Pink dappled the apples of her cheeks.

Night after night he'd lain in his bed, imagining her expression of ecstasy as she writhed beneath him and he brought her to release.

And it could not compare to the vision before him at that moment. Those who believed fantasy surpassed reality hadn't been under the spell of Priscilla Pratt.

Fear rose from deep within and inched up his spine, vertebrae by vertebrae. Warning sounded in his brain as surely as a soldier's trepidation before a battle.

If he proceeded, he headed into very dangerous territory from which he surely would not escape unscathed.

He should stop this madness, send her home, and claim his victory.

Instead, he stepped behind her and began unfastening her gown, mentally raising the white flag of surrender and praying she would show him mercy when she'd finished destroying his heart.

PRISCILLA HAD SEEN STATUES OF NUDE MEN IN MUSEUMS AND aristocratic galleries, and her mother tried in vain to whisk her away before she tarried too long. But cold, white marble did not compare to warm flesh, especially when dusted with coarse auburn hair. Her fingertips still tingled from the sensation.

She wanted to touch him more, but he slipped behind her without a word—except for the strange, feral sound he'd made. She had worried she'd hurt him, but his expression indicated the opposite.

A thrill shot through her. Passion had gripped him.

Would she make such sounds as well? Grateful when he slipped behind her, she dipped her head as a blush scorched her skin.

He used the position to his advantage, placing soft kisses against the curve of her neck as his fingers deftly worked the fasteners of her gown.

A wicked grin tugged at her lips, and try as she might, she could not keep the teasing tone from her voice. "Did I give you permission to undress me?"

Movement behind her halted, then he lifted his lips enough to have his breath brush against her skin. "Permission to continue?"

She couldn't help but giggle. "Permission granted." Contrary to his declaration that he would proceed slowly, he loosened her gown with lightning speed, then tugged it from her shoulders until it pooled at her feet.

He mumbled a curse as he worked to remove her stays, but soon it too fell among the discarded clothing littering the floor.

Only her chemise, stockings, and slippers remained.

When he stepped back around to face her, his breath hitched. As his heated gaze traveled up and down her body, it stoked the fires growing within her. "So beautiful," he whispered, his voice almost reverent.

She wanted so much. More kisses. For him to touch her, hold her. But she only managed one strangled word. "More."

And yet, as he pulled her close, he seemed to understand, as if he'd developed a way to peer inside her mind—privy to her deepest desires.

Unintelligible mutterings poured from his lips as his mouth teased and nipped at her skin.

She sucked in a breath, joining him in nonsensical gibberish as he slid his hand up from her waist to brush the underside of her breast. Her whole body hummed with pleasure.

Right. Lord Nash was right.

It truly was magnified one thousand times.

Or so she thought until he tugged down the sleeve of her chemise, the fabric brushing against her already taut nipple. And even that paled in comparison when Timothy's fingers teased the peaked flesh.

Her fingers dug into his arms, holding on for dear life.

His lips broke from hers and sought her breast, replacing his fingers.

"Oh!" she cried out, much more loudly than she'd expected.

How much more of the exquisite torture could she withstand before she completely fell apart?

One thing was certain. She wished with all her heart to find out.

With great reluctance, she pushed against his chest and took a step back. One side of her chemise drooped down her body, exposing her left breast and riveting Timothy's gaze.

Modesty dictated she should cover herself, or at the very least feel embarrassed in front of a man not her husband.

But she did not.

She felt powerful.

Both she and Timothy had the same number of items of clothing remaining, and she intended to rectify that forthwith—to her advantage.

"Your boots and stockings. Remove them."

She would save the best for last.

He grinned, the effect sending her stomach somersaulting.

Sitting on the edge of the bed, he lifted one foot. "Might I ask for assistance?" The grin turned wicked. "For old time's sake."

The rake!

Two could play at that game, although she had no wish to lob a piece of footwear at his head. If her aim had improved, she might actually injure him.

And she wanted him very much unharmed and alert.

She reached for the drooping fabric of her chemise to tug it back into place.

"Leave it." He rasped the words, then softened his command. "Please."

The position inhibited her movement, so instead—with some difficulty—she slipped her arm from the sleeve entirely, leaving the garment to drape her body much like a Greco-Roman toga.

He did growl then. Or perhaps it was more of a purr.

Muscles she didn't realize she owned tightened at his heated gaze. She strode before him on wobbly limbs. Her hand shook as she touched the leather of his boot, but not from fear.

Anticipation buzzed through her like a horde of bees, setting every inch of her skin tingling. She gave a sound tug on the boot, grateful that it slipped off more easily than when it had encased his swollen ankle.

Still, she fell backward, landing on her bottom. "Ooof."

He sprang from his position on the bed and helped her up. "Are you injured?"

She rubbed her backside. "Only my pride, which seems to be located here."

"Allow me." He pulled her close and, cupping the injured area, massaged it gently. "Better?"

Gentleness shone in his moss-green eyes as they pinned her in place. "I'll manage the other one."

At first, she wondered if he meant the other side of her bottom, but he sat back on the bed and removed his remaining boot and stockings.

He patted the mattress next to him. "Sit."

She sent him her sauciest look. "I'm not a dog."

He tilted his head, his eyebrows raising in question. "I won't attempt to pursue that line of thought. Let me rephrase. Rest yourself while I attend to you."

Once she was seated, he moved off the bed to kneel before her. One at a time, he lifted her feet and removed her slippers. As he slid his hands under her chemise, his fingers left a trail of heat up her leg until he reached the top of her stockings.

In a pace excruciatingly slow, he untied the ribbons holding her stockings in place, then rolled each one down, the entire time his eyes never leaving hers.

Her heart hammered so hard she feared he could hear it. If things continued in this intensity, she would surely combust in flames. A sound like a kitten's mew escaped her lips.

He lifted the hem of her chemise. "Shall we divest you of this as well?"

Thoughts so muddled as if wool filled her head, she feared she stared at him like a simpleton. She choked out something that sounded like "Gah."

His lips quirked in that rakish, mischievous way. "Yes?" Like a stealthy animal, he climbed back onto the bed next to her. "But first, more of this, I think."

Wrapping his arms around her, he laid her back on the soft mattress and brought his lips to hers.

When he cupped her breast, she gasped, opening enough to allow his tongue entrance.

Once again, she ran her fingers across the coarse dusting of hair on his chest. He fit against her with aching rightness, the hard planes of his body molding precisely to her curves.

Perfect.

His sandalwood scent. The sweetness of his kisses. The exquisite sensations he called forth from deep inside her. How would she ever live without this?

She pushed it from her mind, determined to remain in the present in order to remember it completely.

His touch befuddled her. Before she realized it, somehow he'd removed her chemise and had proceeded to suckle at her breast.

"Oh!" She arched back, her body needing something she couldn't name. "Timothy!"

He placed a finger against her lips. "Shush. You'll wake the servants."

❦

Timothy should have known Priscilla would be a screamer. A woman with her fire could be nothing less. His warning to quiet had been half-joking and half-serious. He trusted his servants, but he wanted to protect her, nonetheless.

Her face, so beautiful, had been the epitome of a woman in the throes of passion, and thoroughly put his fantasies to shame.

She cracked open one eye.

He grinned at her. "Although I will admit, I'm very pleased *you're* pleased."

"We're not finished, are we?" The disappointment on her face pleased him even more.

"Not even close." He lowered his head and captured her lips again. Keeping his movements slow, he traced a path down her abdomen to the area between her legs. With his thumb on the little nub of flesh, he inserted the tip of one finger.

She jerked beneath his touch, then grasped his hair, tugging slightly.

And he loved it.

"You're very wet," he whispered, tracing the shell of her ear with his tongue. "And before you ask, that's very, very good."

He pulled in a shuddering breath when she mimicked his movements and inched her fingers from where they played with the hair on his chest down to rest on his arousal. Even through his trousers, her touch set him on fire.

Eyes widening, she stared at him. "It's so hard."

Unable to help himself, his grin widened. "And that's very, very good as well." He hovered above her, his lips a hair's breadth from hers. "In case you harbored any doubts, it means I desire you."

Lust darkened her blue eyes, and she sucked in her bottom lip.

His erection jerked beneath her fingers, demanding to be set free. All his promises to take things slowly surrendered to the overpowering need to unite with her.

But first . . .

"Priscilla, are you absolutely certain this is what you wish? Once it's done, there's no going back."

In answer, she grasped the back of his head, pulled him toward her, and pressed her mouth to his.

Even as wet as she was, he needed her to find completion first. He continued to stroke her, teasing the sensitive area and inserting another finger, hoping to stretch her in preparation.

Tongues performed a frenetic dance. As she matched him in boldness, his fingers matched the in and out rhythm.

She moaned and mewed beneath his ministration, her hands wildly traversing his body. Shoulders, hair, back, groin. Her nails scratched and dug into his skin. But unlike the marks Catpurrnicus had left, he welcomed Priscilla's claim to his body.

At his breaking point, he reluctantly broke their kiss, instead laving and suckling at her breast.

She stiffened. "Timothy! Timothy!" She came apart in his arms. *Huzzah!*

Uneasy emotion poked at his brain—a persistent knock on the metaphorical door he'd kept locked for five years. Briefly—no more than a fraction of a moment—he considered ending things there and then. Perhaps she would be satisfied. He'd given her the passion she desired.

But if he opened that door . . .

If he went the one step further and consummated the passion burning within him . . .

There's no going back.

His unspoken words were not only meant for her.

NEVER IN HER WILDEST IMAGININGS HAD PRISCILLA THOUGHT she could feel as she did at that moment. She floated on a cloud, with fireworks exploding all around her. The delicious tension building within her as Timothy touched her in her most intimate place had seemed unbearable.

And then, when she thought she would expire from the need, it happened. She still wasn't certain what exactly *it* was, but it was more than a thousand times more pleasurable.

If she could ever summon the courage, she would tell Lord Nash he was wrong. It was a million times more pleasurable. Was there a number greater than a million? She was never particularly adept at mathematics. Numbers bored her.

But now. She wished she knew.

Her body as relaxed as a cat's on a sunny windowsill, she stared at Timothy. His face appeared taut. A muscle pulsed in his jaw. Didn't he feel the same?

With his body pressed against hers, the hard bulge in his trousers remained. She swallowed. Mrs. Wilson said the act was a joining of bodies. Surely that meant more than fingers and tongues.

"Isn't there more?" As she said it, she realized she wanted more. She wanted to see Timothy—all of him. To be closer—as close as possible.

Because for her, it was more than physical pleasure.

At first, he didn't answer. Eyelids heavy, half-masking his green eyes, more than his arousal told her he desired her. She seared the image in her mind. Passion. He gazed at her with such desire it made her heart squeeze.

And for a moment, she pretended something else lurked in the depths of those green eyes.

Love.

"There is, if you're certain."

Listen to your body.

Oh, yes, she was more than certain.

An auburn trail of hair formed a line that led down his abdomen and disappeared beneath his trousers. Instinct took over, and she reached for the buttons of his fall, sliding each one out with shaking hands.

She gasped at the sight of him. The only comparison to marble statues was the hardness. Artists had never sculpted men like this— at least to her knowledge.

What a shame.

Her cheeks heated at the idea. Mamas would certainly never allow their unwed daughters to peruse such galleries. She tittered a laugh.

He lifted an auburn eyebrow. "I believe I'm insulted."

"Oh, no." She brought a tentative finger to the tip of his arousal. How could that part be so soft and the rest . . . she wrapped her hand around the shaft . . . so hard? "It's magnificent. I only laughed remembering how it's represented in art."

He coughed—a laugh? "Yes, well. It doesn't always look like this. As I said, it's because—"

"You want me."

He nodded, then slipped the trousers from his body.

Oh, but he was magnificent, and she took her time to remember every inch of his body. A pucker of reddish pink marred his skin at the shoulder, and she placed a fingertip against it. "What happened?"

"Bullet."

Before she could ask him to explain, he kissed her, sending any further inquiries away.

Gently, he nudged her legs apart with his knee. "Relax as much as you're able."

She had no worry there, and she trusted Timothy with her life. He would never hurt her—intentionally. And if her heart shattered into pieces, she had no one but herself to blame.

Ironic, and no less than she deserved. To find love and have to beg for its crumbs from a man who would never love her. To share her body outside the sanctity of marriage and be grateful for it.

Hovering above her, he held her gaze and pressed his arousal against her entrance.

The meaning of Mrs. Wilson's words became shockingly clear. The joining of bodies was with his—

For a moment, she froze, icy panic racing up her spine.

"Relax and concentrate on kissing me," he whispered, then claimed her mouth once more.

If his prescriptive kiss was any indication, Timothy was an excellent physician. Soon, the tension in her neck and shoulders eased, replaced by another tension, one low in her belly and between her legs. No longer fearful of the intrusion, she yearned for it and spread her legs wider.

He entered her slowly, carefully, taking the time for her to adjust to him. Patient. Strange, but she thought it fitting and recalled the Latin root of the word *patient*—suffering, enduring. Was that why physicians called those whom they treated patients?

But was Timothy suffering for his patience?

When she opened her eyes, breaking free momentarily from her lust induced haze, she noticed the pulse of Timothy's jaw and witnessed the muscles in his arms and shoulders bunch with restrained power.

He held back, controlling his desires.

And it was causing him pain to endure.

Participate.

And she would.

She grabbed his firm buttocks and pulled him toward her as hard as she could. "Oh!" she cried, both from surprise and a little burst of pain.

His eyes widened. Much as hers were, she supposed. "Are you all right?" The strain in his voice was palpable. And she loved him all the more for it.

She could form no words, only nod.

"Hold still for a moment and any pain should ease momentarily."

Try as she might to follow his instruction, she could not. The pressure building within her was too great to resist. Skin against skin, his body so fully linked with hers became more glorious than anything she could have imagined. Tentatively, she moved her hips, uncertain if what she did was correct.

Listen to your body.

Her body liked it.

She grew bolder, moving more aggressively against him. Her

nails scraped against his back, her teeth nipped at his neck, her lips searched out his, encouraging him to continue. Before she knew it, he joined her, and they moved together in a rhythm as primitive and natural since the dawn of time.

It felt right.

It felt wonderful.

Exquisite pressure built within in her once again, ready to explode.

And she wept from the joy of it.

CHAPTER 27—RECKONINGS

Fear slithered in Timothy's stomach at the tear slipping down Priscilla's cheek, and he slowed his thrusting. He licked the teardrop away with his tongue, then placed tiny kisses over her face. "Are you in pain?"

She shook her head. "No. Don't stop."

Buried to the hilt, it would have killed him to stop, but he would have if she'd asked.

Thank God she didn't.

He wouldn't last much longer. Heaven knew how he'd managed this far. With one hand braced against the mattress, he used his other to tease the stiff peak of her nipple, while he nibbled at her neck and lips.

Her muscles tightened around him, and he watched her face. He needed to sear the moment in his brain when she found her release. He would relive it many times over.

Not a moment too soon, she threw her head back and screamed, "Timothy!"

As she continued to pulse around him, all he could think about was her. Her screams of passion, the silky softness of her skin, the lemony scent that clung to her hair, the incredible blue of her eyes, the sweetness of her lips that surpassed honey.

He should have pulled out and spilled his seed on the bed linens. She planned to marry another man, and he'd already taken what was not his to take.

But he could not.

If in nine months Priscilla gave birth to a child, he would forever wonder if the babe was his.

It would eat him alive.

Yet, it would still not be enough of a punishment.

With one final shuddering thrust, he gave in to his weakness and surrendered himself fully.

Warmth suffused him, not only from Priscilla's body wrapped in his arms, but from the emotion rising from the fires within his chest like a phoenix. He would deal with it later, or more likely ignore it. Priscilla was the only thing that mattered at the moment.

After settling next to her, he placed gentle kisses on her eyes, her cheeks, and her lips.

Radiant in the flush of afterglow, she was the image of a woman truly and completely loved. Strands of her blond hair had fallen from the restraint of their pins and draped haphazardly across his pillow. Pink colored her cheeks. Her lips were red and swollen from their kisses. The aftermath of lust still darkened her blue eyes.

And his dead heart roared to life.

He stroked her cheek with the tips of his fingers. "Was it what you wished for? Hoped?"

"Hmm." The word came out like a sensual purr. She wiggled next to him, burrowing closer to his body, then laid her head on his chest. "Timothy, I lo—"

With lightning speed, he touched his finger to her lips. "No. Don't say it."

Muscles in her arms tensed against him. "If it's because you don't return my affection, you've made that abundantly clear."

He supposed he had. And it had wounded her. But she was wrong. It wasn't that he didn't return her affection. The emotions he'd buried were clawing their way up from the ashes and protesting the falsity of that notion.

No, if he were honest with himself, which he tried desperately to avoid, he *could* love her—if he allowed himself. But he couldn't say it. Giving voice to it would make it real, would give her hope of a future with him when there was none.

Silence stretched between them, cold and uncomfortable, and he struggled for the words to ease the hurt he'd inflicted.

"It isn't you." The words landed with a dull, resonating *thud*, and he cringed at their absurdity. He couldn't let things stand between them like this, not after what they'd shared.

He called forward the words to explain in the only way he knew how. "You asked once what had precipitated my aversion to passion —to love."

She stared at him with her blue eyes, wide and trusting, and he wanted to believe she would never betray him like . . .

"There was a woman named Merilee. I was hopelessly and completely in love with her, as I believed she was with me." He shook his head. He'd never spoken of this to anyone, not even Bea or Laurence.

"What happened?" Priscilla's whispered words tickled the hair on his chest.

"The day I'd planned to propose, I found her with another man." Unable to meet Priscilla's eyes when he confessed the rest, he tucked her head tightly against his chest. "You asked about my scar. The bullet was from the other man's gun, inflicted during a duel."

Disregarding his hold on her, she shot up and out of his arms, fire blazing in her eyes. "He shot you! I pray he rots in hell, the cur!"

As painful as recounting his past was, a sad smile tugged at his lips at the ire in her voice. "Priscilla, do you understand how duels work? *I* challenged *him*."

"But he shot *you!*"

If only he had a glass of whisky handy. "He did, but that wasn't the worst of it. I had planned on firing at his feet, perhaps getting in a lucky shot and inflicting a minor wound. Even then, I had dreams of becoming a physician—of healing people, not causing injury or"—he gulped, preparing to choke out the next word—"death. When the bullet struck me, it threw me back and my gun discharged, the trajectory much higher than I had planned. I killed him, Priscilla."

Suspicious wetness formed in his eyes, and his throat clogged, inhibiting the next words he needed to say. "When it was over, she ran to him—not me. Her cries and the image of her body draped over his in grief still haunt me in my sleep. She never loved me. My *love* killed a man, and it was all for naught. That's what love, what passion does."

Moments dragged on, and he held his breath, waiting for her response.

"No wonder we are at cross purposes." She traced the puckered scar with her fingertip, the lightness of her touch a healing balm. "You deny yourself happiness because a woman betrayed your love. Whereas I desire it because a woman betrayed mine."

Perhaps the remnants of their passion clouded his mind. "What? A woman betrayed your love?"

"In a sense. My mother. I trusted her, believed she wanted what was right for me. I think, in her mind, she does. But her idea of what will make me happy and what I discovered are worlds apart. She wanted me to marry a title and to do whatever was necessary to secure it. But when I witnessed the love the duke had for the duchess, I realized I had misplaced my trust. I yearn for the happiness passion and love can bring." She paused and ran a finger along his jaw. "However transitory and calamitous it might be."

He grasped her fingers and kissed them. "I'm sorry I can't offer you more."

She snuggled back against him. "Don't be. You've given me more than I hoped for."

Drifting into slumber, he only had one thought.

He didn't deserve her.

Although reluctant to break the spell that had engulfed her, Priscilla slipped from Timothy's embrace.

Sound asleep, he mumbled something unintelligible, then rolled over without fully waking.

Quietly she rose and dressed, struggling with her stays—truly her arms ached from trying to lace and tighten them behind her back.

She gazed down on Timothy, sprawled out on the bed and snoring softly.

Gently, she brushed the lock of auburn hair from his forehead, smiling at how it made him look so rakish. A tiny smile traced his lips at her touch. Pain gripped her heart at the sight of him, and although she had no regrets over what they had shared, the bittersweet memory of it would haunt her every time she gave herself to Mr. Netherborne.

Leaving Timothy, giving him up, was the hardest thing she would ever do. More difficult than becoming Mr. Netherborne's wife in a loveless marriage. Every instinct in her screamed to wake Timothy and insist they marry. Instead, she rose on tiptoe and leaned over his sleeping form, kissing him lightly on the lips.

"I love you, Timothy Marbry. With my whole being. I will *always* love you. Be happy."

Although Priscilla *had* felt remorse for her deception in compromising the duke four years prior, her sorrow had been rooted in how it affected her directly. Shunned by the *ton,* fleeing London for the desolate countryside of Lincolnshire—and sheep— she lost the ability to promenade through Hyde Park, showing off her latest fashionable gown, to attend parties and balls, to receive the adoration of handsome gentlemen. Oh, yes, she missed those things and was sorry her actions had resulted in those pleasantries being stripped away.

Shallow, unimportant things.

Her selfishness pointed an accusing finger at her.

This was her punishment, her penance. With a force that nearly knocked her off her feet, she understood what the duke had tried to convey to her. Now, she truly understood the horror on his face when they were discovered in an unsavory—but orchestrated —position.

She understood the detachment with which he made his proposal.

As she gazed down at Timothy, understanding flooded her. She remembered how the duke had spoken of his love for the duchess and her love for him, the tenderness in his voice and the light shining in his eyes when he said Margaret's name. The pleading tone of his voice when he practically begged Priscilla to reconsider and cry off.

Had her wedding to the duke not been interrupted, her selfish actions would have ripped that from them and destroyed any chance of their happiness together.

And she understood that pain. That despair. That longing. The kind of love so deep that it could crush a heart. And she felt a bitter, cold remorse for injuring another.

Yes, it was a fitting punishment for her sins, and she would accept it with as much dignity as she could muster.

Had the duke and duchess shared their love prior to that fateful evening when Priscilla had made such a poor choice? She supposed something that private was none of her affair, but she was certain of one thing. What she had shared with Timothy a mere hour ago had changed her forever. She would never again underestimate the power a physical coupling could hold over a person, and she was grateful she was left with something to comfort her on cold, lonely nights.

During her exile in Lincolnshire, she had watched squirrels gathering nuts in preparation for the winter, their tiny cheeks sometimes comically puffed out. She witnessed them scurry off to hide their treasure in underground burrows, hoarding them in order to have their fill in the desolate, barren months.

To that end, she stood, silently watching Timothy in his

peaceful slumber, and committed to memory, each touch, each kiss, every precious moment they shared, knowing she would bring them out and feast upon them in her darkest hours.

Once she drank her fill of him, although it would never be enough, she slipped from the room, closing the door behind her with a quiet snick. The sound mimicked the cracking of her heart.

◈

SWISH! TIMOTHY STIRRED AT THE SOUND OF CURTAINS BEING thrown open. Bright light flashed against his closed eyelids, casting his vision in a red glow.

"Good morning, sir. Did you have a restful night?" Rivers' annoyingly cheerful voice asked.

Priscilla!

Icy fear shot up Timothy's spine, and he reached out with a hand to the side of the bed.

Empty.

He ran a hand over his face, clearing away the vestiges of slumber, and sat up.

"What is it, sir? Is something amiss?" Rivers stared at where Timothy's hand rested on the spot where Priscilla had lain.

Was it a dream?

He lifted the counterpane and peeked beneath. A tiny splotch of red marred the white bed linens, confirming he hadn't imagined it. He'd made love to Priscilla, taken her innocence, and now she was gone.

"Sir?" Rivers stood waiting.

Did he know? Timothy studied the man's inscrutable face, cursing the schooled features of his servant.

For an instant, Timothy considered giving his servants' gossip free rein, ultimately forcing Priscilla into a marriage with him, and just as quickly, he dismissed it. His concern for Priscilla, more than his own vow to avoid an emotionally charged marriage, decided the

278

matter. He couldn't, in good conscience, further damage the reputation she valiantly tried to restore.

Had she delivered a message by slipping away in the middle of the night? *"Thank you, Timothy. Now proceed with your life as I will proceed with mine."*

Although he questioned her decision to marry the boring country curate, it was indeed what she had chosen. What right did he have to sabotage it?

He lowered the counterpane. "I seemed to have injured myself slightly." He raised a hand to quell Rivers' concern. "It's nothing. A minor cut. However, please alert Bess not to be alarmed when she changes the bed linens."

Suspicion flashed in Rivers' eyes, but he nodded. He shaved and dressed Timothy in silence.

When Timothy passed Bess, his maid, in the hallway, she gave a curt nod but did not meet his eyes.

At breakfast, his toast was charred at the edges, his coddled egg overcooked, the tea tepid. He pushed his half-finished, unappetizing plate away.

What little food he'd consumed sat heavily in his stomach as Rivers entered, holding a blue cloak.

"Sir. It would seem Miss Emma forgot her cloak when she departed last night."

<hr/>

WHEN PRISCILLA ARRIVED HOME IN THE WEE HOURS OF THE morning, she'd skirted around the house toward the mews. Victor had promised to wait for her by the servants' entrance. After she tapped lightly twice, it seemed to take an eternity before he opened the door.

He'd pulled her inside a bit too forcefully. "Good God. I've been worried sick. I had a mind to go after you." His gaze traveled over her.

Instinctively, her hand reached up to where her once artfully crafted curls hung in loose strands about her shoulders.

Yet it was not her hair that caught his attention. His grasp tightened, and he shook her. "Where is your cloak?"

Chills knifed in her stomach as if she'd had too many ices at Gunter's.

After pulling herself away from Timothy's bedside, her only thought had been to leave the house unnoticed as quickly as possible. She'd completely forgotten Timothy had taken off her cloak in his study.

Batting away Victor's hand, she pulled free. "I'm tired, Victor. I wish to retire and try to get some sleep before sunup."

Muttered curses sounded behind her as she walked away. Then he said more loudly. "Very well. But we will talk about this in the morning."

Not if she could avoid it. However, the only thing she avoided was sleep. She tossed and turned, Timothy's face appearing each time she closed her eyes. Each brush of the bed linens or counterpane reminded her of his touch.

Morning arrived without fanfare and without the respite of slumber.

Priscilla stared in the mirror as her maid dressed her hair, wondering if, somehow, she looked different. Her gaze darted to Nancy's reflection. Could she tell?

As if reading Priscilla's mind, Nancy said, "You appear tired today, miss. Did you not sleep well? Must be the excitement over your upcoming nuptials to Mr. Netherborne."

Excitement and Mr. Netherborne—two words Priscilla never thought to hear uttered in the same sentence. Yet the world remained firm about her. "Of course," she mumbled.

Nancy finished pinning the last strand of hair in place, and stood back to assess her handiwork, giving a sound nod of approval. "Lady Cartwright wished to remind you of the fitting for your wedding gown today at the modiste."

"Of course." Were there no other words she could manage?

Nancy bobbed a curtsy and left Priscilla alone.

A knock interrupted her blessed, but short-lived, solitude. She prayed it was not her mother. For once, that might have been preferable. The door cracked open, and Victor poked his head inside.

"May I come in?"

She waved him inside, realizing she had avoided his interrogation as long as possible.

He closed the door behind him, then paced before her like a caged animal. "I've temporarily detained Mother, but she nattered on and on about your visit to the modiste, so we don't have long."

He spun, spearing her with a glare. "What happened last night? The truth, Cilla."

"I explained that he'd misinterpreted what he'd seen. That it was you and not Mr. Netherborne he witnessed."

His eyes narrowed.

She feared the one thing, which up until that point she'd always loved about her brother—that he would be able to read her as surely as if he peered inside her mind.

"For six hours!" He raked a hand through his blond hair, destroying his valet's handiwork, then he resumed his infernal pacing. "I shall confront him. Perhaps staring down the barrel of a pistol will loosen his tongue."

Bolting from her chair, she grabbed him by the arms, stopping his perpetual movement. "No! You can't."

He shook out of her grasp. "The hell I can't! Watch me."

She darted a nervous glance toward the door. "Keep your voice down. Please, Victor, listen to me. Nothing happened that I didn't want."

"Are you mad?" he hissed, gazing up to the ceiling as if asking the Lord above. "You're to be married in four days."

"Sentenced for my crime, you mean." She could almost taste the bitterness of her words.

He jerked his head toward her.

"Punishment which I accept fully. But before I'm banished to the country to live out my penance with Mr. Netherborne, was it so wrong of me to seek one night with the man I love?"

"Even more reason for him to confess to his seduction. You could marry a man you love instead of one you despise."

Tears clogged her throat and pricked her eyes. "I don't want him like that." She shook her head. "Trapped. Forced. He'd resent me, grow to hate me. I saw that look in a man's eyes before, and I carry that guilt with me always. To see it in the eyes of the man I love would kill me."

"You love him that much?"

Blinking back the tears, she said, "So much it hurts . . . here." She pressed her fist to her sternum. "It's better this way. And I don't despise Mr. Netherborne"—she shot Victor a little smirk—"I just don't like him very much."

Victor snorted a laugh, then sighed. "Oh, Cilla." He pulled her into his arms and patted her back. "What am I to do with you?"

Her mother's voice rang through the door. "Priscilla! We must hasten to the modiste. What's keeping you?"

Victor placed a kiss on the top of Priscilla's head. "Very well. I'll remain silent." He pulled back and met her gaze. "But as you said of Mr. Netherborne, I won't like it very much."

CHAPTER 28—ADMITTING THE TRUTH

C rumpled pieces of paper littered the floor at Timothy's feet. Try as he might, the words he needed to say—wanted to say —wouldn't come. The blue cloak lay folded neatly in a box on his bed.

Exactly where Priscilla had lain in his arms a mere four nights before.

Damnation!

Selfishly, he'd held onto the garment, even though he should have returned it posthaste. When he'd plucked it from Rivers' hand the morning after the blissful night with Priscilla, it was like holding her in his arms again.

His logical mind weighed every scenario.

If he returned it immediately with a note written in his hand and someone other than Priscilla received the package, he would expose her without her consent—effectively betraying her trust.

Having been on the receiving end of betrayal, he could not countenance being the perpetrator and categorically dismissed that option.

If he returned it sans note, she would think him cold and unfeeling, callously disregarding what they had shared.

And although he couldn't promise her love, he had no desire to sully the memory of what had transpired between them.

Delivering it in person was definitely out of the question, for obvious reasons. Even using one of his servants to return it would raise suspicion.

Inspiration struck with the idea he could use a third party to handle the matter. If she had left it at a party, the hosts would have seen to its return. He searched his memory. Had she worn it to Bea's garden party? Chances were unlikely, as the day had been unusually warm, eliminating the need for an outer garment.

Besides, what would he say to Bea to explain why he had it in his possession? Although he trusted his sister, she still had reservations about Priscilla and Timothy's involvement with her.

And so the cloak had remained with him. He'd held it to his face, breathing in the lemony scent that clung to its fibers. At night, he'd placed it on the bed beside him and touched it, imagining Priscilla's body encased within its folds, her blond curls peeking out from beneath the hood.

Each day when Rivers entered Timothy's bedchamber to wake him and perform his daily ablutions, the valet cast a castigatory glance at the blue material. And even if speaking the words wouldn't have been out of line for the servant, they weren't necessary—his expression spoke volumes.

The damn garment had become an obsession.

Timothy wondered if perhaps Priscilla would return to retrieve the cloak herself. He clung to the hope he'd see her, to gaze into her eyes and see if she still held him in regard—perhaps even tell him after much thought, she'd cried off and sent Mr. Netherborne back to Lincolnshire.

Yet she did not.

And her wedding was to be held the next day.

Timothy's time had run out.

She'd made her choice, and he should make his.

After calling Rivers in, he dictated the brief note as his valet transcribed it in his precise hand. Then he instructed Rivers to hire a hackney driver to deliver it to Lord Cartwright's address under strict instructions the driver should not reveal the sender.

It was a simple solution, one he should have thought of immediately—a fact Rivers' quiet acquiescence to his task confirmed. In fact, the man didn't bat an eye at the package's destination.

Had Rivers known all along that *Emma* was Priscilla Pratt?

It was a stark reminder of how much servants observed and knew about their employers—not to mention how well they held their tongues.

Once he married Honoria, Timothy would raise Rivers' wages substantially.

Honoria.

He'd put it off long enough. With Priscilla wed, no excuse remained to delay the inevitable. Timothy needed a respectable wife with a large dowry.

But he couldn't bring himself to do it quite yet.

He would call upon Honoria the next day—Priscilla's wedding day—and make his offer.

The thought did not bring him joy.

⁂

THE DAYS FOLLOWING PRISCILLA'S MAGICAL NIGHT WITH Timothy passed with both blinding speed and interminable slowness, the contradiction of which was not lost on Priscilla.

For the former, it seemed she could barely blink an eye, and her wedding day to Mr. Netherborne loomed one day closer.

And the dreary, priggish curate's arrival in London was precisely the reason for the latter.

Each morning for the past two days, he appeared at her father's townhouse promptly at nine o'clock, much earlier than was customary or proper.

Her mother dismissed the blunder, citing Mr. Netherborne's ignorance of city manners.

Priscilla's father hid behind his newspaper or excused himself to go to his club.

Would that she had such luxury.

Instead, she sat hours upon hours listening to Mr. Netherborne wax poetic about the benefits of physical mortification, which brought to mind her trick of pressing her nails into her palms to keep her awake.

Unfortunately, she performed the ritual so often little half-moons appeared to have permanently indented her skin.

The day before the wedding, Mr. Netherborne arrived even earlier to accompany them to Sunday service. As he sat beside her in the pew, nodding encouragingly at each word the vicar uttered, Priscilla's mind drifted, imagining her wedding.

Seasonal flowers would drape the front pews, the fresh fragrance filling the nave.

Dressed in the beautiful pink gown decorated with tiny, embroidered rosebuds the modiste had artfully crafted, Priscilla would enter on her father's arm. He would give her hand a little pat of encouragement and reassurance.

Then she would gaze up toward the transepts to see her groom waiting for her. Timothy would look so handsome in a perfectly cut superfine black tailcoat, a crisply starched white linen shirt, and an emerald-green waistcoat. There would be no dull browns or grays for him on their joyous day. The intricately knotted cravat would summon memories of her shaking fingers as she untied the cloth securing the shirt at his throat.

He would send her a tiny, secretive smile, conveying the promise of what lay ahead when they were alone later that night, sending a thrill of anticipation through her.

She sighed audibly at the image.

"Shush," Mr. Netherborne admonished, poking her in the ribs with his bony elbow.

The beautiful bubble burst, drenching everything in a slimy miasma of disappointment.

When the vicar greeted them after the service and enquired as to their anticipation for the next day's ceremony, she gave him a wooden smile, much like the dolls she had as a child—their painted lips cracked with the strain of overuse.

Wedged between her mother and Victor on the carriage ride home, she turned her gaze away from Mr. Netherborne, who occupied the rear-facing seat next to her father. Queasy unease roiled in her stomach at his stoic, censorious expression, and although she'd eaten a meager breakfast of toast, she feared she would cast up her accounts on Mr. Netherborne's boots.

Victor leaned toward her, touching her hand, and whispered, "What is it? You look positively green."

She shook her head, fearful if she opened her mouth to respond more than words would spill forth.

Mercifully, they arrived home without incident. Priscilla planned to make her excuses to her family and Mr. Netherborne and retire to her room, but before she had an opportunity, Digby stopped her.

"Miss, a package has arrived for you."

"Oh, I wonder what it could be," her mother said, all aflutter.

Brown paper covered the large, rectangular box with no name or address written on the wrapping.

Mr. Netherborne leaned in, eyes fixed on the package. "If you have ordered another new gown, you must curtail such frivolities after our nuptials. Frugality is imperative. Your frequent change in attire concerns me."

"I didn't order a new gown." Priscilla hoped the dolt heard her muttered response. She turned toward the butler. "Are you certain this is for me? There is no name."

"Yes, miss. A hackney driver delivered it. Said his instructions were to give it to you alone."

After unwrapping and opening the box, Priscilla gasped at the sight of her blue cloak folded neatly inside. A piece of paper lay on top.

Her eyes darted to Victor's.

"Why don't we adjourn to the parlor and leave Priscilla to her package?" he said, doing his best to usher everyone away.

Her mother would have none of it. "Is that your cloak?" She reached for the note, trying to snatch it from Priscilla's hand.

Victor grabbed their mother's hand, holding her back. "Mother, it's Priscilla's. It's rude to read someone else's correspondence."

Her mother frosted him with a glare.

With her fingernail, Priscilla broke the wax seal, which bore no imprint.

My dear Miss Pratt,

I apologize for the delayed return of the cloak you left in my safekeeping.

It is my fervent desire that its warmth gives you comfort on cold nights in Lincolnshire, most especially should you find yourself caught in a snowstorm.

Although the handwriting was unfamiliar, and the missive bore no signature, the message was unmistakable.

Or was it?

The unease she'd experienced on the ride from the church overpowered her again, this time manifesting in a light-headedness. "If you would forgive me, I feel rather tired."

Her mother made a quick excuse, directing her comment to Mr. Netherborne. "It's very common for young ladies to be overwhelmed with excitement the day before their wedding."

Mr. Netherborne appeared neither concerned nor affronted. He simply nodded.

Digby held out his hands. "Shall I relieve you of the cloak, miss?"

She should allow him to store it, but she couldn't bear to part with it just yet. "I wish to have Nancy brush it for me first."

Everyone, except for Mr. Netherborne shot her a questioning glance. It was a request Digby could have handled for her. Yet, she didn't care if she raised suspicion, and she raced upstairs to seclude herself in her bedroom.

Once she'd turned the lock, she pulled the cloak from the box and held it to her face. Hints of sandalwood mixed with the lemon verbena of her own perfume. She brought it to her nose and inhaled deeper.

How had Timothy's heady scent permeated the fabric to mingle with her own? He must have held it close to him.

She read the note again, puzzled at the seemingly contradictory message.

Mention of Lincolnshire indicated he'd accepted her decision to marry Mr. Netherborne, but other words jumped from the paper as if vying for her attention.

Safekeeping.

Fervent desire.

Comfort on cold nights.

Caught in a snowstorm.

Was a secret message encapsulated in code?

Or was it merely the wishful thinking of her desperate heart?

Someone tapped lightly on her door, and she quickly deposited the cloak in the box, slipping the note within the folds of fabric, then slid it under her bed.

"Priscilla, it's Mother."

Ugh!

On leaden limbs, she trudged toward the door.. "What do you want?" she asked through the wooden barrier.

"Priscilla." Her mother sounded nervous, unsure, which was completely out of character. "We need to . . . talk."

"What about? I don't feel well. I'm trying to rest."

"I understand, dear. I think I know why, and I wish to address the matter. To ease your mind." She didn't sound angry or upset. In fact, gentleness laced her voice.

Nevertheless, Priscilla's earlier churning stomach returned at what her mother might "know." Reluctantly, Priscilla turned the key, unlocking the door, permitting her mother entrance.

Her mother's usual confident stride had vanished, and she darted a nervous glance at Priscilla as she shuffled to a chair by Priscilla's bed. "Have a seat, dear."

Like a recalcitrant child, Priscilla plopped down on the mattress in an ungraceful fashion.

No censure or look of reprimand from her mother followed. *Strange.*

After taking a seat and fussing with her the skirt of her gown at length, her mother cleared her throat. "I wished to speak to you about your wedding night."

Oh! Oooh. No wonder it looked like her mother had swallowed something distasteful.

"As your mother, it's my duty to prepare you for the marital act. It's been four years since . . . well, since I prepared you for your marriage to the duke." She cast her gaze to the tortured handkerchief in her hands. "Do you remember our talk?"

Priscilla searched her memory and came up short. "Not really."

Her mother nodded, still refusing to look her in the eye. "I fear I may have failed in my duty, thinking since the duke was a physician he would explain things to you. But Mr. Netherborne is an entirely different type of man."

Of that, Priscilla had no doubt.

Her mother cleared her throat. "You must have many questions, and your curiosity over what will happen has made you rather anxious. I remember the night before I married your father. I was at sixes and sevens the whole day. Why my mother—"

"Get to the point, Mama." Priscilla took an evil satisfaction watching her mother squirm. Although Priscilla was sorry for many of her sins, she had a long way to go to achieve sainthood.

Another strangled sound rose from her mother's throat. "Yes. Well. There's nothing to worry about, dear. Mr. Netherborne will handle everything. I recommend indulging in a little more sherry than usual, or perhaps a glass of port before bed. If you think pleasant thoughts during the . . . act, it's not so bad, and it's usually over quickly. Personally, I enjoyed thinking of the new gowns and bonnets I would order, or a particularly lovely bracelet of emeralds and—"

"Mother."

Her mother's eyes snapped to hers.

The temptation was too great, too delicious to resist, and she had years and years ahead of her to serve her penance. She schooled her features to the most innocent she could manage. "What exactly will happen?"

Red flushed up her mother's throat, traveling to her face until the whole thing was the color of a ripe apple. "Well, I . . . that is . . . the man, lies on top of you, and he places his . . . member inside your . . ." Her mother made a circular motion with her finger pointed low at Priscilla's abdomen.

Oh, yes. Priscilla was courting the fires of hell, but she didn't care. At least Mrs. Wilson hadn't made it sound like the ultimate punishment. "And why, pray tell, is this coupling necessary? You make it sound like something I wish to avoid at all costs."

Her mother seemed relieved not to have to further explain the how-tos. "It can be pleasant, especially as affection grows between you and your husband. And the why, my dear, is to have children. Before you know it, you'll be bouncing an adorable baby boy on your knee. Children make it all worthwhile."

"What if I have a girl?"

"Then you will keep trying. Of course, since Mr. Netherborne isn't titled, there is no need to worry about producing an heir, but all men want sons."

As if daughters were an afterthought and a consolation prize. The thought rankled.

"Besides"—her mother straightened her spine, assuming the demeanor Priscilla was most familiar with—"if you have a daughter, you will find yourself delivering this same speech one day. It is most disconcerting, I confess."

"I'm sorry to have caused you distress, Mama." Her mother's woefully inadequate explanation of lovemaking did, however, precipitate a question. "How does a woman know she's with child?"

"Well, your courses will stop. Which I admit is a benefit. There are unpleasant signs, however. I was horribly nauseous with both you and Victor. I could hardly eat a bite and cast up my accounts at the very smell of food. Oh, and dizziness. Why I had to take to my bed for the first five months."

Her mother droned on with more accounts of suffering, the sound like an annoying insect, but Priscilla stopped listening after the mention of nausea and dizziness.

Aware that her mother had stopped speaking and was staring at her, Priscilla forced a smile. "Thank you, Mama, for telling me everything."

"Not at all, dear. I'll send Mr. Netherborne home and tell him you need your rest before tomorrow. After our talk, it might prove too embarrassing to be in his company." She rose from her seat. "I'll have cook send up some chamomile tea to help soothe you."

"Thank you, Mama." And for once, Priscilla meant it, truly grateful for the small kindness of not having to deal with Mr. Netherborne.

Once alone, Priscilla's hand involuntarily slid to her abdomen. Could she be?

The idea filled her with both panic and joy.

And relief that at least she would become a married woman before anyone was the wiser.

⚜

TIMOTHY STARED IN HORROR AT LADY HONORIA'S DETERMINED face. "I beg your pardon? Would you repeat that?"

"I will not marry you, Dr. Marbry."

"But your father has agreed. He's given us his blessing. I don't understand."

"My father and I have yet to agree about whom I should marry. He's never taken my wishes into consideration."

Honoria's face softened, and she took his hand. "Don't misunderstand me, sir. I have the utmost fondness for you. And for that reason, I feel I must speak my mind and release you from your pursuit of a union with me. You don't love me. You love Miss Pratt."

When the bullet that changed Timothy's belief in love had struck him in the shoulder, it had effectively knocked the air from his lungs. With less deadly consequences, thank goodness, Honoria's words carried the same impact.

"Bu-bu-but." Timothy blubbered like a child trying to explain themselves after having been caught pilfering freshly baked biscuits. He wanted to protest, but found he could not. The truth of Honoria's statement would not allow such a falsity to fall from his lips. He'd tried to shove it down, keep it contained. Had he failed so miserably it became obvious to everyone but him?

As if reading his mind, Honoria continued. "It's true whether you will admit it to yourself or not. I've seen it when you look at her. The longing, the affection. I know it well. Not to mention when you see her with Lord Nash, or any other gentleman who shows interest, the anger passing across your face belies your protestations of indifference."

"You're suggesting I'm jealous of Nash?" He choked out the words, knowing as he did so they were the truth.

A knowing smile curled Honoria's lips. "It is you who have said so. Perhaps not in so many words, but every fault you've found in each suitor she's had gives testament to it. And they do say actions speak louder than words."

"But she's getting married—*today*. If I interrupt her wedding, I'll sully her reputation further."

In a display unexpected from a lady of her class, Honoria gave a magnificent eye roll. "Have you ever listened to what I've said? Perhaps, Dr. Marbry, she no longer cares. Consider what matters most."

She squeezed his hand. "As I said, I do care for you, but my feelings are as one would have for a dear brother. And at least one of us should have the chance at happiness. Wouldn't you agree?"

He expected regret or sadness to show in her eyes. But instead, he saw strength and relief. "I'm not worthy of you, Lady Honoria."

She gave a little laugh and brushed his compliment aside. "Pishtosh. Now, I suggest you stop nattering and go stop that wedding. St. George's in Hanover—go now!"

Like a man possessed, he grabbed Honoria by the shoulders, and kissed her full on the mouth. A gasp arose from her maid, standing in the corner of the room. He pulled back, noting the shock on Honoria's face. She laughed and placed two fingers on her lips. "As I said, like a brother."

It was true. Kissing her was like kissing Bea, although admittedly, he'd never kissed Bea on the mouth. However, it was the same sensation. It would appear Lady Honoria had saved them both from a rather disconcerting relationship.

Without another word, he raced off, hoping to make it to the church in time to stop Priscilla from making the biggest mistake of her life.

And of his.

***

"Is it much farther?" Priscilla asked, her voice shaking. The journey to St. George's seemed endless.

Her father smiled from across the carriage seat. Thank goodness Victor had taken their mother ahead in a different carriage. "Anxious? Or is something else bothering you, my dear?"

Definitely the something else. Why on earth had she agreed to marry Mr. Netherborne and be relegated to the country, boring sermons, and sheep for the rest of her days?

She twisted the lace handkerchief with her fingers. "I'm just nervous. Given what happened at my last wedding."

"I doubt Mr. Netherborne will run off to rescue another woman." Her father reached over and patted her hand, his knowing gaze studying her. "If you wish to cry off, I would understand."

"Am I doing the right thing, Papa? Is there no one else who would want me?"

"There *is* still Mr. Ugbrooke. He left in a huff the other day when I informed him of your pending nuptials."

Gah! Mr. Ugbrooke and his brood of unruly children. Although, in fairness, two didn't really constitute a brood, but it always seemed as if their number multiplied whenever she was near. She exhaled a heavy sigh. "No. I suppose Mr. Netherborne it is."

She glanced down at the lovely pale pink dress. Black would be more fitting—along with a heavy veil covering her face. Before she could delve deeper into her misery, the carriage slowed to a stop, and she peered out the window at the church.

"Ready?" her father asked.

"Will you give me a moment?"

He nodded and, when the footman opened the door, exited, waiting patiently for her to descend.

While she tried to gather her courage, her father's attention jerked away from her, his expression startled. "I say there. What are you doing?"

Suddenly, the carriage jerked forward, throwing her against the squabs. The open door flapped wildly, slamming against the side. She scooted forward, grabbing it as it moved back against the opening, and closed the latch.

Twisting in her seat, she stared out the back window at the sight of the driver sprawled on the pavement, rubbing his jaw and her father, running after the carriage in vain, shouting and waving his cane.

What was happening? Was she being abducted? And by whom? Thinking back to her failed wedding with the duke, terror froze her in her seat at the thought of that horrid man and what he did to the duchess. Was this an act of vengeance against her? Would her abductor demand a ransom?

She needed to think and develop a plan to extract herself from the situation. In an attempt to gain her bearings, she peered out the window, desperately looking for familiar landmarks to gauge her location.

There! On the side of Regent's Park near Camden Town. The carriage slowed, and she frantically searched about the compartment of the carriage for something to use as a weapon. Her father's black umbrella! Thank the stars!

Holding the instrument like a club, she readied herself and pulled in a deep breath when the carriage door opened.

She took a furious swing, hitting Timothy soundly on the head.

CHAPTER 29—WHEN PASSION PREVAILS

O w!" Timothy howled. "Must you always be lobbing things at my head?"

"Timothy!" Priscilla had the temerity to look aghast as she fell back inside the carriage. "What the devil are you doing?"

Not able to resist the grin spreading across his face, nor the opportunity to tease her simply because vexing her was so much fun, he answered, "My, my such language from a gently bred lady. As to what I'm doing, I would think it would be perfectly clear. I'm stopping your wedding."

When she remained firmly ensconced in the carriage, he held out his hand, motioning for her to place hers in it. "Well, are you going to sit there all day?" He tilted his head in question. "Or do you wish me to return you to Mr. Netherborne, who is no doubt wondering what's happened to his bride?"

Her mouth opened and closed several times, making no sound, which, although completely out of character for her, at this point of things, was a blessing.

"Well, whom shall it be? Me or Mr. Netherborne?"

Her eyes narrowed to slits. *Ah, there she is.*

"What do you mean, you or Mr. Netherborne?"

He exhaled a purposely dramatic sigh. "And here I thought you were an intelligent woman. Allow me to state it plainly so you may comprehend. Whom do you wish to marry? Me or Mr. Netherborne?"

"But why? Hadn't you planned to propose to Lady Honoria?"

He shook his head. "She pointed out the error of my ways. Informed me in no uncertain terms that I love you."

At that, she slid from the carriage, although perhaps slid was not the precise word. He wouldn't describe her movements as graceful. It was rather like watching a reanimated corpse, stiff and jerky, as if the brain no longer controlled the muscles. Not an attractive image for the woman he wished to marry, but if nothing else, he was an honest man.

And he loved her nonetheless.

Loved her.

No matter what.

All the years he fought it, pushed the painful memories down, vowing never to become vulnerable again. He'd dismissed any romantic feelings as balderdash and for weak fools, leading only to pain and grief. Believed people, men in particular, deluded themselves to the existence of that simple four-letter word.

Love.

Instead of weighing him down, the reality of it spilled through him like lightness flowing through his body. He felt practically giddy and dangerously close to giggling like a child.

Thank God he held the urge in. Priscilla would never let him live that down. She would hold it over his head for the rest of their very long married life.

Which speaking of . . .

"So, whom shall it be? Me or Mr. Netherborne? If it's the latter" —he pulled out his pocket watch and took a peek—"I had best return you posthaste. I believe the wedding was scheduled for—""

She hurled herself into his arms, knocking him off balance, and they both tumbled to the ground, Priscilla landing atop him, arms and legs akimbo.

Although not precisely a giggle—thank goodness—he emitted a rather high-pitched laugh, drawing attention from people passing by.

He lifted his head enough to whisper in her ear, "I believe we're gathering a crowd, Priscilla. Perhaps we should right ourselves and proceed inside my home for some privacy?"

She rolled off of him, none too gracefully, he had to admit with some satisfaction. It gave him joy that he'd flustered her so. He rose, held out his hand, and helped her to her feet.

Horses' hooves pounded against the cobbles, and carriage wheels rumbled their syncopated response. When the conveyance came to a halt behind the purloined carriage, a young man bolted from the compartment, followed by Lord and Lady Cartwright.

The younger man approached, and as he grew closer, Timothy recognized the similar features in his face to those of Priscilla's. Clear blue eyes narrowed to slits, and his mouth was drawn so tight all that remained was a thin, straight line.

"Unhand my sister, you cur!" The man—Victor, if Timothy recalled correctly—pulled the glove off his hand and stepped closer.

Timothy braced himself for the challenge. Of course, he wished to avoid a duel, but skirting tragedy or possibly prosecution was not the deciding factor in how he would respond. He would willingly— no, eagerly—promise to marry her.

The rightness of it settled within him, down to the marrow of his bones. Although she hadn't officially accepted his rather gauche proposal, her reaction indicated she was more than amenable.

"Victor, no!" Priscilla leapt between them.

Did she really doubt his intentions and worry that he would rather face her brother in a challenge?

"I've already struck him with an umbrella. Please don't inflict any further injury upon him."

Ah. He chuckled. So it wasn't a matter of doubts.

"You find this amusing, sir?" Victor pushed Priscilla aside none too gently.

Timothy's own rage surged. "Do *not* manhandle the woman I love in such a manner, or I shall be the one to demand satisfaction."

Priscilla emitted an exaggerated huff, drawing their attention. "Will you two dunderheads cease this ridiculous masculine posturing immediately!"

"Priscilla!" Lady Cartwright said, her hand clutching a handkerchief to her ample bosom.

Both Timothy's and Victor's heads jerked toward Priscilla.

Lord Cartwright's calm voice of reason broke through the chaos. "Dr. Marbry, if you would kindly explain the meaning of this. There is a groom waiting at the altar for his bride. It would be, at the very least, common courtesy to inform him if she has cried off."

All eyes landed on Timothy, each pair exhibiting a different emotion.

Lord Cartwright's seemed concerned, and as they darted toward Priscilla, the love they held for his daughter was evident.

Lady Cartwright's appeared calculating, a spark lighting behind them as she no doubt realized an heir to a viscountcy—regardless of his financial state—was a far superior match than a country curate.

Skin on Timothy's neck itched from Victor's perceptive gaze as if he were privy to what had transpired between him and Priscilla.

And Priscilla's eyes sparkled with amusement. The termagant.

But she was *his* termagant—if she would have him.

He cleared his throat, which had suddenly become clogged with emotion. "I've asked Miss Pratt to marry me, but she has yet to give me her answer." He faced Priscilla. "Will you do me the honor of becoming my wife?"

Collectively, all eyes turned toward his—hopefully—future bride, waiting.

She tapped a gloved finger to her lips and tilted her lovely head, as if pondering the simple question.

He exhaled the breath he hadn't realized he'd been holding when a grin broke across her face.

"I suppose I could bear being a physician's wife. Yes, Dr. Marbry, I will marry you."

"Huzzah!" Timothy wanted to pick her up and spin her around, then thoroughly ravish her. He refrained from both. There would be a time and place for the latter. Hopefully, in the not too distant future.

Filled with new confidence, Timothy addressed his future father-in-law. "If it's agreeable, may I call upon Miss Pratt tomorrow and discuss the marriage contract with you, sir?"

Lady Cartwright dabbed her eyes with her crumpled handkerchief. "Someone needs to inform Mr. Netherborne."

Victor darted a glance toward Priscilla, then addressed his parents. "Let's spare Cilla the discomfort of facing him. Why don't you two go back to the church? I'll stay here as chaperone with Cilla and Dr. Marbry in case there are any repercussions from Mr. Netherborne."

Fear notched up Timothy's spine. "Do you think there will be?"

"Pfft." Priscilla's unladylike response brought a smile to his face and a reprimanding look from her mother. "I highly doubt it. He will likely count himself fortunate to be rid of me and my scandalous behavior."

Timothy smiled inwardly, anticipating all the scandalous behavior on his and Priscilla's horizon.

And it didn't matter.

PRISCILLA PRESSED HER NAILS INTO HER ABUSED PALMS ONCE more. This time not to keep her alert, but to verify the recent events were not a dream.

Victor positioned himself in a chair at the back of Timothy's small parlor, his eyes never leaving Timothy seated on the sofa next to Priscilla. Each time Timothy would inch closer, Victor would make a noise from the back of his throat.

"Are you growling at us, Victor?" she asked. "Do relax. After all, Timothy and I are engaged."

Timothy leaned closer, eliciting another growl from Victor. "Is he always like this?"

She shook her head. "No. He's really harmless and actually quite charming. I think you'll like him once the shock has worn off."

"I can't offer you much, Priscilla." He motioned around his minimally furnished parlor. "If you haven't heard, my father has left us in financial difficulty. If it hadn't been for Montgomery, we would have been completely ruined." His Adam's apple bobbed.

Was he nervous?

"I'm not proud of it, but it's one reason I sought an attachment with Lady Honoria. She had a substantial dowry."

Priscilla nodded. "And she's respectable. Something I cannot give *you*." Was nervousness contagious? "You may well regret your decision to take me as your wife."

He didn't hesitate. "Never. I've learned what's important. My employer, however, may prove to be a challenge. But if I've learned anything about Ashton, he's a fair man. With time, he will come to accept you—us."

"I hope so. What if there's something I can do to win him over? I shall make it a priority to find a way. Perhaps Honoria could assist me. She does seem to love solving problems."

Timothy laughed, the bright carefree sound sending gooseflesh up her arms.

"As for your other requirement. Have you forgotten about my rather large dowry?"

He blinked, and red tinged the tips of his ears. "I didn't ask you to marry me because of that."

She reached over and squeezed his hand.

Another growl rose from the corner.

"For goodness' sake, Victor, will you please cease that nonsense?" She squeezed Timothy's hand again. "As I was going to say, I know that. The look in your eyes when you defended me from Victor confirmed it."

"What look was that?"

"Everything I ever hoped to see. Passion. Love."

She schooled her face into her most serious expression. "However, it doesn't change the fact that my funds will do wonders to restore your coffers. I do have my standards, you know. This place needs a woman's touch. I think I shall start with a fresh coat of paint, and this sofa needs to be reupholstered or replaced. And some brighter paintings, those are so drab—"

He pulled her into his arms and kissed her soundly, driving any other thought of redecorating from her head.

Victor growled more loudly.

"Quiet, Victor," Priscilla and Timothy said in unison, then laughed.

"I love you," Timothy whispered, pressing his forehead against hers.

"I'll be sure to remind you of that the next time I throw a boot at your head."

❦

FOUR WEEKS LATER, TIMOTHY STOOD AT THE FRONT OF THE church, waiting for the ceremony to begin. His fingers itched to reach for his pocket watch and check the time.

Where was she?

Laurence poked him in the ribs with his elbow.

"Ow," Timothy said, keeping his voice low.

"I vaguely remember someone telling me it would be over before I knew it. Interestingly, I found my wedding ceremony to be only the beginning."

"I meant the ceremony, you dolt," Timothy hissed back.

"As I said . . ." Laurence grinned, then poked him again.

"Will you stop—" The next words screeched to a halt on his tongue as Priscilla entered the nave of the church on her father's arm. She hadn't left him at the altar as he feared.

Breath hitched in his throat, and his eyes never left her as she made her way toward him—to become his forever.

And he couldn't be happier.

Once he'd decided to marry her, his whole life seemed to click into place. When he'd lost his faith in love and refused to succumb to its passions, it was because he'd placed his trust in the wrong woman, and the guilt over taking another man's life was the price he paid.

But rather than use and trap him, Priscilla had proven time and again she only wished to protect him, even if it meant sacrificing her dreams.

There would be trials and struggles for certain. Harry had expressed his doubts about the match, but had still wished him joy and promised to keep an open mind.

Likewise, Bea had expressed reservations about Timothy's choice of brides, but confessed that upon witnessing the joy on his face, she would make allowances. Timothy rather thought it had more to do with Priscilla's interest in Bea's scientific articles. More than once, as Bea rambled on and on about her latest interest, Priscilla had sent Timothy a discreet wink.

It would appear his bride had a way with people if they gave her half a chance.

When she reached his side, his only thought was that once they were wed, she could have her way with *him* as often and in any manner she wished.

The rest of the ceremony was a blur.

After a hastily eaten wedding breakfast, he whisked her away from the well-wishers and back to his—their—home.

Rivers hadn't blinked an eye when, prior to their wedding, Timothy announced her as his betrothed. However, a certain twinkle of both amusement and awareness shone in Rivers' eyes when he correctly addressed her as Miss Pratt. With Priscilla's dowry, which was indeed more than generous, Timothy planned to make good on his promise to raise the man's wages.

Finally, he had her alone and wrapped in his embrace. "Ashton's given me leave from the clinic if you would like to travel anywhere?"

She shook her head, and the blond curls, freed from their pins, brushed against his chest. "I don't want to move from this room or this bed."

Nudging her chin with his finger, he met her gaze. "I knew there was a reason I married you."

Her blue eyes widened. "You said it was because you loved me."

"It is, and I do. But there is a decided benefit to marrying a woman of such passion." He brought his lips to hers, brushing gently at first, then growing insistent.

Soon, they were both spent and satisfied—at least for the moment.

Trailing a finger over the hair on his chest, she sighed. "I have a confession."

He waited for the tightening in his chest, but surprisingly, it didn't come. Was that what trust felt like? "Continue."

"On my wedding day to Mr. Netherborne, I thought I might be with child—your child."

What? "Priscilla, it had only been a few days since we had made love. There would be no way to tell." The implication of her statement registered. Over four weeks had passed. Excitement built in his chest. "Have you missed your menses?"

"No. My courses came the next week. I wasn't going to tell you at all, but, Timothy, what if I can't have children?"

He wanted to laugh at her notion that it would only take one time together to conceive, although it had been known to happen. However, her voice was so solemn he bit back his amusement. "Then we won't have children. The world will continue on, and there are many other people to contribute to the population."

"You won't be angry, disappointed with me?"

"How can I be angry or disappointed in something you can't control?" Still, something niggled at him. "When I proposed, why didn't you tell me you thought you were pregnant?"

Her finger traversed a circular path around his nipple, making it more difficult for him to concentrate on her words. "I didn't want you to feel obligated or think it was the reason I agreed to marry you."

"Why don't we make a pact? Rather than worrying about what the other may or may not think, why don't we agree to be honest and open with each other from this point forward?"

A sly grin spread across her face. "Truly? Then I already have something to tell you."

"Will I like it?"

She pursed her lips. "I'm not certain."

"Then, before you tell me, let's make love again."

As things turned out, he liked both the lovemaking and what she had to say.

EPILOGUE

Ten Months Later

"Mая I have your name?" Priscilla asked as she gazed up from her desk in the waiting area of the Hope Clinic.

"Maisie Hendricks," the middle-aged woman said.

Priscilla jotted the information down on the paper before her, which listed patients' names and ailments. "And what seems to be bothering you?"

The woman leaned forward. "Terrible pains, here." She rubbed her abdomen.

Priscilla made note of the complaints and added a little "S" next to the information on the list.

"Dr. Somersby should be with you shortly. Please have a seat."

Upon speaking with Honoria, Priscilla discovered she had a talent for organization, something Timothy had mentioned the clinic sorely needed. Priscilla had witnessed the rather chaotic nature of the waiting area herself when she'd brought in the child who had nicked her reticule.

Timothy received her idea with both enthusiasm and admiration—resulting in another round of lovemaking.

With the duchess's assistance and suggestions, the duke agreed to a trial period whereby Priscilla would perform an intake and assign each patient to a physician based on the doctor's special talents and the urgency of the patient's needs. The trial period passed with great success, and Priscilla had become a rather permanent fixture at the clinic.

Although her system was far from perfect, order had, for the most part, been restored to the clinic, and patients who had been treated before Priscilla's arrival commented on the improvement.

Priscilla's heart swelled with pride. It was the only payment she received—or needed.

Of course, not everyone was happy about the arrangement. Her mother had swooned and cried for her smelling salts, detailing the impropriety of such an endeavor.

Victor had come to Priscilla's defense. "Mother, she's a married woman. Being by her husband's side is both recommended and admirable."

"That depends," her father had said, giving his newspaper a little shake. "Aurelia, now that Priscilla is married, why don't you go back to Lincolnshire and give me some peace? What you don't see won't upset you quite so much."

Priscilla's heart did not break when her mother complied. The sheep could have her.

She continued to make inquiries about Fingers, the young urchin she'd encountered, but to no avail. Dr. Somersby said Pockets had been rather tight-lipped when questioned. She hoped the child would reappear for treatment, and she hoped he was doing well.

The duke emerged from the treatment rooms, escorting another satisfied patient. "Who's next, Mrs. Marbry?" His smile was genuine, and the tension between them had eased.

In private, he'd even asked her to call him Harry. And although she requested he reciprocate and call her Priscilla, each time someone addressed her as *Mrs. Marbry*, joy bubbled within her.

She ran a finger down her list, landing on the entry with an R beside it. "Mr. Johnson, Dr. Radcliffe will see you now." After giving Harry a brief account of the patient's complaints, she went back to her work.

She and Timothy had yet to be blessed with a child, although not for lack of trying. However, one thing she'd learned from her new sister-in-law, Bea, was the pride in being productive. The clinic filled her days and Timothy filled her nights, and she found that, for her, it was quite enough. Neither of them missed the trappings of society.

They attended small parties with family and close friends, the circle of the latter growing slowly as the duke's influence began to change minds. And although she still enjoyed going to balls and dancing, she found its appeal faded compared to the slow, sensual moments she shared with her husband in private.

"Deep in thought?" Timothy's sultry voice whispered as he leaned down and touched her shoulder.

She smiled up at her handsome husband. "Just happy."

He gave her a little squeeze. "There is no *just* in being happy. Now, who's my next patient?"

As she called a young boy forward, Priscilla knew he was right. Being happy was everything.

Timothy escorted the lad back to the examination rooms, and Priscilla grinned to herself. The boy had described receiving a blow to his head when his sister had thrown a shoe at him. Of course, she had to assign him to Timothy.

A bark of laughter echoed from the examination rooms, and no doubt Timothy would have to explain to the lad he wasn't laughing at his injury.

When Timothy finished his examination and returned to the waiting area, he did his best to send her a reprimanding look, which she returned with her most innocent expression. Which made him laugh all the more.

"Wha's so funny? There's sick people here," an older gentleman complaining of gout said.

Timothy pointed at her. "My wife."

"Ah," the man nodded, as if those two words said it all.

THAT EVENING, WHEN THEY TRAVELED HOME IN THEIR CARRIAGE, Timothy sighed as Priscilla snuggled against him.

"Is it a sin to be this happy?" she asked.

He tugged her even closer. "If it is, I'm guilty as well. We shall burn in hellfire together." He lifted her chin with his finger and gave her a kiss. "Although I take issue with your sense of humor when assigning me patients."

"I couldn't resist. I hope his injury wasn't serious."

"Nothing time won't cure."

"I wish everyone could be this happy."

"So that everyone would burn?"

She slapped him on the chest. "No, silly. I was thinking about Lady Honoria and Lord Nash."

"Ugh! Now why did you have to go ruin my mood by mentioning him?"

"There's something sad about him, Timothy. I don't know what, but I think everyone has done him a disservice. He's not as bad as everyone paints him."

Timothy shot her a dubious look. "Perhaps someone has whacked *you* on the head with a shoe. Shall I examine you?"

She giggled. "Later. When we're home. But seriously, perhaps Lord Nash needs someone to save his reputation as you tried to save mine."

"It would be a tall order."

"Was I worth it?"

"Every torturous moment," he teased.

He pulled the curtains on the carriage closed, deciding not to wait until they were home to show her just how much saving her meant to him.

Wondering about that rascal, Lord Nash Talbot?
He's no one's hero . . . until he's hers
Scan the QR code below to find out how hard he falls.

Redeeming Lord Nash

CURIOUS ABOUT HOW TIMOTHY AND PRISCILLA ARE DOING IN the future? For a free extended epilogue with a peek nine years into their future as well as other free offers, sign up to my newsletter. Scan the QR code below.

Saving Miss Pratt Extended Epilogue

IF YOU LOVED TIMOTHY AND PRISCILLA'S STORY, WHY NOT LET other readers know? You can leave a short, honest review by Scanning the QR code below. Easy peasy.

Saving Miss Pratt Review Page

AUTHOR NOTES

Research is a must when writing any work of historical fiction, even romance. For me, it's part of the joy of writing in a time period prior to my lifetime. (Contrary to my oldest son's belief that I "remembered" the American Civil War, I have not been alive that long. He will never live that down.)

With each book in this series, I've found myself exploring ideas that necessitated additional research. This book was no different, some of them being as entertaining as how to play Whist and trick horseback riding.

Needless to say, when writing a series that revolves around a group of physicians in the nineteenth century, I find myself digging deep into medical practices and procedures that existed during that time. As you can imagine, we've come a long, long way from leeches (bloodletting).

The physicians of The Hope Clinic have some very advanced ideas about practicing medicine, but that's not to say they're completely anachronistic. I may have taken a bit of creative license with Harry's practice of using chlorinated lime to wash his hands after treating patients. The first *documented* use was in 1847 by Ignaz Semmelweis in an obstetrical hospital in Vienna. But it's not impossible that Harry might have stumbled on the fact that by washing his hands with a disinfecting solution the number of patients presenting with the same ailment dropped (as mentioned in *Healing the Viscount's Heart*).

In *Saving Miss Pratt*, Timothy becomes ill after taking shelter in Mr. Thatcher's cottage during the snowstorm. He develops an ear infection. Fresh out of medical school, he would be full of new innovative ideas. The *concept* of bacteria had existed for some time, although the term bacteria did not. Instead, in 1670 Anton Von Leeuwenhoek named the tiny living organisms "animalcules." Unlike the predominant theory of miasma (which translates to "bad air"), later scientists posited that it was the living organism that could be transmitted via air not the air itself which caused the disease.

If you scoffed at Timothy for thinking he'd developed the ear infection from the wind, I don't blame you. He'd probably contracted it much earlier, but the brutal wind could very well have increased his pain, so it's logical (at least in my mind) that he would have attributed his illness to the storm. Keeping in character means keeping their knowledge within the realms of their time period.

Any inaccuracies are strictly my own, and I take full responsibility, hoping you will forgive me for perhaps "bending" things a bit to fit the story.

On another note, you might be wondering why I chose to write a story about Priscilla Pratt, What does an author do with a character readers love to hate? Should I just throw them under the proverbial double-decker bus and say good riddance? As someone with a background in psychology, in good conscience, I couldn't do that.

People make bad choices. We make mistakes. That's what makes us human. Are there intrinsically evil people in the world? I hate to say it, but, yes, I think there are. But, I believe, the vast majority of people fall somewhere in that gray area between all good and all bad.

There is a principle in psychology called The Fundamental Attribution Error. In short, it basically says that we often discount environmental or "outside" forces that affect behavior, instead attributing it to the core personality of the person. That guy who cut you off in traffic? Well, he's just a jerk, right? Hmm? But is he? Maybe he's rushing to the hospital because he got a call that his infant son had to be airlifted for emergency surgery? (My daughter used to say "Maybe he really has to poop." Which always made me laugh and wiped away any anger I had toward that person who cut me off.)

So what about characters in novels? They're fictional, true, but if they're a well-rounded, truly fleshed-out character, they've had things happen to them that may lead them to make bad decisions, or maybe shape the way they behave or who they listen to. In other words, they all have a backstory.

So how did I try to *Save Miss Pratt* and *Redeem Lord Nash*?

If you haven't read the book yet and read on, we'll I'm not the boss of you, and you're an adult. But just be warned there are spoilers a'waiting.

In *The Reluctant Duke's Dilemma*, Priscilla Pratt was the woman who almost cost Harry the love of his life by orchestrating a compromise with our beloved duke. Readers hated her. Goodness, even I disliked her. I even gave her a really unflattering name. As a discovery writer, I didn't really want to "examine" her very much, but I began to see her as a very young, malleable girl, who was spoiled and self-centered, true, but also easily persuaded by her mother to do some pretty despicable things.

At the end of *The Reluctant Duke's Dilemma*, we saw a little chink in her selfish, self-centered personality when Harry pleaded with her to call everything off and when, during the wedding, she told him to go rescue Margaret. At the end, when she admitted to the scheme (said scheme assisted by our other questionable character, Lord Nash) she asked Margaret if it was as wonderful as it seemed to be loved so deeply by someone. Of course, Margaret tells her it is. It was when I wrote those words that I saw Priscilla in a new light. Rather than a scheming manipulator, I saw her as someone desperate to be loved.

Obviously, in her book, she is paying a heavy price for her horrible choices, and she has a long, long way to go to redeem herself. Her growth is slow, and I'll admit (and as my critique partners will attest) she still has some moments of self-centeredness and selfishness in the first part of her character journey. But I really liked her character arc as she learns what's most important in life and what it's like to put someone else's wants and needs ahead of her own. It was a harder task to redeem her in one book than I'd imagined.

I'll leave it up to you to see if I was successful at "Saving Miss Pratt."

Which leads me to Nash Talbot. Unlike Priscilla, Nash's character arc occurs throughout the series. So hopefully, by the time we get to his book, people will be a little more in his corner at the beginning. That's not to excuse the horrible thing he did in *The Reluctant Duke's Dilemma*. It's something he will have to come to terms with in a personal way. I won't say that it's a lot easier for an author to write a character's arc over the course of multiple books, but it gives the author more "time" to examine the inner workings of the character and get the reader onboard.

With Nash, we saw a little flicker of his humanity at the end of *A Doctor for Lady Denby* when he helped Oliver escape a horrible fate. And of course his matchmaking efforts in *Healing the Viscount's Heart* are not entirely altruistic. His animosity with Laurence Townsend is a driving force behind his machinations. After all, it was Laurence who exposed him as one of the perpetrators in Priscilla's orchestrated compromise of Harry. But we see a bit of acceptance (or maybe it's tolerance) between Laurence and Nash going forward in the series.

Nash is truly one of those complex characters that every author loves to write. There will be a big revelation in his book that is vaguely hinted at in the previous books of the series. And it's there the reader will finally understand the reason for the ongoing animosity between him and Harry. I've written a prologue (which may or may not be included in the book, but if not, it will be available for free to my newsletter subscribers) that goes into depth about it. As I wrote it, everything truly clicked into place with amazing precision, and the duplicitous nature of one character (who is only "seen" briefly in the prequel and "kind of" in the beginning of the first book) shows the lasting effects of one person's cruelty.

To sum things up. How does an author redeem unlikeable characters? By making them well-developed, fleshed-out characters with backstories.

ALSO BY TRISHA MESSMER

The Hope Clinic Series

No Ordinary Love (Prequel Novella)

The Reluctant Duke's Dilemma

A Doctor For Lady Denby

Healing The Viscount's Heart

Saving Miss Pratt

Redeeming Lord Nash

Coming Soon

The London Ladies' League

A Duke In The Rough

Contemporary Romance

Different World Series

The Bottom Line

The Eyre Liszt

Look With Your Heart

ABOUT THE AUTHOR

৩৯৩

Trisha Messmer had a million stories rattling around in her brain. (Well, maybe a million is an exaggeration but there were a lot). Always loving the written word, she enjoyed any chance she had to compose something, whether it be for a college paper or just a plain old email. One day as she was speaking with her daughter about the latest adventure going on in her mind, her daughter said, "Mom, why don't you write them down." And so it began. Several stories later, she finally allowed someone, other than her daughter, to read them.

After that brave (and very scary) step, she decided not to keep them to herself any longer, so here we are.

She hopes you enjoy her musings as much as she enjoyed writing them. If they make you smile, sigh, hope, and chuckle or even cry at times, it was worth it.

Born in St. Louis, Missouri, Trisha graduated from the University of Missouri – St. Louis with a degree in Psychology. Trisha's day job as a product instructor for a software company allowed her to travel all over the country meeting interesting people and seeing interesting places, some of which inspired ideas for her stories. A hopeless (or hopeful) romantic, Trisha currently resides in the great Northwest.